BRIDE OF
LUCIFER

BOOK 1: HELL ON EARTH

EMILY SHORE

CBRIDE OF LUCIƑER
BOOK 1: HELL ON EARTH

Cover and Interior Design by We Got You Covered Book Design
WWW.WEGOTYOUCOVEREDBOOKDESIGN.COM

OTHER WORKS
BY EMILY SHORE

AUTHOR'S NOTE

Bride of Lucifer: Hell on Earth is an ***18+*** dystopian fantasy. This book is spicy, gritty, and intense with high heat levels, a Hell on Earth **"Vegas-on-Steroids"** tourist trap, sexual tension battles, murder, sexy angels and demons, bride trials, and more! This book ended up much more humorous than I'd intended, but I blame Astraea.

Heroine: Astraea is badass, sweet but a bit psycho, salty AF, and has past trauma. I torture my ladies so I may chisel them into their destined goddesses! When she gets knocked down—even by the dark love interest/s—she comes back swinging. Astraea gets to be as aggressive, as powerful, and as toxic as the alpha-holes around her because women shouldn't have to be perfect to be valid.

Anti-Hero: Lucifer is sexy, scarred, and a somewhat of a stalker. With his own trauma, he's tortured, possessive, aggressive, cunning, and broody. He owns his demons, and he's pretty damn proud of them. And Lucifer *loves* his dirty talk!

Anti-Heroes: (Yes, there is more than one love interest. No, I'm not telling you. This is a **SERIES.**) I write dark love interests who straddle the border between alpha and alpha-hole. The kind you love to hate AND grow to love along with the heroine since they'd burn the world for her. And maybe—just maybe—they have a heart of gold beneath their assholery. They are the ones who know how to prioritize a woman's pleasure (and pain) and make her moan and swoon and drool and scream and beg for more.

Author is very responsible for any drooling, moaning, fantasizing, clenching, panty-wetting, and/or obsessing over sexy characters. Author advises keeping a partner or vibrator close.

I write enemies-to-lovers and hate-to-love **NEVER** insta-love. My works are not for *everyone*, though *anyone* **18+ or older** and especially lovers of spicy fantasy romance will fall in love. My work features themes of trauma-healing, sex positivity, positive sexuality, and feminism.

Bride of Lucifer is perfect for spicy book lovers with angels and demons/monsters. And *Lucifer* on Netflix, of course!

I write spicy romance, and queer inclusivity because we are normal, we are valid, we are here, and Reverse Harem/Polyamory because "why choose?" Queer identities and lifestyles are all normalized and respected in my fantasy universes as they should be in real life. Everyone deserves respect and humanity. Learn more about my platform on my social media pages. Or subscribe to my newsletter at www.emilybethshore.com.

SUPPORT/CANCER FUND: Last year was my husband's cancer battle with surgery and chemo. This year, it's mine. It's likely that I will need surgery on my tongue to remove precancerous cells. Kindle Vella kept our family afloat through 2021 and part of 2022. Please consider voting for any of my books on Kindle Vella and supporting me as an author and cancer medical fund. The minimum to vote aka **Top Fave** is literally less than $2.00 a month. I love to treat my Vella supporters to special art postcards and exclusive super fan group perks like helping me on names, fashion, and even getting advanced chapters! Learn more at "Emily's Vella Verse on Facebook: a public group where I share fun memes, teasers, games, and giveaways.

Please follow my TikTok: @authoremilyshore and my IG: @emilybshore.

FINAL P.S.: This book ended up being WAY longer than I thought it would. I blame my attention-whore Lucifer and his sexy, brooding monologues. So, I divided Bride of Lucifer into TWO books. Hell on Earth and The Bride Trials. Thank you for your willingness to binge-read. And you will not have to wait long for more Lucy and Astraea spice as Book Two will be released in the same month as Book One.

BRIDE OF
LUCIFER
PLAYLIST

ASTRAEA'S SONGS:

"Sweet But Psycho" – Ava Max

"Pretty Little Psycho" – Nine Shrines

"I'm Gonna Show You Crazy" – Bebe Rexha

"All the Good Girls Go to Hell" – Billie Eilish

"Devil in Me" – Halsey

LUCIFER'S SONGS:

"Enemy" – Imagine Dragons

"Hate Me" – Blue October

"The Devil's Dance Floor" – Flogging Molly

"Cryin Like a Bitch" – Godsmack

"Sympathy For the Devil" – The Rolling Stones

GENERAL:

"Demons" – Imagine Dragons – Nightcore Cover

"Angel With a Shotgun" – The Cab – Nightcore Cover

"Take Me to Church" – Hozier

"Boulevard of Broken Dreams" – Green Day

"Monster" – Skillet

"Dark Horse"/"Monster"/"Take It Off" – Nightcore

"Runnin' With the Devil" – Van Halen

"Haunted" – Evanescence

"All Around Me" – Flyleaf

"I Dream" – Nightcore Fanatics

"Dirty Angel" – Courtney Jenae

"Wrong Side of Heaven" – Five Finger Death Punch

"We R Who We R", "Your Love is My Drug" – Kesha

"Saints and Sinners" – Bullet For My Valentine

"Circus For a Psycho" – Skillet

"The Monster" – Rihanna & Eminem

"Love the Way You Lie Pt. 1-2" – Rihanna & Eminem

DEDICATION

To all the spice-loving, smut book-clutching, badass ladies who fall for the morally gray, tail-whipping, dick-growing guy with a side of monster. Even if he's the Devil himself.
If they come for our spicy books, it'll be over *their* dead bodies!

Emily E Shore
Fantasy Romance
Author

For the ***uncensored*** version, please subscribe to my newsletter (www.emilybethshore.info) or follow my FB reader group (Emily's Vella Verse) and learn how to become a super fan!

PART ONE

HELL ON EARTH

ONE

PENNIES FROM HEAVEN

——ASTRAEA——

Welcome to Hell on Earth. All are welcome in the City of Sin unless you are an angel, of course. All angels, not fallen, are banned by order of Lucifer Morningstar, King of Hell on Earth, Ruler of the Nine Circles. We trust you have good intentions since the road to hell is paved with them. Welcome again, and have a devil of a time in Hell on Earth.

I roll my eyes at the derogatory holo-sign pulsing above the gates of Hell on Earth and flare my common but keen golden wings as the security demon barks, "Your kind isn't allowed in here!"

Agitated, I ruffle my feathers, blade-sharp at their tips and edges. The hair on the nape of my neck stiffens from the demon's refusal. Although he's three times my size, I imagine the multitude of ways I could decapitate him. Each would take an average of 3.8 seconds.

"I may be a weapon of mass destruction, hellion, but as you can see, I bear no sword," I point out to the carmine-skinned beast, smirk, and do a twirl for his satisfaction, remembering he's doing his job.

Unsurprised when the demon's eyes linger upon my figure, I resist the urge to swallow any revulsion from the costume—a stereotypical get-up befitting a Victoria's Angel ever since she lost her secrets after Lucifer bought the franchise and released his line of glitter body paint. No hope of hiding so much as a knife in the sheer, white negligee with a lacy bralette that barely covers my full breasts. Or the matching panties with the word "Angel" embroidered on the cheeks. Not like I haven't attempted a multitude of other ways to get into Hell on Earth.

I inwardly curse Camio for this last resort of a suggestion. He will get a good laugh out of this. Once I make it beyond the gates, he'd better meet me at the Devil's Due Nightclub.

Rest assured, I will not stay in this for the masked gala. I'm here for one reason. This is my only chance to meet with the ultimate fallen angel face to face.

"Lucifer's Law: fallen angels only, little cherub," the security demon grunts. I wonder if he only speaks in grunts and barks. I resist the urge to bare an angel fang at the mention of those brow-beating bullies forever blowing their horns and smoke out of their alpha-hole asses. Thankfully, they don't patrol the Outer Circle, or I'd be doomed since they love preying on female angels like me. One of many reasons I'm here.

Behind me, several humans and lower demons show their impatience and frustration from an angel holding up the line. Oh, hell no, I didn't spend all night flying from the Celestial City, where I was the laughingstock of my countless older brothers, nor did I wait all day with every race drooling over me for this meat-headed hellion to deny me entry.

Come hell or high water, I'll get Lucifer to the Tribunal so he may face justice for his crimes, public and personal, past and present. If I can't, I'll stab a knife through his black heart.

Where the hell is Camio?! I feel an angel scream coming on, but I plaster on my sweetest-wrapped psycho smile and creep my fingers along the demon's bulging chest to coo, "Surely one of Lucifer's finest demons can bend the rules…"

He flares his nostrils, and I crook my smile into a grin, knowing the pheromone oil Camio gave me is working its magic. "Catnip for demons", he'd said.

The demon falters, and I close in, parting my plump and pouty angelic lips rouged with the same oil. I flutter my wings until I hover at his level, casting the demon catnip around his bulging atmosphere.

"Now, where's that devil-may-care attitude?" I sweet-talk and toss my silky curls to the side.

He blinks and parts his lips. Guess he never had a chance. I'd say poor soul, but demons have none.

By the time I've lowered myself back to earth, the security demon has swiped the button on his holographic console to grant me access. I blow him a kiss and dance inside before he can get wise to my machinations. I've traveled into the Outer Circle before through other routes thanks to smugglers, but Camio assured me I'd make it beyond the main gates this time. Until his pass failed after the parking lot.

I fully intend on giving him shit for it. I don't have time to fuck around. Not tonight.

Tension invades my stomach as I take my place on the high-speed tram which transports tourists from the main gates to the Vestibule of Hell on Earth: the Outer Circle with its nightclubs and restaurants. Provided Camio comes through, I'll enter the Nine Circles soon. Sure, we warrior angels have placed bets on who can sneak into the Nine

Circles, but Lucifer's security is too powerful.

Fake passes to access the Devil's Nine Circles are reserved for spy angels—but never his Underworld. And I failed spy training.

Spine prickling, I pinch my lips and ignore the echoes of my older brothers guffawing at my plan. They'd slapped their backs and cackled countless cheesy jokes while ruffling my hair and jerking on my feathers: "Aww, look at our adorable, little scrapper wanting to earn her wings,", or "Remember, Trinny, if you can't take the heat, get out of Hell's Kitchen!", and "Don't forget your fire-retardant suit."

Tossing my blood-red curls over my shoulder, I snap my wings shut behind me. I may have common wings, especially compared to archangels and seraphs, but mine are sharp enough to slice. A fluffy lightness fluttering in my chest, I lift my proud chin. Halo currents rush through my blood, gilding my skin's early dawn gold to a rich sunset hue. Head-hovering halos are for cupid or cherubim angels while mine resides in my chest.

Out of habit, I creep my fingers to my side but find bare skin. Ugh, I feel so naked without a weapon.

At eighty-six, I may be a novice warrior, practically a teenager by angel standards, but I've experienced my fair share of skirmishes and brought in a few bounties with my hunter rank. Unfortunately, as far as my brothers go, I'll always be their baby sister, the scrapper, the runt of the angel litter.

Off to my right, a demon and his family sit in the first five rows. I nod and offer a faint smile that confuses them. The mother shields her baby with his adorable, tiny horns curling from his head. Not that I blame her, considering most angels don't exactly associate with demons apart from hunting or spying purposes. Guess I'm the exception since I prefer them to fallen angels. Demons, I can handle, especially when most are Hell on Earth security. They act according to their nature compared to those black-winged, fallen parasites who want to drag every angel down with them, especially any with ovaries.

Not like I can claim any moral ground over demons anyway.

While waiting for the tram to push off from the station, I tap the iNK-Link embedded in my wrist and cue up my Hellify-No Playlist, another one of Lucifer's contributions. I can't rightly complain since it's ad-free. Seconds later, I hum to the old song, "Demons". Moments after, the tram lurches. I steel my spine, bracing myself for the views—heaven-shattering ones according to the ads: Lucifer's joke.

Beyond the window, flicker cars and hover bubbles filled with elite tourists zoom past the tram on their way to the Nine Circles. The Outer Circle, aka the Vestibule, is made up of mostly shopping and nightclub districts for cheap, hell-themed souvenirs and thrills. Lucifer's way of reeling in the "common folk".

I glance around at those lower-pass holders. Toward the back of the tram, a group of humans chats about their cosplay costumes—probably for a convention—and I commend them for doing their homework since the professional craftsmanship of their faux elf and fae ears proves they bought them from native artisans. In the center are a few half-elves since elves are the most willing to reproduce with humans. A nearby dwarf couple wears matching "Hell for Honeymoon" t-shirts that brings a smile to my lips. One or two daemons of the cat variety. Two harpies dressed for nightclub-hopping.

Like any other tourist trap, Hell on Earth is a melting pot of diversity. Hundreds of millions visit every year. Few wish to leave. So, Lucifer expands, much to the chagrin of our races. I sniff. And a few others. My spine prickles at the thought of the fae and elf territories to the north and east.

Brand new tourists gush when the barriers clear to showcase the Nine Circles in all their glory. Understandable. My first reactions were similar.

Sighing with conflicting emotions, I prop my elbow against the window. I can't exactly give the devil his due for the originality of basing his tourist trap on Dante's Circles. But redesigning hell and opening the fiery gates to the public, now that took grade-A flaming balls. Two middle fingers right up heaven's golden ass!

It's five times the size of New York City—no longer considered the City that Never Sleeps—which has been dormant since Lucifer opened Hell on Earth. I snicker because he outright put Las Vegas out of business.

Gives a whole new meaning to "have the devil to pay" since Lucifer is the world's richest man. Richer than God, I smile at my joke. Hell on Earth, as decadent and sinful as it may be, pales compared to Lucifer's true crimes. I swallow the ache in the back of my throat and crush the pang in my chest, not wanting to think about my real motive for sneaking into Hell on Earth. If hell has no wrath like a woman scorned, this pissed-off angel has officially met her boiling point.

Evangelina. The name haunts my mind like a specter. I close my eyes, scrape one claw down the curvature of my throat, giving myself enough of a sting, and concentrate on breathing deeply. I banish the nightmare resurfacing.

The tram pitches to a stop. Thankfully, the Devil's Due Nightclub is right inside the main Vestibule sector, the nightclub sector.

Once I step off the tram, the warm night air ruffles my sinful garnet curls. Currents of glitter-laced steam drift through the street vents to speckle my sheer dress. I weave around them to avoid the shimmery smithereens. My breath hitches from the glimmering nine mega-towers so close, their spires fracturing the moon and prodding the stars. Lucifer paid the highest fee for astronomical-defying towers with their space transports to Hubble City constructed upon the moon last century.

But Hubble City can't compare to the Celestial City bordering the expanse of Hell on Earth. The height of irony: Lucifer raised hell, and my brothers sunk heaven. Well, at least a chunk of it.

I blink from the moonlight reflecting off my home's gold spiral towers cresting the floating mountains in the distance. To the untrained eye, the pinpricks of light twinkling around the heavenly realm could be stars, but I know what they are: flying angels. My family...well, 360,000 of them, give or take. The rest reside within the seven levels of heaven, accessible via portals on the Celestial City.

I stream my fingers through one of many multi-colored water jets shooting from the ground to prance, dance, and leap into enormous fountains. Like kaleidoscopes of liquid ribbons, they capture the attention of any children still awake after a busy day at the amusement parks. Countless tourists of various races from the Djinn to elves to changelings, and humans, cast halluci-coins into the fountain. I smile at one little elf boy whose eyes catch the light of the streamers until they fill with gold from gazing at...me. I wink. He blushes and buries his pale face in his mother's shoulder. Shrugging, I move on.

I failed the breeding program by choice.

Scarlet neon holo-lights parade the title of the Devil's Due a short distance away. Lust cloys the air as couples, throuples, or more kiss from the romantic elements of the nightclub sector.

Thanks to the digital shield-domes, the night sky is right out of a fantasy. Not even I object to gasping. The height of irony considering the majestic views of my home. My lips part. Wonder thickens my throat from the constellations and shooting stars smothering the royal violet skies.

To think, I'm so close—one more tram ride to the Nine Circles. Lucifer resides deep inside the earth within the Ninth Circle closest to the Pits of Hell. Except for tonight: he will make his appearance for the first time in one hundred years at the grand anniversary masked gala.

Outside the mile-long line of young tourists waiting to get in the Devil's Due, I scan my iNK-Link under a carrier bot. Two seconds later, its robotic, feminine voice alerts me, "Astraea Eternity, please accompany me to the Devil's Due." I shake my head in disbelief, my chest tight. A carrier bot, seriously? "Don't be mad, bitch," Camio's melodramatic voice cuts in, far too whiny. "You know I love you, but if you woke up right next to the sexiest demon serpent—"

I swipe the "pass" icon and roll my eyes. Camio's the only one who's allowed to call me bitch. But it doesn't give him a free pass to share all his dirty bedroom details.

Squaring my shoulders and avoiding the lustful gazes of nightlife demons and other races salivating over my wings and my angelic glow, I follow the escort bot to the Devil's Due Nightclub.

In the meantime, I envision all the ways I will unleash heavenly wrath upon Camio.

"There's my favorite she-wolf!" Camio half-teases and half-mocks, kissing each of my cheeks before roaming his eyes across my sheer outfit, the one he suggested. "Or should I say she-cat, meow!"

"Careful, Cam," I purr next to his ear and sweep my tongue across his cheek, "you look tasty enough to be a mouse right now." I bite my bottom lip suggestively and waggle my brows, referencing his sinful dark attraction. Not quite original sin, but pretty damn close.

He flinches from my gesture but doesn't hesitate to add another kiss. "Aww, now, bitch, we know your bark is worse than your bite without your sword. How many inches is it anyway?"

I stick out my tongue and snort, "Bigger than yours."

"Oh, you wound me!" he guffaws and slides into a center stool at the nightclub bar.

The club vibrations purr into my body. My heartbeat times to the rhythm as I scoot into the seat next to him and tap the gem-tech bar menu. "That's what you get for leaving me high and dry at the main gates."

A hover tray sweeps past me, carrying a few drinks to a corner booth where a gorgeous fae with wings decked out in gold lining and holo-gems flirts with a tall elf, her hair like a waterfall the deep color of forest moss. All welcome, save for angels. Only fallen angels roam free in service to Lucifer and his high demons. After all, why remind people of morality or justice when they can get an express elevator right into the realms of the seven deadly sins?

Camio waves a hand dismissively and orders himself a gin and tonic, believing it makes him look like a classic. Which he is. Down to his core. "If you couldn't talk your way past the inner gates, Astraea, you're not cut out for our little scheme." I love how he sounds out my name one syllable at a time: "Ah-stray-yah".

I curl my upper lip, exhibiting a sharp angel fang, one of my many pride and joys while placing my order. "If this scheme doesn't pan out, I may retract my offer to donate one of my ethereal eggs for you to fertilize."

He sighs. "Our little secret, right? Don't need all those big brothers of yours deciding you need a chastity belt."

"They lost their pinkies the last time they tried," I say casually and inspect the menu with a devilish smirk, remembering that night Sariel and Uriel had ganged up on me. Thanks to Asmodel, I hadn't severed their remaining fingers. "I vowed to cut off something that would not grow back next time."

"Before or after you chucked the infernal belt into hell's pits?"

I can't help but mirror Camio's smirk. He's the only human who can travel back and forth between the Celestial City and Hell on Earth. Most live on one or the other and never in between. All thanks to the brand on his forehead.

"I thought Aamon was coming." I glance around the nightclub, expecting Camio's demon partner to appear.

Hundreds of hover-orbs flame about the club while holo-demonesses dance in cages for the bypassers. In the center is a sweeping sculpture feat of gem-tech lights. Like a disco ball on steroids, it pulses the music to resonate into the bodies of every club-goer on the main floor. This is nothing compared to the elite nightclubs of the Eighth Circle. Or the Ninth Circle, which boasts of the most expensive mile-high club.

But underneath that super tower is the Under-City: Lucifer's reverse skyscraper burrowing deep into the earth's surface. Urban legends state that the penthouse delves into the pits of hell and leads to the entrance to the Unconsecrated Crater. Regardless, that reverse skyscraper is the heart of Hell on Earth, pumping out hundreds of thousands of employees and security for every race. The nine megatowers comprise his pleasure super center to mirror Dante's nine circles.

Once the VIPs indulge in the Nine Circles of Hell on Earth, they pay extra to suck up to Lucifer in his Under-City. Tonight, I will become one.

"Alas, my sweetheart, Aamon cannot join us tonight. And stop fussing about the menu." Camio softly nudges my shoulder. "You know I got your back, gorgeous." He nods to the holo-bartender, who nods back. A moment later, the counter before me caves in to thrust a glass of fiery red liquid into my waiting palms. Dragon's blood.

"Angels don't have a heart," I remind Camio, but flutter my eyelashes and lean in, kissing his cheek and tapping his nose. Celestial souls, yes, but not hearts. Hearts aren't necessary to fulfill our duties. Sure, we still have blood born of star fire to power our haloes that reside in our chest cavities. But no hearts. Hearts are fickle. Hearts get us killed.

"And you could never handle my back. Not on any good day," I add to the immortal human, raising my glass before downing the dragon's blood in one swig. Its bitter and smoky aftertaste tantalizes my tastebuds as the liquor heats my blood. Curlicues of smoke flit out of my pores.

"You're my last hope," Camio confesses, ordering another with a deep sigh. "Aamon is so busy commanding the Ninth Order of the infernal legions. But if I take Lucifer's place for the next quarter, we'll be married within a fortnight, and you can put those eggs to good use!"

I chuckle and lean toward my friend in the loosest sense of the word. Warmth radiates through me on account of the dragon's blood. The hairs on my arms tingle, and my wings lift until I'm subconsciously flaring my feathers to protect my territory.

"After all, Cam, everyone knows you're the real big bad wolf of hell, aren't you?" I tip my glass to Cain, teasing him. Sure, my friend might have committed the world's first homicide, but now, Cam is as soft as a cinnamon roll, the kind with rainbow icing and sprinkles.

He gives me the pouty lips at his one weak spot. "Lucifer this, Lucifer that. The "Angel of Pride" tries to take over heaven, fails, and falls from grace. And what do those bloody seraphs do? They let him be the King of Hell on Earth. Meanwhile, I kill the first human ever and my own brother! And all I get is this fucking mark!" he jabs a finger at the mark on his forehead of a reverse "L" with a semicolon surrounded by a near-enclosed circle. "And yet, Lucifer is charged with all the legions of hell, opens it as a tourist trap, and still retains the title of "Morning Star"?"

I order another dragon's blood, down that one. "Morning Son," I correct."

He shrugs. "I've heard it both ways."

"Life sucks, Cam. Then, you never die."

"Wonderful words of purity."

I stick out my tongue. "We both know you haven't killed one being since that day, Cam." Unlike me with all my bounty hunting kills as the lowest warrior angel rank. It doesn't matter if I'm not the executioner. I hand-delivered my bounties to the Tribunal.

He shrugs. "Roaming the earth homeless for eons and seeing countless wars ironically softened all my hard edges. I've seen enough bloodshed."

Decades of battle training have hardened mine. Not that I've had many opportunities to use that training beyond a few skirmishes. When you're one of few female angels and the personal charge to the biggest, baddest archangel, you don't get to see much action. At least not the action I wanted.

Seven-year-old horrors are the main reason I'm here.

"Do you have the key?" I lean in to whisper, referencing the Eighth Circle VIP pass, eyes darting to their corners, sensing someone watching us. The hairs on the back of my neck bristle, but there's no one, aside from the naturally curious. And the club shadows.

As long as Camio's plan works out, I'll breach that Ninth Circle after midnight.

Before Camio gets the chance to transfer the digital key to my interface, a rowdy demon interrupts us, stepping in front of me as a barrier. I wrinkle my nose from the stench of sulfur and iron and too many fruity fire shots.

"Did it hurt?" he slurs his words, and I knead my brow, a headache brewing from his predictable and stereotypical come-on. With my halo glowing all over my skin, I might as well be a heaven-dusted demon nip launching a radar for a seven-minutes-in-heaven wingding.

Camio snorts, sputtering his gin and tonic before whistling. "You don't want to be doing that, mate," he warns the demon.

"When you fell from heaven?" finishes the demon, leaning against the bar, whirling his head to me.

I glance beyond him to Camio, winking. "Guess," I urge.

He shrugs. "4.6 seconds."

I snatch up my next dragon's blood and down it in one gulp. "Oh, ye of little faith."

As soon as I finish, the cheesy demon touches my waist. Big mistake. I've had enough of all the ogling, the salivating, and the angel ass-pinching for one night. My vision mists crimson—if mist is acidic.

First, I snap the demon's fingers. Next, I thrust my fist into his windpipe, then hook my arm, bending at the elbow to throw the demon to the floor until part of his horn splinters. "Stay down," I coo in the demon's ear as his eyes roll to their ceilings. "Or you'll learn what it means to catch my devil."

Camio sips at his gin and tonic, wide-eyed as I rise and blow a strand of ruby hair out of my eyes. No others interfere with my little skirmish, though plenty murmur. They won't mess with a warrior angel, even if they doubt I am the real gold-blooded thing. Cosplay convention, after all.

I shrug and scoot onto the stool, checking my time. "3.4 seconds. Personal best."

"I wouldn't want to be Lucifer tonight."

"I'll carve a pretty "L" into his forehead for you, Cam." I lean in and peck his cheek.

"You'll need this first." He peers around, double-checking. It's why he chose this location. Outer Circle clubs aren't monitored as heavily as Inner ones beyond the Vestibule.

Once the new song pulses, Camio grabs my hand and leads me onto the dance floor. "They're playing our song," he murmurs in my ear.

I roll my eyes and laugh as the music resonates in my ears and the bass thrums into my body. Camio twirls me, and I snap my hips, careful my sharp-edged wings don't brush any crammed bodies around me. Camio's soft dark locks eclipse his eyes as he tugs me back, stationing a hand chastely at my upper waist. Though he leans in, he keeps his chest well away from my breasts.

"This implant will get you to the VIP level of the Eighth Circle," Camio says before pricking my wrist. I don't flinch, but grin cunningly as he spins me again. The crimson ink forms into a tiny set of curling horns above my iNK-Link. Nine Circle security. "Hope you brought that hidey skin pouch."

"Always."

At the song's climax, Camio jerks me to him and bumps my nose while slipping a cold and metallic, yet feather-light, object between our bodies. "Put it to good use. That was fucking expensive."

I kiss his cheek again, tucking the mask into the secret skin pouch I'd had specially designed. Sealed in such a way, I'm able to carry a small weapon—or a mask—but to the unobserving eye, it simply resembles the fleshy part of my inner thigh.

"I'm doing this for love, Astraea," Camio references the song "Angel With a Shotgun" streaming all over the club. "But are you certain about this?" My smile slips, shoulders tensing as he continues, eyes creased in concern. "I know what the past seven years have done to you. What happened that night—"

"Don't," I snarl a warning, baring my keen, angel teeth.

Camio sighs and touches the back of my hand. "It wasn't your fault."

I hiss but swallow a hard lump in my throat because I shared in the responsibility. I've spent seven long years chiseling away at my grief, at my guilt. And traded them for icy revenge. The deeper layer to my superior yet superficial layered motive for justice.

"Lucifer has had his fun for far too long," I point out, falling back on justice. "After midnight, I'll drag his ass back to heaven, and the archangels will put him on trial for opening Hell on Earth. He'll have hell to pay, you'll get your time to shine, and I'll finally earn my celestial stripes and trade them in for the best rank and sword I can get! Now, if you'll excuse me, Cam, I'm late for a party." A grand, masked ball of a party.

As I prepare to exit the club, I lick my lips, considering Heaven's Seventh Level. No more pathetic bounties far beneath my skills. No more constantly beating the shit out of my brothers when they get fresh with me. Okay, the second one since it's pretty fun.

By this time tomorrow night, I'll kneel before the highest archangels, my bond-keep included, claim my true sword and assume my rank in the holy war against the legions of hell. I'll spill a river of blood from the fallen angel throats I'll slit.

"Good luck, Astraea," Cam kisses me back.

"Who needs the luck of the devil when I'm bringing pennies from heaven?"

ONE POINT FIVE

AN ANGEL IN THE DEVIL'S HOUSE

——LUCIFER——

I never fuck angels, but I may need to make an exception.

Foolish girl believes she can enter my realm, and I wouldn't know. After all, I am the ultimate stalker, prowling the world like a ravenous lion. And this little angel has entered my den. I'd rolled my eyes when she met with that preening peacock of a scheming son of Adam. Should have known Cain was involved. I'd chuckled in the corner of the club, clothed in smoke and shadows, curious when she overcame the drunken demon. Undoubtedly a warrior angel, bounty hunter, I'd wager. She doesn't carry herself like those annoying archangels, overcompensating with their enormous swords.

This little angel doesn't need to overcompensate for anything. Regardless of her plain but pretty gold wings. A common hue for angels, but it's clear she takes great care with them.

I'll give the Tribunal credit. They've certainly afforded their assassins more liberties than usual. I'll give her more credit for standing in line for hours outside the Gates and swallowing all that wrath and pride whenever she was groped or hit on. I smirk to one side, fantasizing about what else I'd have her swallow.

It's a new tactic. Angels never stoop to raw, sexual power. They're far too superior. With my Eighth Gala's upcoming appearance and announcement, the Tribunal must be desperate. Tonight, I'll change tactics and use a double, but I'll let the little angel be for now. Heaven forbid I send her flying high when she's knocking on Hell's door.

I haven't seen an angel's body so unclothed since the time before I fell. All my muscles tense, my spine tightening. Indignation fills me since I didn't fall. That would imply an accident, a chance to rise. But no. After the war was lost, those sanctimonious seraphs chose to make an example of me and sent their best warrior to send me falling to earth. They're sorer than ever at how I've risen from the not-so-shallow grave they sent me to. Pride simmers within me at how they formed the Celestial City during my construction of the Nine Circles.

They've sent countless angels into Hell on Earth as spies. None like this. It would be too simple to order security to stop her before she reaches the Eighth Circle. Or program the advanced gem-plant in her iNK-Link to refuse her entry. As enjoyable as it would be to ruffle those pretty feathers, I'd prefer to watch this angel in the streets a little longer...

TWO

THE EIGHTH CIRCLE

—ASTRAEA—

I swear I must have a heart since it's probably crashing against my rib cage. Hot blood rushes in my veins, causing beads of sweat to pool along the sides of my face and the back of my neck as I exit the tram inside the Circles for the first time. Camio's pass worked like a gem—literally since it's enhanced gem-tech. Another due to the Devil, who franchised crystal-harvesting of the pits of hell. A veritable, endless oil well reserve since crystals can always be grown.

Swallowing hard at the sight of the eight super-towers surrounding the final one, the Nine Circles, I lower my gaze to the thousands of humans, demons, and countless other races forming lines hundreds deep to enter the First: the Chamber of Eye and Root—the lowest of the symbols. Each Circle's chamber symbols grow in rank and power. Ruled by overarching principalities of eight governors and political chambers formed of various races, Hell on Earth forms the most elite and democratic government in the world. Not to mention diverse since this is the largest tourist trap in the world.

Ahead of me, several security holo-gems, incapable of being hacked, pop up like flicker figures—far more enhanced than the Outer Circle's pixelated holograms—designed to scan rings or gem-plants like mine. One holo-gem greets me as soon as I disembark from the tram. I smile at the projected image of a young daemon—part panther and part demon—who prepares to scan my ring or mark. On Hell on Earth, daemons are ironically far more popular than demons. Not so ironically since they are bred for beauty, agility, and strength while remaining the kindest and most courteous race on the earth. Perfect for tour guides or holo-gem security.

I offer my wrist, and the daemon flickers a dark scarlet color representing the Eighth Circle.

"Trinny Malak, please follow me to the upper platform to your left, where your transportation awaits to carry you to the Chamber of Smoke and Flesh, the Eighth Circle."

Grimacing and gritting my teeth, I try not to let the inside joke of an insulting name needle under my skin. Since childhood, my brothers nicknamed me "Trinny" from my "Eternity" surname, rarely calling me Astraea.

I am going to decapitate Cam for choosing Trinny, gods be damned if his head will grow back! No, I'll carve my initials into his pretty forehead, one on each side of his mark. Or once I reach warrior rank, I'll get my holy fire and arrange a quick barbecue. The possibilities are endless.

I follow the flickering holo-gem escort to the upper platform, where a private hover bubble awaits me, and I eagerly slide in. Not as good as flying, but it's close. Once inside, the holo-gem program offers me an app to select my ideal host. I smirk and select my favorite daemon actress: Indraa. A flush burns along the back of my neck to my ears. I fan myself, swooning unashamedly at the elegant demon/tigress hybrid with her golden sienna skin accented by sinuous tiger stripes of pure white and deep mahogany. Her hair cascades in a silver waterfall, mirroring her glowing flame eyes. A lithe body with a swinging tail and prick of ears. Decorated in gold details, her purple gown shows the white undersides of her beautiful arms and upper chest.

"Welcome, Trinny Malak."

Indraa's smoke and velveteen voice makes me forget all about the nickname. I love how the tigress is not simply a phenomenal actress who diversified old Hollywood—Hellwood now—but she works as an international humanitarian and activist for the rescue and rights of young daemon women. When war has ravaged the daemon territories outside Hell on Earth, daemon girls often become prisoners of war or refugees in tent cities.

Not that the archangels have done much to stop the war. I shiver and battle a lump in my throat when I consider my family in the loosest sense of the word. My brothers take great pains to remind me of my lowest race of angels, how they generously adopted me into their fold since I flunked out of every form of angel school, from guardians to messengers to weeping angels to ambassadors. Thankfully, Abaddon, my bond-keep, spared me from the breeding program. Not that I'd let any angel cock get anywhere close to my priceless pussy.

"Thank you for your generous donation to the Daemon Restoration Center and the Underrepresented Daemon Actors Guild," announces Indraa, proudly exhibiting her deadly, scythe-sharp fangs.

So, that's how Cam got the ticket. I smile to one side, thinking I can almost forgive him for the nickname. Almost.

"Please help yourself to any of the refreshment options," Indraa extends her hand to the menu before me.

"Don't mind if I do." My eyes feast on the endless options, but I settle on my traditional favorite. Stomach fluttering, I lean closer to the holo-gem screen as a pedestal appears from the hovercar center to offer me the lemon bar.

"Now, you will enjoy a splendid view of the Vintage District as you are transported to Hell on Earth's Grand Station. Would you like a historical address?" asks Indraa as I fold the bright lemon custard into my mouth, my tastebuds singing the "Hallelujah Chorus" from the flawless balance of tart and sweet filling with a tender crust.

"Why not?" I shrug. I don't intend to be in Hell on Earth for long, but any information about the cityscapes surrounding the Nine Circles will be helpful. I must remember why I'm here.

Once the hovercar passes over the Vintage District, I can't help but admire the aged architecture. While Indraa regales me with the Vintage District that Lucifer took great pains to preserve against the desires of the Chamber that wished to demolish it for building corporate centers, I inhale a variety of new scents. Programmed to mimic the environs, the hovercar dispenses the scent of smoked meat and spices from a festival in the central square along with hellfire ale, grilled fish, flame wine, roasted nuts, and more. One scent is familiar. I narrow my eyes, astonished at the trees surrounding the square, recognizing them as Dream Trees. Kneading my brow, I'm incredulous, wondering how Lucifer found the swift growth seeds that originate from the Celestial City and cast a sweet and light scent with hallucinogenic effects.

Even the temperature has changed inside the car to a humid summer night.

At the edge of the square, I sigh longingly at the brass band playing with countless races dancing in the streets under hover-streamer lights. Despite how battle training is similar to dancing, we never dance. Dancing is strictly for the seraphim and cherubim, not warriors. I straighten my shoulders, remembering I have something better than dancing. After decades of using other methods, save for my sexual, angelic appeal, it's time to pussy up. Denying it won't get me a backstage pass straight to the Ninth Circle.

I flex the muscles in my wings, fidgeting as I grow anxious and tune out Indraa's soothing voice. My stomach churns from knowing what I must do while my brothers' bellowing laughs thunder in my head louder than heaven's crashing cymbals.

This is the greatest risk I will ever take, pitting myself against Lucifer's security of fallen angels who rule the skies of Hell on Earth. They'd love nothing more than to get their claws on the highest prize of a female angel.

It's why I can't fail. I won't fail.

The hovercar arrives at the Grand Station a few minutes later. The lemon bars have turned to rocks in my stomach. I double-check the time, registering how I have over an hour before midnight. Perfect, barring any delays.

At least the hovercar stopped at a private platform meant for VIPs since similar ones have docked nearby. Skyway bridges crisscross above the cars while hundreds of trams embark through various tunnels to lower Circle levels.

The magnetic belt doesn't release, nor do the car doors slide open.

Puzzled, I narrow my brows until Indraa announces, "Thank you for your patience, Trinny Malak. You will arrive at your connecting transport to the Eighth Circle soon."

A wave of dizziness drifts over me. I can't believe I'm doing this. I can hardly believe I'm this close to the second most powerful tower next to Lucifer's.

The hovercar drops.

At first, I hold my stomach from the plunge, but decades of flying have accustomed me to the sensation. Most would need anti-sickness patches. Darkness encases the car a few moments later, and I register we've dropped into a tunnel far below the station. All the lights in the hovercar have dimmed. Even my halo has dimmed as an innate security measure while the hairs on my arms and neck prickle, sensing a predator. A fucking powerful one.

I swallow, sweeping my gaze around, finding nothing but pitch black. My breath echoes in the hovercar until the thundering groan vibrates deep into my body. My blood turns to ice in my veins. I widen my eyes as the monstrous creature sweeps past the windows, its scales glimmering light into the darkness to show a cavern-like tunnel.

"Introducing Geryon, Lucifer's finest, oldest, and greatest wyrm," proclaims Indraa.

Transfixed, I put my nose to the glass and crane my neck as the trained wyrm crawls along the cavern to grant a full display of its amassed muscled body hundreds of feet long, its hundreds of sword-like spikes serving as a fringe, poisonous barbed tail, and several rows of saber sharp teeth.

"You are perfectly safe," continues Indraa. "Please enjoy the ride as Geryon transports you to the Eighth Circle station."

"Holy hell's balls!" I gasp as the hovercar lurches forward, bound to the wyrm whose scales must be programmed with centrifugal force technology. Or magnets.

Throughout the journey, which lasts a few minutes, thanks to the wyrm's speed, I still can't settle. My inner predator angel understands I am the weaker hunter. The hairs on my arms and the back of my neck don't stop pricking the air. My halo doesn't glow until after the hovercar docks at the station when Geryon returns to the underground.

As soon as the doors slide open, I stumble out of the hovercar, battling a wave of nausea. Why should I be surprised by the wyrm when monsters fill the pits of Hell on Earth? Monsters who respond to their ultimate master's command.

I must get a hold of myself. After midnight following the Gala, I will meet that master.

Steeling myself, I straighten and sweep my eyes to several holo-gem advertisements streaming around the private dock. A few other VIPs pause to stare at me, and I shrug and smile sweetly, maintaining the ruse.

"Thought it would be a fun and ironic costume for the Gala tonight," I say to a teen fae close by.

"Your designer must have worked for months!" gushes the fae with her silver piercings, ink across her brows, and preppy purple hairstyle. Her leather and lace gown is a popular design in most shopping districts.

I twirl, fluttering my wings, then lean in to whisper, "They used real angel feathers collected by scavengers from the Celestial Plains below the city." I'd prepared the story in advance, keeping it as plausible as possible.

Once the older fae, whom I assume is her father, judging by his war-torn wings, scar fracturing his face in two at a diagonal, and well-tailored suit with armored elements, clears his throat, the fae teen spins, and retreats. I'm thankful they are headed in the opposite direction since a veteran fae such as himself would be able to scent my ethereal essence and peg me for the genuine article.

I beat a hasty retreat out the opposite exit.

Once I issue beyond the station, I nearly shriek from the enormity of the Eighth Circle. Slowly, I make my way to the lookout point with its decorative railing—finials and a gargoyle on each side. If I had a heart, it would be spasming in my chest. As it is, I'm breathless from the sight. Several levels below me surge with skyscraper corporate centers, elite hotels, entertainment centers, sky-high restaurants, an arena in the distance—for demon sport, I assume, shopping centers, and more. Breezes from the various hovercars sweep past me, carting citizens every way except upward.

According to the holo-gem billboards flickering with actors issuing welcome greetings, this is the Media Central and Club District. It's not long before all the billboards showcase the Masked Gala, which will be held on the Penthouse level above my head. For obvious reasons, it's not visible from the lookout point.

Cam mentioned how I would have an hour until the Gala. One hour to prep my body for the main event. And that my VIP ink implant includes all expense-paid access to the most elite boutiques.

I have the perfect idea for my costume.

TWO POINT FIVE

FOOLS RUSH IN

—— LUCIFER ——

Fools may rush in where angels fear to tread, but it's clear this little angel was born without a healthy sense of fear.

Of course, I'd seen those fine angel hairs on her body prick to life when her celestial senses felt Geryon's approach. Not even my wyrm deterred her. An angel has never made it to the Eighth Circle.

Pride warmed my blood and bones from her expressions in the hovercar. Naturally, I may up-link to any mode of transportation in my Circles to monitor the car's inside. I'd expected her to wrinkle her nose, repulsed by the opulence and splendor. And while that pert little nose is still high enough for her to drown from a sprinkle of rain, I can't deny how much I enjoyed her expressions. My cock had throbbed when she'd perched her bare legs on the dash of the hovercar while lemon bar crumbs flaked onto her chest. I imagine she would taste similar: the honeyed crust of heaven paired with the lemony tart filling.

If she proves not to be an assassin, I'll give her all the lemon bars she wants.

She'd welcomed the virtual tour, admired the sights and sounds, and appreciated the smells of the Vintage District: one of my greatest accomplishments. Hell on Earth has something for everyone. A realm where anything is possible. My domain is where one's deepest desire may come true. So, what sort of desires does this little angel have?

As she gazes at her introduction into the Eighth Circle, I study her from the shadows, tilting my head, too curious than I should be. She has as much chance as a wax cat in hell at defeating the Devil incarnate. Thousands have tried throughout the ages. But when she'd also sighed longingly at the dancing, I couldn't help but play with heaven's sweet kitty cat a little longer.

"We will dance soon, sweetheart," I assure her.

THREE

TRAPPED BY ALPHA HOLES

—ASTRAEA—

I secure the eye mask to my face.

The moment it touches my skin, I inhale sharply as it hums and tingles, shifting and molding to the contours of my heaven-high cheekbones. Camio must have spent days, if not weeks selecting the perfect mask since the eye slits are wide enough that they do not eclipse the sultry intensity of my golden eyes with the deep smoky shadow, black liner, and fierce elegance of the eye wings. Gold glitter to add a hint of sweetness. I smile when I consider the nickname my brothers adopted that I love: Dr. Jekyll and Mr. Hyde.

Making faces in the mirror, I cross my arms, lean against the grand fitting room wall, and prop my bare foot on the solid surface behind me. I love how I can go from sweet to psycho in 0.2 seconds—from Victoria's Secrets angel to assassin angel.

Spreading my flawless cupid's bow lips and tossing my thick and full blood-red curls, I wink at the mirror and affirm, "I'm a devil-fucking nightmare wrapped in a voluptuous daydream package." On wings. Lucifer won't know what hit him.

I slide into the high heels, which extend my 5'6 inches to 5'10. Perfect addition to this "costume". While I admire my lithe stems with their lean muscle, especially in my thighs, a fantasy lurks in my mind of pressing the point of one heel into Lucifer's skull until he screams for mercy only an angel can grant.

"With that honeyed smile, you can trap every spider-demon from here to the pits of hell," Camio had told me the first time he met me at the Devil's Due, and we've been friends ever since.

What the designers had done to my body was sheer, fucking genius. Or rather, I should state the makeup artists, considering I don't have a designer scrap of fabric on my skin—apart from the lace thong and transparent swathes cascading down my legs. And the white ribbons they'd attached to my wings. I'd pressed my lips together and showed no pain as they'd stitched the tresses to the edges of my "faux" feathers. At least it's the outermost wing layer vs. my most sensitive inner-third layer. Later, I'll carefully remove them.

I twirl in my heels and slide my hands across the pure gold leaf pieces the makeup artists had sealed in chaotic flattery over my body. The gold leaf gives the illusion of frozen shimmery butterflies fluttering and twisting around the center of my throat to sprinkle down my upper chest, curling sinuously upon much of my breasts and nipples but sparing their generous outline. Gold leaf speckles my toned stomach and the fronts and backs of my nude legs and arms. Between my long wings, the tulle ribbons, and the thong, I'd opted for no gold leaf on my too-curvy but thankfully packed derrière.

Damn right, I'm proud of my body. I've had to fucking work for this sexy angel with an inner beast since I practically emerged from the womb eighty-six years ago. Well, the D-cup-sized, bundle of joy breasts and striptease-worthy hips came from whoever belongs to that womb since Abaddon himself doesn't know.

I shiver at the thought of my guardian—the one who found me as I was flying around the clifftop towers of the Celestial City as a newborn. Well, more like getting tossed by the wind currents and laughing and gurgling like a baby bat who'd shot the fuck right out of hell. An extreme rarity for a newborn to fly. A born passion for flying and fearlessness of heights were my saving graces and why I was allowed to grow up in the Halls of Warriors.

And because I have no angel marks. Unlike all my brothers gifted with celestial ink from birth, my wings are bald as mole rats. And more naked than I've ever been at the moment, save for the sexy gold leaf and the halo gifting my body with its natural glow. Tonight, I'll earn the mark to match my fucking stripes. Stripes I'd ensured I'd covered before I left the Celestial City. Camio has never seen them.

I don't need to scan my implant on the way out of the Eighth Avenue Shoppe. Once I'd read about the body painting services, I knew it was a perfect idea.

I smirk, wondering how large of a dent the gold-plated high heels would leave in Camio's budget.

Double-checking the great tower clock in the Central Shopping Square, I nod: thirty minutes. Plenty of time to get to an elevator, scan my implant, and get transported to the highest balcony level for the Gala, which Camio assured me would be within direct sight of the platform where Lucifer is due to arrive.

After waving my implant before a directory to order a hover-form,

I step onto the steel floor plate and scan my implant for the Gala destination. The motion propels me forward, but I don't lurch or flinch. Compared with flying, this microscopic bit of inertia is nothing…even with the four-inch heels. As it transports me beyond the Shopping District, I absentmindedly hum "Boulevard of Broken Dreams", my proud hips swaying from side to side. Currents of adrenaline eddy inside my blood. My skin tingles, and the hairs on the back of my neck stand on end—ever alert by instinct and training. No such thing as intuition. This is all nature and hard-ass labor.

Still, I haven't enjoyed myself in far too long, so I twirl and slide into the elevator, my halo glowing more than usual. My blood hums. No, it practically sings the highest operatic octave when I curve my fingers around the railing and stare out at the expanse of the Eighth Circle's Hotel District from beyond the window.

Kaleidoscopes of butterflies flutter in my stomach—half-expectant and half-terrified at what I'm about to do. All Lucifer would need to do is blink and order a squad of fallen angel freaks to surround me and cart me off to the pits of hell.

I'm staking my wings and this manna-from-heaven milkshake on Lucifer loving the bit of devil inside me enough to invite me for an up and close interview. I'll go straight into the belly of the beast: the Ninth Circle Penthouse.

Tapping the railing on each side of me, I take a few practiced deep breaths to calm the halo inside my skin. It has a mind of its own most days.

Heat radiates through my body until all my hairs prickle to static life, sensing a predator. No, predators. Several shadows douse any heat in my body. Icy fear chills my blood, and I grip the railing tighter but don't dare turn around. I should have expected this. Even in a place as low-key as the Shopping District and the private elevator.

A low voice chuckles darkly behind me. I bristle from the powerful presence like a wraith drifting toward me. My breathing turns shallow, which I know he can detect since that chuckle ripples into a steady laugh. Fucking freak. I've spent all my life avoiding these black-winged parasites like the cockroaches they are. Too bad they're also lethal as nightshade vipers. Some more than others.

Goosebumps needle my flesh.

"My, my, my, sweet thing," the dark voice mocks me, but I still don't turn around. Not even when he sifts a hand through my curls and raises them to his face. "You smell divine, little star shine."

Another manifests at my ear and nips the lobe, so I flinch for the first time. He cackles, following with a whisper, "Looks like this heaven-scented one is a fool who rushed in where real angels fear to tread."

Fucking marvelous.

I'm trapped in an elevator, one of the worst of confined spaces, with a squad of fucking fallen angel alpha holes.

"Easy, boys," I croon, pouring acid-laced honey into my voice while turning around, hoping they don't pick up on the hints. For all they know, I'm a lowly guardian angel. Barring any weapons, surprise is my best one. Well, and my claws and angel fangs.

Their eyes mark me, pupils dilating. I'd bet my wings they're already fantasizing about clipping my feathers, keeping them as trophies. Or dumping me headfirst into the Unconsecrated Crater: with its horrors that brutalize the blood, body, and wings of any angel who plunges into its shadowy depths. The initiation and rite of passage for all fallen angels. They surrender their soul to Lucifer and gain a heart in return. Real angels don't need hearts. Hearts bleed. Hearts crack. Hearts break. After all, life as an angel, especially a warrior angel, is not for the faint-hearted.

Hell-pig pussies.

The one with the sharp-boned features, muscles, and mirthful eyes glittering, who clutches my curls, is the highest rank. Captain, I judge from the insignias tattooed along both sides of his neck and sides of his face: marks from his kills. I'll need to take him out first. My stomach churns from their eyes lusting after me—my wings most of all—thirsty tongues preying on their lower lips, feathers ruffling eager. Their dark crimson leather signifies their rank along with their black wings, tattooed insignia, and dark veins. All dead giveaways to their fallen status, but I'll still go hell-bent for leather with them.

You're so fucked, my inner psycho cackles.

Shut up! I'm about to fuck these black sheep's world up! I grimace and cross my arms over my chest, giving them my best, shining smile, but my posture stiffens along with my jaw.

"A long way from home, isn't she?" The captain's second slides next to me and props his elbow up on the window above my head, leaning casually and sporting a set of pointed teeth as white as pearls and sharp as serpent fangs.

"Give me your hand, love," the captain advances next while the others form a rank behind him. With the second hemming me in on the other side, I don't get an opportunity to dodge out of the way before he seizes my palm. "Now, I know what it's like to be touched by an angel." He lifts my hand to his lips, but there's nothing gentlemanlike about him.

I spit the ruse out of my mouth like it's poison. Oh well, never been good at acting. It wouldn't take them long to scent the warrior on me anyway. Why bother with pretenses? So, I snap the captain's wrist, revel in his howl, and shove his limp hand down to his cock. "Try your own hand, asshole." Muscles thrilling from the familiarity of battle and the concept of a challenge, I bring my knee up hard, slamming it into the captain's jaw before stabbing my heel right into his chest, so he hurls into the rank of angels behind him.

One knocks an elevator button, launching it upward with a fierce jolt.

The captain growls and barks, "Strike." One word order, but the five remaining angels march toward me. Skillet's Monster echoes in my mind. I feel a devilish grin coming.

A sudden pain howls through my wings. Adrenaline sprints through my blood to numb my senses—not my instincts—, and I spin from where the second has gripped the upper muscle, digging his claws into the sinew. There better not be one feather missing! With a squall of heat flushing my body, I thrust the lower part of my hand to the second's nose, breaking it, and gliding away before the blood splatters my gold-leafed skin.

Out of my peripheral vision, three other angels move toward me as the captain recovers. I ease into a low crouch, flare my nostrils, and rupture the claws right from my fingers. "I'm going to light a fire under each of your asses. With a match made in heaven!" I wink and spread my lips into a wide grin, unleashing the front and bottom row of keen angel fangs.

They don't falter, and I'm half-tempted to agree with the invisible devil on my shoulder: I might be fucked.

THREE POINT FIVE

PRIDE GOES BEFORE...

——LUCIFER——

The seraphs are proud of their swords, status, and their sublime cities of gold.

This sweet celestial is proud of everything else. Justifiably so. Proud and vain but not pompous. If she were pompous, she wouldn't have gritted her teeth through the pain as the designers stitched those ethereal ribbons into the edges of her wings. She'd held her chin as high as a queen through it all.

My cock had done far more than throbbed. The damned serpent reared its crowned head, ready to play snakes and ladders and climb right into her abundant bosom. Curves in all the right places, despite how average her height is. If it weren't for the lethal, little weapon she's concealed in that cunning and captivating area so close to her celestial center, I'd assume this angel is simply here to play a little seven minutes in Hell on Earth. It's clear she's frequented the cruder Outer Circle of my domain where angels are permitted, yet rarely go. Unless they're spy angels hoping to sneak in or those artful ambassadors with their scheming, seraphic-driven tongues I loathe most.

She is neither. Spies don't resort to sexual plays. Nor would they maintain such a high profile. High profile to me. Amusement heightens the nerves in my veins. It's a shrewd tactic. Everyone believes she's hiding in plain sight. Apart from me, but I'll give the celestial sweetheart an A for effort. A+ for everything else.

I adjust my breeches and crack my neck from side to side as her halo lights up, and she twirls into the elevator. Light as a feather, I'd say...and chuckle internally. Until the squad enters the elevator.

If I wasn't so interested in her response, curious if she will act on that ferocity in her expressions, I'd end the conflict before it may begin. I grunt and excuse it as a chance to assess her battle skill level.

But when she snaps his wrist, stealing my chance, and responds with the wicked retort and the mocking gesture to back it up, I find myself smiling more. An unfamiliar heat prowls my blood. I chalk up my lust to some long-lost affinity for the angelic. Except no angel in heaven is dressed like a wet devil dream. I admire her form, honed from years of training. A violent grace. She goes for the easy shots. Like a cornered creature, she acts in defense.

Oh, bloody hell. My devil dick points straight to heaven when she crouches. Every drop of blood in my body hardens my organ from her forbidden fruit swaying at the action. When she unleashes those claws and fangs, I fear my balls will burst. The little she-demon-wrapped angel is all in now.

But her playful pun covers up her fear. It can't hide the gooseflesh, her pupils dilating, nor her shoulders tightening. What I love most is how the fear doesn't drain the color from her cheeks. That moralistic superiority is on full display in the red rage. Unbroken pride at its grandest. It's like looking into a mirror. A twisted mirror of my crazy female twin.

Now, I wonder what she will break next.

FOUR

THE GRAND GALA

—ASTRAEA—

The second charges for me, and I jam my elbow into his ribs, knocking him back. His wings crash against the elevator corner. I breathe windstorms through my nostrils and swipe my leg to trip two of them, rise, and jab my heel into the third's shin. Two more rush toward me, eyes pinned, wings rigid. Thunder battering my eardrums, I claw at one of them, slashing through his leather and drawing blood. But my good luck runs out.

Once the captain stops the elevator, it lurches. The second goes for my wings again while the remaining angel shoves me hard against the side, knocking my head hard against the glass. My vision splinters. The next thing I know, two alpha holes are gripping my arms. They could substitute for a worthy torture rack from how my limbs shriek.

Snapping his wings behind him, the captain advances to me as the others hold me down. I jerk my head to the side where the second circles me, swiping the blood from his nose and snarling.

"Careful, you've got blood on your hands," I snicker, falling back on the same mouth that got me kicked out of the ambassador angel program.

Leering down at me, the captain flexes his fingers and twists his now-healed wrist that I broke while cracking his neck muscles. "I'm going to enjoy playing seven minutes in heaven with you, little warrior."

"Oh, trust me," I say, voice breathy and rasping from my dry throat, "with how much pain you'll be in, it'll feel a lot longer than seven minutes."

He snickers to his buddies. This time, the second goes for my hair, yanking it back to expose my throat.

"Don't worry, sweet girl," croons the captain, lowering his head toward me. I hide my grin behind pressed lips and clenched teeth. He shouldn't have called me sweet—not this close to me. "We'll pretty you up nice before your unholy baptism," he references the Crater.

Blood flushes my vision. I yank my hair back from the second and head-bash the captain, breaking his nose this time. Snarling, he stalks toward me, balling his hand into a fist, raising it to strike. I don't bother flinching.

The elevator dings. The doors slide open.

And I shake my head in disbelief and groan at the seven-and-a-half-foot familiar figure with his hands stuffed in the pockets of his black leather trench coat, which is not as long as the glory of his hair he keeps in a high ponytail. The same dark hair I loved to braid once upon a time. Memories burn in my mind of gripping that hair by the handful when his face was between my thighs right before he speared me to the wall of his clifftop manor suite with his impressive cock. Fucking nephyl warrior.

As soon as he takes in the sight before him, the nephyl shakes his head with a low chuckle, eyes green and glittering as gems. "Astrea fucking Eternity."

"Jack fucking Tempest," I mimic him, matching his smirk.

"What did I tell you about hosting wild parties without me, gorgeous?" He steps inside the elevator, but those hands don't leave his pockets... yet. Once they do, they'll become weapons in their own right.

The fallen angels stiffen around me, but I raise my chin and flick my head back and forth, glowering at the fallen ones.

"Hey," I protest and toss my curls onto my shoulder, thrusting my chest out for Jack's benefit. "I didn't ask to be voted hell-coming queen angel."

"56th Legion squad business," barks the captain, sizing up the nephyl and flaring his feathers for an intimidation tactic. "Piss off, Cyclops."

I whistle low as all the muscles in Jack's body bulge, surging to life and nearly shaking the trench coat from his body. Throwing my head back, I laugh, gaze at the squad, and announce, "You guys are so fucked!"

Jack still doesn't bother removing his trench coat. But he does make a sucking noise with his tongue and teeth before snapping his eyes to the captain, lowering his chin to eye him in contempt. The deep chuckle rolling from Jack's throat is both amused and vexatious, as if the fallen angel below him is worth less than a crumb of grit in the nephyl's boot. Which is about accurate.

I take a few deep breaths, my chest eager and expanding, imagining which body parts Jack will break first.

Stepping forward until his shadow capsizes over the captain, the nephyl leans forward, so a fair portion of his dark tresses eclipses one side of his face. He might not have diamonded cheekbones like us angels, but I've always loved Jack's more rugged features, the rough masculinity that befits the descendants of the nephilym. Among other impressive features.

For once, the fallen angel presses his lips together and swallows, uneasy and intimidated by Jack's prowess and muscles. "An impressive specimen", I'd labeled him the first time we met. He hadn't stopped impressing me since, considering he was the one flightless being to ever catch me.

"Trust me, quisling…" Jack alerts the captain, curling his upper lip in disgust, "it would be no difficult feat for me to shatter all your bones within seconds. Ripping your wings off would take less; imagine a child tearing off a butterfly's wings before pinning its thorax to a photo frame. But since I'm late for a party, and Astraea is, too, I will extend the following warning: if you care to fuck with Abaddon's bond-keep, I won't hinder you."

All their faces turn pale from the mention of Abaddon, and I pinch my lips. My stomach lining hardens to iron from frustration, vowing it will be my name that strikes fear into the blood of every mother fucking fallen angel, demon, human, fae, angel, and even Lucifer himself. The alpha holes' grip on my arms loosens.

Jack gives a snort and shrugs. "But considering his patrol territory is the Unconsecrated Crater, I imagine he will learn of your transgressions soon. And we know all it takes is a single molecule of that unholy smoke to snuff your fallen souls from all eternity," he adds the little pun at the end for my benefit, and it's my turn to fucking snort.

Once the captain lowers his shoulders in defeat, I jerk my arms free, rise into a seamless stand, and grip their arms. I wrench them hard to dislocate their shoulders. Before the second can scuttle away, I slam my elbow into his balls and thrill in the sight of the rest scrambling out of the elevator. All but the captain, who glares at me, eyes narrowing predatory.

I blow him a kiss. "Don't let the elevator doors hit your wings on the way out, asshole."

As the captain stalks past Jack, I flinch when Jack's one hand flees his pocket. In less than an eye blink, the nephyl warrior has severed one wing right down to its bloody stump. The captain's howl ebbs from Jack shoving him out of the elevator, pressing the button for the penthouse, and sealing the doors closed.

Turning to face me with the wing still in his hand and dripping blood, he deadpans with me, then chucks the cleaved wing to my feet.

I cross my arms over my chest, careless of how it plumps my breasts more to his eye. Not like it's anything he hasn't seen and felt. "Abaddon sent you, didn't he?" I blow a devil-red curl out of my face.

He shrugs, sticks those hands back in his pockets, and approaches me. His shadow has never intimidated me—better than a fucking shield.

"Can't blame him for being worried. The Angel of Destruction is far too high profile to enter Hell on Earth, and I was in the neighborhood."

"Let me guess…" I roll my eyes and squint at him, cheeks flushing as he closes the distance between us, smile spreading. "Here for the Gala. So you can schmooze every fae, orc, vamp, elf, satyr, shifter, centaur, or gorgon lord you can."

"Got me an appointment with the Pan." He waggles his brows.

"Fuck, Jack!" As he leans closer with that crooked grin that liquefied my limbs all those years ago—before I was jaded, scarred, and snarky—, I scoot back against the corner of the elevator and add, "You're so predictable, Tempest." My pained lungs struggle from how much breath escapes my nose as I try my hardest to keep my chest from bursting. Still, I don't want to know how he secured a meeting with that satyr demon.

"And you're as unpredictable as ever, Eternity."

"Cut the fuck out," I hiss when he props his lower arm on the glass above me. His heat slithers across my flesh. My halo practically swoons, causing my skin to glimmer—the glimmer Jack has always loved. Those silky dark tresses cascade over my cheek, casting the scent of mist and snow from the clifftops where he lives. That sexy as fuck manor where we...*ugh! Get your thoughts out of the gutter, Astraea.* The nicest damn gutter.

I thwack those strands away, half-tempted to duck under his arm, but he'd simply thrust me right back. And I don't need any excuse for him to touch me, considering he'd probably have me up against this wall with my thighs spread and that thirteen-inch cock shoving my thong out of the way.

"What are you up to?" His eyes roam across my body, lingering on my breasts. "We both know you're not here for the Gala. I saw you through the elevator windows before I arrived. You were pulling your fucking punches."

I sniff, stiffen, and lift my chin, averting my eyes. "Didn't want to get blood on my wings."

He makes that same sucking noise—his one flaw that ever got on my nerves. "You didn't answer my question."

I heave a sigh, then bare the underside of my wrist to reveal the VIP mark. All the veins in his neck surge, his muscles tensing. "Fuck, Eternity. There's only one way you got that pretty implant. If Abaddon knew you were keeping company with Camio again—"

"Abaddon doesn't have a fucking leash on me, Tempest," I snarl, muscles in my wings quivering as I flash my angel teeth. "Besides, he knew I was coming here."

Shaking his head, Jack gazes at me, deep gray eyes softening to resemble that clifftop mist that once drenched our naked skin every night for months, frolicking with our sweat. "Offer's still on the table, Astraea."

I sigh, reflecting on the hundreds of times Jack tried to persuade me to join his rebellion of nephyl warriors battling the Queen of Demons in the northern territories of Gemterra: the nation's new name. Not that Lilith submits to its laws. Or Lucifer, who controls the western territories. Everything else falls under the provinces of Gemterra, from the Orryna Forests of the fey and elves to the Thinyon Mountains of the orcs to the moorlands of the vamp castes.

"You know if I make you mine, I'll worship you in the bedroom, right on the edge of Mount Yvos or wherever the fuck you want for all our immortal years," adds Jack, his warm breath a hint from mine.

I roll my eyes in disbelief, but Jack lifts a hand, curls his fingers, and trails them across my cheek, causing me to freeze in my tracks and rousing goosebumps to tingle my skin. "We both know you laid down your armor for me before anyone else, Stargirl."

At the sound of his old term of endearment, it takes all I have to reinforce that armor, to keep myself from trembling—especially with nothing covering my body but the gold leaf and a fucking thong. I remember the night I gave him my "purity", which stirs the heat between my thighs.

Beyond my desire at sixteen to stay as far away from the angel breeding program as possible, Jack and I had collided like burning flames in the night. We sprang up fast, driven by the same idealistic passions. But after a few years of tug of war with us fighting on the crest of Mount Yvos followed by makeup fucking, it was clear we were on opposite ends of a bridge the length of a country.

"I respect your cause, Tempest. Always will. But you know I won't abandon my family, Jack. My brothers."

"Same brothers who gave you the scars on your back?" he challenges, those heated eyes wreathing with shadow and flame.

"Don't you fucking dare, Tempest. Not when every one of them shares the same scars." I stab a finger at him, flaring my wings.

"Funny how I was there to wrap the wounds in Dream Tree oil and fucking pieced you back together every night for years."

"Fuck you, Jack, I'm alright." I glare, using the old euphemism, and stick out my tongue. "So, either steal second-base or go back to Fuck Mountain where you can be King Shit of the nephyls for eternity. I'm going to be late for my date with the Devil."

Jack bristles and frowns at me, pushing off the glass. "I remember when I had far better uses for your tongue."

"Sorry to disappoint." I shrug and set my hands on my hips, thrusting out my chest. "All tongue-in-cheek now, Jackie boy. And if you don't mind, this little angel's about to play the devil with this Gala. Don't worry, it'll put Pan in a real good mood."

"You're no match for Lucifer," he warns me as I push the button to open the elevator doors.

I pause, shift my chin back to glower at him. "Unlike you boys and your dick-sized wars, I don't need to get in a pissing match with Lucifer. Not when I got the forbidden fruit that's gonna fuck him over to kingdom come. And while you and I will never be a good match, Jack, I'm more than happy to play seven minutes on Mount Yvos with you— after I drag Lucifer's sorry ass to the Celestial City and drop him off tied in a fucking bow for the Archangel Tribunal like it's Christmas Day."

"Good luck, Stargirl."

I flip him off, exit the elevator, and scan my implant to the first holo-gem that flickers before me. Unfortunately, I still can't get the first song Jack and I danced to out of my head. He played "Take Me to Church" within his manor right before he gave me my first fucking.

Putting it out of my mind, I dismiss the masses waiting in line to get into the Gala. Though I can't see anything from this smaller vestibule-like area, I hear thousands in the distance and the thundering bass of pulsing music.

After a quick ride on a hover-form to another elevator—a private one this time—the doors slide open to reveal the personal VIP balcony box. One of ten with a bird's eye view of the entire Eighth Circle penthouse. Make that angel's eye view.

"Holy hell's balls," I gasp and wander out onto the balcony. The music explodes into my skin, quickening the blood in my veins. My adrenaline thrashes, and all the hairs on my body prick to static life.

Eight Gothic mansions fused into a massive circle make up the Gala. And in its center is one enormous arena of a nightclub with thousands dancing under holo-gem disco balls as large as houses and gem-tech laser prisms showering the audience with hallucinogenic effects so strong, no one requires drugs tonight.

Trinny fucking Malak forgotten, I'll kiss Camio later. Because not a hundred feet from my box in direct line of sight is the exact pedestal where Lucifer will rise for the grand ceremony. Tonight, I'll dance with the Devil, and no one will ever forget the angel with the golden wings who stole his thunder, lightning, and limelight before bringing him to his mother-fucking knees on the seventh level of heaven.

FOUR POINT FIVE

A DATE WITH AN ANGEL

—LUCIFER—

A date with the Devil, I muse. Oh, she's adorable. Fierce, tongue as sharp as a seraph sword, but adorable.

"Rather impressive, however strange that the King of the Nephyls would be on the side of angels," I quip alongside Tempest in the elevator as he stops it one floor down.

Jack lifts a brow, hands shoved casually in his pockets. If he knew who I truly was, he'd raise them in defense and bow his head, but the Devil is a grandmaster of disguise.

"One angel," he corrects and shrugs. "And I was not King when I met her. Do I know you?"

I chuckle darkly, tap my elbow from where I hug my chest. "Not yet."

When the veins bulge in his neck, I harden my wing muscles just in case. While I'd win, of course, it would be an intriguing battle, perhaps a challenge.

"Stalking my angel, demon?"

"And if I were?" I toy with him, leaning my wings back against the elevator wall, more casual than him. When he tenses, rising to his full height, a head taller than me, I am tempted to reveal myself. Especially considering he used the term "my angel".

"I'd say she's not worth the trouble, but it would be a lie. And not just because her pretty face can make the angels weep. Among other notable features."

I resist the urge to growl, curl my upper lip and showcase a fang. My throat tightens. "She laid down her armor for you," I muse, coming off the wall and beginning to circle him, tapping my elbow again. It doesn't take much to deduce the hidden meaning.

Jack snickers and tilts his head down while his notable ponytail curves along his shoulder. "Care for the details of how she screams louder than a banshee when she comes?"

Smirking to one side, I shake my head. "Not necessary. But I would care to know how a nephyl warrior successfully caught an angel."

"I didn't catch her. She never fell for me, demon, though I was the bounty she was hunting. Just so happens that I trapped the little sprite instead. Couldn't out-hunt her. No match for her wings. Entrapment was the best solution."

"Fascinating. A trap implies bait."

Jack pauses and narrows his eyes, scrutinizing me. "If you're planning on trapping *my* angel—"

Agitated feathers tightening from the repeated statement, I interrupt, "I meant my bait, Jack Tempest. Not yours," I deepen my voice and borderline snarl. "After all, a meeting with Pan is not so simple to secure. But should you wish for his aid in your cause, I'm afraid nothing less than a recommendation from the Devil will persuade him."

"Ugh…" he groans and kneads his brow, his other hand retreating from his pocket, flexing before it hangs in defeat at his side. Good boy. "I said she was no match for you."

"True," I confirm, returning to my original form, thickening my hellfire and shadows. Not in a warning but for the theatrics, of course. "But I enjoy playing with fire. She proves to be quite an irresistible challenge."

Heaving a sigh, Jack drags a hand down his face and grumbles, "I've been around long enough to recognize a deal with the Devil in the making. So, I get my recommendation, and you get…?"

"Information." I gesture to the Nephyl King. "Bait, for example."

"I treated her to a personal tour of my manor. She was quite impressed with the king-sized bed."

"Careful, Jack. I might just decide I like the King of the Nephyls. Even if your race is far better at chasing their tails than anything."

"Last I checked, your kind have the tails, Lord Lucifer." He salutes me and dares to wink.

"And they call me cheeky!" I guffaw. Jack nods to me.

For a few seconds, our eyes cross—a shining green that would make emeralds envious meeting my constellations within darkness. I tap again, waiting, waiting, predicting. A slow smile spreads across my face. The King is the first to blink, to relent, and sink his shoulders. He opens his hands at his sides in surrender.

But I am the next to speak. "Your information was quite helpful. Thus, your recommendation to Pan is secured. If you'll excuse me, I have a date with an angel."

"So tempted to sell my soul to the Devil incarnate to watch, but Kingly duties, you understand." He shoves his hands back into his pockets.

"Not too concerned about your paramour?"

The Nephyl King shrugs, the ends of his trench coat flaring. "She can handle herself. While I'm certain you'll have a hell of a job taming that tongue of hers, I think it's about damn time Astraea Eternity learns the Devil is not so black as he is painted."

An interesting turn of events. I give him my best devilish smirk.

Sweeping a hand to the elevator doors opening to his floor, I usher Jack out in a gesture of farewell. "Oh, and Tempest..." I pause with my finger on the button, admiring his height and form once he's outside the doors. "It won't cost you your soul, and I would offer you the friends and family discount. I'm certain you would be most impressed, if not floored, with *my* king-sized bed."

Jack shakes his head with that comic grin again. Side turned to me, he lifts his rugged chin, exposing the strong muscles in his thick neck, and retorts, "Or perhaps another recommendation sometime."

I grin. "It's a date."

FIVE

WINGING IT

—ASTRAEA—

Ten thousand little thunderbolts rumble into my body from the music bass growling from the club. Hover-bubbles flutter above the twirling revelers from those who've paid extra fees. One flickers right past my balcony, imparting me a view of a fae couple shamelessly fucking to a glitter flurry. I shake my head with a laugh and blow them a kiss, but their eyes are too glazed to register.

Leaning forward, I catch a few glitter flecks and beam, recognizing the scent Lucifer franchised: Sinful Seduction. "Don't mind if I do," I trill and swipe my tongue across the hallucinogenic speckles— programmed to read the tastebuds and instantly transform according to the individual's desire. Sighing deep from the Moonblood Tears and ginger ember cake's aftertaste, I inhale a windstorm through my nose from the insta-shock to my system. A few more, and the bliss would shimmer in my nerves so much, I'd be reduced to nothing more than thrumming flesh, pulsing blood, and a lucid spirit.

My hips swing to the Nightcore mashup of "Dark Horse/Monster/ Take It Off", and I sparkle a laugh from the too-fitting irony. Roused from the music, my halo gleams to life, scintillating the gold leaf upon my skin, but I duck back against the wall to get control of myself.

Tapping a holo-gem screen hovering above the balcony center, I select a setting for the ambiance of holo stars and lasers—they surge warm currents into my pores until it feels like liquid gold melting on my bare skin. And since I have the attention span of a bipolar and ADHD squirrel on crack, I switch it a few more times from rainbow streamers purring static tendrils to a glitter rainfall to bubbles that pop with the ember-like kisses.

A sheen of sweat coats my body, but I'm careful not to overexert myself. Not when the main event is yet to come.

Giggles flitting right out of me, I lurch, catching myself on the railing to eye the skyway bridges connecting the mansion levels where thousands of rooms overlook the grand spectacle of a nightclub. Countless grand staircases sweep down to the club floor to welcome more elite visitors. Thanks to Camio, I'll make my grander debut in far more eye-catching style. It takes all I have not to leap off this balcony and soar all over the club until every molecule of energy engulfs me. Dancing simply doesn't cut it.

I'll make the dust fucking fly, and he'll have no choice but to eat it!

As the song winds to its finale, I tap into the holo-gem one last time, blinking and tucking curls behind my ears, curiosity burning inside me. I swipe through countless features, but when the lights dim, my breath hitches from the deafening screams blaring in my ears. Inside the arena, every light darkens until not even a glitter fleck dares to glow. All my hairs prickle. Muscles twitching from the ominous noise of ancient battery-powered car horns setting the suspenseful tone, I can't help but roll my eyes. Of course, Lucifer would choose a mother-fucking classic!

Come on, come on, come on! I wince, panic pulsing into me from the audience screaming to ear-shattering levels. Out of the corner of my eye, the pedestal erupts with hell flames and fireworks. Real ones since I can feel the damned heat from a hundred feet away. I curse the holo-gem feed until my eyes finally latch onto the setting.

The song's rhythmic bass pulses the iconic staccato beat.

Yes!

At the same moment, dozens of gem-lights train upon the pedestal. It shivers. I take a deep breath through my nose, tighten my wings, and hold my exhale, knowing the entire Eighth Circle is doing the same. The raw violence of Van Halen's "Runnin' with the Devil" sets the tone, mirroring the crowd hungry for the fallen Morningstar.

Flaming holo-cars glide down from the air—flawless replicas of the ones the band owned—and form a circle to dance around the pedestal.

All my muscles tense as the indomitable black-feathered wings are first to ascend from the darkness eclipsing the lower part of the pedestal. *Fuuuuuuuck*, I clench the muscles in my jaw, burning with fury at the powerhouse of those wings that could beat a tempest to knock me right off this balcony.

If I didn't have supernatural angel hearing, my eardrums would bleed with permanent damage from the howling crowds. Of course, he's beautiful: he's the mother-fucking Morningstar, still retaining the title despite his fall from grace. Long silver hair collected into a knot at the crest of his head to exhibit his towering cheekbones. Fire and fury wreathe his persona from the black robes dripping with gem-tech to mimic hot blood to the ends of his hair—each one like the tip of a burning star.

Lucifer spreads his arms. The crowd roars. If I had a heart, it would stutter, but I furrow a brow. A million moths fluttering in my chest, I lift my wings in preparation. The Devil glories in the crowd's emotions: a tsunami to engulf the very Nine Circles of Hell on Earth.

It's so tempting to select Breaking Benjamin's "Dance with the Devil", but the worst thing I can do is throw down a challenge. Instead, I shove the warrior to a dark island in my mind, push my shoulders back, and control my breathing. Tonight, I need to be bait. Angel-acid temptation his tongue will taste. Gold venom he will suck into his veins. A huntress in masochistic clothing. Or gold leaf upon halo-kindled skin.

Smirking to one side, I wait until the near-final beat of the rock n' roll song, ensuring he won't escape. Pussy devil didn't even leave his pedestal.

I'll knock him right off it!

Before the crowds may thunder into applause, I tap the song, knowing the holo-gem tech was an after sight. Or no one ever believed in a million years one would dare to overlap Lucifer.

For eleven pure seconds of the eerie introduction of Evanescence's Haunted, I linger in the darkness, savoring the sight of Lucifer's pinched eyes, at the ironic bobbing of his Adam's apple. For those eleven seconds, I struggle to rein in my halo until it roils heat in my belly. Finally, I lift my wings, crouch, then lunge, leaping into the air and diving right off the balcony.

Lucifer flinches.

Before I may glide beneath his level, I flare my wings to catch the warm breeze, thrill in the thickening of my wing sinew, and soar right past the Devil. No matter how much I may want to pucker my lips in a mocking kiss, I weave around him, coming full circle. Here, I hover, studying the tensing muscles in his neck. Keeping my eyes soft, warm, and sultry, mesmerized by his pupils dilating unfiltered darkness, I curl my seductive fingers.

Dozens of fallen angels charge at me from all sides. I hold my breath and lower my chin in a delicate bow while staring at the ultimate fallen angel.

Wings beating the air, chest seizing, whole body trembling, I open my mouth to whisper the words of the song, "Fearing you, loving you…", hold my breath, and—

Wait, Astraea, I command my burning lungs to unleash my breath, but with countless fallen angels raising swords of black-shadow metal mined from the pits of hell and capable of slicing an angel's wing in two, nothing but panic spikes in my blood. As the chorus crescendos, I imagine those angels hauling me to the Unconsecrated Crater and lowering me into its spectral shadows. They will blacken my halo and wings. Worst of all, they'll darken my soul until I'm fallen and shackled to Lucifer's blood service for all eternity.

Until a slow smile spreads upon Lucifer's wide lips. With one flick of his eyes, the fallen angels retreat into the darkness.

My lungs unleash too much breath, and I fall, eyes rolling to their ceilings. The screams and gasps of the crowds nearly overwhelm the thrashing finale as I crash hundreds of feet in seconds.

Below me, the crowds scatter, waiting to know if the Gala's highlight will be pancake a la angel. But once the wind spirals around me, playing with my exposed skin, my halo awakens, warming me. I close my eyes and take a deep gust. Adrenaline storms through me. Grinning playfully at the confounded audience, I embrace the heat like golden waves washing over me, tuck my wings at the last second, and hurl my body into a sudden roll. My curls sweep the floor.

As I finish the roll, I violently unleash my wings. Tears slaughter my cheeks as my limbs and muscles howl from the savage force. Careless if it doesn't sound graceful, I open my mouth, so a primal angel scream tears from my throat—the sonorous, soprano roar of a divine predator. The heat detonates inside me. I beat my wings, striking the air and propelling myself into a long-range glide. My chest quakes as I soar throughout the arena. But my wings are steady as an arrow. Weightlessness, this familiar sensation, early as my newborn memories, overcomes me.

Pride thrilling me, I thrust my chest out, driving my wings forward, curling them to throttle the air. The inertia propels me back. Laughing, I throw my head, tipping my whole body upside down—until two sulfuric heated hands seize my waist, forcing me into a 180-barrel spin. My wings knock against his body, and I come face to face with those dilated pupils, as deep and dark as the Unconsecrated Crater. Those supreme wings crush the air around me, stirring wind into my curls.

My breath spasms as Lucifer presses his substantial chest down upon my breasts. His hands are flaming coals upon my flesh, and it takes all my strength to swallow my revulsion, the inner need to cough. Faced with the first and ultimate fallen angel and our ancient enmity, all my being desires nothing more than to expel him. My fingers ache to grip the weapon hidden in my skin pouch.

The Devil leans in and whispers seduction in my ear, "Impressive, little angel. You will join me tonight for a private engagement. Prepare yourself. I will summon you soon."

I hardly know where I am until Lucifer has deposited me right onto the same balcony where I'd previously stood. Smirking to one side, the fallen angel slides his hands along the sides of my body, fingers roaming across the gold leaf, lingering upon the swell of my breasts. Bile rises in my throat, but I force it back down, masking my distaste behind a sweet smile.

Lucifer nods to me, then turns, splays his wings out, and returns to the pedestal with the crowd wailing like psychopaths.

My knees buckle, but I crumple against the railing instead, beyond breathless. Still, I manage to close my eyes and gasp, "Mission accomplished."

FIVE POINT FIVE

SETTING THE TRAP

—— L U C I F E R ——

How ironic to play guardian angel tonight.

Every roll of her eyes and subtle huff were dead giveaways regarding her disdain. But she never lost her smile, or stopped swaying her delicious and dangerous body to the music. She couldn't conceal her elation, whether in her dancing eyes or glowing figure. So full of life and passion despite her motive for coming here. After all, I admire a woman who can mix business with pleasure. In her case, the scale tips to the pleasure side. As if she's ready to say "to hell with it all", fall in love with her lust, and unleash the wild, dark creature living inside her.

Tempting this little angel would be a thrill. Taking an angel mistress without consuming her soul would be the ultimate challenge. Not to mention a one-finger salute to the Tribunal. Perhaps she may be of some use regarding the latest occurrences in Hell on Earth. Appeal to whatever divine decency she bears.

My pulse quickens from the approach of more predators hiding in the shadows and making a beeline for her balcony. Whether hunters or hedonists after the prize of the first angel in Hell on Earth, they won't get the chance to breathe the same air as she.

When she plunges from the balcony, I recognize how she'd saved herself, all her energy, for the ultimate temptation. Not a challenge, though there will be time for that soon. This is her dance. A thirst, a long-lost dark hunger, ignites a shiver of desire within me. A feverish heat simmers in my blood as my eyes prowl every inch of her body as she dives and dances in midair. Twirls of torture. What's worse is how they are unintentional. In these moments, nothing exists for her but her wings. The high-pitched wallop she belts out confirms it.

A greater irony: races from all over the world will come to Hell on Earth to fulfill their deepest desires. Not once have I encountered a being with a ravenous appetite so close to mine. Until tonight...

If it wasn't for her recoiling and swallowing hard in obvious disgust, I'd be tempted to incinerate my double for touching her despite my command to maintain the ruse. Anger flares within me, quivers in my wings, and kindles my hellfire to rear. He should have known better than to let his hands play merry hell with her body. I'll arrange a quick combustion later. A shame when I've had so few rare doubles throughout the centuries. Can't master perfection.

Ashes and cinders are all that remain of the hunters approaching her. Heaving breaths and fluttering her wings, she sags against the railing, oblivious to the demon dust drifting on the wind.

And the ultimate fallen angel waiting for her in the shadows.

SIX

THE DEMON IN THE NIGHT

—ASTRAEA—

"That was quite a performance."

The low and heated voice stops me in my tracks. I turn to the stranger a few paces away.

"Some would say it was downright divine," he continues in a voice as ancient and dangerous as a double-edged blade.

All the hairs on my flesh prickle. I flare my wings, my body rigidifying as I spy the two crimson pupils, like blood moons, surrounded by winter storm irises gazing back at me from the dark entryway bordering the balcony. I narrow my eyes and survey the outline and subtle ruffling of wings, of black feathers mingling with the darkness.

On my guard from the fallen angel interloper, I stiffen and clench my fingers but play it cool. For all I know, Lucifer has sent a fallen angel to escort me to the Ninth Circle for his private engagement. "What can I say?" I shrug, then cross my arms over my chest, tilting my head toward him. "Perhaps I'll start a religion."

"Consider me your first and most ardent convert," he seductively purrs, touching a finger to his brow.

Surprised, I lift my wings and lower my hands to glide along my hips. "Well, be that as it may, you know what they say, unconsecrated one. The bigger they are, the harder they fall."

He steps out of the darkness, and my breath seizes in my chest as he counters, "Or the higher they will rise. And I assure you, I'm sizable enough to satisfy any angel in the streets but a devil in the sheets."

Daaaaaayum. It's the first time I open my mouth, but no words come out.

Not just a fallen angel, then. Wings relaxing to curl behind me, I roam my gaze up and down the beauteous being who is far more demon than fallen. Heat curls between my thighs, and my halo kindles a delirious glow upon my skin. Fallen angels mating with demons, while not unheard of, is still uncommon. His skin is dark and gray as thunder clouds vowing a great storm, but his silver mist hair falls in long, graceful tresses to his elbows, accentuating his four obsidian-like horns. Two curl in thick crescents along the sides of his face. The other two twist to sharpened points above his head. Scars pucker one side of his face and disappear beneath the collar of his open black robe but do nothing to dim his beauty.

"Is it true what they say about female angels and foreplay?" he croons, circling me. I mirror that knowing grin. I swear his voice was forged within the lightning kilns of heaven before falling mid-burn into the Unconsecrated Crater. It's sensual as a dream ending with a smoldering nightmare. And I fucking love it.

The air grows thin upon his approach. My lungs burn as if he's seduced my very oxygen to himself. Despite embarking from the darkness, more shadows pull to him, trimming his body. Fuck. It should be a crime for a specimen already as sinfully delicious as him to have tattoos swirling along his honed biceps. Serpents are no surprise, but I'll give him points for the flaming eyes they sport.

My eyes follow his, glimpsing his deep, scarlet wings, fallen ones of feathers hard as Diablo ore. "Oh, you mean the part where we make you get on your knees and beg to suck our celestial pussies, and if you do a fucking good job, we will claw the sides of your face and sing the gods-damn Handel's Messiah in every language?"

He comes full circle, lips twisting to a beguiling smirk. "Which part is true?"

"That depends."

"On what?" He draws a hand to his chin, stroking the dark stubble there.

"On what Legion you're in. And rank," I snivel, wrinkling my nose. Even half-breeds like him will enter Lucifer's mighty army and align with the fallen assholes to attack women angels, which is why so few leave the confines of the Celestial City. Heat simmers inside me when I remember one such young woman as a gang ripped her flight feathers and nearly dragged her into the Unconsecrated Crater.

Her screams haunt my memories to this day.

"Hmm..." he lowers his hand so the fingertips may kiss his others along with the heels of his hands. "My interests and profession may be more business-oriented." The two blood moon pupils under the deep hoods of his eyes gleam and turn sultry and tempting as his long, dark lashes descend to the halfway marks.

"Is that why you're here at the Gala?" I wonder, scrutinizing him as he circles me again. Not that I mind him spreading his fragrance. With my heightened senses, I analyze blood roses, smoke, spices, and a hint of Vetiver. A gentleman's scent. I fantasize about him in a corporate business suit overlooking the penthouse of the Eighth Circle. He'd survey the view, swirls a glass of fire-dream brandy, then turn to gaze at me as I'd roll onto my stomach with nothing but thin, cool sheets around my nude form. Bedroom-soft eyes and sex-messy hair. My body spasms from the fantasy, my nervous system nearly short-circuiting.

His low snigger wrenches me out of my fantasy. "I enjoy mixing business with pleasure." Those eyes roam lower, beyond my pelvis to the thong covering my pussy. His smile grows because he sees the wetness there as much as I feel it. The veins along his neck pulse, and I offer a like-minded grin from the serpent tattoos coiling around his arms, their hellfire flaring with obvious lust.

I almost lurch right into him when he projects his demon pheromones, a raw intensity that stir heat and hunger in my blood. "Oh, fuck!" I gasp, a sheen of sweat breaking out on my brow as my nipples pucker, straining against the gold leaf covering them. "That was more than pleasure," I brandish my eyes upon him with a snarl.

"Turn around is fair play," he goads me. "Your essence has been crawling all over me like a fucking spider siren since I landed on this balcony."

I raise my chin high and regal. "And I'm supposed to believe you're simply here for some heavenly hanky panky?"

He shrugs and hugs his arms to himself, ruffling his wings. "If it eases your concerns, there were more contenders."

"Oh?"

"I was the first and ensured I'd be the only."

"Oh…"

I weigh the risk, wondering if Lucifer will be offended or envious. My shameless cunt weeps with need, and I flick my eyes to his. I haven't had a decent fucking since Jack, and that was more than a few decades ago. At least not of the cock variety. And this demon screams lust and danger. Judging by the thickening bulge beyond his breeches, he wasn't lying about that "sizable" part.

Before I may respond, the demon curls a hand in a gesture to my mask, his fingers hovering above my cheek. "Quite a becoming mask, I must say. But not as becoming as the face it conceals, I imagine."

A blush rises to my exposed cheeks, and I touch a finger to the gold mask molded to my features. When I'd first secured it, I was simply grateful Camio hadn't chosen something angel-themed. Everything about it is enchanting and flawless, from the gold phoenix curving its head and beak at the very center of the eye mask. Sinuous gold and silver curls sweep and spiral beyond the phoenix body and below the asymmetrical mask.

"Nothing for you, Mr. Fifty Shades of Gray?" I quip, my eyes lingering on his skin…and scars.

"I do not need one."

He closes the distance between us. At least a head or two taller, he overpowers me with those fuck-me-hard pheromones, so I have no choice but to press against him for support. My whole body tightens from his eyes piercing mine, from his fingers teetering above my skin to radiate energy but starving me of touch.

"Surely you must know," he continues, lowering his rigid jaw, his mouth floating above my lips, beguiling me down to my bones, "that according to Dante, the Eighth Circle was reserved for wretches who'd committed fraud. And for all your adorable playing, will that halo inside your glorious flesh dim once your sins are exposed?"

At first, I open my mouth until my lower lip trembles. My sins won't ever steal my halo. Not when it shined brightest in darkness. I shiver from the memories of those haunting screams. How the Crater's deathly powers had destroyed her wings, but I'd pulled her out before it could steal her soul.

Evangelina.

The name burns a dangerous trail in my mind, capable of lighting more like mental watchtowers—solar flares of powerful neural signals to trigger my deepest sins. Tonight, I'll atone for everything.

Battling those pheromones, I expel my breath and revert to my inner psycho, who wants nothing but her own needs fulfilled. And right now, all I want is to get my first demon dicking until I feel nothing but my cunt being fed, see stars in my eyes, and forget all about that night and why I'm here. Until I get the damn Devil's summons.

"If you're such a fan of shiny things, demon," I counter, scooting forward, my breasts rubbing against his adamantine abs, nipples chafing the gold leaf, "I can think of far better methods of exposure."

He presses his lips into a tight seam as if annoyed by my banter. I clench my teeth on a hiss in response because any other demon would've jumped my bones by now.

"No qualms? No concerns about the cost?" It's the first time he touches me. His thumb traces my lips, eyes roving lower to where my breasts suffuse with warmth. "After all, with your body in such a state, you could catch a cold."

I stand on my tiptoes and whisper the hint in his ear, "I'm certain you could warm me up, demon. And as for your cost, for a face as pretty as yours with your scars and tats, I won't make you beg. And I'll sing whatever song you want."

Less than two seconds later, the demon presses my back against the alcove wall, pinning my arms above my head, possessing my mouth with his, and sliding his knee between my legs to stab against my core.

SEVEN

MEETING LUCIFER

—ASTRAEA—

"Oh, god!" I yelp against his lips before a violent growl rumbles from deep within his chest, rattling my blood and bones.

My eyes fly open when those two blood moons dilate with heat and danger. A long, thick, and ribbed tail with an arrow-tipped end appears from behind his body, curling toward me. Holy fucking devil daddy!

Silver strands eclipse his eyes, but I read the hard lines of his mouth, the jaw tensing, and the tick there hammering with lust. When his hellfire power sizzles a predatory warning to prickle the hairs on my arms, and that tail strokes my face to curve curls of my hair behind my ear, I moan an apology for the insulting curse.

Snarling his approval, he crushes his mouth to mine again. The kiss is hard and demanding. He tastes erotic like the seven deadly sins live inside his tattoos. My lips cave, opening to his hot tongue forging into my mouth, claiming me, and triggering more heat and moisture to pool from my core. That knee drives deeper into my center, soaking my thong with my fluids. I flare my hips as my nipples nearly protrude through the gold leaf. Liquid heat engulfs me, and tremors erupt over my skin as that tail journeys lower, seeking my breasts.

The tail pauses, and so does his mouth, taking pity on my swollen lips. "You're wet for me already, sweetheart. Oil of the angels…" He opens his full mouth in a shit-eating grin and taunts me with his sharpened teeth while grinding that knee into my pussy. I snap my teeth in playful response. But that tail circles the gold leaf coating my areola, spiraling closer and closer to the nipple, prompting me to lean forward and moan.

His scarlet serpent tattoos undulate within his deep gray skin. I swear they spring to life, baring their fangs. But my eyes are too glazed to recognize much, so I dismiss it. My body is a quivering mass of need. I can't even muster the protest to his "sweetheart" term. A firestorm brews inside me, the tension coiling tightest in my pussy. I groan in pain and clench my thighs around his hips, grinding against that demon dick bulging through his pants.

He snarls against my ear, "Last chance to run, little angel."

I nearly melt against him, my mouth open, breath heaving. "And why in the hell would I do that?"

"Because it won't be me on my knees begging for you to sing to me," his tone darkens, currents of his power seeping into my pores, charging my blood with electricity. I throw my head back, and he strokes my throat with his hot, rough tongue, so I whimper. "You will be on your knees singing my praises and begging me to fuck you. Or I'll give you one opportunity to run, sweetheart."

I gasp when that tongue trails down to my breast. And jolt from his tail shoving my thong to one side, arrowed end sliding along my swollen, slick folds. "You're a hunter, aren't you?" I wonder, seeking to confirm his title. Not a soldier, but he's equally as deadly.

He chuckles against my breast and fondles the other, pinching my erect nipple through the gold leaf. "Whatever I am, sweetheart, my offer still stands. You should run."

"And how far will I get?"

"Clever girl."

When the arrowed tip rubs my distended clit, I give a deep groan and tip my forehead onto his shoulder. Breathing in the vetiver, I listen to his deep voice hum, "Not far, little angel in hell. Not far."

"Well, you know what they say about a woman scorned. And I'll warn you, demon. Hell ain't got nothing on this angel. I'm a very, very sore loser."

"You'll be sore, sweetheart. I guarantee," he purrs a trail along my throat.

I don't even get the chance to tense or relax my muscles. He plunges that arrowed tail deep inside me, twisting, thrusting against my inner walls. I gasp. Sweat cleaves to my brow. I swear that tail is licking flames into my chamber and stabbing the hidden pleasure knot. He works a sensory maelstrom inside me, carrying me so close to the edge again and again until I'm fucking singing, begging for him to finish.

Lips settling against my ear rouse the fine hairs along my neck to needle high. The demon hums, "Mmm, you are soaked to the core for me, aren't you? I look forward to tasting your golden flesh, little angel. Would you care to know what nerves my tail contains?" He rumbles laughter, swiping that pleasure knot inside.

I snap my head to the side and bare my sharp angel teeth, bounce them against his throat. "You are getting on my nerves, demon," I snarl, thrusting my pelvis in a feral need for that tail to rip through my pussy.

"Demanding, aren't we?" He strokes his tongue across the side of my neck. I flinch, moaning. On the verge of detonating. He doesn't give me what I want. The tail eases away inch by inch, and I open my mouth to yell my protest, but the demon adds, "What will happen, sweetheart? When Lucifer discovers your fraud? How you're nothing but a wild and lustful little cherub who's pricked herself with her own arrows?"

"Call me a fucking cherub again, and I'll prick your demon heart with my sword."

"The Eighth Circle is for liars. The Ninth is for betrayers. Why do I get the feeling that you are betraying someone quite close to you even now?"

"I can't help your fucking feelings, asshole. If you're worried about my guilt, you can light a candle and say a few mother-fucking Hail Mary's on my behalf. I can mix business with pleasure, too. But I'm still waiting on the latter. So, if you're too impotent to put out, then you can go to he—"

The tail plunges deep inside me. I throw my head back. And scream. My halo erupts, showering the edges of my skin with gold beams. Stars explode in my vision, and I breathe a silent prayer of gratitude that the nightclub drowns out the sounds of my orgasmic cries. The demon's eyes burn against mine, igniting flames to charge inside my blood.

Nearly limp with pleasure, I drop my head onto his shoulder. And dive my hand down to his pants, eager for far more beyond simply his tail to fill me. Until the gem-plant on my wrist vibrates, pulsating and stinging my skin. I straighten. Above my VIP mark, a holo-gem pops up with an automated message:

"Trinny Malak, Lucifer Morningson, Dawn-Bringer, High Lord of Hell, has summoned you. Make your way to the nearest Eighth Circle

Station. A private hover-bubble will be waiting to transport you to the Ninth Circle."

I sigh deeply, touch my lips to the demon's, and shrug. "Looks like our time is up. Raincheck?"

That shit-eating grin again threatens to turn my legs into golden goo. "It never rains in Hell on Earth, sweetheart. But rest assured, you'll come back for a ride on my dark side. But it's a one-way ticket. So, when I fuck you for the first time, you will belong to me. And you'll sing those pretty, heavenly anthems for me alone."

"Yeeeah…" I push off him, adjust my thong, and toss my curls onto my back, posturing high. "I'm not so into ownership. But I hope you enjoyed the show."

The demon swings his tail, still coated in my fluids, to his lips where he sucks on the arrowed tip, grinning to display a full row of pointed fangs. "It was a real treat, sweetheart."

I shake my head and roll my eyes but conceal my smirk. Guess I've always had a thing for the bad boys. The sycophantic suck-up angels with their sperm-surging balls in the breeding program, always ready to get on their knees and worship us rare female angels, have never interested me. Even if the women get to claim their own harem.

As I climb into the awaiting hover-bubble, I prop my elbow on the glass and contemplate how it takes far more for a man to get a woman to submit to him on her knees. Jack came fucking close. He's always respected me, treated me like his equal, believing what's inside me is strong enough to hurt and heal me. But Abaddon was the one who got me through my darkest night, my true hell. And he's off-fucking limits.

A wave of ice overcomes me. Tears threaten to blind me when I consider all Lucifer has done to rattle the foundation of this world, how much he's fucked heaven and earth with his alpha hole legions, and how much he's done to us. Never just me. I choke back the emotion and strangle the nightmarish thoughts darkening my mind.

Five years in the making, we've planned this: our dark secret we've kept from everyone else. He could never make it to the Ninth Circle. Tonight, I'll be damned if I don't get vengeance for us and all gods-damned heaven.

When the hover-bubble's centrifugal force latches onto a set of tracks, I know it's about to take the plunge. The announcer proclaims how the shields around the car will prevent motion sickness while imparting the adrenaline rush. I snort laughter, considering how I've taken plunges higher and steeper than this one since I was a toddler.

But I still rake my nails into the sides of my seat from the sheer drop. Adrenaline thrashes in my veins, stirring my halo to shimmer along the edges of my body. The one light in this darkness since Lucifer would never allow anyone from chamber dignitaries to the highest princes of Hell on Earth to know the twisted routes of the Ninth Circle.

Once the hover-bubble slows, the dark window technology fades to offer me a view of an enormous dragon frozen in ice with its mouth wide open. At first, I flinch from the lifelikeness until my mind registers the frosted ice encasing the scaled monstrosity.

I sigh as the hover-bubble stops before the frosted staircase leading up to the mouth. Several demon guards equipped with hell pit-forged blades stand on each side. Climbing out of the bubble, I square my shoulders, wishing I wasn't so impressed with the frozen dragon.

"Gotta give him points for ingenuity," I mutter to the demons, but they don't so much as flick an eye in my direction. Stiller than statues, as frozen as the dragon. I'm half-tempted to make a few faces at them, poke one or two, but I've had my fun for the evening.

This angel is all business now.

"Trinny Malak," the holo-gem flickers from my wrist, alerting me. "Progress into the dragon's mouth and follow the arrows to your meeting with Lucifer, High Lord of Hell on Earth. Thank you."

I don't waste time. As the darkness folds around me, I creep my hand toward the skin pouch, toward the one weapon I could manage to smuggle in. Much like me, she may be little, but she is fierce.

Gem-tech hums its energy to prickle the hairs on my skin to static. Arrows in the shape of a devil's tail light the way, but my halo gifts me all the glow I need. On each side of me, shadows lurk upon black walls that thrum with dark energy I've never seen. But once it slithers along my skin, I jerk back, hissing, flaring my wings. It's Diablo ore. Mined straight from the Unconsecrated Crater, the ore is the hardest substance upon the earth—harder than diamonds—with an echo of the same lethal, otherworldly force haunting the crater.

A shiver trails down my spine, but I press onward and ignore all the voices in my head that warn me to turn and fly in the opposite direction. They remind me too much of my brothers.

Finally, the stone walls open to a waiting room, a lobby of sorts, if a lobby is located inside a massive cave system. Shaped into a circle, the waiting room's center is a pit with a roaring fire in its center. No wood or tinder lights it, but its source is gem-tech or Lucifer's hellfire magic. Seated around the flaming pit are long couches broken by end tables. At the edge of the waiting room is a single staircase leading to an upper level with two balconies.

The arrows light the way to the staircase.

Keenly aware of the exits and angles of the cavern system, I step onto the staircase and turn away from the multiple arches leading to halls reeking of sulfur and smoke. Bloodcurdling screams disturb the air, echoing from those halls. Grateful for the barriers of flaming light that mask the source of those screams, I ball my hands into fists, tense all my muscles, and advance to the upper level.

Two great doors of Diablo ore lie before me with intricate, coiling serpents trimming them. No handles or cracks. The dark energy pulses onto my skin, raising gooseflesh.

Before I may knock on the doors, they open. For the first time, I turn to look behind me, my head dizzy from my hesitance, from anxiety. The demon's words about the Eighth Circle, about fraud and deception, haunt my mind. No, this is what Lucifer wants. Fucking drama queen directing me into the literal mouth of a monstrous beast. I'll give him points for suspense. I wouldn't be surprised if he wrote this as a morbid film script. Too bad it's so cliché.

Body and breath shuddering, I lick my lips and press them to steeled resolve, cracking my neck. I enter. Inhaling deeply, I stride down a hallway lined with more Diablo ore. Walls of pure hellfire on each side. The nerves in my feathers sense the heat sizzling from the walls, preying on my skin. I quicken my steps. The last thing I want is for any of this gold leaf to melt.

The hallway clears to a suite. Not any suite. I slide my hand down a railing and descend a few steps into the heart of the suite. Staring above my head, I marvel at the expanse.

"Hells bells and buckets of blood!" I gush from the chandelier of countless chains of diamonds cascading from the ceiling, each shimmering a dim light to the room.

Off to my left is a fully-stocked bar with a back wall of skulls wreathed in hell flames.

Curved and spanning a great L-shape, the glass windows form all the walls, sweeping from floor to ceiling and offering an overpowering view of the Ninth Circle's downtown district. Thousands of VIPs, political gurus, and staff fill its swirling sub-towers. In the distance, I make out hundreds of points of light. Narrowing my eyes, I weave around the lavish furniture and get as close to the windows as possible. My chest spasms from the realization of those points of light: the Lava Pits of Hell. The one place on the earth capable of forever destroying an angel's wings—never to grow again.

"Admiring the view, sweetheart?"

My blood freezes in my veins. Fear engulfs me, and I stiffen. And yet, my body tightens from the familiar scent of smoke and vetiver, of spices and blood roses…and the memory of that delirious tail stroking my heated inner walls.

Crossing my arms over my chest, I slowly turn to face the demon from earlier, spreading my lips into an angelic smile.

"I'll give you something far more beautiful to admire," he proclaims, spreading his arms, vast wings lifted high as he makes his way down the staircase from the upper level. Donned in nothing but a scarlet velvet robe.

Self-loathing rises within me at what should have been so obvious— bloody Prince of Lies. I narrow my eyes, ruffle my feathers in a flirty gesture, and sweet-wrap my psycho to play the lustful ruse, "Hello, Lucifer."

Once he crosses the distance to us, I'm not surprised when he chuckles darkly and waggles those brows. Nor when he sets his crater-deep-hooded crimson eyes upon mine. I'm not surprised when he seizes my waist, taps the edge of my backside with his claws, and draws me closer to drag his full and sensual mouth across my jawline until he arrives at my ear.

But when he whispers, "Welcome to my suite, Astraea," I know that if I had a heart, it would have plunged into my stomach, crawled right out of my asshole, and rolled out of the penthouse as fast as its strings could carry it.

The Devil knows my fucking name!

EIGHT

A BATTLE WITH THE DEVIL

—ASTRAEA—

"Holy shit," I snarl and shiver against the Devil, wishing I could shake off the encounter from earlier. Or how my skin tingles with every tap of those claws close to my ass. The scars puckering one side of his face do nothing to eclipse the rest of his dark beauty. And prowess.

Amused as I shake my head violently, struggling against him, Lucifer tightens his grip on my waist, permitting me to lean my upper half away from him. "Unholy," he corrects, casting warm breath across my cheek. Strands of his silver hair mingle with mine. Much of them he's gathered in a man bun, and it's criminal how sexy but sinful it is, especially with his black horns.

"Ugh…" I roll my eyes and glance to my left at the flames swirling from behind the bar. "I seriously need a drink."

He loosens his hold. One hand slows as it slides from my waist while he gestures with his other, "Please help yourself. But if you're truly thirsty, sweetheart, I'll be more than gratified to provide you with a cocktail delicacy your angel tongue won't soon forget."

My eyes grow wide at the implication, and I gulp when that bulge behind his robe boasts how he is more monster than man. His tail swings to the side. And I swear it waves at me.

Turning to the bar to regain my composure, I stiffen and tap the gem-tech menu, peeling aside my mask to rest it on the counter. "As much as I enjoy a mouth-watering cocktail, I'm afraid it plays the devil with my stomach."

His laughter, heated and knowing to mirror his smirk, rumbles from his chest, stirring the serpent heads tattooed there. They narrow their eyes upon me, sultry and warm as fresh blood. Flames trim his wings, and I imagine if he desired, he could command them to charge at any time.

Monster moonshine," I order without hesitation, sliding onto a bar stool.

"A bold choice," declares the ultimate fallen angel, sitting next to me, tapping his thumb to summon his own. "Dragon's blood." I swallow hard, refusing to give anything away regarding my usual favorite preference.

Lucifer's wings are close enough for his talons to brush mine, but I fold my wings in tight behind me, beyond uncomfortable at the most sacred part of me touching any part of him.

Straightening, I raise my chin to him and lilt, "I need something stronger to wash the taste of Satan from my mouth."

Lucifer leans in and thumbs the center of my chin, casting that sweet and spicy scent all over me, igniting my pheromones, so I lock my aching thighs. "I don't recall any complaints from your pretty pink tits or that heaven-scented soaked pussy when it rubbed against me as your fucking tongue was down my throat like I was your fucking manna from gods-damned heaven."

I glower, try to jerk my chin away, and protest, "And how much was your damned unconsecrated power seducing me while my guard was down?"

"Trust me, sweetheart…" Lucifer retains his hold, mouth prowling, a subtle growl rising in his throat, "…if I wanted to use my power, your guard alone would not be down. You would be down on your knees crawling on the floor like my bitch, begging to worship my cock and fold your pretty, angel lips around it until I fuck that tight throat and teach your tongue a lesson in manners." He twists his lips into a sardonic smirk, glancing down to where my nipples have responded to his touch, predatory eyes, and authoritative words.

Arrogance in power and a sharp tongue always get me wet, and the Devil knows exactly when and how to wield both. Unlike me, who can't ever fucking shut her mouth. It's why Jack and I worked so well, but while Tempest is a playful cocky, his ego could never match Lucifer's—however well-earned. I have no doubt the Devil could follow through with his words. Not that I wouldn't go down swinging…and biting.

I frown and huff, thankful the circular opening in the bar thrusts the two glasses to the surface. Lucifer captures both before I do, and our fingers brush. I recoil as if electricity has stung me. Lucifer rolls his eyes, threads his brows, then hands me the glass of monster moonshine. I waste no time tipping the glass back, downing the two fingers in one hard gulp. Then clutch my throat burning on the inside. Fire engulfs my blood, and my insides protest from whatever wild magic roars there. My cheeks redden to a boiling flush.

Lucifer nods, raising his glass to me as smoke gushes from my mouth. "My compliments, sweetheart. My moonshine is made with something extra: a hint of lava spice straight from my pits."

Coughing more puffs of smoke, I pull at the anger flowing in my veins. "You could have warned me."

Wicked smile creasing his lips, the Devil sips at his dragon's blood, winks at me, and shrugs. "What fun would that have been?"

I cross my arms over my chest and sneer. "If you'd wanted fun, I have a host of ideas," I hint, steeling my spine. Regardless of him knowing my identity, nothing has changed. I may have lost an edge of surprise, but I came here for one purpose. My soul screams for vengeance, but I contain that and curl my fingers, extending my claws, relying on my training. And my reflexes, my sharp instincts, my wit. I'll need everything to beat the Devil.

"Hmm…you mean this fun?" He retrieves a tool from his robe, wagging it in the air with a devilish grin.

I get to my feet and flare my wings, dropping my hand to my thigh, to the skin pouch where my one weapon has disappeared into Lucifer's fucking hand.

"Bloody hell," I seethe and bend my knees, lift my wings, preparing to pounce.

Lucifer shakes his head in warning, but his voice is casual. "I wouldn't advise it, little angel. After all, you have no one to blame but yourself. Perhaps you shouldn't spread your thighs so freely, however ample and lovely they are." His smirk is beyond wicked. It's wolfish.

Triggered, I unleash my claws, curving my wings with their talons primed. My skin turns gold from the halo radiating through me. I harden all my muscles.

Snorting, Lucifer balances the point of the blade on the counter, downs the rest of his dragon's blood, then tightens his robe sash before rising to face me, mirroring my offensive body language. "You want to dance then, sweetheart?"

A rare vibration rears inside me, and I narrow my eyes. One I've made once—too close to the Unconsecrated Crater. Angels' vocal cords have more abilities than humans, and while the stars may bow and bleed from our screams, the sound surging in my chest is a shrill, rattling trill. A soprano, celestial warning.

"Now, that's a sound I haven't heard in a long time," remarks Lucifer, straying from the bar counter with the weapon still clenched in his firm hand. "And far more rapturous than any other in my centuries. Will you sing for me, too, sweetheart?"

"I'll sing the Rapture down on your head, pretty demon," I snarl, revealing all my honed angel teeth.

"So fucking adorable!" Lucifer grins as our eyes hunt one another— two predators sizing each other up.

The moment after he spreads his hands wide, goading me and swinging that tail, I lunge. Swiping my claws at his bare chest, I thrill when I draw first blood. Lucifer glances down as I dance out of his arms' range, swaying my hips.

A violent sound reverberates from his chest—the counterpart to my angelic trill. A dark demonic call. If thunder could purr, it would sound exactly like that. When his scent and pheromones and a sizzling current ride across my flesh and slither into my pores to stoke my blood, I realize what he's done. Those power tones have my body trembling and knees weakening. The thunder-purr that was not a demon growl but a fallen angel call, I grind my teeth and snap my eyes to his.

"Did you fucking lust-hum me?" I seethe, shaking off the wealth of warmth from that thunderous purr before tensing my wings.

Lucifer bobs his brows, ruffling his dark feathers, scarlet eyes turned to mere slits. "Your game, angel. Appropriate for me to get an edge when you're standing there looking like sin and smelling like you need to be devil-fucked."

"Oh, I'm more than ready to fuck you up."

I swing toward him, claws and teeth prepared. He's faster than I expect. Curling one hand around my arm, tugging me toward him, Lucifer thunder-purrs again. Holding my breath, I use the momentum to pitch my body into a violent spring while beating my wings. I use his shoulders as a launchpad, careful to evade those sharp horns, but before I can take to the air, he grips a handful of my hair and drags me in a powerful arc. Then shoves me against the bar.

Winded and breathless, I close my eyes to ward off the dizziness from the brutal impact. He presses his chest down upon mine and clicks his teeth. "Tsk, tsk, tsk, the first rule of fighting: always keep your hair up." With a proud pat on his man bun, Lucifer gives me a shit-eating grin, lowering his head toward me.

Before he can purr thunder and pheromones again, I reach up and rip those silver tresses from their bun. The Devil growls from the invasion, putting a gap between us. Enough for me to drop my weight and beam when I claw at his nude legs, stripping dark flesh. I'm rewarded with a raging demon howl. As he turns, I roll into a crouch and jerk my chin to him in a mocking nod.

Inhaling deep, I bring my claws, still dripping with his flesh and blood, to my lips and angel trill, "I love the smell of devil blood."

Up till now, that smirk has remained on his lips. Now, it falls as mine grows. Lucifer tapers his brows, eyes turning to pure hellfire. He swipes a hand down his face and seethes, "Fine. You wanna play, dirty angel?

No more Mr. Nice Satan. I'll show you how I got these scars." For the first time, he extends his claws and fangs.

"I know where you're next one will be," I hint dangerously, biting my lower lip in a taunt.

His body moves, wings spreading into an upward curve, legs tightening. My blood boils as I launch to meet him in mid-air until we crash into a tangle of claws, teeth, wings, and talons.

"Mmm, so this angel likes kink!" Lucifer growls and grips my throat in a chokehold, smothering my breath. "I should break out the fluffy cuffs."

Hissing, I tuck my chin low, bring my palm down hard on his wrist, and thrust my elbow in a brutal blow to his jaw. Enough that he breaks his hold. "I'll be your daddy, Devil," I taunt and blow him a kiss, strutting my hips and flaring my feathers.

Lucifer charges for me, so blindingly fast, that it rips the air from my lungs when our bodies knock against the glass. But it doesn't crack or so much as tremble, so I know it's reinforced. I shred the flesh on one side of his neck and shriek in pain when he rips into my back, reopening old scars beyond the sealer I used to cover them. Wings beating, talons vying with the other's, we trade crushing blows until I've broken his ribs, and he's dislocated my shoulder.

Embers from the flames around his wings crackle and spit at my body. I don't flinch.

The demon captures my jaw with his claws and claims my mouth in a kiss. Carnivorous and captivating. That power current binds around me like a cage and tightens my throat, restricting my breath. All so he may force my lips open. Once his tongue snakes out, I seize the moment and bite hard, drawing blood. Growling, he charges his power around me. My lungs burn, darkness clouds my vision. I have no choice but to collapse against him, registering I'm about to pass out.

The split second his mouth crushes mine is when air fills my lungs. He's fucking feeding me air.

As soon as he pulls away, that power strangles my throat again. Despite our wings whipping wind around us, my whimper is sliced off by a lack of oxygen. I snap my gaze at him, gritting my teeth.

"Bite me again, Astraea, and I'll take everything," he warns with a fierce glower before gripping a handful of my curls to jerk my head back. And forcing my mouth to open. Again, he crushes his lips to mine and gifts me with blessed air.

Unable to do anything else, I gulp it down, drinking whatever he gives me, moaning from his tongue tasting mine, flicking the roof of my mouth. No, I can't bite him, so I improvise. Relieved by the precious oxygen, I drive my powerful knee in a solid stab straight to his balls. Wings giving out, the Devil roars, gripping his wounded pride as he crashes to the floor.

More than anything, I want to have another go at him. By now, my dislocated shoulder and back wounds have already healed due to my angel blood. But my brothers trained me better: know your opponent, assess their skill level, and most importantly, know when to cut and run. My body is tired. I've lost track of how long we've battled in this suite. Minutes? Hours? Regardless, I can't risk that power force suffocating me again. He won't let me get anywhere near his balls again. I've won this battle, but if I don't get the fuck out of here now, he'll win the war.

Lamenting the loss of my little but lethal weapon, I pulse my wings, swing my body forward, and charge for the suite exit, for that Diablo ore-layered hall. Chest expanding with fresh air and the thought of freedom, I laugh while my halo radiates warmth throughout my body, lighting my skin at its edges.

And as I cross the verge of that hallway, something sturdy and strong lashes my back. I freeze midair.

"Did you just fucking whip me?" I gasp, spinning my head, struggling to stay aloft, battling the familiar feeling

That powerful tail swings again, striking harder. It's too late. The storm of Déjà vu memories devours me. Hundreds of training marks earned from failure.

I seize up as hot blood pools down my back. Pain erupts there but most at the back of my throat.

Stars explode in my vision, and I hear a crack—brutal and bone-deep. I know I'm screaming from the wing fracture, but the storm of memories clouds everything, including my hearing.

Like an instrument of torture, reality bends and curves, twisting my mind into its illusion. I pass from the training field to a deeper horror. Wings of ash, nothing but ashes—glittery sprinkles in my hands, coating her flesh. A dead halo. Breath of sulfur, eyes weeping acid, blood flowing down my back. I can't breathe.

Reality springs back into place when a figure blocks my vision. A formidable silhouette against the light of the black diamond chandelier dripping from the ceiling. I fantasize about them falling like a tiny black army, blades ready to beat the Devil, who kneels and stares down at me, tracing one finger over my cracked wing.

"Naughty, fucking angel."

I quiver from the tender assault and trill a warning before moaning and rolling onto my side. The Devil yanks me hard, so I'm on my back again. I gulp a whimper, cringing when the hard floor presses against the fresh lacerations from his tail. When he slams his knee down on my chest, drawing the breath right out of me, I cough. Then freeze from the thrust of the familiar celestial-forged blade that he presses to my throat.

Lowering his head, Lucifer purrs that lustful thunder fiercer. It ignites all my nerve endings and flushes liquid heat throughout my body until I'm spreading myself—hating myself for parting my thighs, for splaying my wings, arching my neck, and thrusting my chest to rub his. More than ever, his power guts me until tremors rack my body. Blood hammers my ears, but I can still hear my primal, trilling screams filling the entire suite.

None could drown out the sound of Lucifer humming in my ear, setting all my hairs to prickle, "We have unfinished business, Astraea."

NINE

ESCAPING LUCIFER

—ASTRAEA—

"I must commend you on your choice of blades, little warrior," expresses Lucifer as he caresses the knife hilt while dragging its point across the curve of my throat. "An archangel's talon. Forged within the kilns of heaven from the fabric of the stars. Small enough that you could fit it into that cunning location so close to your tantalizing cunt. But deadly enough to pierce and cut an angel's wings."

Lucifer's eyes don't leave mine. I glare coldly at him and swallow my fear, treating it like a poison I'd vomit out later as I always did.

He then taps the knife point across my cheek, his grin twisted and malevolent. "Now that your sins are laid bare, your deception confessed as I predicted, what shall the cost be? Hmm, it would be a shame to mark up that pretty face, especially when I will enjoy those cheeks blushing and your eyes rolling back when I fuck your little throat while your pretty pink lips suck me off."

Anger pushes through me with an angel's wrath trailing its heels. I rear up and spit in his face. "Or you can suck my hind tit!"

With my blood racing in my veins, competing with the galloping adrenaline, I grip the opposite edge of the knife, careless if it cuts me. We become a stalemate of wills, our eyes burning against one another. His tongue snakes out in a lascivious taunt. And though he has strength on his side, I fall back on my decades of training, the trauma-filled scars on my back, and the screams I will never forget. Everything fuels me. More blood trickles from my hand as I push the knife back, back, back until the Devil blinks.

Not wasting that eyelash beat, I twist my wrist, grip the hilt, and thrust the knife right into Lucifer's collarbone. He roars, loosens his hold on me. I scramble out from under him, beating my wings and crouching to seize the air.

More blood streams from the wounds on my back and my hand, but it doesn't matter. I sweep through the Diablo ore hall, take a deep breath to catch all the fresh air I may, and swing beyond the mouth of the dragon. No hover-car waits. So, I charge for the nearest tunnel, hoping it will lead me out of this fucking hellhole of the Ninth Circle. I haven't stopped tensing my muscles but feel numb from adrenaline— no pain from the wounds, and by the time I would, they will have probably healed.

Hope catches in my chest at a light in the distance, but I cough and fling it away because it's too delicate, too breakable. Hope has failed me too much. Blood pulsing, body quivering, I whip my wings onward in a seamless glide, exerting muscles like old friends until I arrive at the light. Less than a second later, wind rifles through my hair. My reflexes kick in, and I swing back in the nick of time. One centimeter—or less— more, and the hover-tram flying past would have turned me into an angel pancake.

It's a convergence point. Like the spoke of a wheel with several other tunnels leading to various destinations.

I recognize the silver capsule disappearing like a needle into a tunnel on my left. A tram: equipped with protective shields, they enable VIPs to cruise the Nine Circles above the surface and tour the pits of hell where Lucifer's demon spawn are birthed.

Within moments, more hover-bubble cars and smaller trams whirl past me, each faster than a shooting laser. With all the transports surging past, a deep part of me knows it would be near suicide to fly into that wheel. The hairs on the back of my neck prickle, whether from fear or insanity or fucking panic, I can't tell.

Behind me, dozens of snarls reverberate off the tunnel's walls, and I spin my head to none other than a squad of fallen fucking alpha holes. Flaring my nostrils, I ignore the tremor in my fingers, slow my rasping breath, and focus on the flying silver bullets and bubbles before me. I track whatever patterns I may within a few seconds, already sensing the chill pebbling my skin with goosebumps from the fallen angels closing in.

"Now, now, pretty angel…" one in the front ranks mentions, his voice guttural with the sensation of scraping against my spine with rusty nails. "Don't want to get those shiny wings crushed, do we?"

Of course, we wouldn't. As if he has any claim to my wings.

The pattern is subtle, chaotic, but I've broken it down as much as possible. No more time to tempt fate. I hover here with the squad encroaching, cautious and slow as if I'm a doe-eyed deer they don't want to frighten.

Out of the corner of my eye, the squad leader stretches his clawed fingers to me, mere inches away. "Lucifer wants a word with you, little warrior."

"Sorry, boys!" I finally chime in and bolster the muscles in my wings, turning my head at an angle to wink. "I've got a train to catch!"

The trill that flees my throat when I sail into the hub and seize the 300-mile-an-hour wind current along with a metal rung on the edge of the tram is a rare one—one I haven't felt since before Evangelina. My hair flies far behind me like a banner. The air chafes all my exposed skin, ripping off flecks of gold leaf. But I have to credit those artists for the pieces living up to their promise: the gold leaf will stick to me for twenty-four hours in any type of weather or environment. I wonder if they could have predicted an angel riding a silver beast of a tram like a lady boss making it her bitch!

Blisters form on my hands from gripping so tight to the rung. I drive my wings harder than ever, losing a few feathers to the wild current. The last time this euphoria hit me, I was leaping off the clifftop of Mount Yvos, diving through patchworks of foggy clouds and scaring the shit out of Jack. Now, I'm scaring the shit out of myself, but damn—what a rush! I'll need to add this to my scorecard of flight triumphs. Not that I haven't already broken every record in the Celestial City. A sense of wonder fills my hollow chest cavity, lighting up all the neurons and synapses in my mind like a gods-damned disco ball.

When the tram approaches another hub, I know I can't risk flying through another tunnel on one of these. Never thinking because I hardly ever do, I leap, snapping my wings midair, tucking my body into a tight roll to narrowly avoid the self-flying helicopter blades roaring above my head. Blood pounds terror in my ears. I hold my pained chest together as the blades loom closer. I gasp when they slice off a few curly tresses and knock my body around, but my well-trained wings serve me with their strength. My training, my angel reflexes do the rest.

I land in a flawless crouch on the closest hover car, grateful it's much slower than the tram, moving at a leisurely pace, probably headed to a Ninth Circle casino or hotel. As long as I can catch a ride back to the surface, I'll be home-free. The gem-plant will give me access to anything. I could probably hide out on Hell on Earth until the heat dies down. After all, it's not like Lucifer is going to drop everything to send a legion after one little angel, I sniff. I could shack up with Camio for a few days. He always throws a great party.

On both sides of me are dozens of landing platforms for the hover bubbles with holo-gem directories to various Ninth Level districts. Determined shoulders pushed back, I take a deep breath, preparing my muscles so I may launch at any one of them. Wings fluttering to mirror the butterflies in my chest, I rock forward onto my toes.

Steady, Astraea. It sounds eerily like Abaddon's voice inside my head. He's taken me under his wing all these years, so to speak. I giggle. My guardian angel. The hovercar may be slower, but it doesn't mean it isn't dangerous. One wrong move, the barest flick of a wingtip or a muscle tweaking at the worst moment, a ninety-mile-an-hour wind could still batter me against these walls and pulverize me to a bloody angel pulp fit for a monster's stew.

Taking a deep breath through my nose as all my brothers have trained me, I study the placement of the platforms. How far apart they are. How wide and how high they are. How fast the bubble car is rushing.

I thrust my chest out, spring from the hovercar, contort my wings within a second, tumble into a seamless somersault, and use the platform as a launchpad.

Another thrilling trill of jubilation scrambles up my throat until something iron-hard slams into my body, battering me against the wall. Knocking the wind out of me. Bones crack. My breath wheezes. Ears hollow out. My mouth opens in a silent howl from the pain, and I swear something slams against my rib cage walls. The coppery taste of blood engulfs my mouth. Tears burn in my eyes. I spit the viscous fluid. And a tooth.

Head pounding, vision dizzy, I struggle to get up. Can't stay down. Down is where it's dark, where it's cold, where I can't breathe from the dark shade magic of reapers and soul hunters. A whimper leaves my mouth as I swipe at my lips, discovering three blurry fingers that remind me of twisted, gnarly branches. While on my knees, dark, winged figures approach me.

"Fuck, my King!" a familiar voice bellows as I struggle to get to my feet. The voice of a pretty beast I have heard before. "I could have stopped her without such violence. Astraea, Astraea, dear!"

Bile churns in my belly. Nausea migrates in the wrong direction until I retch my guts onto the platform. Acidic pain sears my throat.

A heated hand bearing claws as long as daggers but deadlier and sharper touches my face. I wince, registering the legion of bruises on my body. The cracked ribs. Bloody mouth. Hours at least to heal. Massive warm wings, raven wings, fold around my body. The giant serpent tail and the wolf teeth define him.

"Aamon," I whisper the name that soothes, that calms my mind.

"I have better things to do with my time than chase this little daredevil with a death wish all over the Ninth Circle," snarls Lucifer from the opposite side. I shake my head because the blurs impede my vision grow, turning dark. Oh shit.

"Daredevil," I mutter, holding on tighter than ever to my sarcasm and spit, splattering blood upon the ends of Lucifer's long, black robe, projecting a couple of chunks of vomit for good measure. "What, what, what I wonder may be the dare from the Devil?"

"She's in shock," Aamon deepens his voice, but it sounds like desperation, like panic. "I have to get her to a med-room. Now. Or the damage to her wings could be permanent."

Permanent. I can't contrive what the word means. But I know it's wrong. My eyes roll to their ceilings.

"Go on then. Bring the little hummingbird to the closest med-room."

Lucifer's final words are wronger. Worse than the Unconsecrated Crater. But it's too late for me to protest. I'm already passing out.

TEN

THE DEVIL'S WARNING

——ASTRAEA——

Hundreds of thousands of tiny prickles stinging my skin wake me. My eyes fly open, panic spreading them all the more: I can't move one fucking muscle. And I'm naked, lying on a cold, metallic table with my wings splayed out on each side and a gem-stitcher above my head.

"Relax, bitch. It's nearly finished," a familiar tenor resounds from a speaker above my head.

Camio. I clench my teeth. Around me, the walls hum with gem energy, the fluorescent lights flooding all of me as if I'm a fucking bug under a microscope. A warm wave streams across my body in a slow pass-over, retrieving what I assume are the microscopic gem-bots programmed to repair any broken bones and flesh and restore the fabric of my wings. Nowhere near as effective as our star pools in the Celestial Mountains, these gem-bots could never hope to edit or sequence angel DNA or genes. All they do is manipulate my cells to swifter healing.

As soon as a final wave pulses and the prickling sensation is gone, the numbness subsides, and the feeling returns to my quivering muscles. Chin lifting high, I face the large one-way mirror opposite the table, giving it my best angel-with-a-dirty-face glare, followed by my middle finger.

"Now, that was quite rude," Aamon's voice flows through the speakers, and I wish it weren't so gods-damned tranquilizing. Understandable why he earned the title of the Demon of Reconciliation. "Robes off to your left, Astraea."

No time wasted, I climb off the table, my knees wobbly. While approaching the robes, I raise my wings, ruffle the feathers, flutter them, and do a slight wingbeat, satisfied by the range of motion. No feathers missing, so I lower my shoulders, heaving a deep sigh of gratitude at their healing.

At least my thong was preserved. After shrugging into the panties and the silky black robe, I tie the sash tight and sweep my curls out from the robe's inside to ripple down my shoulders. A door swings forward into the med-room, nearly clocking me in the head. Camio hauls me into an attached observatory room and swings me into his arms. I wheeze when he hugs me so tight, it cuts off my air.

"I'm so sorry I got you into this mess, Astraea," he apologizes and cups my cheeks as Aamon glides toward us upon that massive serpent tail glimmering like liquid sapphires—a contrast to his black feathered raven wings. One curves around Camio's shoulder, tapping his arm in a soothing gesture that radiates an encouraging warmth into my body.

"Cami has been beside himself ever since your aerobatic display at the Gala: gemming me every five minutes," he indicates to his gem-plant, "and paying Ninth Circle security to learn where Lucifer summoned you. He even arranged a private transport to help you escape."

A vein in my neck twitches, and I wrinkle my nose, eyeing my human friend. "Could've given me a heads up, Cam. Hell, I'd have taken a toenail's up before Lucifer royally rattled my bones." I don't remember much from the incident, but after our time in the suite, I know what Lucifer's body feels like when it slams against mine. The sharp masculinity of his armored muscles, the powerful sinew of his wings, his thighs roped with solid muscle. I stop myself and replace the memories of my legs wrapped around his hips with the one of me kneeing him in the balls in midair and sending him crashing to the suite floor.

"Couldn't risk gemming you or anything else, love. Once you were on Lucifer's radar, the gem-plant was compromised."

I guess that makes sense. Camio touches my upper back, sliding it around my shoulder in a one-armed hug. Hard to believe the world's first murderer turned reformed cinnamon roll cares about me this much when a mere twenty-four years spans our relationship: an eye blink of time for the immortal human. If I had a heart, it would sputter a bit. My blood warms when Camio rubs his lips on the side of my head, stirring heat to my cheeks. I hug my chest and flick my eyes to Aamon, who smiles, revealing his predatory teeth.

"So, I take it he contacted you instead?" I throw the prince a side smirk and lower my hands to my hips, knowing he will have his hands full with the demon legions he commands.

"You should know by now, Astraea, if push comes to shove, and I must choose between calming and reconciling Camio or the hundreds of demons within my care, it will always be Camio."

Warmth floods my chest cavity as the demon slides his tail around my immortal friend, drawing him close for a kiss on the cheek. Camio waves a casual hand, but I love how hot and bothered he gets from

Aamon's public displays of affection.

"Oh, come now, Aamon, you'll make me blush."

I beam at the two of them. At heart, Camio is an attention man whore—so adorable when he pecks the demon's cheek and starts playing with the ends of his flirty serpent tail.

A chill slithers up my spine when I remember the unfortunate circumstances that necessitated Aamon's interference. Exhaling with my wings drooping ever so subtly, I glance at the demon prince whispering sweet nothings into Camio's ear to turn the human's cheeks even redder. I dart my eyes between them, admiring the contrast of Camio's dark skin against the demon's deep blue sky. On the rare occasion that Aamon blushes, his cheeks turn a lovely shade of violet.

A twinge of guilt knots my stomach lining because the last thing I wanted was for either of them to get involved in this—at least nothing beyond Camio using his slush fund and resources for the gem-plant and mask.

I imagine I'll be sent back to the Celestial City with my tail between my legs in no time. But if Lucifer does anything to my boys, I won't stop until I've personally dragged Abaddon to wreak havoc on his ass. As long as I get to mount it on my wall afterward.

"Humph," I snort after the observatory room entrance door opens, revealing multiple fallen angels girded in black gem-tech armor. Far lighter and more effective than body armor since it must be strong enough to take a blow from a centaur's hoof to vampire claws to demon fists. I recognize their rank insignias: blood and fire but with a gray background vs. the black that signifies the military. No, these are Ninth Circle conveyors, but I prefer the term "escorts". Makes it easier to imagine them in high heels, hoop earrings, and leopard print. Not that there's anything wrong with—oh, forget it.

My chest tightens, and I return to crossing my arms, tensing my wings at the fallen ones approaching me. They don't speak, but my gem-plant does, conjuring a holo-feed of a woman who resembles more of an escort—except a high-ranking, classy type with thousand hell-credit heels, fresh-caught pearl earrings, and potentially leopard legs. Like a daemon.

"Astraea Malak, Lucifer Morningson, Dawn-Bringer, High Lo—" I shut down the feed and roll my eyes before it continues its long-winded titled summons.

Heaving a sigh, I turn to Aamon and Camio and shrug. "Guess I'm going to the principal's office before I head home." I advance toward the conveyors with their lips pressed into a tightly-sealed seam. Their job is to escort, not talk.

"Astraea," Camio's concerned voice stops me in my tracks as does his hand on my shoulder. I pinch my eyes, puzzled when he squeezes my shoulder and scrubs a hand down his face. "I know your ultimate reason for coming here. But if you have one infinitesimal speck of respect for his authority and power within his domain, please don't…" he trails off, swallowing far too much as if he's already predicting a poor end for me.

"Camio, you know I'm Abaddon's bond-keep, right?" I have no shame for falling back on my guardian. Not when he's shown me the most respect. Not with how he found my newborn self flying around the heights of the Celestial City like a crazy, little cupid. Not with the deep bond we share—a bond beyond blood.

Camio drops his hand, averting his eyes and shuffling his shoes backward until he huddles into Aamon's arms. The skin around his eyes doesn't stop creasing, triggering my stomach to churn. But I shake my head and harden whatever whirlpools in my stomach to solid ice—cold, brutal, and bitter. All I will ever feel for the one responsible for my greatest loss, for the scars Abaddon and I bear. And with the Devil's too-personal history with my guardian, the last thing he wants to do is piss him off.

With that knowledge, I glide on my bare feet into the center of the conveyors. Guess Lucifer doesn't care much for decorum. I glance down at my robe and shiver. My halo is restless, testing my skin with fine nerve tingles, eager for action.

"You know they say silence is golden, not black, right?" I mock their wing color once they surround me inside the elevator. Not one blink or clenched jaw.

One angel taps his insignia, and the elevator rolls upward, which surprises me. If it leads me to the surface level, all I need is a wing's gap of distance to fly out of here like a bat out of hell.

Flexing my fingers, I study the two wings on each side of me, protecting the slit of a gap in their armor. Despite how they're not military, they're still trained. The higher the Circle, the better the security for any threats to Lucifer.

"Ve haf vays of making you talk," I slip into the poor accent, a misplaced lightness in my chest that must come from surviving a battle with Lucifer and a near-brush with death.

I narrow my eyes. At their belts are black-iron swords, sheathed, but judging by their straight-backs, squared shoulders, and muscles brimming with tension, it wouldn't take them much time to retrieve them.

I snicker to myself. Bet I could do it faster. Ugh! Psycho Astraea rears her head at the personal challenge—the one I call the devil on my shoulder who baits my proud angel. Not like it takes much since the angel became her bitch long ago. All I have left is Abaddon's voice of conscience commanding me not to do anything stupid, bide my time, and be patient. But Asmodel is the Angel of Patience. Not me. I shed my celestial title when I was sixteen and went into heat for the first time, sweating it out in Jack's mansion and fucking on Mount Yvos. I'd rather have free will than a purity title.

The elevator pitches to a stop. My inner psycho slaps a collar on her angel bitch while roaring loud enough to smother Abaddon's chastisements.

As soon as the doors slide open, and the fallen one to my left moves his gem-armored boot by a mere inch, I act. I lunge, gripping the sword hilt and swinging it around to clash with the alpha hole behind me as predicted. Thrusting it away, I duck under the swing of another sword and jam the hilt into one's balls. I don't get to revel in how I made one do more than simply talk. Pulse elated, my insides vibrating from the action, and wings quivering, eager for freedom, I bring the heavy sword up and plunge it through the slit in the nearest fallen one. Blood pools on the floor. The fallen angel falls—I don't have time to quip on that either—and I leap through the gap his body made.

No sooner than I do, something presses to the side of my neck, burning my skin and freezing my muscles. The sword drops from my hand while my body crashes to the floor. Even my wings lock up. Nothing like the med-room paralysis. This is electrical current pulsing into my skin, lightning playing my nerves like a fucking fiddle.

And a deep and husky and unfortunately too-familiar voice croons, "That will be quite enough. Valiant effort, but you won't escape me again, sweetheart. I trust you've received the message?"

He removes the device from my neck. The lightning ebbs instantaneously. No trace of the current under my skin or wrecking my nerves. This simmering burn will soon fade.

Tossing the curls covering my face onto my shoulder, I glare up at those blood moon eyes and grit my teeth to say, "Clear as crystal."

ELEVEN

LUCIFER'S OFFICE

—ASTRAEA—

After traveling to a separate Ninth Circle elevator with Lucifer leading the conveyors, we pass through a series of back hallways of what reminds me of an elite, multi-billion-dollar corporate office high-rise. I snivel at the boring décor of black, white, and red aesthetics broken by the impressionistic serpent and skull motifs.

More than once, I consider another escape attempt. But after my last, Lucifer vowed that any more would result in more burns—and no more robe. As thrilling as the notion of exhibitionism is, and despite the honor I'd pay any observers, I'm quite attached to the silky robe. When I leave, I fully intend on taking it with me. With its breathable silk, flowy sleeves, and sweeping silhouette, I feel like an angel swaddled in a cocoon of clouds.

Better to get this over with.

We progress down another hall that expands. On one side, tall, rectangular glass holders filled with fresh diabolicus orchids—named for their devil's head reproductive structure and claw-like petals—line the walls. On the other side are sleek black office chairs bearing the insignia of the double serpent tattoos on Lucifer's skin.

I wrinkle my nose when I consider how his chest pressed to mine, how the heat buds between my thighs even now. I stare too long at the muscles rippling along his back, visible beyond his thin robe. His wings are lethal weapons in their own right. Like mine, well-earned sinew ropes the framework from chronic training or battles while the edges and points may turn sharp as dragon fangs. However, while mine bear an angel's pride and sensuality bred into their fabric, Lucifer's are dark and musculature. I frown, fingers fidgeting. In Lucifer's case, those dark wings bear the imprint of the Unconsecrated Crater. Fallen angel wings. Demon wings.

If I held the powers of a seraph, I wouldn't rest until I'd found a way to destroy that evil cavity responsible for the death of billions of souls.

The promise of power exudes from Lucifer's being as he leads me to a set of double-arched doors formed of Diablo ore. Never once does he glance back as if he knows I won't risk running anymore. I touch the fading burn mark on my neck. Veins slither along his wings and neck, kindled with eternal hellfire. I clutch my arms, gripping the elbows and willing away the sudden heaviness in my body. He didn't specify gem-taser burns. He had no qualms about breaking my bones. Perma-burns from his hellfire wouldn't be much of a stretch. I chew my bottom lip and remember his power electrifying my blood with pleasure and stealing my breath with pain.

My gut clenches. I press my lips into a frown. The Devil is, first and foremost, a deceiver. Why should I be surprised by his machinations and schemes? Or his violence? Too bad he isn't an ordinary half-breed. My imagination conjures all sorts of dirty scenarios of that VIP room with my back against the wall. Until today, I didn't believe it was possible to loathe myself more, but life is full of surprises. Is there enough time to make it to Mount Onys above the Celestial City? One petal from the forget-me plant will erase hours from my memory.

Camio's reminder invades my mind, pricking the psycho inside me. For once, it gives her cause to pause. He might be right about keeping my mouth shut. The quicker I get this over with, the better.

Lucifer plants his palm upon the Diablo ore. I part my lips, fascinated when his smoky gray skin glows with an amber radiance. I have no idea why my halo surges its warmth while goosebumps conspire with the tingles upon my skin. I chalk it up to his power drifting in the air around me.

The doors open to darkness. It's the first time Lucifer turns, but his command is to the conveyors. "Leave us. Return to your posts."

I will myself not to squirm like a hooked worm when he puts his arm around my back, marking me with those blood moon eyes surrounded by depthless shadows.

I stab my chin out and dig my heels in. "If you want another battle in the bedroom, you could simply ask."

Dark, throaty laughter rolls from his mouth, and he lowers his head to me, brandishing a wicked grin. "You're the one who flew the coop, little bird. Couldn't handle the fox's teeth." Sparks erupt from his ruddy tattoos and flicker onto my skin: a flirtatious mock.

I roll my eyes, contempt squeezing through my clenched teeth. "She who fights and flies away will live to fight another day. And I recall, you couldn't even catch me without going all Fifty Shades of tail-whipping me. And I still escaped you."

He pauses and leans against the door, twisting his mouth while looking down at me. Damn that jawline as sharp as the edge of a seraph's blade. "You kneed my balls, sweetheart. I'm quite attached to them. And you stabbed me. Consider us even. But I vow this to you,—" he lifts a finger, raising his chin and straightening his back to his full height that towers over me, "—if I choose to whip you again, it will be after you've begged me for it."

His lips are closed into a cocky smile, but his chest betrays a deep sigh of satisfaction. Dismissing the phrase, I breeze past him with my cunning retort, "I'd stake my tits that you have far more experience whipping your dummy."

Before I take another step, Lucifer seizes my wrist, wrenches me back, so I crash against him, and bends my arm behind my back. Narrowing those carmine eyes to slits, he pushes his body against mine, and I seethe when he thunder-purrs. Unholy doses of rage, fear, and lust prey on my nerves, weakening my legs. My vision spirals. More power in that lust-hum than ever. It vibrates from his chest onto mine, sinking past the thin, silk robe to beguile my very blood. In the bare moment I falter, Lucifer's lips spread into a wicked grin.

He doesn't need to do anything. The intense heat of his gaze is enough to squeeze my lungs until my breaths turn shallow and short. He adds insult to injury by releasing those sex-on-a-Satan-stick pheromones until I inhale blood roses, smoke, and spices. The heady, masculine scent oozes into my pores, and I can't help the whimper escaping my throat.

Dark laughter ripples from Lucifer's throat, timed to my body tightening, my thighs clenching. Hissing, I harness my senses, vying with his power until I unleash the claws. Wise to my reflexes, the Devil twists my other arm behind my back until they strain in protest.

With his raw hard-packed chest bearing down upon mine, Lucifer maintains a firm grip on my wrists while the other grabs my hair to yank back my neck. Like a massive serpent coiling around my neck to squeeze, that invisible force tightens my throat. At least he leaves me with more air this time.

He presses his lips to my throat, snaking his tongue along my skin. More pheromones, more of that carnal power as Lucifer sucks the flesh above my pulse and warns, "I'd be very careful before betting those tits of yours, Astraea. Especially when they are as ripe and angelic as if formed within the heart of Eden." His head lowers to the V-line of the silk robe, tripping warm breath along my skin. I trill a warning from his nose slipping through the slit to stroke between my cleavage—pitted between those globes. "But…" he raises his head, eyes burning again upon mine, "…if you are dead-set, sweet girl, I will take your wager."

"Oh, yes, I know how you love to mix business with pleasure."

He releases me with a rolling chuckle before proclaiming, "Lex! On."

At once, the lights slam against my vision, and I adjust my pupils to the sudden shift. One glance at the floor, and I yelp. Petrified, I swoop into the air and cling to a large statue of Diablo ore. My whole body trembles. And I could care less that it's a statue of Lucifer—a very naked statue of Lucifer.

"What the—" he spins his head, then rolls his eyes. "Hell's balls, woman…" he strides forward upon the liquid magma like he's the mother-fucking Messiah walking on water. "It's perfectly safe. Come down from there before you break my favorite statue."

I violently swing my head back and forth, eyes wider than church doors. My thighs are practically wrapped around Lucifer statue's head, verging on fucking it. Oh, I silently vow I'll be a saint if I make it out of here! I'll even do weeping angel duty if the Tribunal commands. I choke on fear. Other than the Unconsecrated Crater, that magma may destroy an angel's wings.

Lucifer grunts and jerks his thumb to the liquid lava that pools around his ankles, indicating it's harmless. My claws rake into the Diablo ore from how hard I'm gripping it. My limbs don't stop quaking.

"Astraea, I'm giving you a proper warning," Lucifer hardens his voice, sneering up at me, tension coiling in his neck. "If you don't stop humping my statue and come down immediately, I will bend you over my knee and spank you like the child you're being right now."

I part my lips. Hesitant, I lick them. All I want is to fly out of here. My wings flare with the need, but there's no making it past the Diablo doors like angel-proof forcefields. This close to the statue, I'm already fatigued from its energy, my muscles weakening. Soon, my vision will blur, and I'll drop anyway. And I don't doubt Lucifer will make good on his vow. So, I take a flight of faith and push off the statue, dismissing the fantasy about knocking it over and smashing it to smithereens.

Instead, I hold my arms to myself and flutter my way to the floor until I hover above the magma. Its heat drifts across the soles of my feet. Bubbles boil to the surface as it branches off into tributaries all over the room, which is a penthouse office.

"Thanks to Diablo ore construction and a gem-tech program, the magma flows through a sealed chamber beneath the transparent floor," he explains, cocking his head to the side as my wings quiver. "If I'd known a bit of lava was enough to control you, I'd have summoned you here first. But then I'd have missed out on our amusing bedroom battle."

"Is that why I'm here? For another battle?"

He snorts but doesn't respond, beckoning me forward. So, I survey the area. Off to my left, a staircase with fused bones for a railing winds to the second floor. On the walls, in alcoves and frames, are more bones and skulls—ones coated in everything from gold to rubies to black diamonds. We pass large, glass display cases, but they might as well be caskets. I shiver from the demon frozen in death, preserved like a trophy for display. Sweat breaks out in my palms, and I make a brief list of the races housed in the caskets: a nephyl warrior, a fallen angel, a fae, a were-cat, an elf, an orc, a vampire, and I finally lose track. Relieved at the absence of humans and daemons, I lower my shoulders. The lava still takes getting used to, but after a few minutes, the tremors stop. Swallowing the pain in the back of my throat still takes work.

Finally, Lucifer directs me to a chair constructed of skulls and jeweled serpents situated before an enormous desk. His chair is far more of a throne, of course. Huffing, I slump down into the chair, prop my elbows on the desk, and start to pick at my fingernails.

"I don't suppose we can chalk all this up to a mistake and part ways as archrivals, can we?" I attempt, flicking my eyes to his where he stands above me.

"No, we cannot."

Before I can ruffle a feather, Lucifer retrieves something from his robe. Warm metal bites my wrists, coils around them. I grit my teeth and shake my head in disbelief. "Diablo cuffs, seriously?"

Lucifer takes his opposite seat, straightens like a sovereign, and smiles, showcasing his demon teeth. "Merely a precaution so we may have a proper conversation, unlike last time. Make no mistake, Astraea, you are in deep shit, crater-deep," he emphasizes to rattle my nerves, but all my blood chills when he adds, "You will not be leaving Hell on Earth. And I have every intention of making you my celestial bitch."

TWELVE

THE PITS OF HELL

—ASTRAEA—

D espite the cuffs, I still pick at my nails, avoiding Lucifer's hooded gaze. And his chiseled cheekbones. And his hard-packed chest from his parted robes. And his vast wings curled around his throne-like chair to cast seductive shadows close to mine.

Instead, I focus on the room. It's difficult not to cringe at the lava streaming below my bare feet, humming warmth into the soles. One wall of floor-to-ceiling windows overlooking the hotel district of the Ninth Circle lies behind Lucifer. I imagine charging my wings, tucking my body into a roll, crashing through the glass, and disappearing into that bustling district with its shopping malls and restaurants. My skin tingles at the thought.

"You're well trained," Lucifer notes, claiming my attention, gesturing to how my eyes have swept the room. I've taken a moment to study the exits, the angles, and the details. "But trust me when I say this: you are in my domain now." A trace of a smirk crosses his lips. When I blink, offering nothing but my frozen stare, Lucifer continues, "Would you care for a drink?"

I twist my lips to one side and decline. "Sorry, I don't suck dick. But if you care to suck a donkey's hind tit, don't let me stand in your way."

He gives me a flat look. I'm tempted to roll my eyes.

Placing my shackled wrists on the desk, I fold my hands and survey him, "So, what am I doing here? If you'd wanted to kill me, you would've done it already."

He shrugs and waves a hand to me. "The thought had crossed my mind. I fantasized about those pretty angel screams as I dipped you inch by inch into Hell's fire blood pits…starting with your toes."

I yawn and drum my fingers on the table before peering around. "What time is it?"

"Why should you care?"

"Counting the seconds until he shows up." I slump back in the chair and pick at my fingers, ignoring the glorified fallen angel. I dart my eyes back to the windows, map out the trajectory to the closest hotel, and expand my angel pupils to determine the location of the allies.

Leaning forward, Lucifer props his elbows on the table and steeples his fingertips, the heels of his hands not quite connecting. "If you are referring to Abaddon, I'm afraid he will not be joining us. Despite our rather turbulent history—"

"I know your fucking history," I lurch and snarl, baring my angel teeth. The evidence is all over one side of Lucifer's face: the brands puckering his otherwise dark, velveteen skin. A small price to pay when Abaddon has suffered far worse with internal wounds. Not even I can fathom the demons stalking my guardian's tattered soul. I dig my nails into my palms over and over until several crescent moons form on my skin.

Out of the corner of my eyes, Lucifer's security manifests. Alerted by my snarl, they shift through the walls, through the windows, shadows wreathing from their figures. Without turning or issuing an order, the Devil merely lifts a hand to dismiss them. They shadow back to their hiding places.

Defeated, I slump in my seat, pick at my nails again, and grumble, "Ghouls. Impressive." Flesh-eating specters. No flight plans anytime soon, I sigh, shaking out my hands.

"As I informed you, Astraea: you're in deep shit. Mercifully for you, Abaddon and I have agreed to an understanding. So, I will throw you a line of a shovel to dig yourself out, so to speak," he levels with me, leaning forward, his horns casting shadows on the table.

I snap my gaze to Lucifer and stiffen in my seat, hoping I appear more arrogant than uneasy. Something in his relaxed shoulders, in how he does not smile with his lips but his eyes, as if he knows he's got me dead to rights, feels like I'm caught between the devil and the deep blue sea. And angels aren't designed to swim with our fucking wings.

Before I may open my mouth, Lucifer taps the gem-plant upon his wrist, conjuring a holo-feed with my profile on it along with documents of information.

"Rather lengthy file," he surmises as he scans, but I can't judge whether he's impressed or merely observant. Posture unchanged. No muscles twitch. No jaw clenches. He barely even blinks. Damn, I expected the Devil to have more fire in him. Lucifer could pass for a grumpy garden gnome.

"Quite an amount of potential from an early age but lacks discipline and motivation," he reads in a monotone, not betraying anything. He sets his jaw, eyes focused on studying the content. "Poor execution marks."

I snort and flex my fingers. "Tell that to all the rogue angels squealing like pigs when I tossed their asses to the Tribunal."

"Poor execution marks in every other field of training. Your first task as a Guardian Angel was to care for a mere goldfish."

It's the first time he shows any semblance of emotion with those dark eyes squinting, twinkling with traces of mirth as he had when he'd bantered with me on the balcony. A chill slithers across my flesh, and I shudder, remembering his tongue stroking my throat.

"The goldfish lasted a total of 1.2 hours," he concludes, a wheezy breath escaping through his nose. I know he's pressing those lips tight to prevent himself from chuckling. That playful devil is in there somewhere.

I shrug and lean over the table, extending my shackled hands. "I swear the thing was mocking me with those chronic kissy lips. And those things dare to be called "gold"? I'm fucking gold!" I flutter my wings, so they catch the chandelier light above our heads, casting my proud prisms across the room. That's when I realize his red eyes are gone, replaced with irises as dark as midnight, but I swear I catch a dusting of gold inside them.

"You lost your virginity at sixteen and were disqualified from the breeding program before you'd even entered," he observes.

Not bothering to lift my chin from the table, I beam at him and waggle my brows. "Oh, I guarantee you I didn't lose it. I traded it for a long night of no-strings-attached, super-size-me cock happy meal. And I was one fucking happy girl." I wink and pucker up my lips. The back of my neck overheats from memories of that night with Jack. Not that I could have anticipated all the strings that would follow—ones we forged together.

"You tried your hand as an angel spy." I press my lips hard to contain my laughter, but more scuttles up, ready to burst through my clenched teeth as Lucifer remarks, "Made it as far as the outer gates while attempting to impersonate a…naughty priest."

Shameless when I cackle so hard, and the spittle flies right past the holo-gem to speckle the Devil's cheek, I rattle the cuffs and knock my head gently against the table to get a hold of myself. "Oh, come on! The fishnet stockings were Camio's idea. And how was I supposed to know the humans in line would suddenly grow a conscience and want to go to fucking confessional?"

"The outhouse as a substitute was your downfall." Lucifer clenches his fingers, lips pressed so tight, they turn thinner than a thread, but I swear I catch a hint of a blush in his cheeks—as if he's trying his damned hardest not to laugh with me.

I throw him a look. "Figurative or literal downfall?" When he blinks, I giggle, touch a hand to my ailing ribs, then lean back in my seat to spread my fingers and add, "Hey, shit happens."

His brow furrows as he studies me beyond the holo-gem. "You received more strikes in warrior training than any other novice."

I lift a finger, reminding him, "But I did pass."

"By the skin of your teeth."

I grin and flash my fangs. "Rawr."

"In one area have you ever demonstrated any proficiency: flying."

Pushing my shoulders back, I tap a finger to my proud lips. "What can I say? I love winging it.

He gives me a blank stare.

Oh, come on! I fidget in my seat. I'm pulling out all the stops, and he's giving me nothing! The most Lucifer shows are those hellfire veins gleaming hotter under the high collar of his robe, barely peeking from beyond its edges. I swear the crimson serpent heads upon his upper chest stick their tongues out to hiss. I already suspect where he's going with this whole build-up. So, if I'm going to be stuck in Hell on Earth any longer, then the least he can do is lighten up.

"You took the plunge off Mount Vesyna at the youngest age known to any angel novice: two years old."

"Twenty-two months, swine-ass," I substitute the word, not wanting to insult Jack. Even if he does have a fine ass. Unfortunately, so does Lucifer. Ugh, I wince, remembering his hands cupping my bottom, squeezing my heavenly haunches.

"Tread carefully, Astraea," he warns, voice deepening as he taps his gem-plant to close the holo-feed before folding his hands on the table to scrutinize me. "Otherwise, I may be tempted to take a whip to your smart ass. Again."

To hell with Camio's suggestion. I cock my head to the side and thread my brows, denying myself the urge to swallow or rub my arms. Instead, I dish out more bullshit to cover up my anxiety. "Is that your idea of punishment? Or incentive?" My stomach churns. I can easily take a whipping. But I loathe each one.

A heavy sigh breaks from his mouth, and the Devil kneads his brow. I preen but can't help my flinch when he sweeps into a stand. Muscles swell, blood moon eyes return—the predator of the ultimate fallen angel. And a demon on full display. Hellfire strains from inside his balled fists while smoke curls from his pores.

I slide my lips into my sweet-wrapped, psycho smile, but when Lucifer plants one firm hand on the table before me, taps the ebony, and lowers his head to me, I sense he can see right through it. Of course, he can: fucking Prince of Lies.

He brushes his knuckles across my wings, and I jerk from the too-intimate gesture.

When he leans in and grips my jaw hard, forcing my eyes to his, waves of heat and ice compete with my body. One-half loathing, one-half desire. The heat of his eyes burns me, the telltale smirk hinting that he's waiting to play his trump card.

"You try my patience," he breathes against my mouth, a subtle dare edging his words.

His power grows thicker. His dominant energy poises in the air and trims my body.

"Ugh…" I groan, tipping my head back, the comeback on the tip of my tongue.

"Don't fucking think about it," he warns, growling low in my ear, tracing a single claw across my throat.

"Too late."

More hellfire spews from the outline of his body while something vibrates from his chest. The sound reminds me of a death rattle. I stiffen and shut my mouth but clutch my chained hands close to my chest, comeback slamming against the backs of my teeth.

Slow and cautious, I lean as far from Lucifer as I can.

Despite the predatory warning in audiovisual form, the comeback slams against the inner walls of my mouth until I finally burst, "My brother Asmodel is the "Angel of Patience", and I could put in a good word for yo—"

I don't get the chance to finish.

That power plunges into my body. Lucifer grips my throat with one hand, my cuffed wrists with the other, and hauls me to my feet. The world caves in around me, matter imploding as the Devil transports us through the fabric of the world. Hundreds of billions of cell particles dance a whirlwind around my body, shattering my blood, rattling my bones, and rearranging my insides. Seconds later, the earth rises to meet me. Too hard when my knees bruise from the landing. My breath heaves and cleaves. Bile rises from Lucifer's sifting act, but I force it down, swallowing hard.

My curls eclipse my vision, but the sensation of flaming coals erupts on my kneepads. Countless embers spit at my wings from behind, threatening to simmer the resolute feathers. I spin my head and bite back a scream, scrambling away from the edge of a precipice. I know exactly where we are. Sulfur and heat and smoke smother my flesh and nostrils and eyes. Burning them. Wrenching tears to blister down my cheeks. Liquid flames shoot into the air hundreds of feet high like hellfire geysers.

The Craters of Hell. Nothing but an endless chain of lava pits—not to mention giant iron instruments operated by enormous orcs for the sole purposes of gem fusion. Not simply the fire geysers, but the air surrounding the pits is so hot, it would damn well destroy my wings if I fly too close.

A scream catches in my throat when I knock against a familiar robe. Lucifer lowers his hand to stroke my curls. "You look so gods-damn pretty on your knees, Astraea."

THIRTEEN

MARKED BY THE DEVIL

—ASTRAEA—

My breath quickens, but every time I struggle for air, heated smoke is all my lungs take in. I double over and cough before thrusting my neck up and snapping my wings behind me. Despite my blurry vision, I still make out those blood moon eyes.

Lucifer grips my underarms, wrenching me so hard, the ties on my robe loosen. The fabric at my chest parts, so my cleavage presses against his stomach. With my shackled hands against his chest for support, I cough again. And lower my head so my curls protect my eyes. But the Devil captures my chin and arrests my face to his, tossing my blood-red hair onto my back.

"Prepare to listen like a good little angel, or we will return to my first option of dipping you inch by inch into my lava pits, starting with your pretty, little toes." His voice has sharpened to blades forged of lighting. Even the shadows flickering around us bow to him.

"Such sweet words."

I learn the hard way when the hellfire swells around us. My throat closes up. My lungs burn. So, I nod. Anything to get out of here. The heated air, laced with embers, threatens to burn my silk robe from my body. The ends catch fire, but Lucifer directs his power to coat my skin. His shades act as a shield against those flames without snuffing them. They slow and dim, and Lucifer's chuckle is all I need to know he's controlling the flames. A slow taunt of the robe burning thread by thread.

I whimper and clench my eyes shut, locking my wings tighter.

"Good girl, Astraea," he commends me and lowers his mouth to rub his lips across mine. I wish I could deny the hot fuse igniting inside me, the heat he triggers between my thighs to compete with his hellfire. He brushes those lips across my earlobe, whispering, "I can taste your fear. And your lust..."

The flames climb until the robe smolders at my knees.

Lucifer licks the side of my neck, and I bristle. My blood turns to ice, all the hairs on my neck prickling. Nothing I can deny. Like upon the balcony when I'd believed he was simply a beautiful blend of demon and a fallen angel. My halo quivers, warming my insides more and kindling my skin. While shadows pull to him, bathing him in darkness, more robe burns, exposing my nude thighs. His pheromones overpower me again. I arch my back, careless of the remaining robe reduced to ash until I'm utterly naked—apart from the thong—and pressed to him. His silver hair tickles my arms. My nipples grow hard as little rubies, and moisture drips from my cunt.

"You're gods-damn right, you should be terrified of me," he snarls, latching onto my fear, feeding on it. That hellish energy, like storm currents, bind me, then drag me right to its eye. "You've danced with the Devil tonight, little angel. You've played with him. You've taunted him. And now, you will pay the price of your lies."

I battle the onslaught of heat between my thighs, strain against the shackles, and brutalize my eyes against his. "Get it over with, Devil. Do your worst and drop me in your pits so demons can torment and torture me forever."

His chest rumbles, and I cringe from how it reverberates into my breasts. "I have a far better idea."

"If this involves dropping me in the Unconsecrated Crater, I'd rather drink orc venom," I hiss, referencing the deadliest toxin in Hell on Earth, known for its slow-acidic melting of the flesh when ingested. The worst of torture methods: one survives if they've built up immunity with much pain. I have, but Lucifer doesn't know that. Unless that's in my fucking file, too.

"Trust me, Astraea, as effective as my Crater is, even its spectral power has limits. You are already impure enough for my purposes." He hints and rubs his thumb across my bottom lip.

I bring my hands to rest under my neck, so my arms straighten and overlap my breasts. "I'll take that as a compliment. And what fucking purposes?"

"Remember..." he lust-hums against my ear, nipping the lobe. My knees weaken, and I moan from that low, subtle thunder purring into my flesh, warming my blood. It thrusts heat to my pussy until it clenches with need, dripping more fluids.

Before I can so much as blink, Lucifer grips my arms, wrenching them down to my belly and holding them there. I open my mouth to scream, but he captures my lips, a low growl rumbling from his chest into mine.

Dark magic skitters across my flesh like hundreds of moth wings perched, their antennae tickling my skin, thread-like legs humming energy into my blood. Tempting me. I can't think. I can't move. Not with Lucifer's sinful tongue scrawling his fucking unconsecrated name along the walls of my mouth. And then, the Devil's hand slips between our bodies and brushes over my left breast before that hand slides up to grip my throat.

I flinch from the memory of him strangling me, but he doesn't squeeze. I can breathe but barely blink.

Sudden pain sears me, rocketing into my flesh. I screech into his mouth. I've felt the burning pain of a flaming whip across my back, but this is different. This is Lucifer's hellfire power and unholy shadows—raw and carnal and branding my flesh. It's ancient and slithers into my skin, smelling like sweet pomegranates and spicy incense, but underneath that first layer, it reeks of thorns and deception, of the first lies that ever stalked the earth.

Now, the Devil's ungovernable soul of an untapped well of the seven deadly sins storms into me. His mouth doesn't leave mine, and I gasp for breath. He's gifting me air again. More than air. He feeds me his pride and lust, and I loathe myself for swallowing them like seductive poison, for fucking devouring them. Loathe myself more for the heat gushing through me. His knee stabs between my thighs, and I part them, bowing to every impure desire rioting inside me. I tilt my neck, tongue greedy, eager to explore his mouth.

The power probes me, and my skin sizzles. More pain penetrates the underlayer of my skin. As soon as I groan into his mouth, trembling from whatever he's branding into my flesh, Lucifer breaks from my mouth. I cry out until he lowers his head to suck my nipple into his wet, heated mouth. The pain bows to the primal pleasure he's igniting inside me.

He pauses, grinning up at me.

"I-what?" I close my eyes, shake my head, and grip his neck, urging him toward me again—overcome by the lust. Once he swirls his tongue around the puckered bud, I alternate between gasps and moans, pushing my breasts toward him. I trill long and slow from desire. His tongue isn't silky but rough, long, and skilled.

"Hmm…" he murmurs against my nipple. "I love the sounds you make when I suck your tits, Astraea. Give me more, sweetheart."

I don't have a heart. My throat is too dry and cracked to speak. Endorphins of pain and pleasure engulf my body, adrenaline charges through my blood, and a deeper heat unfurls in my belly. His tongue laves at my nipple, taking the edge off the pain. Off that hellfire wreathing into my chest. He traces the other nipple with his thumb, pinching it and transforming it to a puckered bud.

"Oh!" I moan and trill, arching my neck and thrusting my pelvis, presenting my pussy to him.

I should shove him away for this. I should unleash my fucking rage and ruin and show him the real meaning of a destroying angel. But I can't deny the predatory heat staking its claim. My inner psycho practically sways her hips while the angel in me gets on her hands and knees, submitting to the Devil, to Lucifer.

When his fingers tiptoe lower to slide beneath my thong, I buck. The inferno around my throat burns into me, scrawling its black energy into my flesh and blood. But all I can focus on are those fingers crossing my mound and trailing over my sleek opening. I shiver from his erotic magic, agonizing in its build-up.

I'm in the eye of his storm, but it feels like the eyewall ripping me apart, waking a part of me, granting my soul permission to drink those seven deadly sins until they explode into every celestial cell in my body.

That pure, carnal force bores into me, penetrating. My skin wails like the entire bloody book of Lamentations. At that moment, Lucifer slips his finger into my center, stabbing deep. My bound hands grip his robes, then his silver hair. My pussy pulses from that finger. His teeth catch my nipple, tugging until the raised peak stings and burns, diverting me from the pain around my neck. Sweat cascades down the sides of my body. My soprano trills flood the air.

"You'd look so beautiful with my teeth marks on your beautiful breasts, angel."

The fire coils a circle around my throat, smoking and simmering. Hot tears stream from my cheeks, but the pressure on my breast is gone. When I look up, Lucifer is staring dead-on at me with that finger still pulsing inside me. As if he's got a built-in fucking vibrator! I part my mouth and lick my lips, eyes watery as the tension coils tighter. I'm on the verge of convulsing. All he needs to do is flick a fingernail across my clit, and I'll dive right off that edge and erupt into flames and feathers.

Everything burns inside me as if wrath and envy ripple into my hollow chest and my halo. All from Lucifer finger-fucking me. The last vestiges of his power form an eternity circle around my neck, and he seals the brand with pure hellfire. I trill, high and shrill from the pain, squeezing my eyes. Growling, Lucifer grips the back of my neck, bringing my gaze back to his. Two blood moons crash against my golden suns. And he kisses me brutally, violently, until I collapse against him.

I'm addicted to his touch.

When the fire geysers rocket up to the cavern ceilings, I tip my head and open my mouth on the barest edge of a scream, ready to fly off that edge.

The storm passes.

All is silent and black as pitch. Nothing but two blood star pinpricks gazing at me. My pussy thrums in the aftermath, my limbs quivering with the need to climax. A dark chuckle rolls across my flesh.

He produces a gold mirror so I may view the mark. "Feast your eyes, sweetheart," commands Lucifer.

I bite my tongue to prevent the shriek from escaping. Sealed upon the flesh around my throat like a collar and undulating with blood fire magic is a black, curling serpent tattoo.

"What in all unholy fuck?" I scream and ball my hands into fists, shaking the chains wildly.

"Insurance, Astraea. Now, I'll always know where you are, nor can you leave the boundaries of Hell on Earth. Consider it your shock collar. You're my celestial bitch, sweetheart. You're mine."

FOURTEEN

THE DEVIL'S BITCH

—ASTRAEA—

his time when he sifts, I land on my hands and knees before his desk, dry heaving. Naked as the day I was born. The shackles have disappeared, which proves the Devil has no concerns over my escape attempts. My fingers stray to the raw mark upon my neck, to the inflammation puckering my flesh—one easily healed, but I imagine it's a stinging reminder of his previous words. I may be Lucifer's bitch—whatever the fuck that means—but I'll be damned and fly into the fire geysers of hell's pits themselves before I ever belong to him.

With blood pounding in my ears and violence in my fingers, my soul rampaging for slaughter, I tense all my muscles. Something heavy and soft falls over my back, distracting me. It's dark and abundant as a shadow. A robe. I thread my brows lower, waiting for another trick from the Prince of Lies.

At first, I wince, curling my fingers upon the floor. My wings push against the heavy fabric, and I grip the black robe around my neck before it may fall.

"Do you know what I normally do to liars and little angel thieves, Astraea?" Lucifer asks while I rise, securing the boundless robe around my frame, thrusting my wings upward until they drape across its back.

Shrugging my arms through the sleeves, I clench the robe tighter, incensed when he steps closer and drapes his knuckles across my cheek. I cage a moan in my throat from how his touch purrs static electricity across my skin.

I jerk my chin up and burn my eyes onto his, matching his will. "I'm guessing you don't blow them a kiss and let them be on their merry way."

A light breeze slaps my flesh, and before I know it, he's spun me around and shoved me into the chair opposite his. I hiss through bared teeth while he makes his way around the desk. Those wings lift ever so subtly at their tips as if mocking me. The first chance I get, I will test his little shock collar. Lucifer is a fool if he believes he can cage an angel in hell.

"For the ones I do not cast into eternal torture, I find they have their uses," he relays and sweeps into his desk throne, adjusting his robe. "While your file leaves little one would find impressive—" I snort a minor interruption and hitch up the robe until it nudges past my cleavage, "—your flight skills will be quite valuable. If not, my dungeon pits are a suitable option unless you prefer my bed. It's quite extensive and may accommodate another warm body." His eyes travel up and down my figure as he leans forward.

Wrinkling my nose and huffing, I remove one hand from the robe, release my claws, and tap one along his desk, wondering what he'd do if I scrawled my name upon it. "Why my flight skills when you have legions of fallen angels who may do your bidding in the blink of an eye?"

"True." He nods and props his elbows on the desk, fingertips kissing so his chin may poise at their crest. "But not one of my fallen ones would have dared follow you into the tunnel to ride the Ninth Circle wind currents—apart from myself, of course. You proved your reflexes and instincts well, and I know you can handle yourself and don't scare easily. Most of all: not one race in Hell on Earth—subject, tourist, servant, citizen, or ruling entity—would ever believe an angel is the Devil's spy."

I blink. And toss my head back with a cackle. "You're a fucking fool. Guess you didn't read my file closely enough. Remember? I failed spy training."

Lucifer leans back in his seat and gives me a shit-eating grin. "I pride myself on high-pressuring a stone until it becomes a prized diamond. And make no mistake, Astraea, I am an avid collector of shiny things. Given time, you may be my shiniest pet."

"You don't own me, asshole." I glare.

"The collar on your neck says otherwise."

Digging my claw along the desk, I lean closer, matching him battle for battle and demand, "And what's to say I won't try and kill you again?"

He smirks to one side and lowers his shoulders, relaxed. "You may try. I truly hope you do. I haven't enjoyed a spar as good as you gave me in my suite in quite a few decades."

"Oh, I'll be more than happy to knee you in the balls as much as you want if it means I can get the fuck out of here."

Lucifer chuckles darkly, and out of the corner of my eye, his tail swings up, slapping the desk and causing me to flinch and jerk back. "Before or after I whip your pretty backside?"

I snarl at the demonic weapon, feeling a flush at the back of my neck, remembering how that strapping tail is masterful in both pain and pleasure.

"I'd shut your mouth and listen if I were you," continues Lucifer with a low growl of warning. "It's why the gods gave you two ears and one mouth, however sharp a tongue it contains. I am going to tell you three very important things. One: even if you could kill me when millions in the past have tried—including your own Angel of Destruction bond-keep, Abaddon, your collar is equipped with a self-destruct implant: if I die, you die, sweetheart. Two: corpses are showing up in dark corners of Hell on Earth; the Chambers have called for an official investigation and have dispatched their agents to deal with the threat, but you will be my secret weapon, my fly on the wall as it were. Three: I am doing you an enormous favor. Gratitude is in order." He finishes his statement with a lust-hum which prompts my back to arch. I gasp a few deep breaths, not knowing which annoys me more: his condescending arrogance or how my body responds to that dark, rippling purr.

"A favor because you offer me a job playing your bitch spy as opposed to getting tossed into your pit of nightmares or fucking raped in your bed like a fawning whore?"

Lucifer deadpans with me, his pupils turning black with that shimmery glaze and dilating to seductive onyx. His feathers ruffle and flare, and his neck seems to crouch in a warning. I almost flinch as lethal shadows breed with hellfire around his figure. The lava inside the floor beneath my naked soles grows hotter, rumbling from the undercurrent of the Devil's temper.

When he rises to a stand, eyes pinning mine as he weaves his way around the desk toward me, an icy current skitters along my spine. I stiffen, turning to look him in the eye as he leans over and places one hand on the desk before me and the other on the back of my chair. His chest nearly brushes my feathers. I snap my wings shut as the hairs on the back of my neck rise. My breath deepens, growing heavier.

Once he taps his claw along the desk, I flick my eyes to it. Then, the Devil acts, launching his pheromones at me in a deadly, erotic assault. More dominant than ever. The predator of Hell is on full display. My body responds, shaking with need. My spine arches, lips part, and thighs clench. I throw my head back and grit my teeth to force a sob down my throat. Hot tears burn my eyes, and all the ice I'd felt before transforms into a deep, needy heat stoked by the Devil himself.

"I don't need to rape, Astraea." I nearly fall to my knees from the vindictive thunder-purr in my ear. Instead, I drop my hands from the robe to rake my claws into the desk as he proves his point. "Not when races all over the world come to Hell on Earth and pay the highest price for the Devil to fuck them into euphoric oblivion. The arousal you feel now is nothing compared to what you would feel in my bed. Your cunt creaming itself is a wet dream, unlike the ecstasy I'd gift you with my cock buried inside that sweet, angelic pussy. I could have you on your knees so fucking fast, begging me for the honor of sucking me off before I fuck you so hard, your halo itself would shatter from the pleasure. I am the addiction and the cure, sweetheart. I may be a kinky fallen bastard, but I have never once raped a man, woman, or any fucking gender of any fucking race. Rapture has nothing on the Devil, sweetheart."

As soon as he stands, he obliterates those pheromones. I fall over the desk, winded, lips trembling. Fucking hell, the seat below me is slick, as are my thighs! Throat dry as a bone, I groan and lightly beat my brow against the desk, tempted to do it harder until I knock some sense into my skull.

Of course, I believe him. The memory of that balcony taunts me with confirmation. His history of lovers of all races and genders—so measureless, I can't fathom how many times it would have circumnavigated the earth—confirms it most. All virgins would sell their souls to him for one night in his bed. Billions of deals with the Devil. And payments of blood, flesh, and spirit. No, Lucifer doesn't rape. He fucks. He fucks in a multitude of ways, from the flesh to the blood to the mind. And even the soul.

Sighing heavily, I lower my shoulders, and my wings follow, sensing an inevitable surrender as I lift my head. "And what's to stop me from a desperate cry for help?" I hold onto that Abaddon anchor for dear life.

That knowing smirk returns along with his usual scarlet orbs as he lowers himself opposite me again. "Not even your guardian may reach you here, little angel. Moreover, I may be the King of Hell, but it doesn't mean I don't have an ear to heaven, your Celestial City. I have it on good authority your divine realm is the last place you wish to be at this time."

My chest tightens, anxiety-ridden. I wish I could exchange that paranoid discomfort for heated anger, but my toes curl as if bracing for worse.

"Why?" I dare to ask, my breath hitching.

"I learned of a significant trial which concluded at dawn while your body healed in my med-room. A trial seven years in the processing."

My whole body turns rigid, wings flaring. I trill a warning as anger spikes within me. The urge to escape rears, and that window looks appealing regardless of the ghouls. Ghouls who would love to taste angel flesh. Pain explodes in my throat. I hug my arms, sealing the robe tight to my skin, protecting the halo inside my hollow chest. Will it crack from the rampage of my dark memories?

Three angel screams pierced the stormy, black night. Thunder crashed to consume those screams. Claws and teeth and barbed whips. Shadows clawing at our ankles. And the dark matter threatening to drag us deep into the darkest abyss of time. Blood and shattered wings.

"That was your true reason for coming here, wasn't it, Astraea?" Lucifer hums, leaning back in his seat.

Clutching the robe, I shoot to my feet and snarl, "You have no fucking right—"

"Sit down, sweetheart. The Tribunal and their self-righteous trials bore me to tears. And seven years is but a blip of time for immortal angels. Hardly worth glancing at compared to the trials they've held, which at least make double or triple digits. While I may be curious about yours, I ultimately care about their sentencing, not the history."

"And...?" I ball my hand into a fist, recalling the conversation Abaddon and I had, how I'd planned to return at dawn with Lucifer in tow and drop him right before the Tribunal's front door before they could announce their sentencing. I broke probation by leaving the Celestial City.

Lucifer grins a full set of demon teeth. "Guilty on multiple counts."

I press my lips into a frown and drop back into the chair. Nothing I hadn't expected. "Why should I believe you?"

"I'll be more than obliged to show you a recap of the trial's conclusion. My ear to the Celestial City pairs well with an eye, specifically one equipped with holo-recording." He starts to summon the holo-feed.

I raise my hand in dismissal. "Not necessary. But the punishment?" I move on because the last thing I want is to watch the feed. My halo burns, but my blood chills as my emotions war. Grief, rage, guilt and fear battle for supremacy.

"An angel always receives two options. For your crime, the seraphs' motives were clear: your wings clipped or the First Level breeding program."

Yes, the motives are clear. I'm a loose cannon. I'm too dangerous even when on probation. A leash isn't enough. The high seraphs sentenced me to nothing less than a cage. The First Level breeding program. My stomach churns, and I nearly dry heave again, my head dizzy from the fate equally as horrific as the loss of my wings.

So, I drum my fingers on the table and droop my wings lower, in defeat this time—not simply surrender. Being Lucifer's bitch leaves me fucked six ways from Sunday. But the Tribunal would leave me fucked seven ways. Even with Abaddon pleading my cause, I'm no more than a bastard angel to the Tribunal. This sentencing is solely to prove a point to all lower angels: no one is untouchable.

Straightening in my seat, I lean forward, narrow my eyes to burning gold, and point my index finger on the desk to demand, "I want a salary."

Lucifer spreads his lips into that Cheshire cat smile and nods. "I guarantee you, Astraea, you will want for nothing when you work for me."

"I want to go anywhere I please in Hell on Earth. If I want access to the fucking deepest prison in your pits, then slap a fucking Warden's favorite VIP sticker on my head."

"That particular sticker is already embedded in your collar, sweetheart." He nods to my throat.

I seethe at the mocking term of endearment but let it go. "One final and of the utmost importance."

"Pray tell, angel."

"I'm fucking famished," I grumble, crossing my arms over my chest. "And I get really cranky when I'm hungry. So, you'd better feed me now, or I'll show you what it means to be a destroying angel."

"I'll cue up a holo-menu, and you may order whatever you want, and we will discuss details for our first stop."

I lift a brow. "First stop?"

"Didn't I mention?" Lucifer taps his desk, true to his word about that holo-menu. As I salivate over the options, my belly growling its hunger, the Devil sits back, appraises me, and gestures. "Your duties begin immediately. No rest for the wicked, Astraea."

I swipe my fingers through the options, select a banquet, and then lean so far back in my seat, I prop my naked tootsies on the Prince of Darkness' desk. "Ruff, ruff, Lucifer. Where do we start?"

FIFTEEN

THANKING THE DEVIL

—ASTRAEA—

"Are you quite finished yet?" asks an agitated Lucifer as I chomp into my fifth chocolate-coated strawberry, dripping juice down my chin. I don't bother to wipe it away.

Wagging my toes above his desk, I shrug and gesture to the variety of plates I've sampled, careless of how the robe has dipped below my shoulders to showcase my cleavage.

"Are you sure you don't want anything?" I grin and flutter my wings, half-tempted to blow the Devil a kiss. "The sushi rolls were delicious, but I can order more!"

Lucifer sweeps to a stand, tugs his robe, snaps his wings shut, and curls his upper lip to bare a demon fang. "Contrary to what imaginings your pretty little head may have conjured, my universe does not revolve around you."

I reach for a petit fore this time and wag it in the air. "If I'm going to be the King of Hell's bitch, I might as well milk it for all it's worth."

Brows bobbing with obvious intent, Lucifer folds his hands behind his back and strides around the desk to me. Already, those pheromones trace the edges of my skin. I plunge the strawberry whole into my mouth, resisting the urge to squirm. At least he doesn't lust-hum yet. Still, I can't help but arch my neck when he lowers his head toward me, breath drifting through my curls at my ear with his power trimming along my body.

And then, Lucifer lust-hums, charging a live wire right for my pussy. "If you don't get your ample fanny out of that chair in the next three seconds, I'll have you bent over my desk with your pretty, little cunt milking my cock, and I'll ram balls-deep inside of you until you scream my name for all the demons in my deepest pits to hear."

I'm scrambling out of the chair so fast, my wings lose a couple of feathers. Lucifer chuckles, giving me a cold smile. I huff, rolling my eyes with a sneer. "All you had to do was say please," I point out.

"Where's the fun in that?" He jerks a finger at the winding staircase leading to the second level. "An Infinit-i chamber in the suite upstairs. Change quickly."

"I get a choice?" I lift a brow.

Lucifer rolls his eyes with a sneer. "Unless you require my hand to strip you naked, select proper attire, and dress you, but last I checked, you're my bitch. Not my fucking barbie doll."

I smirk and set my hands on my hips while turning to the staircase. "That may be the nicest thing you've said to me."

"Yes, I'm practically a saint. Get your ass upstairs. I pride myself on punctuality, and I won't be late on account of your gluttony," he barks while summoning his gem-plant and gathering those long, silver strands into a half-man bun.

Out of the corner of my eye, I observe him as I make my way up the iron staircase, marveling at how the artificial sunbeams streaming through the window, along with the incandescence of the lava, conspire to turn his hair to gleaming, silver gold strands. I stroke my hand along the railing, pausing to study his features. What a fool I was to believe the double who'd captured me at the Gala was the true Lucifer. With that faux fallen angel, I'd wanted to spit, to retch. He'd filled me with nightmares and revulsion. But the genuine Devil does not repulse.

No, the real Lucifer enthralls. He turns his back to me, rolling the muscles in his shoulders that the robe cannot hide. Despite how his dark wings betray him as a fallen angel, they are still unearthly in their beauty. Whatever else he is, not one being upon heaven or earth can deny his origins: once the most transcendent of all the angels—a beauty excruciating and exquisite. Despite how he's fallen and scarred from that fall and the battle that came before, Lucifer is still beautiful and brutal as a deadly sword forged from a dying star.

He had me hook, line, and sinker.

"Planning to eye-fuck me all day, or are you going to get dressed?" Lucifer mocks me without turning, tightens his wings, and flicks his tail in a subtle taunt.

I shake my head out and try to cover up my minor transgression. "Any hints on where we're going so I know how to dress?"

"It's no flight of fancy if that's what you're wondering."

Good enough for me. I hasten up the stairs, welcoming the breeze of air from my wings to cool my flushed cheeks. I have to pause and catch my hitching breath from the beautiful suite. Smaller than the first. But other halls downstairs branch off to more rooms. This one boasts double-height ceilings, a massive bathroom, and a domed terrace complete with a whirlpool and stunning, expansive views of the Eighth Circle tower.

Not to mention the Infinit-i chamber. I remember how the earliest versions of this used to be a wardrobe. Now, the technology scans the body to accommodate custom-sized fittings along with virtually millions of fashion choices due to the universal Infinit-i app. Choosing not to stoke the Devil's temper over potential impunctuality, I opt for a comfortable and suitable option for my recent spy title. However, I ensure it comes with a thick band of a collar around my throat to conceal the mark. Just because I'm Lucifer's bitch doesn't mean I want anyone to see his brand of ownership.

Ugh…I swallow a bitter taste and stand still as the Infinit-i chamber seals the outfit to my figure. After, I sweep my curls onto my back and gather them into a high, messy bun, careless of the strands that frolic around my cheeks.

Finally, I take the steps two at a time to return downstairs and part my lips in surprise that Lucifer also took the time to change. With a high and close-knit collar, the form-fitting black coat binds to his frame before parting midway at his chest to sweep at his sides to the floor. Despite the leather buckles strapped to his breeches at his thigh to holster a gun and the sheathed sword of Diablo ore at his belt, they are mere props compared to the Devil's true weapons beneath those black gloves.

I bite my lip, remembering the searing pain from his palm around my throat. Heat gushes my blood from the knowledge of that brand that is part-collar and part-VIP card according to him. My insides twist because he could have simply given me the pain. He could have sizzled my flesh and boiled the unholy signature in my blood when he transcribed that serpent mark upon my throat. The urge to unleash my claws and angel teeth from where he'd touched me, sucked at my breast, and pulsed heat from his finger inside me tempts my violence. Until I register how much I loved his "mixing business with pleasure". And how I'm more incensed that he denied me a climax that would have rivaled what his tail had given me on that balcony.

Barely acknowledging me, Lucifer swipes a holo-feed above his desk. I furrow my brows, curious at the replay of the masked Gala with his double of a mask spreading his arms wide to the audience. Countless news articles flicker around that Gala image, and I murmur headlines:

"Wedding Bells in Hell", "The King of Hell to Host Bride Trials", "Trials by Hellfire: Lucifer Morningstar Seeks a Bride,"…" I trail off as he closes out the feed and approaches me. "Planning a special Bachelor-style reality show? Aww, I'm sorry I wasn't invited."

Twisting his smile to one side, Lucifer advances to me, stares down at my ensemble, and tucks his fist beneath my chin. "If you'd care to play a battle of the sexes, Astraea, I will personally extend you an engraved invitation to my bed."

"I'll bring Abaddon as my plus one," I taunt, only to be met with Lucifer's cold smile.

"The more, the merrier." I ease a heavy sigh, knowing he's got this one. "The announcement was made shortly after your summons. Trials will commence within the month, and the wedding will take place on Samhain."

"A perfect date to be hitched in hell."

When his eyes roam down, I'm about to interrupt in protest until he remarks, "The black bodysuit with its coat overlay is an appropriate choice, but your chest is rather unprotected." He growls low and trails a claw-tipped index finger down the low V-neckline, prompting a subtle hiss from my teeth when he brushes my cleavage.

"Angels don't have a heart. And my halo is practically indestructible," I dismiss his concern, standing by my choice.

I tense as Lucifer slides a hand along my equally-suited arm and coasts it up. What I love most are the off-the-shoulder sleeves and how the fabric arcs to bind to the band at my neck, ensuring the outfit is comfortable yet tempting but not obscene. Especially with the scarlet bodice, which hugs my curves and meets in a V pointing straight for my celestial center.

Once he rubs a curl between his fingers, Lucifer folds his hands behind his back, making no motion to depart.

I squint and set my hands on my hips. "Waiting for something?"

"A simple thank you will suffice," he hints, lips contorting to a beguiling smile.

When his tail nips my ankle, I lurch and lose my balance, startled. Of course, Lucifer is there to catch me by the waist, sending a wealth of heat rushing to my pelvis. And beyond when he tugs me back, so my wings press to his substantial chest. I bite back a gasp and clench my eyes as he slides his hands to my hips, stationing me, and lowers his mouth to my ear.

"With the countless Hell on Earth laws you've broken, I could have easily thrown you into my pits, Astraea. Or head first into my crater. But…"

He grips my chin, and wrenching it up, he cups the front of my throat. His raw, dominant power brutalizes me as if he's shoved lightning into my veins to strike my blood. His hellfire swarms into my body and mind until sulfuric tears burn my eyes. I gulp down the painful knot in my throat and shudder as he rubs his lips along the edge of my jawline beneath my ear to the side of my neck.

"You are fortunate to intrigue me enough that I see fit to not dispose of you, and you have a skill I may put to good use. Yes, I am the Devil incarnate. I will not be held to your Celestial City's high and mighty standards, but the Devil looks after his own."

"You don't own me, assh—"

He jerks harder until I yelp, but he cuts it off when he scrapes his teeth along my throat. "Make no mistake, Astraea. I. Own. You. You're not in your precious city of gold anymore. You are my little angel in hell. And you will flap those pretty wings wherever and whenever and however I desire. Your heavenly fate would have been nothing short of a prison and one you may not have survived. But if you are a good girl and my obedient stool pigeon and, in the rarest of chances, manage to aid me in the growing threat to my realm, I'll remove that collar from your exquisite throat and personally escort you wherever the fuck you want to go."

Hysteria and fear swarm my body, igniting my nerves. Cinders simmer beneath my flesh, and sweat breeds beneath my body suit. His power plays with my body, with my blood, blazing a path straight for my mind. My halo spasms, sputtering flickers of light on my flesh. Pain flares my thoughts, and I struggle for breath and claw at his robe. My eyes roll to their ceilings, my lower lip trembles, and my knees weaken, but Lucifer holds me up and brushes his mouth across mine.

"But…if you fuck with me, little angel, you'll get first-hand experience of what it feels like when I play the devil with you," he utters huskily. "I'll break you, little cherub. I'll wreck your entire being, thrust my hell inside you, and then remake you one piece at a time until you belong to me: body, mind, heart, and soul. You won't have a fucking prayer, sweetheart. Unless it's when you're on your knees worshiping me like your idol and praying to me like I'm your mother-fucking god. I'm the scripter of sin and the god of pain and pleasure. I'm the King of Hell on Earth and under the Earth. I'm the Son of Dawn who battled death and destruction through shooting stars and black holes and survived with the fucking scars to prove it. I'm the transformer of realms. And as long as you wear my mark around your throat, I'm the center of your fucking universe."

Through the tears smoldering my vision, I study his eyes and the naked hunger of his gaze as he slides them down my body. My eyes lower to his full and utterly sexual mouth, to that tail that caresses the inner leg of my bodysuit until it flicks my thigh, and I nearly buckle from the lustful onslaught. My mind whirls from the delirious fantasies needling into me, from my flesh's cravings.

Everything about this is wrong. Fucked up and fucked over wrong. But a deeper part of me recognizes how natural it is: needs must when the devil drives. Right now, Lucifer is driving me to madness. But madness is necessary for Hell. Yes, I hate myself for this betrayal, but I swallow that bitter poison and use it to sear my insides with even more hatred for him. Time to let go of the anchor of the inner angel I'm holding onto and give my psycho demon the keys to my fucking kingdom.

Lucifer is a transformer of realms, but I can transform, too. He wants a flying angel. I will be an avenging one. And the moment I get rid of this fucking mark, I'll plunge my fucking claws into his chest, rip out his black heart, and eat it right front of the Tribunal of High Seraphs. This desire, this need, this vow brands an unbreakable seal inside my soul. From now on, whenever he does these mind fucks and wreaks havoc on my body, I'll imagine those claws goring his chest, my angel teeth severing his jugular, and my trills filling the air until all the realms of Gemterra hear that an angel fucked the Devil. And won.

"You will bow to me later, Astraea…" Lucifer calls his power back from my mind, so the tears stem, the hunger abates. The prickled hairs electrifying my skin with goosebumps settle. But my vision is still red when he concludes, "But for now, you will fucking thank me."

He shoves me hard, so I stumble, catching myself with my hands. The energy of the lava below me pulses into my fingertips, radiating heat into their already sweaty pores. Yes, for now…

Throwing my chin up to the scripter of sin leering down at me with his arms folded across his chest, muscles rippling, I wrinkle my nose in disgust but adopt my sweet psycho-wrapped smile. I finally respond with the poisonous words, "Thank you, Lucifer."

Without another word, the King of Hell grins, hoists me to my feet, and sifts us through matter until we arrive in a glorified morgue right in front of a metallic table holding a naked and mutilated body. I clench my normally-iron stomach because I'm suddenly regretting those sushi rolls.

SIXTEEN

THE BODY IN THE MORGUE

——ASTRAEA——

Thankful for my presently iron stomach, I study the mangled body, picking out details one by one, determining the corpse was once female. Most of the spine has shattered along with countless other bones, as if she sustained a great fall. But it's not the shattered bones, caved-in head over the crushed skull, or the limbs twisted like a pretzel that captures my attention most. My mouth turns dry, and my chest tightens at the familiar extension of bone, muscle, and skin branching out from midway down the spine.

Up till now, Lucifer has paced a few steps behind me. Now, his energy cloys my back, raising the hairs along my arms from where his chest brushes my lower shoulders. I need to outfit him with a bell or two.

I bristle when he lowers his head to ask, "Notice something familiar?" His voice is a sharp flame sparking the back of my neck.

"The body is human, there's no doubt," I determine since angel bones would never shatter so simply. Or crudely. We are made of stronger stuff, and our halos gift us with otherworldly healing. Thanks to those elemental circlets formed of star fabric, our celestial DNA has no choice but to bow to the superior force until our cells repair themselves. Plus, the first thing angels learn in flight training is how to fall—a feat I've mastered since an infant. If we fall a great distance by some rare chance, our wings, our greatest strength, will break our fall.

"But…" Lucifer trails off, hinting as he moves to the side, swinging his tail beyond his dark cape.

"These bones protruding from the skin…" I shiver and hover a finger above the popped limb because I can't bring myself to touch what is so sacred. Feathers are one thing, but the bones and sinew swarming with nerves are another. "They are angel anatomy. The very same as our skeletal structure." I trace a line across the bare flesh, to the familiar tendons and veins. Portions of the skin have flayed off, even down to the wing socket.

"You are certain?"

I turn to the side, meeting his eyes as his heavy breath drifts along my face, carrying that familiar scent of vetiver, smoke, and roses. I nod and gesture to the portion of wings lacking skin, exposing muscle. "This group of muscles is secondary deltoids and triceps. They connect the humerus," I trace my finger above the wing tip, drawing a line down and across the primary bones, continuing, "the ulna and radius, and manus to the spine. I know these like I know my name." I deadpan with him this time, noting those pinpricks of silver in the black velvet of his eyes before his irises once again turn crimson.

"Thank you, Astraea. Your confirmation has proven valuable."

"Confirmation." I lick my lips, treading on the word while clenching my trembling fingers. "You hardly needed me for this. You suspected. Is this what you meant by corpses?"

"Of a sort," he responds and begins to pace again, scrutinizing me out of the corner of his eye. "This one was discovered floating along the Elloria River."

One of Hell on Earth's four rivers that surround its vast expanse. Nearly converging, they act as a power and water source. I stiffen, reading between the lines.

"The Elloria River is to the northeast." I taper my brows, twisting the corners of my mouth low. "Closest to the floating mountains and the Celestial City."

Lucifer pauses and cocks his head at me. "You said it, little angel. Not I."

I slam into him until his wings collide with another metallic table. Lucifer chuckles darkly, his eyes glinting in amusement. "Careful, sweetheart. I'd rather you not get blood on this suit. It's one of my favorites. And there is much more I plan to share with you."

Pausing with my hands gripping his collar, I wrinkle my nose, scorn written all over my stiffened body. I don't care what the Devil says. Angels are not behind this savagery. Nothing more in the world I want to do than wipe that impish expression off his face, but I calm the heated storm roiling inside me.

Lucifer shoves me off him and continues pacing again, needling my nerves. "A few reports have surfaced from my agents about human tourists going missing from the Outer Circle."

I grit my teeth. "The outskirts of Hell on Earth. The underprivileged sectors." My throat narrows in resentment.

"Ones with less security and not patrolled by my legions."

"And how do you know your fallen alpha hole legions aren't behind this?" I nearly snarl the challenge and step toward him. "A squad could have easily plucked unwilling humans and experimented."

Lucifer presses his lips into a frown. "I know."

"But how can you—"

His hellfire rears up, writhing around the edges of his robe and wings. I flinch from the heat scalding my coat. His anger treads across my body in a predatory warning while those serpent tattoos on his chest coil upward, twisting their heads beyond the collars of his robe. They bare their fangs as they slither along the sides of his face. A shiver crawls along my spine from his eyes turning to orbs of black ice, threatening me if I protest further.

I clamp my mouth shut, though I'm not about to play devil's advocate any time soon. Instead, I examine the body again, strengthening my stomach lining.

"Notice something else about the corpse?" hints Lucifer from the side, and I'm seriously considering enrolling him in a course on personal space…with me as the instructor. I shake my head to rattle my thoughts before the teacher-to-student kink fest in my mind grows.

I narrow my eyes to angel slits, bottling the breath in my lungs to concentrate until I make out the faded markings upon the skin of her wings. Exhaling a gasp through my flared nose, I turn to face him, posturing. "Puncture marks. But they aren't from angel teeth."

"That much I knew. All the blood has been drained from her body as well."

I hug my elbows, tapping one as I survey his expression. He hasn't lost his knowing smirk, but his eyes are creased. They stray to the corpse, gaze turning blank from confusion.

"How many bodies like this have turned up?" I wonder.

"This is the second with twenty-three humans missing from the Outer

Circle projects."

I lift a brow, tapping my elbows again. "Out of hundreds of thousands of humans and lower races in the projects, why does the King of Hell show an interest in their fate?"

Before I may flinch or jerk away, Lucifer grips my chin, wrenching me toward him. I flare my feathers, but he stems the threat with one deep demon purr rattling from his chest. His power thickens, cloying my nostrils. My breath leaves in shudders.

"Contrary to the propaganda you subscribe to from your heavenly homestead that was once my birthplace, I maintain a certain level of law and order within Hell on Earth." When I snarl and try to jerk my chin away, he digs his fingers into my hip, tugging me closer until his pelvis nudges my upper stomach. "It takes extreme work and careful delegation to maintain such law and order. Thanks to your interruption, Astraea, I have been treading a very thin line."

"Glad I can make the Devil sweat." I grin but part my lips when his energy travels down my spine like a current. It doesn't stop when it hits my ass. I clench my thighs and wince from the fire and ice tethering my core, knowing I'm the one who's sweating beneath my suit.

"If it becomes public knowledge that humans are disappearing within Hell on Earth, it will create more than a headache for me," Lucifer prattles on. I roll my eyes at his ego trip, concerned his pride is so inflated, it would be a pretty long fall. "Samhain is in a few brief months."

"So, why are you doing these Bride Trials?" I spit out.

"A diversion."

This time, when I tug my chin away, he releases me, collects his cape, and paces again. His shoulders curl, his wings fold behind him, and I determine how overwhelmed he is by his body language. But I remember how he's the master of deception, not to mention his gigantic ego.

"I may be a damned demon and the Devil incarnate, but I am not without my enemies. You should understand that better than most. The Chamber is watching my every move," he explains. "Ever since I opened Hell on Earth, locked the higher-ranking demons in the pits, and passed laws welcoming all races to the Ninth Circle while prohibiting their abuse, they're seeking any excuse to overthrow me."

I raise my chin high and tighten my wings, regarding him. "Perhaps they should."

Bristling, Lucifer growls low, narrowing his eyes on me. "You will think better of me after you live with me for a time."

Wings flared, I set my hands on my hips and stalk toward him, glaring the whole time. "Live with you?"

That feral grin returns, pointed demon teeth on full display. "Oh, didn't I mention? I plan to keep my eye on you for as long as you are in my domain. What better way to do that than to have you as the guest of honor in my home?"

Closing the distance between us, I stab a finger in front of his face and seethe. "Only when hell fucking freezes

over would I ever consent to live with you!"

His grin grows, twisting into a wolfish one that tugs at my very pussy. Before I have the opportunity to blink, Lucifer hauls me into his arms, covers my scream with his hand, sifts out of the morgue, and pitches me right in front of a sidewalk within an attraction district. I stumble, fall to my knees, and catch myself with my hands with a hiss. Ice drifts across my skin, chilling me until goosebumps form beneath my suit.

Lucifer combs a hand through my curls. My breath spasms when he grips my hair and yanks my head up until my neck strains. All so I may eat my words and face the enormous attraction with the title in massive, bold letters chiseled in pure, eternal ice:

Hell Frozen Over

I shiver as the Devil lust-hums above my ear, "Satisfied, Astraea?"

SEVENTEEN

ASTRAEA'S SUGGESTION

—ASTRAEA—

"**D**amn devil dick," I spit at Lucifer from the private hover car two hours later.

Leaning back in his seat with ease, he touches his fingers to his brow in a mock salute and retorts, "Naughty angel."

I stiffen, cross my arms over my chest, and slump lower, dragging my wings against the seat behind me. His double horns twinkle their pride at my expense.

Lucifer had dragged me inside Hell Frozen Over so he could shove humble pie down my throat. Even now, I can't deny the aftermath of my skin tingling from the walkthrough of the ice castle of a winter wonder-hell-land. The shifting backlights of golds, crimsons, and burning amber spun a flaming masterpiece through the translucent prisms. It was an icy labyrinth complete with tunnels, slides, and a scavenger hunt of various levels for children and adults, with an award of fireworks to whoever arrived at the Devil's throne at the end: the picture-perfect prize.

An attached fire and ice-themed restaurant clothed in illusory fog featured everything from flambé to fondue to a five-course cold dessert of blood-rose ice cream adorned in edible gold leaf. A more elite tour included a sleigh ride over a snowy landscape pulled by real hellhounds followed by a grand, demon fire-breathing presentation.

I grumble under my breath and stare out the hover car window as Lucifer chuckles across from me. "Sore loser, Astraea?"

I stick out my tongue. Unfortunately, my stomach flutters a betrayal, and I must work hard to contain my psycho angel who wants to grin. Oh, she wants to do other things, too—all of them ending with me on Lucifer's lap. Thankfully, I still have a shred of pride left.

"Where are we going now?" I wonder, lifting my chin to survey the passage through the Seventh Circle.

"This is a longer route to the Outer Circle, where I will inspect a few of the zones where humans have gone missing. At times, I will pass through unbeknownst to security, so I may perform a private inspection," he informs me, gesturing as the hover car slows upon a balcony overlooking multiple levels.

Pressing my hand to the sides of the car, I peer out the window to eye the hundreds of races in line for a special event inside an amphitheater. I blink a few times, trying to see beyond the crowd. When Lucifer directs my vision to the inside of the car, where he summons a holo-feed of the stadium's inside, I part my lips and lean closer, my blood giddy as it rushes through my veins.

"Hell on Wheels," expresses Lucifer, tapping the feed. "In this international sensation, sparks are guaranteed to fly when demon drag racers burn up the track. Place your bets with your good intentions to pave the way. And remember: all roads lead to hell..." he finishes with a cheeky grin, prompting me to shake my head in disbelief. Still, I can't help the little twinkle of mischief glowing inside me, amused by his humor that echoes mine.

I lurch from the car pitching forward off the balcony and traveling a private route above the crowds and into the stadium. More cars pass us, heading in the opposite direction, but this one journeys down a secluded route with gem-tech grown trees flourishing around us. I can tell the difference since the trees outside Hell on Earth are nowhere near as vivid. These are also programmed with the perfect space between each one, so the branches barely skirt one another, unlike the closely-bundled woods beyond this realm's borders. They're also programmed with perma-leaves that never fall but can transform into a kaleidoscope of colors.

Upon noticing my gaze lingering on the trees, Lucifer remarks, "Remind me to take you to the Hell on Earth National Park Preserve. It spans seven levels within the Fourth Circle and boasts wildfire-proof woods teaming with creatures ranging from wild hellhounds and cats to boars to firebirds and even the mighty hellephant."

"You sound like a holo-tourist ad," I mutter.

"No need to be uncivil, Astraea," he lifts his voice an amused octave. "As I stated before, you will be my guest of honor."

I tug at my collar and throw him a glare, referring to the demonic-inked collar around my throat. "You could have—"

"Could have what?" he growls a low warning, and I press my spine against the seat, curling my wings around me for protection in this small space. "Could have let you be on your merry way to your divine city where you would have become nothing more than an angel's whore to be bred? Or your pride and glory plucked and stripped from your back, reducing you to no other option but the former fate? As I stated before, law-breakers in my realm meet one of three fates: banishment, pit-bondage, or my bed. Unless I recognize their skill and indenture them into my service. I am the ruler of Hell on Earth, and I will protect what is rightfully mine and maintain authority over my realm as I have for centuries."

I feel the defensive color rising in my cheeks as I burn my eyes onto his. "Rightfully stolen, you mean," I say with my mouth dry.

One second, I'm gazing out the window, and the next, Lucifer slams me against it, ripping the breath from my lungs and pulsing his power all along my body until my vision spins. The tattoo on my throat singes my skin. I bite back a scream, but Lucifer chuckles, savoring my fear. "Don't pretend you came here under morally superior convictions, little angel," he snarls in my ear, thrusting my wrists above my head even as I try to wriggle out of his grasp. I shift my wings, hoping to gain momentum, but he's too powerful. After bucking once, I regret it when he flicks his tongue against my ear and unleashes a deep thunder-purr. My legs drop open—all instinct. Lucifer pushes his knee against my core, heating me with that single gesture.

"Stop!" My whisper comes out more of a desperate rasp. I open my mouth to trill, but he wraps a firm hand around my throat, shredding my breath to thin threads. He knows the exact pressure to enforce without harming me, to restrict my breath to its barest vestiges, but without causing any permanent damage. Tears rage in my eyes from the fear and adrenaline spiking inside me because he commands my body and maintains ultimate control. A thrill electrifies my spine, and I wish I could shut down that reward center in my brain.

Lucifer flares his nostrils and snarls, "I've read your records and history. I know your sins and guilt and shame and why the Tribunal brought down such a harsh judgment. We have far more in common than you believe, sweetheart."

"No!" I muster a whimpering squeak as my eyes roll to their ceilings. My halo dims.

Something dark and wild swirls in my chest. I extend my claws, straining against his hands because I haven't felt this emotion in seven years. Not since that horrific night. A wave of ice threatens to rip me under until I'm slipping beneath the cracks, falling into a darkness that blinds my vision. I remember the claws goring into my flesh. Her screams ring in my ears. I'm fucking shutting down all over again.

Her name is an inferno scorching every neuron in my mind: Evangelina.

When Lucifer grinds his knee against my center, I gasp, astonished at how he manages to bring me back. So, I banish the memories, trade them in for the heat smoldering my cheeks and my body growing wet with a primal need. I cling to that lust like it's my last fucking lifeline.

Lucifer's eyes turn dark and predatory. "Scared, little angel snared by the Devil?" he taunts me, and I shiver, my chest heaving in my struggle for air.

All I can do is nod. Smiling to one side, he loosens his hold on my throat, gifting me with a few blessed breaths. "You should be. You should be gods-damned terrified of me."

My nerves are hypercharged, and I smell every scent bewitching my nostrils from his body. I feel his hellfire energy tickling into my pores to penetrate my blood until I'm sweating straight through my suit. I hear his lust-hum as if I'm inside my body with it bleeding my ears. I taste his sweet and spicy essence curling across my lips, parted to welcome the author of sin and seduction. And I see nothing but black depths within his eyes—the full power of the Unconsecrated Crater gazing back at me.

The fear stokes and excites me until I want to destroy my inner psycho for being such a hypocrite. Instead, my lips tremble, and I moan when he brushes his fingers across my center that has soaked right through my suit. With my nipples hardening, I flick my eyes down to where he's touched me. I wince, but it's too late. Lucifer chortles and captures my chin, rubbing his lips across mine.

"I could have simply branded you with my hellfire, but I love smelling how wet you get for me, angel. I could have given you nothing but pain. Hate me for it if you wish. I don't rightfully give a fuck since all of time and history has made me the big, bad guy—a role I've never denied. But I thought it better to distract you with pleasure when I adorned your lovely neck with this collar." I hiss, but one more thunder-purr is all it takes for my body to turn supple, bending to his will because he'll have his say. Gritting my teeth, I listen and swallow hard as he concludes, "Yes, Astraea, a collar to defend myself from any more of your abduction attempts because I don't have fucking time for them. A collar to keep you in line. A collar to prevent any further escape attempts where you run the risk of killing yourself. And most of all: it's protection, Astraea. It's the most powerful protection I may offer you. Soon, you will understand."

I search for the lie inside his eyes and study those depthless orbs, free of bloodlust. Regardless of his thunder-purr, of his advances, all he is now is an undiluted predator guaranteeing me a promise and not a threat. At first, I want to believe him, let go of my pride for one fucking moment, but the battle rages inside my head. My emotions betray me, prompting me to rationalize his words until I remember how I can't rely on them. Emotions are what betrayed me in the first place.

"I'll never understand you. And you sure as hell will never understand me," I lash out.

"I'm more interested in your understanding of those marks," he refers to the mutilated body. "You may not know what being made them, but surely an angel with your hunting history—" he drapes his knuckles across my cheek, and I freeze from the intimate gesture as he leans in and finishes, "—either knows of or knows an individual who may have more information."

"You're the ruler of fucking Hell on Earth." I roll my eyes.

He grins, far too close to my face, and I catch myself mid-betrayal for staring at his full and supple mouth too long.

"My days of roaming the world back and forth are long over. This is my realm now, and while my history and network may be longer, yours includes your celestial realm and its hovering mountains."

"Ugh…" I shift my head, so his lips rub my throat instead of mine.

Wait…mountains. My thoughts drift to Jack and Mount Yvos for a fleeting moment which triggers a memory of a remote underground route on the nearby Mount Asharya: of children crying in mothers' arms, of the gnashing of teeth, of claws scraping across the gem-mag train, of my thrilled muscles burning as I ripped their fangs and broke bones and gored their flesh with my claws, until the predators flew away with their tails between their legs.

As Lucifer's mouth arrives at the base of my deep V-neckline, I find my pride and composure enough to push my hands against his face and shove him off. First, I clutch my throat, rubbing where that serpent collar stings my skin with the reminder. Back in his opposite seat with his legs crossed, wings curling at the edges, chin propped on his fist, and tail flicking back and forth next to him, I chastise the traitorous psycho inside me rubbing her eager hands from that charming glint in his eye. He appraises me, quirking a brow, obviously waiting for me to speak.

At that moment, I realize my mouth had parted. So, I gather my wits, ignore the heat between my legs, and respond, "I may know an acquaintance, though I'm surprised you didn't suggest her since she lives in the Second Circle. Well...last I heard, she was taking control of it."

Lucifer's eyes tighten, and he scrubs a hand down his face with a muffled "fuck". I lower my brows, confused, until he growls out, "I'll trade a whole fucking fallen angel legion if you don't say the name—"

"Mira Paler," I announce, squaring my shoulders because now I'm the one who's amused.

Clenching a fist and wings snapping shut, Lucifer snorts. "Of all the little, fucking angels I collar, it has to be one who fucking knows Mira fucking Paler."

EIGHTEEN

THE TALON IN THE TUNNEL

—ASTRAEA—

I tap on the side of the hover car, flicking my eyes to Lucifer, noting how our demeanors have reversed since the beginning of this little voyage. Lucifer has spent the remainder avoiding my gaze, muttering under his breath, raking his nails into his hair, and wearing a twisted frown. On the contrary, a proud warmth nourishes my chest, and my halo has sparked to life. It practically purrs its glow upon my figure.

As the hovercar passes through the Inner Gates to the Vestibule, I stop tapping and open my mouth to say, "We met on Mount—"

He raises his hand with a snarl. "I don't want to fucking hear it."

"It involved blood and lust," I hint, curling my lips into a teasing smile.

The Devil bares his demon teeth. "I still don't want to fucking hear it."

I shrug. His loss. Sweat blossoms on my brow when I remember that night because violence and pain substitute as foreplay for me. That night, it practically saturated the air. And Mira…well, a tsunami of butterflies whirls in my belly from the memory of her kiss of gratitude. How we'd allied, though we were no more than ships crossing in the night. Two ships anyone would want to fucking ship, my mouth grows wet at the memory of her fingers upon my neck while mine dragged through her hair, unraveling it from its tidy bun. So many times, I tried to breach the Nine Circles to find her again.

And failed.

In any case, the hover car slows, forbidding any more diverting thoughts. After stopping, Lucifer wastes no time climbing out of the vehicle, though he does linger outside and offers a hand to me with a cold, detached expression. Aggravated by his bipolar attitude, I ignore the hand and spring down from the hover car onto the cracked sidewalk with the ends of my coat flicking in the breeze.

We've arrived at a transport station which is a glorified parking garage with an underground network of mag-force trams. Of course, the Devil doesn't have as much gem-tech here in the Outer Circle and sticks to cheaper magnetic-field tech. All designed so people will hunger for the Inner Circles whether or not they can pay.

The ruler of Hell on Earth had to signal our arrival since dozens of security members have regulated the usual citizens beyond the fence-line of the station. In the distance is a residential district of hundreds of sub-section housing, and I imagine they're mostly for service members in the Outer Circle.

The mobs cheering and chanting Lucifer's name from the fences divert my attention. What's worse is when the Devil incarnate himself moves toward the demon security, pacing before the mob grows wilder upon his approach. Disbelief turns my stomach to iron, but I follow at a safe distance, observing as Lucifer sweeps his robe behind him and spreads his arms wide to the citizens. He basks in their applause. I can't help but blink again and again when he takes the time to sign autographs and pose for holo-feeds, smile and converse with the crowd, kneel before any children so he can engage them, and even hold a baby or two. My jaw drops, and that damn collar warms its energy along my skin as if he's winking at me.

Crossing my arms, I stand awkwardly and impatiently, tapping my foot until a demon child peers beyond Lucifer's side and points at me. He turns, smirks at me, and gestures. At first, my mouth goes slack. More than anything, I want to dig my heels in and refuse to spite him, but the hopeful expression on the child's face is irresistible. So, I fold my wings behind me and find my feet dragging me to his side.

"It's a real angel!" gasps the demon boy, shifting his tiny, black horns toward Lucifer. They accentuate his burnt amber skin tone and mirror his dark, expressive eyes.

"Oh, yes," acknowledges Lucifer, winking at the boy. I fight the urge to cringe when he wraps an arm around my shoulder, tugging me closer until his wing nudges mine. "You see, she flew too close to the fire and nearly got her wings burned. Now, I'm having a devil of a job with this one, but maybe you can tame her for me." He snaps his fingers at me, and I flick my gaze between him and the boy who arches his neck, straining his chin toward me.

"Huh?"

"Go on then, sweetheart. Give the boy a kiss," he urges upon my stupefied expression.

All others at the fence line blink, and I prickle before the little demon's cheeks flush to a scarlet gold. Shrugging, I lean down and lower my head to peck his cheek, but at the last second, the boy swings his head and plants his lips in a hard sloppy kiss right on mine. Startled, I lurch back, but the Devil catches me, roaring laughter from his chest to rumble against my wings while I gape. The boy puckers up his lips, then scampers away.

Lowering his head, Lucifer informs me, "Never trust a demon, sweetheart. Even a miniature one."

I huff and roll my eyes. After, he bids farewell to the fawning crowd and leads me toward the nearby stairwell with me blushing the whole time.

"He'll regret it the first time he learns what "no means no" means," I grumble under my breath, my pride wounded more than anything from Lucifer's joke at my expense—his way of getting me back for the "Mira Paler" incident.

"Ahh, we are beyond such pointless mortal sufferance, but if you granted your blessing for kink, Astraea, might I suggest the safe word "Beelzebub"."

At the base of the stairwell, I roll my eyes and retort, "How about the safe words of "kiss my ass"?"

"I'm flexible. But it wouldn't be the only thing I'd kiss."

I'm considering a worthy comeback when his gleaming eyes darken, assessing a view beyond my shoulder. He jerks his chin behind me, and I turn to a section of the cornered-off station. Our footsteps echo upon our approach. The entire station is vacant, desolate, and void of any beings. Off to the right, the tram is abandoned, dark, and quiet.

Before I can ask anything, Lucifer grips my elbow, tugging me along toward the platform, closer to the tram. "Six young women have been plucked from this location."

I stiffen, constricting my feathers. "Women?"

Eyes roaming across the platform, Lucifer sighs heavily. "All the missing humans have been women in their childbearing years and fertile." I press my lips into a frown, observing how his jaw hardens, and he balls his hands into fists. "All worked night shifts in the downtown district of the Vestibule, took public transport, and disappeared into thick air."

I lower my brows, squinting, but Lucifer turns back to me, swinging his cape to the side. "No, I did not speak in error, Astraea."

When he summons a holo-feed from his gem-plant, I purse my lips and approach. Chest tightening, I scan the feed showcasing a woman I'd assume in her mid-twenties with a pixie cut of blonde hair with color-changing tips—a trending hairstyle for the nightclub district. Within seconds, I flinch because Lucifer was telling the truth. Shadows swarm around her, thickening until they clad her in utter night. I lean closer, tilting my head. A few seconds flit by, the shadows clear. The young woman has vanished. My chest hitches, feels like it's caving in.

"A fae?" I question.

He shakes his head. "I know their scent. No fae can hide from the Devil. Higher, ancient beings, yes."

"So, it has to be someone or something—"

"Beyond my borders, yes." His lips twist into a grimace, and I squeeze my arms closer to my chest as he advances toward me, his hellfire growing along the edges of his body. All of him is heavy, from his dark brows knitting over those fathomless, deep-hooded eyes to his hands falling at his side. "As much as the Chambers have done their best to dispel any rumors, they've circulated all the same. A serial predator to a rogue cult to fucking Jack the Ripper raised from the dead." He pinches his lips.

"And what do you think?"

I lift my chin, deadpanning with him following my question, unflinching from the hellfire singing my suit.

"It's not what I think, little angel. It's what I know," he emphasizes, gazing down at me, his chest nearly brushing my arched throat. "I know the Queen of Demons reigns over the Northlands and is always scheming for more power, more blood, more souls to possess. And since her rebellious Hive continues driving out the daemon population, I provide a refuge here for them, which does not win me favor with such races. I know the elves and fae to the northwest have a long-standing alliance to protect their sacred, organic realms, but they crave to overthrow Hell on Earth and drive us back to the deep places of the world. I know the nephyl and human cults have urged me to join them in their long-standing war with the Northlands. I know the witches of the Greylands to the south would rather see Hell on Earth struck from time and history thanks to hell's past and lamentable orchestration of burnings. And the goblins and orcs of the Wastelands and beyond to the east despise all fallen angels and demons. Not even to mention your precious Tribunal." He spits out the last words as if he'd saved the most repugnant for last. His pupils dilate, and I feel like they're black mouths opening to devour me.

"So, Astraea…" he touches his thumb to my chin, chilling my flesh with his eyes rooting me to the spot. My lower lip trembles as he finishes a breath above my mouth, "With enemies surrounding Hell on Earth, unrest brewing from every race within the realms, and the presence of the corpses, do you think this is merely the work of a serial killer or the initial rumblings of war?"

I lick my lips, wavering at first before latching onto his one word. "Killer…are the mangled corpses connected to the missing—"

"Yes," he says without hesitation. His wings are like great black shadows eclipsing us in deeper darkness than this tunnel. "Their DNA has been matched. And you didn't answer my question."

I sigh through my nostrils but steel my spine to reaffirm, "If these are the precursor to war, then Mira Paler is your best source for eyes and ears on the Queen of Demon's Hive and the other realms. And she has the history of war and ancient knowledge of races and their anatomy and physiology. We both know she's the most renowned scientist and her skill with blood types is—"

Growling, Lucifer raises his hand in interruption, stepping away, his body language turning cold and aloof. "Mira Paler would not entertain an audience with me. Recent events have strained whatever thin mutuality we may have ever shared in the past."

I beam at him and tap a solitary finger to my jaw. "But you can get a message to her."

He inclines his head to me and lifts a brow. "And what message would that be?"

"Tell her Ace Raestar wishes to meet with her tomorrow night. And give her this as proof." I curl my left wing around the side of my body, slide my fingers along the inner layer of feathers, and peel one back to retrieve the little trinket I've hidden there for all these years. My inner angel giggles from how I'd promised to keep it close. I hand it to Lucifer, who studies it for a moment before a sultry smile spreads across his face.

"Now, I want to fucking hear it."

Smirking, I start to follow him back up the stairwell. Already, the crowds cheer, but at the last second, I turn, catching a glimmer. With Lucifer preoccupied with his entourage, I hurry down the steps to the grate in the corner of the platform where the glimmer originates. It's sharp and black with a silver sheen protruding from the dirt and shadows. Adrenaline surges up my spine, and I narrow my eyes, reaching into the grate to snatch the object. I close my fingers around it and gasp from the energy coursing into my skin. How it kindles warmth through my flesh and hums into my blood. How did Lucifer not notice this?

As soon as I hear the crowds echoing their farewells, I tuck the lethal talon into the inner layer of my feathers, rush up the stairs, and pretend I was standing in the shadows the whole time.

NINETEEN

LUCIFER'S HOME

——A S T R A E A——

When Lucifer escorts me inside a private tram that will carry us to his home, it dawns on me how I haven't slept in two days, apart from the unconscious stupor in the med-room with my body healing. A wave of fatigue hits me because even angels need their rest. Still, I know I should be more worn out. Maybe it's part adrenaline from all the recent events and the thrill of the unknown. Or this unwitting deal with the Devil. Or the enigma of corpses and a shadow thief. The prospect of living in the Nine Circles, the challenge of this mark on my skin, and even Lucifer himself could all contribute.

I tuck my wings closer to my back and follow him through the private tram until we arrive at an arched door, gilded with a gold trim that he opens and ushers me inside. It's a furnished and ornate travel car, but as soon as the familiar figure at the end of the car rises from his seat and adjusts his robe, I flutter my wings, enthusiastic.

"Cam." I smile, greeting my friend, who doesn't hesitate to pull me in for a bulging hug, restricting my breath.

"He wouldn't stop fussing about your safety and demanding an audience," grumbles Lucifer, voice agitated as he lowers himself into the seat at the head of the tram. Warmth nourishes my chest, triggering my halo to kindle a fervent glow on my skin. "And since the bastard cannot die, and given that Aamon is the one higher-ranking demon I have not imprisoned in my pits, I thought it better to do more than a mere visit."

I nestle into Camio's side but eye the Devil ahead of me. Despite how he doesn't turn to face me, Lucifer waves a hand in a dismissive gesture and mumbles, "He'll be joining you in my home for the first couple of weeks to give you time to adjust."

My blood pulses quicker in my veins, a thrill rushing through me. With my skin tingling and my feathers ruffled, I squeeze Camio's hand but admit in barely above a whisper, "Thank you, Lucifer."

It's the first time I mean it.

"Uh, bitch…" Camio clears his throat and tugs at his collar, his cheeks paling. "Compared to where you get to live, I'm crying tears of fucking poverty."

"Shut up, you spineless rainbow cake before I put a collar on you and make you my bitch," I hiss, overhearing the Devil's chuckle as the tram travels along the ascending roadway lined with gem-tech trees that mimic black willow trees. Except, the leaves on these are tinted red at the tips. It's when I squint and use my angel sight, enhancing my pupils with my halo and celestial blood, that I recognize the leaf tips are rubies.

I huff, wishing I wasn't impressed by Lucifer's estate since it's the one word that can apply. Again, he'd sounded like a walking holo-ad when informing us of how he'd sectioned off the top nine floors of the super-tower with two full levels dedicated to the grounds. My breath hitches as I gaze at the blood-red rose gardens flourishing on each side of the long drive. One wouldn't even know this estate resides within the Ninth Tower, considering the small patches of woods bordering the estate.

A tower within a tower.

Beyond a tower, it's a small castle resting on a foundation of Diablo ore with veins of magma like a network of branches smoldering through the bedrock. Overwhelmed by the unfathomable sight, I clutch at my arms, rubbing them for comfort as I take in the alluring, gothic architecture of smaller spires and pinnacles, grand arched windows, and even a drawbridge. A drawbridge the tram must cross with a slow-rushing current of bubbling magma below it. Shadows and hellfire wreathe the small castle. Behind it is a lake, water so dark, it resembles black ink.

"Penny for your thoughts, angel?" wonders Lucifer, jolting me from my observation. His tone is amused, and I flick my eyes to where he cups an orb of hellfire in his hand, twirling the orb, playful and casual.

"Well..." I stiffen, falling back on my usual pattern as I lean toward him from the opposite seat. "It's clear you need a new decorator."

"Is that so?" he doesn't lose that knowing smile as he barely regards me, continuing to play with that orb.

I pinch my lips, sneering, "What's next? Flying gargoyles? Walls of skulls and tapestries

of bones? Hooded demons standing sentry at every corner? You're such a cliché." I throw out the words, rolling my eyes.

On my left, Camio clears his throat and averts his gaze. However,

Lucifer's eyes don't stray from his hellfire, his indifference raking my nerves.

"The correct word is "classic", sweetheart," he retorts, curving one corner of his mouth into a feral grin to showcase his demon teeth. "I am the author of everything fallen. All manner of darkness and sinful indulgences are associated with me. So give the Devil his due. For anything that arose after is the cliché. I am the fucking original."

I part my lips, but any words I may have had turn to ash. No comebacks for his statement because it's no lie.

After the tram stops beneath a covered entrance before the main Diablo ore arched doors, Lucifer departs first, his iron boots resounding on the ground. He sweeps his cape to one side and offers me his hand, that dastardly tail flicking in the air. At first, I pause, waiting for Camio, who lifts a finger to finish his port. I sigh, shaking my head with a breathy laugh as my friend rises and proceeds to fumble with multiple suitcases. Why would he bother to pack so much when his stay is temporary? I highly doubt the King of Hell is under any budget for providing for guests.

Lucifer kneads his brow, taps his gem-plant, and summons an aid. When he thrusts his hand in a more demanding gesture, I step down from the tram but hesitate before accepting. Even with Camio here, my nerves are still hypercharged. If I take his hand so he may welcome me into his home, will l ever come out, or has he changed his mind and plans to chain me to his bed?

Between the Diablo ore humming its dark energy onto my skin and the heat of the magma cloying the air, it's a flawless trap for an angel.

Biting my lip, I hover my fingers above his open, dark palm, darting my gaze around the area, wondering if there are any escape routes.

Maybe beyond the lake…

"You wouldn't make it, little angel."

I turn to the Devil, who sports a knowing grin, suspecting my train of thought. I firm my lips and press them into a frown, but my insides quiver.

Rubbing one arm with my other hand, I battle my dizzying vision and offer, "Are you sure you don't want to reconsider? I bet you have plenty of instruments of torture in your hell pits. Could be fun."

He sniggers. That palm curves until he strokes his fingers along my cheek, causing me to shiver until he trails them down to my throat and closes his hand around it. And like earlier, my blood quickens, adrenaline pulsing when he restricts my air. No choice but for my body to lurch closer to his. Feathers tighter than new bowstrings, I part my lips, licking them slowly as his eyes lower to my mouth, my throat, and back to my eyes.

"Trust me, Astraea," he lust-hums, leaning closer to touch his lips to the corner of my mouth in a light, near-kiss. "When the time comes for me to torture you, you'll be screaming my name and begging me for more."

I blanch. Lucifer throws his head back with a dark laugh and releases my throat but grips my arm before I can protest. The skin on my throat still tingles, and I wonder if he left a burning imprint there. I blame my lack of a comeback and my anxiety on the environment, then reinforce the mental walls of my fortress.

Overhearing Camio behind us arguing with the aid about his suitcases and how he should have marked them all fragile, I roll my eyes. As soon as Lucifer tugs me along, my body follows, ascending the few black stone steps to the grand dais leading to the doors. On each side of them are gryphon statues. At least three times my size, but my jaw drops from their lifelike expressions and crafted beauty out of place amongst the black and fiery atmosphere. Gold-hued white fur and feathers cover their bodies packed with muscle and power.

Upon closer study, I realize they aren't exactly gryphons since they lack beaks. Their muzzles slope to a softened point while plumes of long, noble feathers extend from the crest of their heads. Smaller ones fan out from the sides of its head, reminding me of a feathery mane. I tilt my head to the side, feeling a soft smile working its way across my face. Their eyes are the most entrancing.

"Daddy's home, my lovelies," croons the Devil, angling his neck down to eye me.

The statues surge to life. Silver flames curl all along the edges of their bodies, crackling fat embers. Startled, I leap away, beating my wings on instinct from two superior flying beings' presences. Before I can hope for any escape, Lucifer grips me harder, holding me in place with his claws. I gulp down breaths and stifle a squeak as the creatures move toward us, shaking their feathered heads and swinging their tails rapidly as if giddy.

No hesitation whatsoever, he raises his hand to the closest beast. It tilts its head to the side, welcoming his palm stroking the feathers on the side of its face. The other thrusts its muzzle against its fellow creature as if jealous of the attention.

"None of that now, Starla," Lucifer coos to the jealous one and tickles the underside of its neck as it stretches, warbling its approval from deep inside its chest.

The other cranes its neck to the side, eyes flicked to me. All white with a silver slit for each pupil, the orbs are long and almond-shaped, ancient and beautiful. I find my fingers straying, curling toward the creature until it puffs smoke from its nostrils and snorts.

Lucifer tugs my hand and shakes his head. "You haven't earned their respect yet, little angel."

"What are they?" My voice comes out in a half-whisper, half-gasp.

"Sylvan-gryphs. The offspring of dragons and gryphons. But the privilege of touching them is reserved for ones who have done them a great service or have found favor in their hearts."

I station a hand on my hip and wrinkle my nose. "So, what did you do?"

Lucifer smiles but not at me—at the ones before him as he strokes their fur and responds, "I healed them."

I taper my brows, beyond curious, but he offers nothing else. For a few more moments, I observe him greet the sylvan-gryphs until Camio makes his way up the porch. When silver flames smolder from the beasts' nostrils, Lucifer wags a finger and speaks a foreign language, mystical and lyrical, calming the creatures.

"Guests this time, lovelies. Not treats."

This time…I muse.

"Cain," the Devil snivels with a roll of his eyes. "You will be in Wing Ignis, and one of my staff will direct you inside. I will escort Astraea to Wing Astrum."

"I thought you had business." I cross my arms over my chest, squeezing my arms and wings shut to avoid brushing the sylvan-gryphs as he leads us to the door.

"Business will come soon, but I won't miss your reaction."

"Reaction to what?"

With a sly grin, Lucifer waves a hand before the Diablo doors, which open inside to his command. No wonder he wanted to see my expression.

TWENTY

THE SECRET OF THE COLLAR

—ASTRAEA—

Before he can touch me, I spring inside, gushing over the vaulted ceilings bearing gem-tech murals of moving star maps. Below the murals, stained-glass windows line up to cast rainbow prisms along the columns and the arched hallways above my head. The colonnaded marble hall stops me in my tracks, and I stare at the stars, which blur from the tears glistening in my eyes.

Compared to the outside, this is nothing I could have expected.

"I may be the King of Hell, Astraea," Lucifer expresses behind me, his voice practically purring across my wings, "but I will never forget my birthright as the Morningstar and the Son of the Dawn."

When I spin toward him, I again catch the echo of starlight within his dark eyes and know it must be from his time before hell when he gazed into the eye of the universe and carried its light within his being. Until he was cast out. I pause to study the markings on one side of Lucifer's dark face, the reminder of his fall from grace. Abaddon has given me bits and pieces of the story of his weeks-long battle with Lucifer, of his responsibility of throwing the Morning Son down to the earth. My fingers stray to my chest, knowing Lucifer lost his halo—the gift of the stars while raw emotion overwhelms me with an echo of that pain.

I swallow the brutal knot in my throat as I gaze at the King of Hell. For once, it's not pride that compels me to deadpan: it's empathy. Lucifer steps toward me, holding my gaze with that dark, seductive stare. His hellfire flames curl and dance with the shadows along the edges of his body, but the embers flickering across my skin and hair don't burn me.

"Astraea," he voices my name in a long and slow lust-hum that nearly sends my knees buckling. I knit my brows into a frown because it's all I can muster for battle right now. "Tell me…" he captures a few curls of my fiery red hair, though his eyes roam across my wings. It's the first time I wonder what his hands would feel like stroking them or his subtle flames warming the gold. "Who gave you your name? It means "of the stars". Your mother? Father?"

I shake my head, pursing my lips and debating whether to share anything of my past. "You have my file."

"I was not interested in your birth at the time, merely your skills."

I lift a brow, curious if he's telling the truth, but I keep my answer brief. "Abaddon."

Lucifer lowers his brows, deepening the shadows around his eyes. "And why did the Angel of Destruction, the Angel of the Abyss, give you such a shining name? Moreover…" he twists his mouth into a grimace, and the heat of his flames simmer against my suit and skin, "why would such a significant archangel as he name a lesser angel and one centuries apart from him?"

He closes the distance between us. I wince from those flames, from his claws burrowing into my skin when he grips my hip. My breathing grows labored from the scent engulfing my nostrils. Dark emotion creeps into my chest to dim my halo when I consider mine and Abaddon's brief but intense history. He's always acted as my guardian, my bond-keep, closer than my adopted archangel brothers. I was not alone on that mountain, but I was the one child he brought back to the Halls of Warriors.

I owe him my life.

Waves of ice wash over my skin, and I shudder from the familiar feeling, ages old. No matter how many times Abaddon trained me to control it, I never have. It swirls in my belly like a cauldron filled with black liquid primed to erupt. I need to get out of here.

"Pretty stars," mumbles Camio behind us, interrupting us, cutting through the tension and offering me relief.

"Wing Ignis," Lucifer barks the reminder, jutting a finger to the left while a demonic staff member arrives to direct him.

Camio settles a hand on my shoulder, squeezes it in reassurance, kisses my cheek, then tottles off to follow the demon.

Moment broken, Lucifer sheathes his claws but grips my elbow, practically dragging me to the marble staircase beyond the center of the arches. I huff but don't put up a protest. Not with my skin crawling and throat burning—the rumblings before the storm. A storm I've shared with one person.

We pass more star-themed murals, but I'm in no state of mind to appreciate them. My vision whirls and I cover my mouth, wishing I could pull my elbow from the ultimate fallen angel with his stiff, hard wings, rigid posture, and eyes cold and distant.

At least the journey to my room is not long and ends after we crest the staircase and arrive halfway down the hall. Without another word,

Lucifer turns the silver knob, opens the door, and promptly shoves me inside the room. Chest lurching, I catch myself before I stumble, only for my arms to hug my churning stomach.

"I've wasted enough time with you today," he snaps, curling his upper lip as I turn to him. "After my business is done, you'll join me for dinner."

"And Cam?"

"Yes, and that traitorous turncoat," he grumbles and slams the door, but I overhear his muffled words—something about having Camio stuffed and served like a flamboyant pheasant at supper.

Ignoring the snide remark and everything about the room, apart from the door to the bathroom, I practically dive inside, open the toilet, and spend the next few minutes retching streams of dark liquid from my guts. Déjà vu returns to me from Jack holding my hair back from my face the one time I did this in his home on Mount Yvos. Not even Abaddon knows this carefully guarded secret and one of my greatest weaknesses and reasons I failed at so many other angel skills. Not that I was trying hard at them.

After choking on the bitter taste that occurs once a month, I swipe at my mouth and face my blanched reflection. Next, I peel off the bodysuit, discard it into a heap in the far corner of the bathroom, then make a beeline for the shower. I spend nearly an hour scrubbing the spider-skittery feeling off my body, that bitter aftertaste from my mouth, and the Lucifer's flames from my skin. Thankfully, my angel heat isn't for another month or so, but I'll have to figure out a way of escaping by then—a way of avoiding the Devil and his wild lust-humming. In heat, I'd never survive them.

Finally, I turn the shower off and weave a towel around my body.

A surge of steam billows into the air once I open the door. I smile, appraising the room from the staircase curling to a second floor with a bedroom on one side and a small library on the other. Floor-to-ceiling windows form an L-shape along the walls, but I breeze past them and head for the Infinit-i chamber, which takes up one wall in the corner.

Flinging aside the towel, I turn to my reflection, smiling in approval of my rose cheeks, the color renewed, vibrancy returned to my eyes, and my damp wings shimmering like sunlight. I select delicate lace lingerie the same color as my hair and slide my hands down my body, admiring the form I've spent decades honing.

"Niccce titsss," a foreign and utterly masculine voice invades the room—far too close for comfort.

I spin my head, seething from the invasion, waiting for a demon lurker to pop his head from beyond one of the secondary little rooms attached to the chamber.

"Come out!" I hiss the demand.

"If you insssissst."

Out of the corner of my eye, I catch my reflection. The inked collar on my throat swirls—pins and needles shifting and twisting. I gasp a windstorm through my flared nostrils as a thick, black serpent rises from my flesh, springing its head back and opening its mouth, so its forked tongue slithers out, and he hisses a greeting, "Pleasssure to meet you."

I stumble back, falling on my rump and shrieking, "Bloody fucking hell!"

TWENTY-ONE

SAMMY THE SNAKE

—ASTRAEA—

I don't think. Grabbing the closest object, I throw the high heel at the snake slithering on the floor toward me. It meets a mark on its back.

He gasps, hissing, "How rude!" I shriek and grab another. This time, he dodges, slinking closer and closer to me. "We got off on the wrong tail, but let me expla—"

I scramble further into the closet, grabbing more shoes with one hand and keeping the other tight around the collar tat. One by one, I chuck the foot weapons at the talking snake, my whole body shaking in the knowledge that that thing was inside me!

"Ow!" cries the snake when the leather boot knocks him on the head. He springs up, baring his fangs. "That wasss jusss unneccccessssary!"

"Don't you dare come snaking back into my bosom," I yell and chuck another heel at the serpentine fiend.

"Fine." The snake weaves to the side as if about to escape. "Sssee how

I can be a cccivil ssserpent."

In barely the blink of an eye, the snake pitches back, but this time, he lunges. I can't cover my neck quickly enough, and it wouldn't matter since he's bound to the collar. The serpent dives into my throat, and I nearly choke on the odd shifting sensation, the pins and needles rupturing as he returns to the supernatural collar. The energy humming beneath my skin is potent, intense—a power I've never felt before that livens my blood and boosts my adrenaline. And I suddenly remember Lucifer's words about protection.

Tentative, goosebumps budding on my skin, I approach the mirror, studying the collar. Unlike before, the ink shifts, undulating and swirling, which I imagine is a sign that the snake is still hovering closer to the surface. First, I knead my brow with a shaky hand, hoping to stem the ringing in my ears. A magical snake is inside me. Lucifer collared me with a motherfucking snake! Not to mention a peeping tom of a reptile.

It occurs to me, then, that maybe I am not the only one who's shackled. The snake could owe a debt to Lucifer, too. Whatever the case, the Devil should be on the receiving end of my wrath, not this slippery, scaled one connected to the collar. Dropping my hand to the side and flexing my fingers, I fall back on rationality: if I can't get rid of this serpent anytime soon, the least I can do is make nice. I grit my teeth around the word. It's never been used to describe me.

"Okay…" I suck a deep breath through my teeth and face my reflection, eyeing the collar. "I'm calm. You can come out now." I tap the center back of the snake tat and yelp from the tiny sting that reminds me of static. "Oh, come on!" I roll my eyes. "You can't blame me for being all shocked. This isn't exactly familiar to me. But I promise I won't throw any more shoes at you."

Once again, I try touching the ink and wiggling my finger across the tail, smirking when it squirms. As if I'm tickling it. The snake's tongue promptly protrudes from the ink with a pronounced hiss, spitting a couple pissed-off drops of venom at me.

"Ugh, what do you want from me?" I snarl and grip the sides of the mirror.

Apologizzze.

I leap back, startled at the demanding voice in my mind. Oh, good grief! I drag my fingernails through my hair, transforming them into claws to rake at my scalp.

Yesss, I'm giving you grief. Now, apologizzze. I'd better sssee some angelic begging, proclaims the serpent, his voice higher-pitched, reminding me of Camio's.

Shifting my weight and staring open-mouthed at the mirror for a second or two, I finally press my lips together and say, "I'm sorry."

You're really bad at apologiesss.

"Oh, gods, I'm really, really sorry! I apologize for throwing shoes at you, and I promise I won't ever do it again. Now, will you get your scaly, crawly tail out of my skin?"

Jussst my tail?

"Don't be a wise ass. That's my job." I stab a finger at the mirror in warning.

The pins and needles erupt beneath my skin, but it doesn't last as long, and it's not as intense. Seconds later, the snake plops to the floor, one half of his body springing up. He tilts his head to the side with his slitted pupils eyeing me. A glassy film coats them, making them look wet and pouty. His tail is equipped with a rattler, but it's currently still and soundless. He doesn't have a cobra hood, and right now, with his head tilted to the side, forked tongue flopping out, oh damn…do I really think a snake is cute?

Sighing, I lower myself to one knee before him and squeeze my shoulders, not knowing the protocol for snake introductions. It's not like we can shake hands. "I'm—"

"Assstraea," he emphasizes, his black scales catching the the chamber lights and glittering like jewels.

"Uh…yeah, that's not gonna work. We can't have you saying "ass" every time you wanna talk to me. Will you call me Raea?"

"Ray-yah," he sounds it out and nods before creeping closer. "I am Sssama'el."

I press my lips into a smile. "Yeah, that won't work for me either. Mind if I call you Sammy?"

"You are my hossst. You can call me whatever you want." He gazes at me, unblinking since snakes lack eyelids.

"Host…right." I chew on the word, then gesture to the collar. "So, how does this all work? Who the hell are you? And how do you know Lucifer?"

"One quessstion at a time. I ssspeak ssslow." Sammy sighs before opening his jaws in a yawn, showcasing his adorable little fangs. "I am here to ssserve you. I have no choiccce. It is my curssse."

"Who cursed you?"

When he stares at me, curling his head to the other side, I read between the lines. "Ahh, Lucifer."

"I dessserved it."

"Oh, I'm sure whatever you did isn't so bad," I deny, but Sammy coils himself onto the floor, turning his neck and propping it on his bunched-up scales.

He makes a sound that reminds me of a hissing chuckle. "Not ssso bad, she sssays. She should asssk Adam and Eve before judging."

I widen my eyes with a gasp. "Oh. My. Gawwwwd. You're that snake?"

He sticks out his tongue again. "Naughty, naughty boy, he sssaid. Lying is an Eighth Circle sssin. Sssince I blamed it all on him, Lucccifer cursssed me to never lie again. Humph." He tucks his head into the knot where his coiled body conjoins.

"Wait, so you can't lie. Oh!" My lips find a grin when I remember his first words to me. "What else can you do?" I wonder.

"Asssk Lucccifer. I need a nap."

"Oh, I'll ask him, alright. Um…exactly where can I find him?"

Sammy lifts his head, tongue slithering out. "Do I look like I know hisss ssschedule?"

"If you were bound to him before me and knew his thoughts like you do mine, and if my assumption about how orderly his schedule is is true, then—"

"Sssteam room…end of Wing Assstrum down the hall."

Feeling daring, I touch a finger to the top of his head and rub the scales a bit while murmuring, "Thanks, Sammy."

"Welcome," he yawns and tucks his head back into his scales.

Meanwhile, I rise, not bothering to do more than shove my arms into a white, lacy short robe.

"By the way," I pop my head back into the chamber at the last second to ask Sammy, "How nice are my tits?"

The serpent nudges his head up, mouth opening ever so slightly, and stares at me with that glazed look to answer, "As niccce as Eve'sss applesss."

I grin. I'll take that.

Sweeping out of the room a few moments later, I make a beeline down the hall in my bare feet. I need to have a few words with a different snake.

TWENTY-TWO

THE STEAM ROOM

—ASTRAEA—

t first, I ended up down the wrong hallway, but it didn't take long to retrace my steps and follow the slight curling of steam drifting from below a black frosted glass door lined with Diablo ore. I imagine it's a protective measure, but regardless, I tug on the handle, relieved that it opens.

Throat burning even before the steam surges against my skin and dampens my wings, I search the billowing layers and discover Lucifer sitting on a bench at the far end of the steam room with a washcloth resting over his eyes. Hands relaxed on each side of him. My lips part from his massive, black wings overshadowing the white stone, nearly filling one wall. Before I may resist the urge, I hone my angel vision where dew drops of steam like liquid diamonds speckle his feathers, transforming them to a far more polished hue. More trickle off the wing edges like tears weeping off feathers. Dammit, why do wet wings have to be so fucking sexy?

Why does everything attached to them have to be so sexy? Black serpent tattoos, conjoined at their tails, rise until their heads face one another over his sculpted chest. The slabbed, packed muscles travel to a flawless V between his impressive hips. Muscles amass in his equally tattooed arms. I nearly drool at his cheekbones as chiseled and sharp as reaper sickles, the five o'clock shadow peppering his jaw, even the deep gray skin—everything about Lucifer was designed to entice, to beguile, to pleasure—to sin.

The Devil Incarnate. And the former Star of the Dawn, I remind myself. I quiver with that knowledge, thankful for the towel covering his lower section.

"Do you plan to stand there eye-fucking me all night with your sweet pussy dripping along with the rest of your body, or would you care to confront me about your first meeting with Samael?"

I lower my brows as Lucifer removes the washcloth, folds it neatly, and places it gently beside him. Tiny droplets befriend his dark lashes that half-eclipse his hooded eyes. He gestures me over, revealing, "I could hear you and scent you before you stepped inside. But it wouldn't have mattered. I wore that collar for centuries. I'll always share a bond with Samael. And now with you."

Hesitant, I rub my arm up and down the silk robe clinging to my skin. The thought of being so close to all of *that* has my nerve endings firing live grenades into my blood. I wonder if he's using his power, but Lucifer's shoulders are relaxed. No veins straining to show tension in his neck.

An inner smirk forms, and I make a command decision, move toward him with my wings drooping lower from the weight of the steam. I sit next to him and glance at the neat washcloth between us. Snatching it up, I bunch it into a ball and chuck it to the floor a few feet away with a satisfied breath.

A vein bulges in his neck. I smirk, but Lucifer snorts while I pick at my nails and challenge him, "Shouldn't you be setting up a meeting with Mira Paler?"

"One matter at a time. How much did Samael share?"

I shrug. "Sammy. And all I know is he is the original snake in the grass. Probably where the term came from."

He chortles at my joke, and I can't help but grin and sit up straighter, squaring my shoulders. "That unfortunate incident has been a thorn in my side for centuries. It took me several ages before I caught the malicious demon, bound his soul to mine, and cursed him for his treachery."

"He's a demon?"

"A demon of death and lies."

"Not anymore." I turn to the Devil with a rueful smile. Warmth engulfs my chest cavity, stirring my halo to glow and tingle the edges of my skin the moment Lucifer mirrors my smile.

"As I am the pronouncer of his Curse, I, alone, may undo it, or transfer him to another. While his freedom is limited, his power is not. But don't get any ideas, Astraea." He lifts a finger in warning when I lick my eager lips, continuing, "I control such power."

"You mentioned protection?"

"Samael acts as a defense, a powerful shield as it were. Only demons on his level may penetrate such defense. No being will touch you without my knowledge…or permission." He returns to resting his head against the white stone behind him.

His last statement turns all the tingles on their heads until they become knife points piercing my exposed flesh. Anger flushing all of me, I rise, ball my hands into fists, every muscle tensing as I confront him, "You narcissistic, gods-damned, slack-dick, dev—"

In less than a second, Lucifer pins me with my arms above my head and back to the bench, wet wings splayed with him on top. Now, his power strokes the sides of my body. Shivering, I clench my eyes, breath quickening to deny the pleasure coursing through me as Lucifer leans in to thunder-purr in my ear. He nips the lobe to get my attention. When I flick my eyes open, that maniacal tail parts my robe, freeing his slabbed chest to crush my breasts. I whimper when droplets tumble off his wings and land on my face.

"Next time, you should consider carefully when you address me in my home. I don't appreciate rude guests." I snap my keen angel teeth, narrowly missing his cheek. He snarls and removes one hand from my wrists to chain my neck. "The devil's in the details, little angel. I specifically stated: no being will touch you without my knowledge or permission. I never said you were forbidden to touch, now did I?"

"What the hell is that supposed to mean?" I blink, then groan when he sports that knowing grin, a muscle ticking in his jaw.

"Just pussies. The only cock that will fuck your celestial center is mine, Astraea. Because you fucking deserve it. You settle for boys when it takes the gods-damned Devil incarnate to fuck an angel."

I hiss, "I'd fuck the Chupacabra before you."

"Perfect." Lucifer wags his brows, beaming down at me. "I'll put in a good word for you. Until then," he shoves off me and winks, "we have a meeting in less than an hour with Mira Paler. I suggest you dress accordingly. While she may reign over the Circle of Lust, and as appetizing as you appear now, you don't want to exhaust Sammy's shield against anyone who wishes to take a bite out of you. He gets cranky if too much power is used. And he will feed on your energy and emotions if necessary."

Grinding my teeth in repulsion, I scramble off the bench, grab the wet, crumped washcloth, chuck it right at his face, and rush toward the door with my wet wings awkwardly slapping my sides.

"Oh, and Astraea..." Lucifer voices behind me, and I turn at the same time that he—

Oh. My. Gods. Holy fucking devil daddy!

"It's anything but a slack dick." He grins, spreading his arms and flaring his feathers...the towel in a wet heap at his feet.

My whole body turns red from head to toe, my eyes rocket wide open, and my jaw drops from his enormous cock pointing like an arrow ready to fire. With a flustered gasp, I spin around, yank open the door, and practically dive into the cold air outside.

TWENTY-THREE

MIRA PALER

——ASTRAEA——

Silence thickens the air between us upon our travel to the Second Circle. Dense as constellations on a clear winter night. I keep my hands firm at my sides to prevent myself from picking at my nails and instead focus on the views.

"I never believed a time would come when an angel would hold the power of possession," Lucifer remarks from the seat across from me. I glance at him out of the corner of my eye, a faint flush warming the back of my neck hidden beneath my curls. Earlier, I'd tamed them into sultry waves. I couldn't help but channel Satine for this night, having gathered one side of my blood ruby hair into a half-updo knot to exhibit the left side of my face and neck. The seductive and classic stage ginger will be the perfect temptation for Mira.

I hadn't anticipated tempting the Devil.

"Warming up to the collar, I see," he adds, gesturing to my throat.

I finger my skin where I've left the ink exposed—bereft of any fabric along with much of my upper chest, shoulders, and arms. Halfway between my shoulders and elbows, rubies cut in the shapes of diamonds weave around my arms while strings of rubied beads drip and coil down the undersides of my elbows to my forearms.

"Or we are warming up to one another," I opt with a sweet smile.

Sammy pops his head beyond my flesh, tongue snaking out to taunt, "I'm cold-blooded."

Beaming down at the serpent, I nudge the underside of his neck and tenderly stroke the scales there. He droops his head lower and sighs appreciatively. "Oh, yesss, higher, watch the earsss, perfect!"

"Who's the cranky ol' snake now?" I coo to the reptile, who rolls his head to one side. I scratch lower.

Lucifer observes us, hands folded neatly in his lap, but he dons a smile of approval, his gaze heady and lurid. Hellfire flickers along the edges of his body, neck, and cheeks as if mirroring the heat of his expression. Ever since we left his castle, I've done my best to avoid glancing his way. He'd slicked his silver hair into a low ponytail to exhibit his statuesque features. He wears a red-lined black trench coat with gold embroidery and ends that remind me of a cape, especially with the collar fanning around his neck. His wings, though tucked behind him, are more polished than usual. A little overwhelming for a brief visit to a Second Circle nightclub.

Upon noticing my glimpse, Lucifer offers me that wicked glint in his eye and traces his fingers down the line of his black tie. My eyes follow those fingers roaming along three diagonal gold buttons on his slate gray vest. The scarlet embroidered vest serpents twist and turn. Surprised by their motion, I part my lips, but they stop as if it was a trick of the light. I don't have time to consider when his fingers travel lower and lower to his thick, gold serpent belt with their bejeweled eyes. And lower, still to the bulge of his black breeches. Swallowing hard, I flick my eyes up, knowing I've been caught when he meets my eyes and gives me a shit-eating grin.

Heat discovers my cheeks, and I clear my throat, turning to the window again, wishing I could forget about the encounter in the steam room. All I know is Jack can never find out about this. Or he'll challenge Lucifer to a dick-measuring contest.

"He'd have a devil of a time, sweetling," Sammy announces, referencing Jack, and I snarl, pushing on his nose until he returns inside my throat.

"Who would?" wonders Lucifer, his hand settling on his lap.

"Nothing." I shake my head and narrow my brows. "How much of a connection do you—?"

"Samael alone holds a mental connection to you. It's limited, especially since he has a practiced filter, but your most vociferous thoughts he can hear."

"Wonderful," I mutter and gaze out the window, focusing on the scenery as Lucifer chuckles darkly.

A sudden warmth engulfs me. I lean back against the seat, squinting and thrusting out my chest because two can play at that game. I draw my own line down the plunging V of the scarlet bodice before curling my fingers down the form-fitting gown. Eyes on mine the whole time, Lucifer twists the corners of his mouth to one side as if knowing something I don't.

When the private tram jolts to a stop, I realize why a second too late. By then, I've lurched, my body pitching right into the Devil's arms.

"Women are always falling for me." He winks. "And men. And every other gender."

"Asshole."

Rolling my eyes, I try to shove him off me, but Lucifer maintains a firm hold on my waist, raising us to a stand. "As I said, Astraea, I will escort you to Mira Paler's Blood club."

"I don't need a babysitter," I snort.

"Trust the Devil tonight, Astraea." Lucifer slides a hand around my waist, tugging me closer until his fingertips caress the barest edges of my backside while that defining bulge prods my stomach. I cage a gasp with a fluttery sensation in my chest as he leans in, casts his fragrance upon my face, and whispers, "With all your sinful curves gloriously accentuated in this gown, my legions would willingly wage warfare to bed you." I gulp, my mouth moistening and my chest heaving as he toys with the ruby diamonds forming intricate floral patterns across my breasts. "You will need much more than a babysitter. But I have no interest in sitting on you, little angel. But you may sit on my face or my cock whenever you wish."

Before I may answer, Lucifer practically sweeps my whole body up with that one arm around my waist and escorts me from the tram and into the Circle of Lust.

"Come to a Match Made in Hell," a holo-ad of a succubus dressed in little other than lingerie beckons in a heated, feminine voice projected from the third-floor window. More holo-ads showcase countless demons and demonesses in various forms of seductive wear who work for the expansive center beyond the darkened windows. "It's our business to do the sin of pleasure with you."

I bite my lower lip, more heat rising to my cheeks.

Since we are on the highest level of the Second Circle, gold signs show awards for "best in service" while elite customers of many races wait in line to enter the matchmaker club.

Pressing his hand to my hip, Lucifer urges me, his magnificent wings brushing my golden edge feathers, so I flinch. Our innermost feathers concealed beneath layers and closest to our nerve-filled sinew are our most sensitive. These edge-feathers skirting one another are similar to a hand caress.

We travel upon a private walkway above the tourist areas, one reserved prior. On the opposite side of the district is another service: Bloody Hell where anyone may pay a fee to torture the worst of the worst. I shiver, but Lucifer pauses and captures my chin.

"With a demon chaperon, Astraea," he indicates. "Care to torment the worst tyrants within history? Or a childhood bully?" he wags his eyebrows, baiting me with that smirk.

Squaring my bare shoulders with pride, I taunt, "What of the Devil himself?"

A dark thunder-purr, followed by a rumble, issues from his chest, nearly vibrating into mine from the thin space between us. "You don't need to pay anything to torment me, sweetheart. You've tormented me since you plunged off that balcony and spread your pretty wings for me."

Heat unravels in my chest, growing like tendrils and spreading to the rest of my body. I sense words hovering behind his parted lips, but he seals his mouth and leads me onward.

After a few minutes, we arrive before the great doorways of the Bad Blood Nightclub. I shake my head with an amused smile. So Mira. At first, I wonder why Lucifer hasn't insisted upon an escort of his own. No

Pomp and Circumstance. No one to announce his presence. No fallen angel squads to surround us.

Once he waves his hand before the doors, which bow to his whim, I understand why. Immediately upon entering, Lucifer projects his power in great currents of shadow and hellfire, which alert all races within the Bad Blood Club to his arrival. Lucifer's shadows suffocate the candle fires and extinguish all lights until his hellfire bestows a dim glow within the atmosphere. And my wings. Chatter silenced, all drop to their knees before him. Blood fountains streaming from the walls into pools of pleasure-bathing and drinking is the only sound.

One being alone stands. I beam from ear to ear at the sight of her—unchanged from the years. Her Gothic beauty is eternal and depthless.

"Welcome, Prince of Darkness, to my domain," Mira proclaims, spreading her arms clad in long black satin gloves that embrace her upper arms. "You've arrived just in time."

She lowers her head to one lone man who kneels before her. I hone my angel eyes, recognizing him as a fae noble. Judging by his crest, he serves the Blood Shadow Queen as an emissary: the darkest and powerful fae who rule over the soul-hunters, among other horrors. The one time I encountered a soul hunter, I flew as fast as my wings could carry me. It was a battle I'd never win.

A chill crawls along my spine as Mira Paler circles the fae in her mermaid-silhouette black gown that coddles her generous curves. A feline predator stalking her prey. As she does, she removes her glove one finger at a time. Upon her back is a skeleton armor piece, the gold filigree contouring to her spine, curling in elaborate patterns from that spinal cord, and caressing the backs of her fair shoulders.

Once she makes a full circle, I freeze and hold my breath. I've witnessed

Mira's bloodshed. I was simply grateful to be on the side of partnership and not on the receiving end.

Lifting his eyes to the Second Circle ruler is the fae's worst mistake. If I blinked, I'd have missed Mira plunging her claws into the fae's chest to rip out his still-beating heart and raise it high. Not once did she growl, snarl, or so much as hiss. The fae's corpse crumples to the floor. Adrenaline stokes my blood, and my breath quickens because she opens her mouth, baring a full set of pearly white teeth—no fangs whatsoever.

Mira crushes the heart to a bloody pulp, lifts her chin to the nightclub crowd, and proclaims, "Let all bear witness: if any dishonors the privilege of entering my domain by abusing the human familiars I have so generously employed, you will meet the same end as the worthless carcass before you."

She flicks her eyes to us, the irises as dark and lethal as I remember them. Heat surges into my core as she nods to Lucifer, who pulls the shadows and hellfire back to himself, alerting the crowd they may rise. However, all their eyes have turned in the direction of Mira. They part for her to make her way to us. My smile spreads as she approaches, my eyes instinctively traveling across her figure and back up to her full and sensual lips rouged in crimson to contrast her porcelain white skin.

"Ace Raestar," she speaks the one name she knows me by.

Though Lucifer's hand does not retreat from my waist, Mira clutches my hand in her gloved one and raises it to her lips, rubbing them across my knuckles. All my nerve endings charge lightning tingles into my skin.

I bow my head in respect. A blush tethers my cheeks when her other gloved hand cups my chin, bidding my eyes to hers. My lower lip trembles as I meet those eyes of pure moonless midnight to respond, "Thank you for agreeing to meet with me, your grace, Countess Dracula."

TWENTY-FOUR

UNFINISHED BUSINESS

—ASTRAEA—

No sooner do I speak the words than Mira simpers and closes the distance between us to capture my lips with her own.

All my thoughts and emotions tangle within the memory of that night on Mount Asharya where the blood of rogue fae hunters seeped into the snows from their broken corpses, bits and pieces of wings coated in crystallized flakes. And while healing overseers tended to the wounded passengers on the train, Mira escorted me into the privacy of a nearby cavern system. There, she promptly tore off my clothes, pinned me against the rock face, kissed me, and gave me the most blood-charged orgasm since my first with Jack on Mount Yvos. I'd screamed her name until the echoes resounded throughout the cavern system while a hoard of bats beat a whirlwind around us.

"Now, we will have no more alter ego names between us," Mira defines, clasping my hands after her lascivious kiss has left me pursing my lips and longing for more. "I am eager to learn your true name, but after we retire to more private environs."

Nearby, vampires, demons, fae, elves, and other races feed upon human familiars. But one glimpse assures me a host of eyes remain fixed on our presence. Blood and lust cloy the air. I hear every moan and whimper along with the pounding rhythm of heartbeats and blood pulsing through veins as swift as fired arrows. I shudder, wincing. If this was like other nightclubs with bodies rubbing to the music, I could fade into the sensations and become one with the crashing bass, harmonizing rhythms, and percussive beats. Not here. The Bloodclub is for slow seduction, languid bodies draped upon sumptuous couches, a cautious lust for the sake of the delicate human familiars.

At the far back of the club, the black iron throne with dozens of spikes protruding from its backing belongs to Mira alone. Upon honing my angel vision, I understand they're no ordinary spikes: they're poles meant for impaling.

The Countess trails her claw-tipped fingers down my arm and to my waist, where Lucifer's hand still warms my skin beneath the gown.

"Hmm…" she observes, pupils dilating upon his firm hold before she flicks them to his face. "Do I take it you'll be joining us then, Lucifer?"

I part my lips, but I shouldn't be surprised that Mira addresses him without a title. Not with the bad blood between them. I snicker internally from the fitting pun.

"For a few minutes to ensure my agent is safe and secure."

At first, she stiffens before waving a hand in dismissal and sniffing. "Try not to set anything on fire, dear Devil, would you? I acquired a new series of skulls." She indicates to the left side of the bar, to the wall of hollowed-out skulls housing various rare bottles of wine, brandy, scotch, and more. My lips find a smile because Lucifer's skull décor has nothing on Mira's. "And my other lovelies don't wish to be disturbed," she finishes, circling her finger to the great domed ceiling above us.

I gasp at how the dome has been modeled to resemble a cavern. Twinkling stalactites drip from the ceiling like organic chandeliers. What's even more impressive is the host of bats dangling upside down in slumber, wings occasionally flapping to stretch.

"No flames tonight, Countess," Lucifer emphasizes the last word as if it's poison, his feathers locking up tight.

"Apart from the ones already stoking our little star's mouth-watering heat, of course."

"Mira…" I groan, rubbing my eyes but following her through one of the grand archways at the far end of the nightclub.

On the way out, we pass countless macabre trees with naked, spindly black branches upon which small, jarred candles hang to complete the ambiance. Gilded coffins are another feature. And more skulls, except stakes have driven through their base, a not-so-subtle nod to the vampire Countess's impressive yet murderous history.

"Oh, for lust's sake, angel, you're in the Second Circle now. Enjoy it," she throws the words over her shoulder.

"We are here on official business, Countess," growls Lucifer through gritted teeth.

As we pass more skulls that act as décor filled with fresh bouquets of black baccara roses and white anemones, Mira eyes the Devil from the side and wrinkles her nose. "Yes, Lucifer, it's always your business that occupies your time. Never mine that you seek to prioritize."

Feathers flaring and prompting me to snap mine shut, Lucifer digs his fingers into my hip and lowers his voice an octave, "You forget, Countess, who reigns over all Hell on Earth rather than one Circle."

"Yes, the one Circle which generates the most profit for your entire domain and still pays the highest rate in taxes."

"And operates at a higher cost per capita if you recall," he counters. "Your visitants and long-term residents will always pay the higher fee for entry and prime real estate within the Second Circle. If you auctioned off rights to your bed, you'd have little place to complain about costs."

Acting the role of a bored angel, I stare down at my feet clad in the rubied high heels Sammy insisted would compliment the gown. I listen with a keen ear. While I know little of the Circles, their Chambers, and their politics and am far more adept with a sword in my hand and most with the wind in my wings, any information I glean may be helpful. Again, I wonder why in the hell Lucifer would choose me as his "agent"? It has to be beyond my flight skills and celestial pussy, though it's obvious what he wants to do with the latter.

Mira snarls, pausing before two arched doors of pure silver filigree. "Some of us prefer not to play the whore, Lucifer."

"Says the woman who plays at everything else," he counters with a devilish grin, and the vampire huffs, tossing her silky black hair to one side. "Besides, I assure you I don't play at anything. Empowerment in whoredom is far more fun. And trending, Mira. Embrace it," he finishes, but his final wink is for me.

"Whatever will I do with you?" snorts Mira before pricking her blood for the security. "Will my dear angel offer a suggestion?" Our eyes meet, and I tilt my head to the side, meeting her smile as she lifts the silver droplet onto the holo-screen, which reads her signature.

"Oh, I've considered quite a few things." I narrow my eyes upon Lucifer. He wags his brows in a challenge. "All of them end with me tying him up, wrapping a big pussycat bow on him, and dumping him at the Tribunal's feet."

Lucifer leans in, a faint lust-hum stirring my curls and pricking the hairs on the nape of my neck. "Would you like to know where the term "God's gift to mankind" came from, Astraea? It wasn't manna from heaven, I assure you. But anytime you care for me to tie you up and eat your pretty pussy out, angel, you won't need to wait for your birthday."

"Enough," Mira cuts us off before I can fire back and ushers us into her office.

It's less an office and far more of a semi-outdoor rotunda with a stone floor, staircase spiraling to a high cavernous ceiling, and arched windows allowing the free passage of more bats that slumber upon the ceiling. Despite the crude environment, the furnishings are anything but. The burning along the back of my neck and cheeks subsides in the wake of several preserved skulls locked in prominent display cases upon nearby ledges. Knitting my brows together, curious, I approach one on the left and read the nameplate at the base: Jack the Ripper. Another reads Vladislav II.

"Is it true you dulled your poles so your enemies would suffer prolonged torture during your war days?"

As soon as I hear Mira clearing her throat behind me, I wince, recognizing my inquiry was too invasive. When I turn, she is seated at the antique, silver filigree table in the rotunda center with Lucifer directly opposite. Their seats remind me of thrones of polished twisting branches. I lower myself into the third, closer to Mira than Lucifer. I lift a brow at the irony of the precious metal, but the Countess shows no signs of weakness or discomfort.

Lucifer takes a once-over at the office and dictates to Mira, "Still a lover of irony, I see."

She sucks a breath through her nostrils and bares a fang. "Sometimes, the best way to deter one's enemies is to hide in plain sight, Lucifer. Regardless, while I am not the sole originator of the classic style, I still played a significant role in it." She glides her eyes to me, lips spreading into a proud grin as she leans back, steeples her fingertips, and continues, "Sweet Bram was only too enthusiastic to protect my anonymity when he wrote his infamous tale with a male Dracula. Of course, the world never imagined Vladimira the Impaler. Nor was it ready to embrace me as it does now."

"I am a woman. Hear me roar," I inject, eyes traveling between each sovereign.

With a lustful glint in her eye, Mira nods to me. "Unchanged as always, my little star. It's what I loved about you since you opened your pretty mouth and unleashed that gorgeous serpent tongue inside."

Sammy stirs, but the pins and needles don't sting as much when he sticks his head out of my lower neck, tongue stabbing the air. "Well, I sssay! Oh, oh, oh!" His protests turn to indulgent moans when I start scratching his scales. "Yesss, gorgeousss, jussst don't stop. Hmm…" he twists his head to Lucifer and mutters, "She jussst wondered if you'd ever make her beg like that."

"Sammy!" I object and shush him but cave to rubbing his belly.

Mortified, I curl my wings around my frame to avoid glancing at the Devil, predicting he has that knowing grin. Thankfully, Mira sits back and raises her brows to remark, "Well, now, Lucifer, you have been a naughty boy. I never believed another would be worthy of carrying that torch since I last returned him to you."

I jerk my head up, but Sammy hisses and nudges me for more attention. While stroking down his back till his tail coils around my hand, I peek above the edge of my wing at Lucifer. "You gave Sammy to Dracula?"

"For a time," she answers for him. "But I'm afraid we ultimately were not a good fit. It took three years before he so much as graced me with his presence. How long have you—"

"Vladimira," interrupts Lucifer, rising from his throne. She stands with him. Without standing, I squeak when Sammy nips the back of my hand like a dissatisfied cat. "I must leave on urgent business now. I trust my agent is safe in your capable hands."

Mira slowly turns her chin to me, her voice deepening to a sultry low, "Safer than a she-wolf in her lair."

"Aww," I comment sweetly, curling my fingers under the serpent's neck. His tail still coils around my wrist, but I love how he twists himself into a ball, head tucking into the center, which I assume is his preferred position for sleep.

Lucifer strides towards my chair, but I don't drop my wings, too tempted to fold them over my head and disappear into their embrace. "I will return for you later, sweetheart. And you will remain within Vladimira's sanctum until I do."

Before I can open my mouth to protest, he fingers a few of my edge feathers in a lustful taunt, triggering a shiver up my spine. He sifts, vanishing into thin air, leaving the seductive scent of blood and roses in his wake. I sigh, sensing the tension fading with his exit.

"Alone at last," Mira states, advancing toward me, kindling a fresh spark that quickly ignites a flame. "We have some unfinished business, my little star."

A long-lost pang invades my chest. With desire instantly renewed and on steroids, I face the vampire head-on, grateful Sammy has fallen asleep. Or at least I believe he has since snakes sleep with their eyes open. Regardless, he doesn't move when I stand and transfer him to the silver chair.

Mira wastes no time seizing my wrist, snarling, and hauling me in vampire speed into a dark alcove within the rotunda.

"Oh, damn me to hell!" I shriek when she slams me against the cold stone wall and strokes her tongue along my pulse, mirroring her actions on Mount Asharya.

"Hell would never let you go, sweet angel. And now that you are here, neither will I." A deep growl issues from Mira's throat, reverberating into my chest. Tingles rupture over my skin, and my halo lights up like a firework. "You made me a promise within that cave, Raestar. Tonight, you will deliver."

I tremble as she raises me higher, my wings sliding along the wall until I'm at eye level with her. Oh fuck, she smells so good! Like pure Frankincense and neroli. Her breasts thrust snugly against the low-cut V-line of her gown bodice, which presses upon my upper chest, so the mounds nudge my chin.

As she lowers her hand to the slit of my dress, grips my thigh, and urges my legs to wrap around her powerful frame, I touch my fingers to her chest, look her right in the eye, and smirk, "And if I refuse?"

Mira's eyes don't leave mine, but her lips form a seamless smile. She chuckles beyond her closed lips. Once she opens them, I blink first. Not a moment goes by. The vampire buries her fangs in my neck, and the bats spiral into a frenzy from my screams.

TWENTY-FIVE

A DEAL WITH DRACULA

—ASTRAEA—

"Vladimira!" I scream, begging her for mercy.

My core pulses, wet and dripping with desire as she works at my clit, rubbing it, pulling away, then languidly stroking it. My thighs clench on either side of her hips. Every time I'm on the precipice, she slaps my pussy hard, destroying the sensation. And there's absolutely nothing I can do. She'd brought me here for a reason, this alcove prepared in advance with the chains strong enough to suspend me, freeing the Countess to do what she does best: dominate and destroy.

She lowers my legs, growls for the seventh time. And crushes her lips to mine but keeps my gown ends firmly bunched at my waist. My panties have long since met their shredded end and lie in ruined scraps on the ground beneath me. "You have no right to beg for your pleasure." She grips my jaw and lowers her hand to squeeze my breast hard, so I whimper. "You vowed to give me your name, and we sealed it in blood.

Now, I have both rings, my little Ace. It's time you paid your debt."

She pinches my clitoris. I push against her hand, my body showing my need. Blood still drips from the wound where she'd sunk her fangs. Her venom courses through my system, warming my blood, playing my nerves like a fucking harp. She tilts her head, regarding me with a raptor-like smile because she knows I'm close to surrendering. I slam my eyes shut and clench my thighs.

"Hmm…I know what will loosen your tongue, my sweetling." She retrieves a familiar device from her inner cape and wags it before my eyes. Then lowers it between my thighs.

"Oh, sh—"

I explode, clenching hard around the vibrator. Muscles burn and tighten as she fucks me with the toy, pumping harder and harder, never offering me a reprieve. With her fangs sinking into my nipples, tongue lapping up my blood, and venom rousing them even more until they're harder than rubies, she draws out the orgasm. She fucks me with the vibrator until I'm screaming. And sweating golden droplets.

"Tell me…" she urges again between my screams. "What does Lucifer want with you, my little star?"

My moans deepen, but when Mira removes the vibrator and relocates it to my clit, I cry out. She stabs her fingers inside me while her tongue strokes along the edge of the vibrator. I part my lips and widen my eyes because she's tasting my fluids while coating the instrument with her venom. Oh, gods!

I don't know how much longer I can hold out. Mira would never consent to tell me anything if I made this too easy for her. This is a lust play and a bloodlust one at that. She needs to know I'm her ally, one willing to submit to her power.

"Did he send you to spy on me?" she wonders and lowers the vibrator to rub against my clit, venom saturating it until it beats like a tiny heart and vaults tremors to rock my body.

"No, I swear, that's not the reason. It was me. He didn't want to—"

She stabs the venom-coated vibrator inside my soaked heat, hitting that magical spot. But I groan deeply when she jerks it out, denying me my climax as I was about to spread my wings and leap off the fucking cliff!

"Good girl, my sweet. Now…" she opens my lips, tongue seducing mine, decorating the inside of my mouth with her spicy venom. "What does he want with you?"

"Mira, for the love of—"

The moment the Countess sinks her fangs into the same location on my throat to suck my blood is when she cranks the vibrator to its highest level. I bite back a trill. All my body locks up, and I splay my wings and rub them against the alcove wall until I lose feathers. My hips thrash back and forth, I clench my hands into fists, strain against the cuffs, and finally scream, "I'm his fucking spy, for fuck's sake! Humans are going missing, he's keeping it a secret from the Chambers, and we need your help! Oh, gods-dammit!" I scream and rock my head back as she twists the vibrator and pumps it harder. "What the fuck do you want?"

"Your name, little angel," she coos in my ear and licks the edge, pressing her breasts to my exposed ones. At the last second, she denies me another orgasm, chucks the vibrator to the ground, and replaces it with four of her fingers.

Tears shimmer in my eyes because this will take us to a new level, a mystery unraveled. And I tremble at what she will think of me when she learns of my bond with the Angel of Destruction. How she will no longer see me as the strange, angelic visitor in the night who helped her slay the fae attacking her familiars. Will she keep her distance as all others have? Or toy with me to bait Abaddon?

"Give me everything," she pressures, tracing her tongue along the seam of my mouth, twisting her fingers deeper.

More tears shed from my eyes as she contorts her thumb to flick my clitoris. My glazed eyes meet her shrewd and cunning ones. Her lips open to exhibit her deadly, beautiful fangs of pain and pleasure. With a deep sigh, she kisses me once more and lowers her head to my breasts to suck each of my nipples. Finally, Countess Dracula does something that triggers a current of lightning to rock my very halo. She kneels before me, takes my clitoris between her teeth. And nibbles. I gasp from the prick of pain from her fangs until the venom courses into that sacred bundle of nerves.

"Oh, holy hell balls! Astraea, dammit! I'm Astraea Eternity!"

"Mmm," Mira murmurs her approval, curves her fingers to that secret place, and licks at my clit. It takes two seconds before I explode, the orgasm tearing through my system, shooting lighting pulses into my very wings. Stars crash behind my eyes that roll to their ceilings until I fucking shatter and drench her face.

Immediately, she rises and releases my wrists from the cuffs. I fall into a boneless mess in her arms, my gown trailing to the ground. She strokes my hair, not shying away from me, and I lean into her chilled embrace.

"I've waited all these years, Astraea. That night, I took your blood and screams, but I knew it would require much more to learn your name. Now that a level of trust exists between us, we can finally get down to your true business."

A few minutes later, I'm still trembling in the aftermath of the several climaxes, but Mira offers me water as well as wine to help while caressing my waves. "You are welcome in my Circle at any time, Astraea. And not solely because your blood tastes like the most angelic of aphrodisiacs," she concludes and pecks my cheek before returning to her throne. Sated in a different way.

While I finish the water, she scoots her throne forward, lowers her hand under the table, and conjures a holo-feed of the mutilated body from the morgue. I choke on the wine. It burns down my throat, and I'm grateful she gave me nothing to eat.

"You knew?" I clutch my throat with a gasp.

Mira leans forward, folding her hands on the table with a closed-mouth smile that reveals her fangs. "Lucifer sent the data to me before our meeting so I could examine it. You might say this was my test, Astraea. Given mine and Lucifer's tempestuous history, I needed to know whether you were an ally or an enemy. And while the Devil incarnate may have you under his wing, so to speak, all three of us are united under a shared interest: the preservation of humanity."

"Hidden meaning: your food source," I tease her, setting my wine glass down and hiccuping, giggling.

"Now, now, Astraea, while humans have a certain appeal, I am no prude and have and will sample many a demon, elf, fae, witch, and otherwise."

I nod, and she circles a finger back to the holo-feed. "I cannot tell you anything about the body mortification itself, but these markings…" she zooms in on the puncture marks along the anatomy of the wings and adds, "are familiar. While I may not know their purpose, I do recognize them. But know this, Astraea: if this is indeed the being I suspect it is, I have encountered this creature once in all my years. And it is far beyond my skill level and yours, my star. Perhaps beyond Lucifer."

A chill skitters up my spine, a wave of ice competing with it. The sensation of frost fills up my veins at the thought of a being that powerful. All I can consider is a monster from the Unconsecrated Crater—like one of the ancient dragons that managed to crawl out from its fathomless depths. Or this is all a machination from the ultimate Deceiver himself. All along, his plan is baiting me into being his spy. An ultimate trick played on heaven. Or revenge on Abaddon. I shudder at the thought, knowing I will need to speak to him soon.

First, I dip my hand beyond the slit of my gown to the skin pouch where I've concealed the object I took from the underground station. I slide it across the table to Mira and explain its recent history. At first, she examines the talon, then taps it across the silver filigree with a knowing smile. Warmth floods me until she rises and weaves her way around the table to me.

"You have heard of the phrase "an eye for an eye", have you not, my star? Or "tit for tat" is a worthier phrase in your case…" she eludes with a grin.

I raise my chin to meet her dark eyes and offer her a meager nod. She closes the distance between us and cups my chin in her hand. "The information you desire comes at too high of a price. I could requisition Lucifer for a lower tax rate for my Circle, and he would be willing to give it. It would humble him and elevate me in the eyes of the Chambers. But my desires transcend such political matters. What I want is far more personal and a priority."

"What do you want, Mira?" I wonder in a soft voice.

"Lord Tanyl Venrys, an elf lord of the Eighth Circle, has taken something precious to me. And necessary to my way of life. You will get it back for me."

I reflect on the name, knowing I've heard it before. Venrys is an urban legend of Hell on Earth. "Isn't he that famous recluse?" I lift a brow in question.

"Yes, and I recently denied his request to buy prime real estate I have set aside for subsidized housing for familiars. I cannot prove he is behind the theft, but my spies have confirmed he is the source."

"Can't your spies or agents retrieve your prized possession?"

"Not without starting a blood feud," she hints and moves toward my chair, fingering the ends of my curls.

I heave a deep sigh. "And I take it due to your checkered history that Lucifer won't lift a finger."

Mira leans over and taps my nose. "Always the sharp mind, my sweet."

"So, if he is a recluse, how do I—"

"Lord Venrys has a weakness," she interjects, returning to her seat. "He is fascinated by angel lore, Astraea."

"So, what? I walk up to his hermit house, ring the doorbell, and tell him I want a sit-down?"

Mira laughs but sweeps a hand to conjure another holo-feed. I narrow my eyes, observing Lucifer in his recent garb, and then recognize the feed is a live announcement.

"All candidates must pay their fee in blood to enlist in the first trial. Bride Trial I will commence on the Summer Solstice. Are you the Devil's final flame?"

I roll my eyes at the cheesy slogan. I'll need a word with Lucifer's scriptwriter. Mira shuts down the holo-feed and folds her hands before her again. I give her a blank look.

"My spies have informed me he has invested a great deal into sponsoring Lucifer's Bride Trials."

Immediately, I rise and stab a finger at her, an angry heat bubbling in my blood. "No fucking way!"

"The preservation of humanity, Astraea," she reminds me, grinning like a fox who's caught the hound in its jaws.

"Ugh, you've got to be kidding me. How would I even do this? Lucifer's always watching me. Escorting me to places, including my room." I realize my mistake as soon as I say the words. Mira's grin spreads.

If I'd blinked, I'd have missed her retrieving a familiar ring and sliding it across the table to me. "A fee in blood Astraea. All you need do is scan it into Lucifer's database, and you will become a candidate. By the time he learns the truth, the first Bride Trial will have commenced. The highest Chamber members will be granted an audience with the winning candidates."

I snatch up the ring, grind my teeth, and flare my nostrils, knowing my cheeks are turning as red as my hair. "How can you be so certain I will win?"

Silence may be golden, but when Countess Dracula does nothing more than beam at me, all I want to do is scream.

TWENTY-SIX

ASTAROTH'S ATTACK

—ASTRAEA—

Shuffling along the outskirts of a lower level of the Second Circle, I consider all the ways Lucifer could punish me if I get caught. Anxious, I twist the silver ring Mira gave me. Entering the Bride Trials is quite possibly the last goal on my bucket list. How do I even know where to begin in Lucifer's small castle of a home? If he has an office, he's likely equipped it with security. At the very least, I'd need his blood.

Cheers in the night startle me. Above a nearby amphitheater, showers of sparkles rain down from the sky while serpent daemons take their place on a stage for a singles' night auction. A few elves, drunk from a night of partying, stumble out of a nightclub. Their eyes shift to my wings, catching the feathers' faint shimmer in their pupils. After one makes a cliché remark about an "angel in the streets", all it takes is one flash of my angel teeth and extending my claws to warn them to keep their distance.

Huffing, I steer away from the bustling lower-level nightclub district because I've traveled to these lower regions for quiet away from the crowded areas of the penthouse levels. I'd never get an opportunity to think, much less plan if I'd waited for Lucifer to arrive and fetch me like I'm a daycare brat.

Just because I'm his bitch doesn't mean he gets to dictate my every move.

After passing a vintage restaurant called Wanderlust, I finally make my way to a boardwalk nudging a large expanse of a lake. Tour boats rock gently, water lapping against their hulls. Halo-like glows from private lust vessels shift from side to side toward the middle of the lake. Sighing, I kick off my heels, leave them along the boardwalk, and descend the muddy slope to the stretches of moss-clad logs and soft grass that form the bank of the lake.

Above the lake is a digital projection of a sky at dusk with a resplendent view of our purple-hued galaxy. I sigh, missing home more than ever. It's been a couple of days, but I miss my nightly routine of flying for a few hours over the Celestial Mountains. Now and then, Abaddon tails me, but I sense his presence and challenge him to a race. I've always won and through no lack of effort on his part since he outshines me in every other area. Abaddon has too much pride to let me conquer him. We both do.

The soonest chance I get, I will contact him, but the method is far too dangerous to attempt here.

With the sounds of the lust districts fading to the watery diction before me, I take a deep breath and relax from the fresh breeze stirring my feathers. The scent of damp wood and faint mist curls into my nostrils. I can lift my wings, arc them, and harness that breeze to carry me across the lake. Flying helps me sort out my thoughts, but I don't want to draw more attention to myself. All I need is a group of passerbys deciding they want to capture holo-footage of a gold-winged angel gliding within the Circle of Lust. Instead, I curl my wings inward and sink my toes into the grass, picking at my nails like I always do when anxious.

The breeze drifts toward me again, but this time, it carries a foul stench. I wrinkle my nose and travel a few paces away, hoping it will get better, but the odor grows. I cough, choking on the stench that smells like sulfur and sewage, fermented fish, and rotten eggs. It burns my nostrils and eyes, triggering tears that blur my vision until I nearly trip over the massive figure sitting along the banks of the lake before me.

I cover my mouth and nose and offer a muffled apology until he turns his head. At a second glance, I freeze in my tracks from the sight of the deep gray horns, one each curling from the sides of his head. A large gray serpent slithers along his bulging arm. He bears two sets of wings—one ragged and worn with holes riddling their dragon-like fabric and another set of smaller fallen angel wings. Like a deep, underwater fish, his flesh is pale and translucent, and when he rises, I shoot my eyes wide open. This demon is naked as scaleless fish. The odor wafts from his body.

Spinning around, I prepare to run from the formidable demon when a deep growl off to my right stops me. From the shadows, an enormous but mangy wolf the color of deep red crouches, licking his chops while his eyes gleam with the sight of a celestial meal. I feel the blood drain from my face and gulp, but the demon approaching me from behind causes my breath to surge and my body to quake.

"Your doubts and fears are delicious, tiny angel," he purrs, voice deep and raspy.

I squeeze my eyes shut and plug my nose from the unbearable scent that pulls more tears from my eyes. The demon's thick serpent hisses, and I clutch my throat, remembering Sammy, remembering Lucifer's protection, his shield.

As the demon circles me, a bitter chill from his naked form preying on my skin, I hug my arms to my chest, not daring to move from the great wolf bound to this demon. All it takes is one command for that wolf to attack.

"You know you do not ultimately possess the power required to conquer any trial Lucifer has conceived. The battle is already lost. And sooner or later, he will grow tired of you as his angelic spy until you become nothing more than a glow-light for his bed or banished into utter darkness after he's used every part of you."

He stops in front of me, tucks a cold, clawed hand under my chin, and raises my eyes to stare into his. Everything is black, from the pupils to the irises to the sclera. I swallow a pained breath. Why does he speak like he intimately knows Lucifer?

"Who are you?" I demand, but it sounds weak from my voice barely above a murmur.

The serpent twists and undulates along his arm, head rearing into attack mode. It hisses and rattles. Sammy's pins and needles are a warm comfort when he emerges, hissing and mirroring the other snake's behavior. They size each other up, much like this demon and I. He is saying the words that have swirled in my head since Lucifer branded me as his spy. It's simply a matter of time, and all I want is a way out.

"I may offer you safety, tiny angel. Safety from Lucifer, a life of ease where your true skills will be recognized and worshiped. Imagine every day spent flying upon wings more powerful and glimmering to blind all who dare to gaze upon you. Imagine how the former Star of the

Morning himself will envy you."

I choke again from the odor, double over, my knees weakening. It's burning my lungs. Strangling my inner throat, restricting my breath. I lick my lips and feel sweat trickling down the sides of my face. My soul feels suffocated, the deeper parts of me slowly stripped away until my broken halo is laid bare.

"Would you care to see your fate, angel? I will show you. I know your past, your present, and your future. Simply touch your fingers to my hand, and you will know the fate that awaits you," he offers, extending his palm. "Touch them and breathe!"

I tiptoe my fingers forward, crawling them at a slow pace, hesitant. The smell deepens, plaguing me, blinding my vision. Hot and sulfuric, it scorches my flesh, my blood, my veins. Are my lungs themselves melting from the acidic air? Everything fades but this desperate need for air.

Sammy wags his head back and forth, but his gaze remains on the opposite serpent. "Raea," whispers the snake below me, "the ring from Dracula. Take it. Ussse it. Ussse the ring!"

Another deep growl. I pause, fingers trembling.

And as I slip my other hand down to my secret skin pouch to retrieve the ring, the serpent springs forward with a snarl. Sammy lunges. My scream is cut short when I touch my skin pouch and fall to my knees from a sudden blast of rancid air. It blisters my face, and the wolf charges from behind me. I hear its paws thundering right before it smashes me to the ground, its teeth tearing at my gown, nose digging into my thighs. It's searching for the ring.

"No!" I screech from the heat and pain and drive my foot as hard as I can to the side of the wolf's face, then scramble for the ring. My lungs feel like they're shutting down. I cough into the ground, tasting dirt.

Cold claws tiptoe along my inner thigh, making for the skin pouch. The collar isn't enough. Defeat sinks me lower when I recognize how powerful this demon is, how he must be higher-ranking, how a mere low angel, a rejected angel, could never hope to combat him.

I fall onto my back, struggling for breath as the demon leers over me. He clutches the lower portion of my face, drawing blood with his claws. "I gave you the choice, tiny angel," he croons and digs his claws into my thigh, but I have no breath to scream. "Now, your death will be slow and painful."

My chest caves in. More tears fall. Blood trickles down my thigh, down my jaw, and neck. As the demon ravages my skin pouch, unearthing the ring until it tumbles to the ground, my halo grows dimmer and dimmer. I open my mouth, but nothing comes out. I close my eyes with the faux projection of the constellations as my last sight.

Right now, I would gladly accept one hundred of Lucifer's punishments, but all that's left of me fades to darkness.

"Your death will be far more painful, Astaroth."

TWENTY-SEVEN

SAVING ASTRAEA

—LUCIFER—

She will be the fucking death of me.

From the moment she leapt off that balcony and dared to tempt the Devil himself, I've wanted nothing more than to fuck her, to damn well destroy her. Every time she opens her salty mouth and taunts me with that wicked tongue, she begs me to bend her the fuck over, spank her so hard, her ass will bear my marks forever before I bury myself in all her wet heat. Seal my hellfire signature in her tight depths until she's ready to ride the Devil and unravel and shatter before me, those gold eyes turning to crashing meteors.

I never fuck angels.

My cock throbs even after I've sifted from the club, the softness of her feathers still tingling my fingers. Everything about her is soft and ripe from those rounded thighs, full breasts, luscious hips, and the curve of her tender throat. I remind myself of my heritage. How I witnessed thousands of beautiful angels, none more beautiful than me.

Astraea is different. She has an angel's flawless face sent to torment me, but the demon inside me can scent her inner darkness—one she's buried deep beneath the fire and salt of her armor.

She is raw need and a brutal mind fuck. A sweetheart full of pain and broken edges disguised within the delicate psycho she holds so close to her. She is everything I hate and lust for. I'm convinced she is the greatest weapon Destruction could have ever set to finish the job he began centuries ago.

Fuck, how I wanted to brand her for my bed. To spread her, chain her, taste that sweet, pink flesh, then drive myself inside to wreck and abuse her until she submits. Until her celestial muscles clamp down and hungrily suck me deeper.

I'd believed branding her would bring me fucking peace. I wasn't prepared for her violent storm of emotions. A mere fucking taste, but I've already dissected the full depth of the seven deadly sins surging inside her.

I've had a multitude of fallen angels—their souls corrupted from the moment their wings brush my entrance to the Abyss, and they choose to accept the demons inside of them.

But Astraea is a gods-damned enigma I'm determined to solve. A dark magic I'd bet my Ninth Circle to feel. She's forged a shield from her demons to protect her pure soul. A soul with a bloody, dirty angel inside it. She wears a pretty mask like the first night I met her. I won't rest until I've melted that mask from her face. Even if it leaves her scarred and branded as mine.

The moment she walked down the staircase in that scarlet gown with her sinful waves, gold wings, skin, and ruby red lips spreading into that self-righteous smirk she loves to wear, it took all my strength to hold my monster back from playing with her. He'd roared all the same. We both wanted to slam her face first against the nearest wall, spread those gorgeous gold wings, hike up her gown, and force our way inside until she screamed our name so all of heaven could hear an angel trilling for the Devil.

That angel trill is a fucking siren mating call to the monster inside me—the beauty to his beast. Beautiful and strong enough to bear Samael—and pure enough to charm the damned serpent. Whatever her soul houses, it's fucking wild and dangerous and deadly as a poison infecting me. She's fucking feeding on me, licking and sampling and nibbling. Soon, we'll devour one another and destroy everything and everyone in our way.

It's why I must destroy her first.

Her kind has taken everything from me, banished me to the abyss where I rose from the ashes and built this empire. An empire she threatened multiple times. I should have dumped her headfirst into my magma pits and washed my hands of her. Or thrown her to the high demons I've imprisoned and enjoyed the fucking show. No, if anyone kills her, it'll be me.

My heart burns with my hellfire armor, the indestructible seal I've inscribed there: the only good angel is a fucking fallen angel...or a dead one.

What I'd give to set her Celestial City on fire, to burn everything she loves, then fuck her in the ashes and flaming feathers until she has nothing left in the world and no choice but to accept the Devil. And then, I'll truly own her and the angel light in her eyes.

My truest victim and beautiful little angel monster that I'll harness and fuck. I'll fucking shatter her, and she'll know it was the drug of the

Devil that got her hooked but left her to pick up the pieces.

She'll carry those broken pieces back to the Celestial City. She'll carry my fucking ghost to haunt her. I'll fucking possess her forever.

She still owes me a fucking dinner.

After I announce the First Trial this weekend, I'll return for her. Our sweet battles will continue. Perhaps, I'll spread her out and taste her golden pussy for dessert. She can't hide her arousal from me. My lust-hum guarantees that she may run but never hide. My brand is the strongest guarantee that she may hide but never run. Whether she realizes it or not, her body belongs to me, and I can take whatever I want from her whenever I desire. But not until she's on her fucking knees with her very soul begging for me.

Until then, the monster inside me can fuck off and starve.

I announce the Bride Trials and thrill in how it becomes the headline for every source of media upon Hell on Earth. Already, the news of the Trials has spread to the furthest reaches of Gemterra. Bitches and sluts and virgins of every race have arrived to compete for the chance to wed the Devil.

Following the announcement, I don't deny my urge to lean back in my office throne, rest my head against the ore, and close my eyes with a gratifying sigh. However, this process drains me and grates on my nerves, it suits its purpose to distract the Chambers from my business. Ever since I took care of the mutiny the high demons plotted when I ordered construction on Hell on Earth, the Chambers and I have been locked in a persistent battle of wills. Most wish me to commute their sentences and send them into the world to subjugate the other races while extending the territory of Hell on Earth.

However, if I go to war, I have a much loftier intention. But after I determine what is happening in my front yard and punish the responsible.

The warmth radiating in my chest turns to icy fear crawling along my spine. I straighten in my throne, wings tightening, pressing my lips to a tight grimace. Beyond fear, it's terror, pain, darkness, defeat. I close my eyes, concentrate on the sensory details of her crushed breath, her thigh and face screaming from the wounds, strained lungs, her choking, mouth tasting dirt with the sound of her blood hammering her ears. And lake water.

I know where she is.

When I sift to the lower level of the Second Circle, the demon and his wolf hover over her. Scraps of her gown sprinkle the ground like splotches of blood.

Astaroth grips her face, raking his claws across her golden skin. Unchecked wrath rouses the serpents upon my flesh as I hear his words.

"I gave you the choice, tiny angel," he croons and lowers his other claws into her thigh. She is beyond battle, beyond screaming, beyond breath. "Now, your death will be slow and painful."

Her tears cascade to unite with her blood. A silver object falls from her skin pouch. By now, she closes her eyes while I accept the serpent power leaping off my chest. It forms into one of my greatest weapons of hellfire and crimson energy. I, alone, may wield such power.

"Your death will be far more painful, Astaroth," I proclaim to the demon whose back is turned.

He whips his head around, teeth gnashing. His wolf charges. I don't care for the buildup of battle unless it's with the little angel below me. Nor does she have the luxury of time. No, she's not dead yet. What I know of her confirms it. Regardless, playing with my old demon toy will come later. For now, it's time to win. And no other being, throughout time and space, is better at winning than I.

With a deep inhale, I have no qualms about plunging my weapon directly into the wolf's spinal cord, pinning the creature to the ground as if it were a moth. As predicted, Astaroth is already up on his hind legs and running. He knows he can't mind fuck his master. If he'd engaged in a battle with my little angel, he would have lost, but he falls back on his demonic power every time.

All my muscles bulging, I close my fist around the serpent staff of my weapon and pitch it to soar through the air as straight and seamless as a shooting arrow until it meets its mark: in the dead center of Astaroth's back. He shrieks, black blood pooling to the ground. As long as the weapon remains lodged in his back, he cannot pull it out, he cannot heal. All he can do is fucking crawl like the worm he is.

By now, Samael has made quick work of the other serpent and slithers quickly back to her side as I kneel before her.

"She'sss not breathing, Lucccifer," he says, eyes glazed and concerned. "But she hasss life."

I grip the fallen ring between her thighs. And smirk, knowing it's the convenient cure. But something else is, too. So, without permitting another moment to pass, I lower my head, press my lips to her sensual pouty ones, open them with my teeth, and breathe life back into her.

TWENTY-EIGHT

TORTURE

—ASTRAEA—

I suck a deep gust of air, waking to Lucifer's full and sensual mouth on mine, gifting me that air. As soon as my eyes fly open, he hovers above my lips with a devilish grin. My chest heaves from how much I breathe, my lungs reclaiming their usage. I'm keenly aware of the rise and fall of my breasts against his chest. And how much of my gown has ripped to shreds.

"Welcome back, sweetheart. Perhaps next time you'll be a good girl and stay the fuck where I tell you to and not go wandering off."

"Excuse you, asshole," I wrinkle my nose and spit in his face. "You're the one who said the collar was fucking protection." Sammy peeps his head up, eyes shimmering and locking onto mine. I reach to pet him and rephrase, "You were perfect, Sammy. Lucifer's brand is gods-damned defective."

"You forget, little angel, my precise words were "only demons on his level could ever penetrate such defense". So happens that the crawling, sniveling manipulator over there is such a demon."

He finally pushes off me, and I hug my arms over my chest and breathe slowly and deeply to stem the tremors under my skin. Out of the corner of my eye, I watch the demon, who is still as nude but with...I squint to make out the weapon before my eyes nearly pop out of my head.

"Holy fucking devil daddy!" I curse and get to my knees as Sammy slithers toward the demon—the demon with a pitchfork plunged right through his back. It's no ordinary pitchfork. This one is on fucking steroids.

"Like my little toy, angel?"

I shift my gaze to Lucifer, who stands above me while I flick my eyes back and forth between him and the pitchfork. "Little toy? That's seriously the sexiest fucking harpoon I've ever seen!" At least ten feet tall with a shaft formed of two serpents twisting like a double helix. Eyes like jewels on fire. And every square inch embellished by flames.

Lucifer sifts one hand into my curls, and I shiver from the intimate gesture as he adds, "You should see my bigger ones." I flinch when he caresses the edges of my wings, going so far as to trail his fingers along the outer feathers. "Wings unscathed?"

I nod, fluttering them and rising until pain surges in my inner thigh, causing me to buckle. The Devil's arms wrap around me, holding me up with my back to his chest. His breath unfurls along my neck, but it's his arms bound around my wings to keep me steady, knuckles brushing the undersides of my breasts that send adrenaline spiking in my blood.

"Astaroth does not attack his victims by force. He manipulates them, but his pheromones and breath are his true weapons. As he diverts your attention with his propositions, the odor does the real work. And his wolf finishes off whatever's left. Next time, little angel," he sniggers and flashes a twinkling object before my eyes, Vladimira's ring, "place this under your nose immediately. The silver acts as a repellent and eliminates the effects."

I throw him a glare over my shoulder, ignoring the heat between my thighs, exposed thanks to the wolf. "So, why didn't you use it?"

Leaning in, Lucifer brushes his lips across my cheek. I grimace despite the tingle of pleasure along my spine. "And miss the expression on your face when you woke to me breathing life into your angelic body?"

"Ugh…" I struggle against him, but he doesn't release me yet.

"Or hear the sweet gratitude from those pretty, red lips…" he traces one finger along my mouth, and I turn stiller than stone, the need throbbing between my thighs. His other hand roams to the bare skin of my curved-in belly, another byproduct of the wolf. Little more than a few ribbons of fabric cover my pussy, and beaded rubies of the bodice were lost, exposing more of my breasts. Warmth flushes them now. I almost sag against him, but he grips my hip with a demanding growl and holds me up. I feel his arousal against the center of my back. "Astraea…I sucked the poison from you, destroyed it with my hellfire. What have you to say, sweet girl?"

I open my mouth, the words lodging in my throat. Astaroth's whimper stops us both, slicing through the thickening sexual tension. Lucifer groans, his grip loosening. "We will continue this later."

As soon as he releases me, I tear into a fierce run. My wings spur me on faster. I'm practically gliding across the grass until I reach Astaroth's side. Sammy poises in front of him, jaws open and fangs bared, waiting for him to make a move. I move instead. I drive my bare feet into the demon's face again and again.

"How do you like me now? Huh?!" I scream and kick his neck. He groans with every thrust of my heel and the ball of my foot, rolling onto his side. More blood sheds from the pitchfork in his back. All the pain from my thighs fades. My vision goes red. "You like the choice I'm making now, motherfucker? Wanna show me my fate now?"

I'm about to kick the fucker right in the balls when Lucifer seizes my wrist and drags me back, seething. "Enough, Astraea!"

"Let me go, you bastard demon!" I kick and thrash at him, and the keen tips of my wings nick portions of his face.

"Oh, let her go, Lucccifer," Sammy pipes up, trailing us but keeping clear of my body. "It wasss getting good."

Spinning me, Lucifer grips my face, his eyes burning onto mine. "You'll have plenty of opportunities to witness his torture soon."

"What?"

"Astaroth is a high demon, Astraea." He gestures to Sammy, but his stare sears into my very soul, triggering my skin to crawl. "On Samael's level. That means he escaped my pits, my prisons, all my gods-damned traps, defenses, and power. I want to fucking know how. And I'm damn well going to find out."

Lucifer calls it a holding center, but I know it's a torture chamber. The kind you'd expect to find in hell. Underground, the chamber reminds me of a dungeon with walls, floor, and ceiling formed of pure Diablo ore designed to repel demonic powers while enhancing Lucifer's. Thick chains and hooks dangle from the ceiling while a massive circle in the center of the chamber is hollow for a magma pit.

"Whatever you hear from this room, you do not enter, is that clear?"

Lucifer commands me, voice diamonded and deep. His whole body wreathes with hellfire, including the ends of his hair. He rolls up the sleeves of his robe, indicating he's prepared to do whatever is necessary to get his information.

"You truly believe this will work?" I challenge the Devil as a squad of fallen angels chain Astaroth to suspend right above that magma pit. The pitchfork is still embedded in his back as the one means of keeping him from sifting. "Hasn't he been locked in worse places for hundreds of years?"

Hands holding his elbows, wings and muscles hardened, Lucifer glowers at me. "And what do you suggest, little angel? A five-course dinner followed by a feather bed? Care to volunteer yours?" He drifts a hand toward my wings. I flinch, drawing them away.

"We're not playing with a fly here, so honey won't work. But neither will torture." I turn around, considering my brief interaction with Astaroth.

"Stay put, Astraea."

Once he's closed the dungeon door behind him, I roll my eyes and repeat his words in a mocking mutter before pacing the floor. It doesn't take long for the screams to begin. Some fade to deep, gurgling groans. Frustration knots my throat. I swallow it back, so it relocates to my stomach, which is growling. I hadn't realized how hungry I was.

By now, whatever adrenaline I had from the attack has worn off, and I feel the fading stings of the claw marks from Astaroth and the wolf. I trace a finger across the ones on my thighs, marveling at my angelic blood and its ability to heal our kind. And fallen angels. Spy angels have shared how it's become a rare black-market commodity. One reason fallen angels will hunt us, especially females. They'll use them however they can, from their bodies to their blood, before dumping them in the Unconsecrated Crater where most are too weak to survive. I rake my claws through my scalp to distract me from the pain in my chest and the tears burning in my eyes from seven-year-old memories.

"Penny for your thoughtsss, Raea?" Sammy coils half of his body from beyond my throat, so he's tilting his head and looking me right in the eye, a tiny portion of his forked tongue darting out.

I smile at the snake, lean toward him, and even touch my lips to his cheek in a light kiss. "Thank you for your help, Sammy."

If snakes could blush, I'm certain he would be right now. "My pleasssure. But Lucccifer sssaved you."

I hug my arms to my chest, shielding my halo that thrums with that knowledge. He doesn't get a fucking pass for bringing me back to life when he's trapped me in Hell on Earth.

Where else would you go? My inner psycho challenges, reminding me of the fate awaiting me in the Celestial City. The Tribunal's judgment. Justified. The memories turn my breathing ragged, and I wonder if I'm still trapped with Astaroth stealing all air from my lungs.

"I feel a hint of your emotionsss, Raea. Your wrath, your frusssstration, your woundsss."

"I'd rather not talk about them, Sammy. I just…I need to sit down."

Without another word, I set my back to the closest wall and ease down to the floor, wrapping my wings around me for warmth. Sammy makes a sound that reminds me of a purr crossed with a warble. A sweet warmth swells in my chest as he weaves around my neck and peeks his head out from my curls on the other side. Perching there, Sammy tucks his head onto the dip above my collarbone, and together, we fall asleep to the torturous groans and screams.

"Astraea," Lucifer rouses me.

I stir, smiling in my stupor from a warmth stroking the edges of my body and wings, combing into my feathers in a slow exploration.

"Evangelina," I murmur, remembering when we were young and swimming naked in the celestial pools. We'd cup handfuls of stardust water and wash each other's curls and our similar wings. We'd bathe beneath the shooting star falls and dry ourselves on the banks with our golden skin shining in the twilight sunset with all the burning light of our halos.

When I open my eyes, it's not her but the fallen Morning Star gazing back at me. As soon as his fingers crawl across my naked thigh and roam higher, I suck wind through my nose and lock myself up tight, knees to my chest.

"What the—" Lids still heavy with sleep, I turn to discover him squatting before me, the shadow of his massive wings devouring my form while the faint constellations twinkle back at me.

"Beautiful," I yawn, my vision and thoughts swirling until Lucifer grins wickedly. His eyes transform into those blood orbs.

Shaking my head out, I rub my eyes but still feel that warmth. I swing my head to my wings draped over my body, discovering Lucifer's hell flames trimming and tickling my feathers. Swallowing the urge to moan, I shiver from the pleasure and how his flames stir the nerves within my surface. And the first layer of feathers. If he pursues deeper, then I'll act.

But it's not his flames, it's the scent of smoke drifting all over him. I narrow my eyes because not one thread of his robes is singed or bloody.

"How long have I been—"

"A few hours." He brushes his knuckles across my cheek.

I lift my brows but don't remove his hand. "He hasn't talked, has he?"

I challenge with a smirk.

A deep growl, but Lucifer keeps it in his throat and shakes his head. "It's not as if I have much experience tormenting my demons, particularly not high ones who used to be my greatest of agents before their betrayal." Shadows breed around him, darkening his eyes—a contrast to my figure with my gold wings scintillating from his fire.

"Let me try."

He threads his brows low and snarls, "No."

"I'm fucking going in there, Lucifer. And I'm going in alone."

TWENTY-NINE

BLOOD AND MIND FUCKS

—ASTRAEA—

Rage vibrates through his body. His eyes narrow dangerously. The lust-hum comes right before he seizes my throat, squeezing even as a flush spreads to my breasts. Alerted by the Devil's action, Sammy hisses and slithers back into my throat, disappearing supernaturally right through Lucifer's hand.

I resist the urge to roll my eyes to their ceilings as the Devil reduces my breath to a mere thread. Instead, I stare at him. There's a raw tension in all his muscles, and his hellfire grows. It sinks deeper into my wings to rouse the inner nerves until my core throbs. Wetness slides down my thighs. He unleashes more growls and lust-hums, one following the other until they become chronic thunder ripples. The sound of the highest demon, the King of hell, when he is proving his power.

Desire engulfs my body until I thrust my breasts toward his chest and spread my legs, my eyes heady with lust. But my determination is too raw and wild. Astaroth attacked me, mind-fucked me, sucked the breath from my lungs, and there's one other time that has happened. Not even Lucifer has taken all my breath, and whenever he's come close, he's gifted me with air. As he does when he seals his mouth to mine. He pushes the breath into me until my lungs and chest swell with it until I kiss him back, devouring him as much as he's devouring me. Our hunger and darkness are hellbent on conquering the other. This time when he thunder-purrs into my mouth, I moan and arch my neck.

His hot power snakes across my skin, raising goosebumps and the hairs to prickle along my arms. Like static electricity, but his sinks into my pores, scribbling its signature like fucking hellfire ink. He's reinforcing how much he owns me. And I'm not fighting him with one iota of my being.

Until his fingers brush against my thighs, tiptoeing higher. I recognize the desperation within them—how all this is a diversion, to keep me out of that room. He spreads my thighs. Pushes them wider.

Before those fingers dip inside my wet heat and I'm too far gone, I ball my hand into a fist and bring it up hard, dusting his jaw and knocking him backward. He grips his jaw with a low growl. The blood fire in his eyes grows. He flares his wings, charging for me. But I unleash my angel teeth and claws, jut out my chin, and snarl, not backing down.

"Alone!" I solidify in a stalemate of wills. "Give me one fucking hour!" I bargain, appealing to his lust for deals.

"You got ten fucking minutes."

Like lightning, a thrill of adrenaline pulses up my spine.

I can work with that!

When I enter, I must hold my breath for more than one reason. The stench is rancid—all blood and burning flesh, not to mention the demon's pheromone odor. Astaroth hangs from the ceiling directly over the molten lava pit, but I lose count of all the burns and brands on his body. Several bones protrude at odd angles. And Lucifer…I pinch my eyes shut, overwhelmed by the sight of half the demon's cock burned off with blood dripping from the rest. He's missing his eyes, but he still jerks his head in my direction, sniffs the air, snorts.

"Reconsidered our deal, pretty angel?" Astaroth tries to croon, but it's a rasp of coughs. When he spits blood, cinders, and fleshy bits, I press the silver ring under my nose and suck a deep breath. Lucifer poured magma down his throat. Any other being would be dead by now, except a seraph, but demon bodies, especially high demons, are far more resistant.

"No. We have a few minutes," I speak truthfully. "I'm simply here to help." And I am.

"Come to offer me salvation?" he spits more ash and flesh and blood.

"No."

I do a wing thrust, fluttering them until I hover before the demon. Swallowing any reservations regarding what I'm about to do, I square my shoulders, ignore my quivering limbs, and extend my claws to their fullest and sharpest length. My inner psycho binds my angel into submission, chaining her up. I embrace the darkness and monster within me. Take a deep breath. Eyes on Astaroth, knowing his pheromones and scent are stronger than his vision ever was, I scrawl the first line across my upper chest. Barely clench my teeth.

He jerks his chin toward me, inhaling deeply, moaning. I grin and slash lower above my left breast. Golden blood drips into the bodice.

Astaroth rattles the chains, covering the sound of my pained grunt, my rushed breath. The endorphins of pleasure mingle with the pain. A thousand thoughts of chasing them down every night for six years plague my mind. How it was never enough. Not until I plotted vengeance. Vengeance that failed.

Could I have killed Lucifer? Brought his head back to the Tribunal? Did I want to fail? Pain and punishment for the demons of my past, for that night seven years ago.

"Angel blood is fascinating, isn't it?" I harden my voice to a deadly edge and slice the faint mark upon my thigh. Nearly healed, I open the wound again and battle the churning bile in my stomach, focusing on my words. "Fae, demons, fallen angels, elves, every race on earth hunts our kind as much as we hunt them. But us women angels bear the sweetest blood, of course. Considered a delicacy, a drug, and a numbing agent. But if too much is ingested, it will cause paralysis and eventually...death."

I grin when the demon's mangled lips part, and he snarls low. Tracking my time, I drag my claw across my arm, then the other, and finally, my hands. The scent of my blood baptizes the air and floods Astaroth's senses. My brand of a mind fuck. Two can play that twisted game.

"Have you ever sampled an angel's blood?" I coo and raise my hand closer to his nose, out of reach. I pinch my eyes shut to clear my dizzying vision from the cuts. But they're superficial. Thin. They've already begun to heal.

"Once. Male," he manages to rasp out.

He groans, straining powerfully against the chains, thrashing, and growling. Biting my tongue hard, I slice the swell of my breast, then down, leaving a stinging trail. My vision blurs, but my mind has never been clearer. Evangelina's eyes burn into mine. I punish myself, fucking bleed for her, but I could never spill enough to rival her pain.

I grunt and swallow the hurt in my throat, slicing my thighs open, then my hands deeper. Careful and precise, I lift my hand to trickle droplets of my blood onto his head, onto his face while keeping his tongue from ever reaching them. He tries. Oh, he tries, sticking it out, twisting and stretching.

This feels beautiful. To mark myself like this with another purpose aside from my guilt, with another goal to center me. Not that I'd ever share with Lucifer. This is fucking mine.

"All I need is a name. One little name. Who helped you escape from Lucifer's pit prisons?" It's the logical explanation—a higher demon capable of defeating Lucifer's security, his traps.

Another growl, another desperate push of his body, another strain and rattling of the chains. I cut again. The side of my neck, nicking the skin above my artery that leads directly to my halo—my purest area of blood. And I know it fucking sings to him. He screeches and vomits cinders, bits of gore, and blood all over him.

"We have a minute left at most, Astaroth," I inform him, knowing Lucifer will barge in and wreck everything. I lean in. Position my bleeding neck a few inches from his face.

"Give it to me!" the demon growls and screams.

"Name!" I demand, baring my angel fangs

"Asmodeus, fucking bitch! Asmodeus!"

Despite how he can't see, I give a mock salute and turn, fluttering back to the ground and moving toward the door.

"Your blood!" he screeches, breaking a link in the chain.

"Oh," I pause right before the door and shrug. "Did I make a deal?

Or promise anything?"

Leaving him to rage, I roll my eyes and knock on the dungeon door. Lucifer opens it, takes one glance at me, and grips my wrist to slam me against the nearest wall of Diablo ore.

"What the fuck have you done?!" he lashes out, and I shudder in wrath and fear from all his hellfire and shadows gathering around me while his hands pin my arms to the wall.

"Get your fucking hands off me!"

All his veins alive and flaming with rage, he narrows his lethal eyes, his voice low and deadly as he eyes my cuts. "What. The. Fuck. Astraea?"

Less than an eye blink passes. He rips the torn gown further, exposing my ragged panties, baring my bleeding thighs. His eyes swell with bloodlust. He takes in my still-extended claws and the traces of fresh blood there. A storm of thunder in his chest, he growls lower than ever.

"It was my fucking choice," I snarl, jerking, but his body is a solid weapon, caging me in. His strong hands chain my arms against the wall.

He flares his nostrils, breathing in the scent of my blood. I love how it tortures him. I smirk from the muscle ticking in his jaw in obvious lust. I beam from the tension in his shoulders and how all his muscles bulge around me. The psycho in me is on too much of an adrenaline high to care about what he might do. She's downright dancing with sexual vapors, our pussy drenched and oozing.

"He's not fucking worthy of your pain or blood!"

"And you are?"

"No! But at least I have the balls to fucking admit it," he roars, fuming fury and sulfur before my face, heating my cheeks.

He flares his nostrils, then reaches down with one hand and grips my thigh. I cry out when he digs his fingers into the wound. I gnash my teeth at him, but my pussy throbs from the endorphins shooting through me. The cream of my heat mixes with the blood on my thigh.

Lucifer raises those fingers dripping with my blood and fluids to his lips, grins, and dips them into his mouth, tasting me. His eyes smolder against mine, but I don't back down. I watch as he taunts me by licking his fingers clean—eyebrows high, wicked glint, and devilish smile.

I shiver from how much my blood and cunt rouse him. His erection is beyond evident, bulging through his robe, in line with his navel. I cage a gasp, remembering the mere glimpse of it in the steam room. Thick and long and branded with the same black hellfire ink that defines his chest. Another serpent twisting and coiling around his dick gives a new meaning to "one-eyed snake".

Clenching my eyes shut and banishing all thoughts of his dick, I snarl out, "I got a fucking name," I divert him from the subject, waggling my brows.

Pressing his lips in a grimace, Lucifer shoves off of me, charges into the dungeon, and slams the door behind him. I clutch my throat, tickling my fingers over Sammy, desperate for a buffer. But he refuses to pop out.

"Chicken," I mutter to the snake.

All he responds with is that forked tongue slithering beyond the ink as if blowing me a raspberry. I roll my eyes, but there's not enough time to argue with him. A blood-curdling scream raises all the hairs on my body before utter silence. Not even the clanging of chains. Not a whimper.

Lucifer emerges. For the first time, blood drenches his robe. My eyes fly wide open at the bleeding, smoking muscle dripping from his open palm.

Curling his upper lip to flash a demon fang at me, the Devil approaches with the high demon's heart, and I press myself against the wall as far as possible. I breathe a deep gasp through my nose as he lifts the heart to my very eyes, proceeding to crush it to a pulp. The blood splatters my cheek. He chucks it to the floor and slams the wall above my head, shaking it until I feel its vibration within my very wings.

I have a moment to act. A moment to leap into Lucifer's arms before the entire wall of Diablo ore crumbles from the force of that hand. Deep laughter from his chest rumbles into mine, and I glance back to the dungeon, now bared from that fallen wall. There is Astaroth, his corpse suspended, the skin of his chest burned to ashes, the rib cage itself missing. Everything is a cavity. A heartless hollow with arteries still flaming.

Gripping my jaw, Lucifer forces my eyes to his and hums hot breath across my lips, "I will never allow a being to live if they shed so much as a drop of blood from you. Even if your hand is the cause. Your blood is fucking mine, Astraea. Your body is mine. Never forget that."

THIRTY

DESSERT BEFORE DINNER

──── LUCIFER ────

uck dinner.

There was no chance in my hell that I could have possibly sat across from her at the table, smelling the aftermath of her blood healing, the wounds closing.

When she'd emerged from that room with blood dripping down her body, I'd nearly ripped off what was left of her gown, drove myself into her, and licked the remaining blood from her body.

The image of her lying there nearly lifeless on the grass with blood trickling down her thighs and face still haunts me. I didn't bring her back to life for her to go and pull this shit.

She still fights me. More sovereign and dominant than ever, my lust called to her. As her fucking trill called to me. I'd projected that hum down to her gods-damn halo. I'd thrust my power beneath her flesh and roused her blood to heat. She'd crumbled, and I felt her hunger when she kissed me back—the same hunger from the first night we met. The one that had my monster rising to the surface for the first time since we fell from heaven. That night, he'd stalked her. It was why I summoned her. Otherwise, he would've fucked her through me right then and there.

Tonight, her hunger was stronger, more passionate, fueled by her hatred...hatred for me. And hatred for herself for wanting me.

Not that she could rival mine.

Vexatious, angelic bitch. I'd come so close, spreading those pretty, thick thighs, eyeing the meager scrap of lace covering her pussy. Utterly drenched, it was transparent enough for me to view her pink folds. They wept for me. Tonight, I'd tasted her blood. And I'd never wanted to fuck anyone harder than I wanted to fuck Astraea Eternity.

I want more. The monster wants more.

I want to watch her eyes fill up with lust as I plunge into her fathomless depths, watch the fire in her ignite as I fuck her hard until she is ready to submit and scream my name to the Celestial City itself.

And once that version of Astraea was gone, fucked to hell by the Devil, I'd destroy her and this divine poison in my blood and my mind.

My monster prowled deep inside me, recognizing her defiance, wanting to fuck it right out of her. Took everything in me to stop the demon, especially with my balls on the verge of bursting. He's a ticking time bomb—countdown already set, hourglass running down. Not even I understand the cosmic being I'd unleashed when I fell. I'd either pulled him from the fabric of the universe during my great battle with Abaddon or an evil spawned from the Unconsecrated Crater. Regardless, if I return to her tonight, the one thing that will sate him is her blood. I'm not her fucking savior. Nor is she mine.

I'm the angel in her. She's the devil in me.

When the time comes, it'll be nothing but blood. Nothing but flames and destruction and death when I slam into that cunt, feel her clench around me, and I take everything from her. I won't need to use my power. I'll always use my lust-hum. She will use her trill against me, causing my cock to throb and ache. She won't escape me. Not till I'm satisfied. Not till her angel is spreading her wings and lifting her ass into the air to give me everything.

For now, I must keep her close. Use her as I see fit. I'd known it could never be as simple as chaining her to my fucking bed, forcing her to submit. I've had plenty of sluts and bitches of every gender and race who can sate my cock and lick my cum clean. Only this little sweetheart of an angel will sate my demon.

I never considered she'd be useful, aside from the skill of a glorified carrier pigeon. Asmo-fucking-deus. A name that has been my poltergeist since I imprisoned all high demons and began construction on Hell on Earth. The one demon I could not conquer.

Until then, I stay in this gods-damned casino with seven sluts hovering around me. Trans fae drag queen who'd gladly mark up my cock later with her ruby lips. An effeminate son of an elf lord who would be the perfect bottom. Two sub demonesses, one fallen angel woman who'd give me her blood, and two human women from the blood district; they'll get paid more tonight than they ever make in a year to gift them six months of peace away from the life. I could care less about their names.

I tip back another shot of dragon's blood, pet the fallen angel and human closest to me, then gaze at the high-rollers at the table: a fae princess from the Shadowstorm caste, a possession demon noble, the governor of the Sixth Circle Chamber of Bone and Claw, and an Unseelie orc lord of the Harvest Caste—my most prominent shareholder in Hell on Earth. Crowds gather around us as usual, ever eager to observe the spectacle of their King.

Wings folded cautiously behind my back, I relax my shoulders as the cards are dealt. And as I touch the edges of my cards, grit and dust sprinkle onto the card table. I flick my eyes upward, tilting my head. A moment passes before the ceiling gives way, and the little mouse crawling through the ducts collapses onto the table, moaning from the hard fall.

"Well now, what have we here?" I lean forward, steepling my fingertips, beaming at the young human woman. She is beautiful in a timid, delicate way with silvery blonde hair, doe eyes like shimmering emeralds, and a petite body but blessed with abundant breasts, full and round hips, and ample thighs.

I raise my hand, delaying the security demons closing in. She coughs and shakes off the dust in her hair, lifts her eyes to mine, and shoots them wide open.

Her lips part in a gasp. "Lord Lucifer..." she bows her head.

"Your name, little mouse from the rafters," I urge her, showcasing my demon teeth. She must understand I won't fuck around tonight.

She doesn't lift her head, but her eyes shift upward, daring yet glassy and fearful. "I-I am Everleigh Beck. My hu-husband was in charge of all your trade routes and your imports and exports before..." she gulps and clenches her eyes before they burn with vengeance, "...before he was murdered. I've spent the past two years tracking his killer."

Curious, I lean back in my seat, remembering the name Beck: a loathsome man but loyal and cunning enough to be charged with the transport routes of my empire. I also remember the news of his death, of sending fire and ice lilies to his widow, who'd inherited his wealth. I'd prepared to transfer the holdings to his partner, the chairman of the board of directors. But after a trial run of the corporation in the able hands of his widow, I'd signed an innocuous document grating her supremacy over the company.

"Ahh, so you are the shrewd and business savvy Ever Hart," I cite the name that reached my ears, her preferred name. "Please…" I gesture for her to continue, "will you gratify me with the name of your late husband's killer as I assume it's the reason you have undergone such a risk as to invade my casino?"

She sighs, lowering her head, taking a few deep gusts before tossing her icy blonde hair back and opening her mouth to proclaim, "Asmodeus."

In the wee hours of the morning, I stray into her room. She's sleeping like an angel. I chuckle internally from my joke. More alluring is how she sleeps in nothing more than lacy lingerie. Her full breasts nearly tumble out of her bra. Ever comfortable within her skin. Beyond that, she fucking owns it. Decades of training and dedication to this beautiful form, her wings most of all.

I approach the bed, memorizing her tranquil breathing, the subtle glow from her halo bathing her skin to effervescence. Fuck, she's beautiful, so gods-damned perfect, slumbering on her side with one wing draped over her belly and leg and the other softly twitching, alerting me to her dream state.

When that wing shifts upward to bare her back, I seethe from the sight of the striations—old wounds, faded gold scars from a fucking whip. In their own way, they are a beauteous pain, no doubt earned during her training. Still, I want to pound my fist against the nearest wall. Blood hammers into my ears. This is not why I came here.

Deep inside me, the monster growls, stalking the corners of my mind, prepared to unleash himself in all his rage and glory. He wants me to ravish her, to infect her mind. Give him her blood and flesh, then burn the memories from her mind so she won't remember. As long as I have one iota of resistance toward him, I will never do such a thing.

As long as I satisfy him to the barest minimum, I will keep her safe from the worst part of my being.

So, I lower my hand to her back and lightly trace a single digit over the tapestry of scars upon her back. She responds as I'd predicted. One split second. Her claws aim at my throat. Before they can so much as brush my skin, I slam her back against the bed, pin her with my weight, and grip her wrists, thrusting them above her head.

"Get the fuck off me, asshole!" She thrashes her gorgeous hips, but I bear down on her harder.

"You knew I was there the whole time, didn't you, sweet angel?" I croon, my eyes lowering to the rest of her.

"Or I felt the presence of a deranged stalker thinking he has the right to watch me sleep."

"As you invaded my privacy, marching into my steam room?" I challenge with a wicked smirk, enjoying her expression when she parts her speechless lips. "Turn around's fair play, sweetheart. Especially when everything here belongs to me, including you."

She rolls her eyes. "What do you want, Lucifer?"

Muscles tight, I sweep a finger down her cheek, trailing it down to her pulse. "Your blood, little angel."

I lower my mouth to hers, a shot of lust charging through me when she extends her pointed angel teeth. That vicious predator of an angel strikes when she frees her hands, grips me by the neck, and tugs me forward toward those snapping teeth. Narrowly avoiding those chomping weapons, I rip her hands from me, needing to gain control before the monster unleashes himself on her.

Whipping out my tail swifter than she may act, I coil it around her wrists, binding them above her head.

"You look beautiful all trussed up, Astraea," I remark, taking advantage when her eyes flick to their ceilings to eye the tail.

I bring my mouth down hard on hers. Her lips bow to mine for a fraction of a second. I resist the urge to groan when she sucks on my bottom lip, until her angel teeth extend to bite. I growl when she latches on, endure the burst of pain until she's drawn my blood.

Grinning, the little vixen sweeps her tongue along my lower lip to capture the tiny droplets from the wound she's created. I gaze down at her cheeks, flushed from her action, and respond, "I'm flexible, Astraea. Care to work out your self-righteous kinks with a little kink tonight?"

"You're an asshole."

"True, but that's hardly a mystery.

As is your masochism. You want pain? Tonight, you'll wear my marks. You get the pain. I get your blood. After, you can go back on your merry way to hating me as much as I hate you."

"Fuck you!"

She snarls, cocking her head back, but I dodge before she can bash me. Damn, I love those shiny wings spread for me. That raw, wild hunger and hatred in her pinched eyes are why I've come.

"Eventually, sweetheart." I wink. "But your blood tonight."

I tap one claw to her cheek, then drag it down slowly. She freezes, and I grin. My cock throbs from her hiss as I scrape my claw along her throat and to her bra, chuckling from those pretty pink nipples pebbling for me, begging me to play with them. I smell her angel pheromones, her heightened arousal. I don't use my pheromones yet, but her blood and breath quickens. My little angel with hellfire inside her.

"You're so eager to punish yourself, sweetheart? Then, why not do it right here right now?" I growl at her, stroking that claw along her navel and beyond to dip beneath her panty line. When she sucks in a deep breath and arches her back, I flick my eyes on her. Wag my brows. She hisses, knowing she's been caught. "Hmm," I croon, drawing that claw to her sexy as fuck thighs, leaving pink marks on her beautiful gold skin. "You like it, don't you? You get off on the pain."

"Thought you said you didn't deserve my pain?" she spits the taunt.

Leering down at her, I harden my muscles against her straining hands, lean down, and hum in her ear, "Perhaps I do. Perhaps I don't. Let's find out," I finish in a whisper.

Tonight, I'll crush her first layer of armor.

As soon as she struggles, I grip her slight throat, cutting off all but the air required for her to survive. High demons have trembled on their knees before me. The darkest monsters have bowed in servitude. And yet, this little angel dares to stare me down with her burning gold eyes even with my hand on her throat. I grind my lower half against her so she can feel my erection. I capture her whimper. Part of me wants to let her go, unleash the wild one inside her so we can go toe to toe in battle.

There will be time for that later.

"You have no power tonight, Astraea," I warn her, denying her the struggle. Nor will she so much as consider fucking fading on me. Tonight will be raw and real.

"You think I can't take whatever you bring me, you gods-damn devil?

I've faced fucking monsters worse than you."

I chuckle darkly and grind against her again before touching my lips tenderly to her brow. "No one is worse than me, sweet girl. But you will own the pain tonight. And as my business is never alone..." I cup her mound. The monster roars inside me when she drips, when she frees those pheromones to leak into the air. Practically howling for my dark demon. Baiting him. Taunting him. The moment I look up, I catch the mocking glint in her eye and her scornful smile.

She doesn't know who she's dealing with. No fucking clue.

"I also mix pain with pleasure, Astraea. But I'll give you an out. Say the word, look me in the eye, tell me you don't want this, and I'll leave now." I remove my hand and gesture to the door. The monster snarls and thrashes me with his dark matter, pressuring me worse than all my centuries until beads of sweat form on my brow. I cringe from the force he exerts. But I reinforce the strength in my voice, stare down at Astraea's burning eyes, and finish, "We both know you'll finish the job yourself while imagining me. Or..." I trail off, knowing the cost will be a life, how the demon will demand a full blood-reaping in return for this rebellion.

But Astraea blinks. Her eyes flick to my hand, to my mouth, and back to my eyes. She opens her pretty mouth to proclaim, "Do. Your. Worst. Lucifer."

I'll do far more than that. I've skipped fucking dinner. Tonight, she's my angelic dessert.

THIRTY-ONE

BLOOD PLAY

—ASTRAEA—

I don't say no.

I'm taunting and tempting the Devil as I let him toy with me.
I don't want to give him the satisfaction of anything. But I know
it's futile. He already knows how much his brand of pain and pleasure
arouses me.

Tattoos are forbidden for lower angels. No markings whatsoever—
some shit about keeping our skin as pure as our souls. Didn't stop me
from cutting myself for years, bleeding my skin so I could scrawl patterns
like celestial ink. No, I've never had a death wish. It's the opposite.

I live for her. I live so they won't win. So that damned crater won't
win. I live out of sheer spite. And for whatever gods-damned adrenaline
rushes I can get.

Whatever superficial pain I survive is nothing compared to my soul's
pain. So, I live inside it, ride the adrenaline of those endorphins to feel
alive, knowing my limits and how far I can go. Because I'm an angel. I

heal quickly. And have blood to spare.

The eager hairs on my arms and the nape of my neck prickle.

This is simply the first time I've never controlled the pain. Will it feel the same? Whatever marks or scars he deals, I'll own them...for me. Doesn't mean I won't have fun at the same time.

"I'm going to destroy you," I vow to Lucifer, unleashing the psycho who's become my lifeline.

"That would be Abaddon's job description."

I spit from his chortle, seethe, and correct myself even as heat roils in my belly, gravitating down, "I'll fucking kill you."

"I'll give you another opportunity to try, Astraea. But not tonight. Tonight, you bleed."

Lucifer snaps his wings shut, his muscles hardening.

"Damn Devil!"

"Little sweetheart."

He slams his mouth down on mine, teeth forcing my lips to open, tongue striking mine. I should sink my teeth hard, but I don't. My angel teeth crash against his demon ones. And I battle his tongue. It takes all my strength to resist the urge to moan with the warmth of his body slithering across me. His flames lick my thighs. My pussy betrays me, growing wet from Lucifer's heat, from him dominating my mouth, from that wicked tail binding my wrists above my head. And his lower half pinning me. .

I still don't say no. With all my inner psycho, I might be as twisted, dark, and disturbed as him.

His mouth is still on mine when he scrawls his claws across my skin, starting at my throat. He scrapes but doesn't break the skin, toying with me. I gasp into his mouth as those claws trail to the crests of my breasts.

I find myself arching. My nipples ache, puckering higher, struggling against the confining lace. As soon as his devilish claw traces around the lace-covered peaked tip, I moan.

"Hmm...you're enjoying this, aren't you, angel?" he pauses above my lips.

"I'll enjoy kicking your ass more." I stick out my tongue.

He laughs darkly, coldly, tightens his tail around one wrist but loosens his hold on the other. "I'd be careful before making such threats, Astraea. Especially when I have plans for your angelic ass. Dirty plans my tail longs for."

My eyes widen from the notion. I remember that tail whipping my backside, but I remember it more inside me. I can't help but wonder what both would be like.

Granting my swollen lips a reprieve, Lucifer lowers his head, tonguing all the pink scrapes from his claw. When he arrives at my breast, pausing, I buck hard. Reach for the back of his neck. Push him lower where I want him.

In response, Lucifer presses the tips of his claws to the upper mound of my breast. And cuts three sudden lines. I groan, but the groan turns into a whimper when he sweeps his tongue across the cuts, licking the blood. The sting fades to the warmth of his tongue. He's using demon venom to enhance the pleasure. I melt into that swirling heat.

"Your blood is so sweet, Astraea. Sweet as honey from the comb. godsdamn delicacy indeed." He swirls his tongue around the cuts, groaning.

He grins devilishly, but when he finally dips his tongue beyond the lace, he traces his tongue around the areola—but not the nipple. "You bastard!" I moan, raking my nails into his back, urging him to that starved tip.

"Dirty little angel," he murmurs against my skin, squeezing my other breast, then fingering the lace. "You want this off, don't you? You want me to suck your pretty, pink tits that get hard at the mere sound of my lust-hum."

"As hard as your cock gets from my trill?"

He chuckles against my breast. I don't have time to brace myself before he slices the clasp of my bra and rips it off, spilling my heavy breasts, exposing them to the room. First, he cups one, fondling its plump weight. But when he flicks his claw across my nipple, I clench my eyes shut, gasping and lifting my chest higher, the need unbearable.

"I'm going to mark these, Astraea..." Lucifer tells me, pinching the bud. "But not with my claws."

His demon teeth sink into my breast. I cry out from his harsh bite. He penetrates deep enough to draw the blood to the surface for his tongue to taste. With another imprint of his teeth on the other breast, I writhe against him, straining against his tail.

"Do you know how exquisite your breasts are with my marks, sweetheart?" he hums low, tongue curling around one nipple. "One day, I'll give you a scar right here..." He taps one claw to the swell. "And here..." he scrapes the underside. "Scars far worthier and more beautiful than the fucking ones on your back. Tell me...did you feel pleasure when you were whipped as I give you now?"

"Lucifer, goddammit!" I thrash and pound my head against the sheets.

Flicking my nipple with his torturous tongue, the Devil meets my eyes, wags his brows, and urges, "Answer the question, Astraea." All the muscles in his wings harden.

"Go to—"

He snorts. "You're already there with me, sweetheart. And you taste like an angel embracing her demons and darkness." He slashes two marks just beneath my navel, and I inhale a sharp breath. "Why were you whipped?"

"None of your fucking—"

In one swift slice, Lucifer does away with my panties and circles a single claw around my clitoral hood.

"Oh, fuck! Fine! All warrior angels are whipped if they fuck up their training." I twist my lips to one side and raise my chin. "I hold the record for the most scars in the Celestial City."

Lucifer growls, closes his mouth around the erect bud, and suckles. I gulp for air. He suckles and tongues harder until I'm damn near keening from the invisible thread connecting it straight to that bundle of nerves between my thighs. He bites the other nipple until it flushes with blood just beneath the surface. More fluids leak from my pussy. All my muscles and limbs begin to soften from the heated aches he's pulling from my womb.

"Hmm, you're drenched for me, aren't you?"

"Is that the question you really want to ask?" I snarl, clenching hard, my wings themselves quivering.

Another slice between the center of my breasts. His tongue comes down again. The moment I open my lips to beg him back to my breasts, he sucks a nipple into his warm, wet mouth while rolling the other between his claws—delicate to keep from nicking it.

"Oh, sweet fucking demon," I moan.

He nips the peak, closes his teeth around the nipple, and tugs hard. My body coils from all the tension building between my heated thighs, willing more moisture to drip. He growls and slices beneath each breast and laps up the blood. The slurping noises turn me on—to know he's feeding on me, drunk on me, fucking addicted.

He looks up from my breasts, blood fire pupils overwhelming his irises. His full lips are wet with my blood and saliva, swollen from sucking my buds. I can't deny my blood sparking from that naked lust, a deep sense of vulnerability in his eyes. "Your blood could turn even the most powerful angels and demons into addicts, Astraea. And it could tempt the strongest of gods."

Two slices each to my thighs. The endorphins pulse into my nerves, igniting them. I rock my head against the pillow. He sweeps up the blood with his tongue, sucking, laving, tasting. All my breath quickens, turning heavier until I'm nearly panting. I dig my nails into my palms. "Please!" I ache, craving his tongue to move higher from my thighs. All my feathers flare. I hate myself for this. Regardless if he's the Devil with centuries of mastery of the art of pleasure—whether he's the author of lust himself—, I still hate myself for my addiction to his touch.

"Mmm...who whipped you?"

He retracts his claws so he may part my pussy lips and blow warm breath across my clitoris. My core overheats. All my limbs tremble with a desperate need.

Tears shimmer in my eyes. Overwhelmed, I shake my head. "Don't ask me that, Lucifer, please." I stare down at him through my blurry vision, pleading silently.

He deadpans with me. Shadows darken his features, but he sets his jaw and says, "When you were whipped, little angel, did it fucking feel like this?"

My screams fill the room from his tongue licking maddening circles around my clit. And once he buries his fingers deep in my pussy, I trill higher than ever. He stokes a storm within me.

"Yes, Astraea. Sing for me, sweetheart." He flicks my clit with his tongue. I gasp when he lengthens it.

"Oh, oh! Unholy fucking devil daddy tongue!" I trill when he lashes my clit with the forked end. I harden my thighs around his head.

"It's not the only thing I can lengthen, sweetheart." My mind nearly wanders down a black hole from all the possibilities.

I can't help it. His lust, his passion, is ultimate and everlasting. A fathomless sea of molten lava. My firestorm of desire latches onto his. He sucks my hood hard, nipping it with his sharpened teeth. I swear he's lathing his venom upon my entire pussy to strengthen my nerves, increasing the arousal. All I can do is open for him, throbbing, rocking against that face as he eats me out, tasting, drinking, and worshiping me. Hellbent on bringing me to surrender. Tears blot my vision from the sinful ecstasy, his fevered energy rolling off him to pulse waves of pleasure across my flesh, raising the hairs on my arms and back of my neck.

One more finger invades my wet pussy. My inner muscles find his pumping rhythm. The need for fullness overwhelms me until I'm squeezing, clamping, and knotting those fingers, desperate to suck them in. For the first time since the night he branded me, Lucifer shows his masterful fingers, vibrating them deep inside me. He curves them to strike fucking gold.

With his tongue twisting my clit and those fingers pumping as his other hand squeezes my breast hard, I explode. Galaxies surge behind my eyes as I shatter, trilling and screaming. Sweat drips down my skin along with whatever blood is left. Lucifer punches his fingers, intensifying the vibration until I'm crashing again, moaning and trilling, and groaning and begging him to stop.

He retrieves his fingers, grins wickedly at me, and laps at my pussy to clean the mess he made. Then, the Devil presses his chest to mine. I quake beneath him. Capturing the side of my face with one hand and urging my dazed eyes to his, Lucifer plunges his fingers slick with my fluids into my mouth. Shutting my eyes, I close my lips around his fingers, sucking and twirling my tongue around the digits. It isn't the first time I've tasted myself, but it's the first time I taste a hint of blood—the aftermath upon his fingertips.

"I've tasted centuries of pussies, Astraea. But none as sweet and heavenly as yours, little angel. You taste like stars and secrets. Do you know how gorgeous you look when you fall apart for me? You fucking sang for me," he finishes in a whisper just above my lips, brushing them softly with his.

I open my mouth, nearly ready to fall apart, but Lucifer growls and vanishes into thin air. I gasp from the power of that sift that stirs my curls and smothers my body with wind. Tingles erupt all over my skin from the hellfire hints he'd left to burn there.

Careless of any blood I get on them or the sheets, I manage the strength to curl into an angel ball, folding my wings behind me. I weep until the salt droplets tumble to sting the slashes already healing on my flesh. Because it was absolutely nothing like my whippings.

He leaves me trembling with the wounds healing, with the endorphins of pain and pleasure swirling through my veins and the scent of my blood in the air.

I still wouldn't have said no.

THIRTY-TWO

ASTRAEA AND ABADDON

—ASTRAEA—

Astraea...

It begins with the tiny waves of pulsations rippling up and down the underside of my body. Like it always does because it's not a new experience. I suppose I have Lucifer to thank for it. Ever since he left, I've drifted in and out of sleep. But an airy static purrs across my flesh. A reminder of the storm he'd awoken inside me. As if energy currents drift along the undersides of my toes, legs, my back. They tickle the nape of my neck to sift into my curls.

I must find a way to escape before he destroys all my resolve, and I end up in his bed.

The pressure swells in my chest until it bursts like a bottle cork has popped. When it had happened the first time, I'd panicked, wondering why I couldn't breathe. Still, I'm alert and awake as the whirlpool of milky, white energy surrounds me in a floating warmth before the silver and black vines twisting together to form a tree of that same swirling energy pull me up. They work with the vibrating waves beneath me. They grow, building in strength and pushing me upward until my soul detaches from my body.

I'm weightless.

The instant I open my eyes, the paralysis binds me to earth.

Astraea…

I close them again, accepting his voice, the call of my guardian angel with his signature inscribed along that dark energy. Freeing my mind to wander, freeing him to tether me because he is the lifeline I trust, I lean into the jolt of my spirit. And let go. I float through the astral waves of energy, never losing the sensation of weightlessness, the vibrations below me, or the spiritual force of those vines carrying me through time and space.

It's the same location every time. At times, I wonder if he truly does have control, if he chooses it on purpose to reinforce the bond we've shared since he found me.

Shivering in the darkness so close to the miles-deep pit of a black inferno of cataclysmic power, of billions of the damned echoing their wails in the distance, I hug my chest. On the verge of tears, I huddle into my spirit's framework—clothed in the lacy lingerie and nothing else. My tears don't fall. They don't get the opportunity.

Abaddon's powerful arms surround me every time. I sigh, leaning into his fortress as his great wings wrap around us. So great, they smother my gold ones, the deep gray shades snuffing the subtle glow of mine. The feathers themselves are long as nephyl limbs, but Abaddon doesn't care if the ends of his wings skirt the ground. He still shelters me with them. Hues of the darkest purple fan out from the base feathers. As if they were formed from a galaxy's innermost eye.

He and Lucifer are matched in the powerhouse department since each tower over me at least two heads. I register how it's the first time I've ever compared Abaddon to Lucifer. More than usual, the Angel of Destruction's power creeps across my soul form, so I'm trembling within his arms.

"I hate this place," I grumble. Icy frustration drifts from me in staccato ripples the color of rotten lemons. While Abaddon can harness his emotional auras and mask them inside his soul, I've never mastered the skill.

"Our souls will always pull our energy here," he explains, gesturing to the Unconsecrated Crater, but I don't want another long speech since Abaddon is fond of his monologues.

Dozens of spirit shades in various hues of deep amaranthine and dusky scarlet soar far above our heads. Forms casting shadows over us. Chills crawl along my spine, and I dip my head, the gesture instinctive over the past seven years. With Abaddon's protection, there's nothing to fear, but I can't fight the trauma stalking my mind and seeping into my blood. My halo itself cowers and darkens from the damned energy here. Not even the destructive Angel of the Abyss can soothe my tremors as he strokes his warm, bronze fingers along my arms.

"W-why didn't you plead my case to the Tribunal?" I throw out the accusatory question, relying on the heated anger. For now, it pulses off my skin like crimson sparks, but it could easily grow.

Abaddon sighs behind me and lowers his head so he may meet my eyes. I still whenever I meet his—an eternity ring of pure golden light surrounds the irises and pupils with no distinction. It's like peering inside a black hole. His energy is no different since he snares me within his gaze each time while his words soothe me.

"I tried, Astraea. I learned of the sentence one day before they announced. I acted quickly. Please believe me. Trust me that I did what I thought was best."

He cups my chin, turning my face to his. Speechless, I crane my neck to him and pinch my eyes in annoyance, feeling my pulse thrumming quicker. Hands slow and purposeful, Abaddon shifts my body until the insides of his wings harbor my back. Facing him, my head barely surpasses his chest. Not once do his eyes stray lower. Sleeping in lingerie is nothing new for me…nor is meeting him in this state.

Thanks to centuries of entering the Unconsecrated Crater, of doing the soul-crushing work of Destruction, black shadow veins riddle his fortress of a body. Whole networks of them swarm his skin—ones I know cause him pain. Like the marks on my back.

His veins don't shift or swell whatsoever, unlike my aura colors. Destruction must always be cold and composed, reserving his energy until he's ready for battle. Wonder still fills me when I look at him. With his fathomless deep-set eyes, throne-high cheekbones, full and curved mouth, and bronze skin as radiant and resplendent as flaming swords in sunlight, Abaddon possesses the allure and rugged masculinity. And he bears the supreme force that earned him the respect of all the archangels. He can bring all races to their knees if he were to choose.

"So, you throw me to the greatest wolf in hell instead?" I spit out, referencing Lucifer.

Abaddon sighs, shaking his head. "I didn't throw you. As I recall, you were hellbent on proving yourself to the Tribunal."

"But you knew. You spoke to Lucifer," I protest, crossing my arms over my chest.

"It was a safety net of a precaution. My greatest hope was for you to escape and hide in Hell on Earth until we could appeal."

"We?"

He drags a hand through his neck-length dark curls, softer than silk, and offers a side smirk and a breathy chuckle. "Asmodel, Sariel, Uriel, Raphael, and all the others in the Hall of Warriors, they're all willing to testify, Astraea. Appeal your case to the high Seraph Tribunal. They even signed a petition in blood."

I gasp. When he manifests the scroll—one of many abilities within the soul plane, threads of bright pink astonishment escape my chest. My halo glows, pulsing swift beats as I take in the multitude of names, among them all the warrior archangels. Tears shimmer in my eyes from the flood of memories of my brothers kicking my ass in training, picking battles with me when I was most vulnerable. Of pranking me endlessly whenever we had free time. And now, they've signed a petition on my behalf. With their very blood.

"Abaddon…" I breathe and cover my mouth, but his wings are too strong for me to step back.

He vanishes the scroll, then kneads his brow, sighing deeply. "A few of them gave me messages. Sariel says, "if I'd known you were going to pull that stunt at the Gala, I'd have chained you to the strongest pillars in the Halls of Warriors". You know how Sariel is." I press my lips into a smile as images rush to the forefront of my older and extremely protective brother. "Raphael says, "If Lucifer hurts you in any way, he'll know what it's like to have hell to pay"." My smile grows at the thought of Raphael. My hardest physical challenger. The hothead of the pack. "Uriel says that whatever pearls of wisdom you may unearth in Hell on Earth may prove their weight in gold when you return to the Celestial City. Asmodel wishes me to remind you that while patience has never been your strong virtue, he pleads for you to channel him as much as possible until they may arrive."

"Arrive?" I lift my brows in a second astonishment.

Abaddon nods. "The four are forging routes, identifications, and disguises so they may enter the Circles. Wait for them, Astraea."

I rub my arms, dropping my head and shaking it, swallowing at the thought of my collar. "They can't, Abaddon. Even if they could make it to the Ninth Circle, it won't matter. Lucifer can find me whenever he wishes."

At first, he tilts his head to the side, studying me. I tremble when he lifts his fingers to cast away my abundant curls from eclipsing my throat. His snarl at the brand comes as no surprise. "Astraea, I didn't know he would…oh gods, what has he done to you? If he's touched you, I won't stop until I've destroyed Hell on Earth's shield protecting the Circles… even if it takes me a decade." He clenches both hands into fists that swarm with shadows.

I touch his chest and shake my head wildly. "No! The last time you two battled, it almost killed you. I'm fine. I'm holding my own." I bite my tongue hard. Self-loathing churns my stomach from the thought of where Lucifer's mouth was a short time ago, how I'd begged him for more, how he took my blood and how I'd agreed to it. "He won't do anything as long as he believes he can use me."

"Use you?" Abaddon lowers his brows, jaw clenching in suspicion.

I smirk at his protectiveness, then lean into him, welcoming his warmth. "Not like that. Oh, Abaddon, humans, young women, they're disappearing from the Vestibule districts. They're showing up…"

I gulp at the thought of the mutilated corpse but manage to describe the bodies and how Lucifer's enlisted me to track down the killer and the motives. Royal blue relief flows off me in long waves as I spill everything about Astaroth and him giving me the name Asmodeus. Finally, I open my palm to manifest the talon I discovered where the corpse was found. Eyes narrowed, Abaddon lowers his head to inspect

the talon but sighs heavily.

"Could it have come from the Crater?" I gesture to my left and wince, grateful his wing shields me from the sight.

"It may have. Beasts managed to escape while I made arrangements with Lucifer, then dealt with the Tribunal and their sentence. But I'll do what I can on my end. I've already caught their scent and planned to track them. Most go into the Wastelands. If I learn anything, I'll send information with our brothers."

Our brothers, right. But Abaddon is not my brother.

Pursing my lips, my emotions project in a woeful dark blue that weeps from my body like tears. "How is she, Abaddon?"

Shadows gather around his eyes, and his shoulders lower with the heaviness we share. "She misses you. Her message was simple: "Come home"."

I hang my head and hold my stomach, but the ache travels to the back of my throat and lodges there. She's never blamed me for what happened that night, but it doesn't matter. I'm still at fault.

"There are times I think you should have left me there, Abaddon. With all others."

A deep and low growl rumbles from Abaddon's throat, and he cups my face with both hands. "I'll never regret that day, Astraea. Yes, I could have taken you to the Tribunal and allowed them to place you. The Hall of Warriors is no place for a rejected angel. But when I saw you playing in the wind currents like a flying daredevil, I brought you home to us. Even if you barely passed your training, you were always this hungry scrapper. You pushed them to work harder, always nipping at their heels. It's why they've challenged you more than any others, why they've singled you out, Astraea. Our brothers love and hate when you give them a run for their wings," he sniggers.

"That makes no fucking sense." I roll my eyes.

"Language," he admonishes.

"I'd say since I'm the one trapped in Hell on Earth, I might as well curse as much as I can until I return to the paths of righteousness."

Abaddon chortles darkly. "Self-righteousness is more like it."

I stick out my tongue, but he grips me by the shoulders, pulling me in for an embrace. "I will begin tracking the Crater beasts immediately. But someone in Hell on Earth may be able to help you. The Diviner."

I shoot my head up. "Fuck, Abaddon! I've heard the rumors about her."

"Regardless of the high seraphs' judgment, she still has her gift. Or curse as they dubbed it. Go to her, Astraea. Pay her price. And she will tell you the identity of the talon's owner."

I heave a sigh, press my lips together, and nod. "Abaddon, I'm entering the Bride Trials." When he gives me a blank expression, I tell him about Lucifer's diversion, about Mira and my bargain with her. "I'm going to see them through to the end. I won't stop until I find a way out of this collar, and when Lucifer brings me to his bed, I won't stop until I've destroyed him."

THIRTY-THREE

THE DEMONS OF THE DEEP

—LUCIFER—

He wanted more.

As I make my way beyond the forge-pits and to the oubliette prisons below, I want more. But anything beyond the sampling I'd tasted would have overpowered me. She would have faced my monster, and she is not ready for such a thing. Nor will she or any other creature ever be ready.

Knowing I was the orchestrator of her pain, controlled it, and tasted her ethereal blood got my fucking dick so hard and fast, I'd come close to exploding several times. She'd believed she was in control, and I proved her wrong. Held her pain and pleasure in the palm of my hand. I love those gorgeous moans and trills as much as I love her pretty pink tits growing hard and swollen from my mouth and teeth. I love the scent of her fluids, how she'd shivered and bucked and trembled beneath my claws and tongue. And how exquisitely she unraveled to my every whim.

Astraea is nowhere close to the purest pussy I've ever licked.

I'd tasted her passion but also her darkness. She must never know what happens when I taste her blood—how I claim portions of her essence, her soul. Never before have I tasted the coldest ice to my hottest fire. Darkness and thunder to my flames and lightning. Never before has a mind worn such a mask, so I could not study the being beyond. And it's driving myself and my monster to madness.

All I know is something slumbers inside that veil and prowls her subconscious like the perfect predator choosing the right moment of when to strike. Something bred of an ancient power that calls to mine. She is a fool if she believes she can fuck with me and hide her true nature. I'll never set her free from Hell on Earth. If necessary, I'll fucking chain her to my bed with Diablo ore shackles, lust-hum her, and lick her until she crumbles and submits. I smirk at the mental image of her snapping her angel teeth, her sunset curls cascading across her gold skin in its naked glory, that siren trill. It all triggers my cock to throb and my balls to nearly burst every damn time.

I'll fuck her and drink her blood whenever I desire because she is the addiction that not even my monster can overcome. The little angel flew into the Devil's jaws to be devoured forever. I'll gods-damn destroy her, unleash whatever pretty thing lives inside her, then tie it down, mount it like the hidden bitch it is, and finally remake Astraea fucking Eternity into whatever I damn well desire.

My heavenly temptation and my ultimate fantasy.

She may burn like lightning at dawn, but her essence is the gray ghosts of winter shrouding the stars. She is the silence of the night, the final shivering whisper of time. And the immovable heart of stone. The angel who holds flaming tears behind her eyes.

I crave that sweet pussy gushing and ripe and begging for me to fuck her hard and raw until her core weeps with blood for me. The one being who could potentially take all my hellfire, my violence, my torture. The marks we'd leave upon our bodies would be our language.

She'd given me a piece of her past. I can already guess more from the sign of her tears. Now, I resolve to learn of her birth—hidden from her fucking files. No information whatsoever about who sired her, who birthed her, what species of angel she is, what star had forged her halo, or which region of the Celestial City was her birthplace. Nothing apart from Abaddon as her guardian, her trainer, her bond-keep.

To imagine that this little, golden-winged angel with her wanton pussy dripping its sweet nectar onto my tongue caused the Devil himself to lose control and explode without warning. The reason I left her so abruptly. As if I was reduced to that lilting cherub whose beauty made every seraph in heaven sing and bow before him. Such a naïve, idealistic boy, filled with dreams of glory and love, I'd taken so many angels to my bed during those years before I was cast out. And none ever fucking trilled to me the way Astraea does.

Thousands of them together were a mere note. She's a gods-damned orchestral and choral-backed symphony. The kind held at a sacred and crumbling temple where spirits of the dead gather to chant. And where every type of race unites dressed in white robes to fight and fuck and flagellate themselves. The kind who dance for hours until their blood floods the threshold of the altar.

At dusk, Astraea's golden goddess would rise from the fire and shadow to the clash of cymbals, the gnashing of teeth, and the rattling of bones to dispense her justice and punishment. And then, I'd seize her, bind her, rip her goddess dress and crown, strip her to nothing. I'd spread her and fuck her on the bloody altar before all, until she screamed my name, so all would know the true King of Hell.

I stem the walls of fire and magma—one of many security measures of my oubliettes. More thoughts plague me, but I shove them into the far corner of my mind, vowing vengeance and punishment against the little angel who made me ejaculate into my damn robe until I'd nearly lost control of the monster inside me. I can't wait to drive her to her breaking point, watch her shatter before me, and fall to her knees with a thrill burning in her eyes because she will know she's lost the battle and who has conquered her. Then, I will fuck the little beastie right out of her.

After resetting the walls to burn and flow behind me, I move through the labyrinthine halls filled with guardians: hellhounds, hellcats, gryphons—creatures bred and trained to answer my voice. Setting my jaw, I dismiss the creatures salivating for my attention and examine for any cracks or veins within the Diablo ore walls and floor—anything that may indicate a struggle or another presence. There's nothing, and I grind my teeth, knowing damn well this is the work of Asmodeus. Little silver Ever was right.

If I weren't so fucking incensed by him, I'd want to commend him. One night two years ago. He's still got this sweet, human woman wrapped around his finger. It's obvious why she's tracked him all this time. Oh, I recognize her hate, her hunger for vengeance, but her body's need and arousal overpowers them. Whatever he did to her that night, he left quite the mark on her. But with the flame in her eyes, I wonder if he will find himself marked first.

Finally, I arrive before the heart of the oubliette: a great domed cavernous expanse with a miles-deep drop-off filled with hundreds of translucent fire gem chambers suspended in midair. Proud of my machination, I posture, admiring the hell flames girding each prison shaped like a jagged egg. Each houses a demon. They spiral far into the depths, disappearing like tiny lanterns until they fade to pinpricks—distant stars within the furthest reaches of the oubliette.

Hardening my muscles, reinforcing my power, I summon Astaroth's chamber. Clear the others and growl at the sight of the prison cracked with crystals in crumbles on the inside. The thin channels of magma mixed with orc venom are designed to burrow into my demons. The combination paralyzes them and leaves them in a state of torture as close to death as possible without stopping their hearts. Several prisons are broken. Their contents long since spilled to disappear in the oubliette.

I hear the sound of frail breath, a wet cough followed by a gurgle. My signature is writ into each chamber. I know the identity and state of the demon. He is dying. Slow and torturous.

Bound to my blood and will, I lift my hand, weave my hellfire to the base of the chamber, and pull it toward me, spinning it until I look upon the being inside.

"Rosier," I snigger, raising my chin and eyeing the demon suffering within a pool of his blood.

Once a Dominion of the second order—a beautiful specimen of bronze skin, dark hair, black horns, and wings of deep royal purple to mirror his mesmerizing eyes—now Rosier is but a sniveling waste. Little wonder Asmodeus dealt him the slow death of a million cuts designed to drip blood, dragging out the torture. As a love demon tempting beings against purity, Asmodeus has always considered Rosier's existence an insult to the high Prince's mantle of lust awakening. The former seraph bastard managed to break the chamber but kept the magma channels intact. He's fed Rosier enough to keep him paralyzed but able to feel every cut and lost drop of blood.

"Tell me what I desire to know, and I'll end your misery," I demand through gritted teeth, pinning my eyes to the demon's. Life begins to fade from them. Asmodeus predicted when I would arrive.

"He is bringing the war to you, Lucifer," Rosier rasps, not wasting any time, his lids heavy as more blood drips from his wounds. "As the true King of Demons, Asmodeus sends the message that he and the Queen have united, and it's time for a new Lord of Hell. This is a glimpse of his power. He looks forward to greeting you soon."

Despite the icy wind of the oubliette crawling across me, it's not fear traveling up my spine. Amusement radiates an eager warmth into my body.

Asmodeus believes he may unite with the Queen of Demons to overthrow the rightful King of Hell? I snort at the hilarity. This is all but a game. Nor do I believe he has anything to do with the mutilated corpses, the missing humans. It's not Asmodeus' style. Not when he prefers to toy with humans as long as they draw breath.

One human, in particular, has captured his attention. And may prove to be his weakness.

I've already put a fallen angel to watch over Ever Hart. Track her, remain in the shadows, and with any luck, Ever Hart will lead me to Asmodeus. I won't show him any leniency as I did prior. Should've known he wouldn't stomach being the Queen of Demons' bitch forever. The demon's Northland vacation has finally ended. Even if he's a fucking master of disguises, if he's in Hell on Earth, no mask will hide him from me. At the very least, he will pop his head out for the Bride Trials. He won't have much time to keep that head.

When I return to the Ninth Circle, to the penthouse where I sift into my office, I discover Astraea has broken in and invaded my private space. With her flushed cheeks and wide eyes, she stands before my desk looking more like a panicky little cherub than a warrior angel. I roam my eyes across her body. My cock throbs from the plunging V-neck bustier that so lusciously tempts one's eye to her generous tits. Her high-waisted mini-skirt hugs those full hips, showing a gap of golden skin between it and the bustier base. The thigh-high stockings hint at the heaven hiding beneath that skirt. The open-cowled coat she wears does nothing to hide those dangerous curves. Inspiration strikes me thanks to the inner blue and royal galaxy fabric.

The monster inside me hums and growls, more eager than ever. She darts her eyes to each side, wondering if she may escape—she wouldn't make it three paces. I grin at her and raise my brows, advancing toward her.

This will be a perfect time for her punishment.

THIRTY-FOUR

HELL'S MARKET

—ASTRAEA—

I hope my stunned and fearful façade has fooled him. He can't know I already succeeded in what I came here to do. The ring is safe inside my cleavage.

Body heating from amused pride, I glance to the door to play up the ruse, fighting the mischievous grin longing to spread. I can't wait to see his expression when I show up at the first Bride Trial.

Lucifer advances toward me, blocking my path with his massive wings. "Try it, Astraea. You won't make it three feet, and your punishment will be more severe," he advises, but instead of closing in, he strokes his jaw and begins to circle me.

A sudden wave of ice overcoming me, I knit my brows together and ask darkly, "Punishment?"

At my side now, Lucifer spreads his lips into a far more mischievous smile than the one I could have donned. "You believe you could break into my office, invade my personal and protected space, and not receive a devil-worthy punishment?"

I swivel my head back to him, hissing, "Excuse you, asshole, I didn't break in. I snuck in. And barely even that." I sniff and cross my arms over my chest, snapping my wings tight to my back the moment he tries to stroke a finger along their length.

"How?"

"I may not be the best at snaking my way into places, but someone else is," I hint and tap the collar tattoo. At first, those familiar, glimmering black scales shift as he subtly pokes his head out. But as soon as Lucifer pins his eyes to the serpent, Sammy retreats.

"And there is the viper in my bosom," grumbles Lucifer with a sneer, arriving at my other side.

"Aww, come on, Sammy. I'll protect you." Sammy charges for the back of my neck, coiling himself around me until he resembles spiraling black jewelry along my throat. I rub two tender fingers along his back, feeling him ripple with that warm purr. "Honestly, Lucifer, you're the one who told me this was my all-access "sticker"," I remind him.

"Not to my private spaces," he growls, and Sammy cuddles close to my neck and hides beneath my hair.

Holding each of my elbows, I stick my nose up at him. "You should follow your advice then: Devil's in the details after all."

"Samael never would have made such a risk."

"Remember the old saying "you catch more flies with honey"?" When Lucifer gives me a blank look, I swipe my finger down to Sammy's tail. He coils it around my finger and pops out from my hair on the other side of my neck to hiss at Lucifer.

"You never gave me squab. Not ever." The serpent sticks his tongue out again and burrows back into my hair.

Lucifer bares his teeth. "If a few pigeons is your twenty pieces of silver, Samael, I should've made good on my threat, peeled off your skin, and turned you into a purse long ago." While I soothe the quivering reptile, Lucifer clenches his jaw and barks at me, "Tell me what you were doing in my offices, Astraea."

My answer perfectly rehearsed in advance, I posture and wave a hand dismissively. "I wanted to read my file."

"Why?"

I glimpse his hand balled into a fist and resist the urge to roll my eyes when he circles me again, mouth turned down and wary. "Do I need a reason beyond curiosity?"

A low snarl builds in his throat. "You wanted to confirm the trial outcome, didn't you?" I stiffen, fear prickling the back of my neck, but Lucifer continues while fingering a curl of my hair. "I offered you the chance to view the Tribunal's sentence, little angel. All you had to do was ask."

I exhale a small sigh, hoping he doesn't notice my relief that he'd referenced a different trial. "I also needed to address something with you," I divert instead, angling my neck back at him, straining against Sammy's tightening body. Ugh, the term "cowardly snake" was never more understated.

"Go on."

Once Lucifer folds his hands behind his back, I set my hands on my hips. "I know someone who may be able to help us with the missing humans…and the corpses. Unless you learned anything in your absence?"

He shakes his head. "Confirmation of the name Astaroth gave you."

"The name I earned in blood," I correct with a proud simper.

With a low growl, he retorts, "Asmodeus is the last one who would be responsible for human deaths. Nor does he need to abduct human women to do his bidding."

"Hmm…does the Devil have competition in the lust arena?"

Knowing smirk growing, Lucifer seizes my waist, and lust hums deeply in my ear until my body turns to liquid, knees buckling. "Would you care to test the theory, little angel?" His eyes descend to my breasts.

Before he can do it again and reduce me to a puddle on the floor, I shake my head wildly, gather my wits, and shove him away, snarling, "We need to go to the Black Market. The Diviner lives there, and she should be able to explain the marks on the bodies. And where the women have been taken. And what this might be." I frown and dig into my coat pocket to retrieve the talon, presenting it to him. "I found it at the station."

Lucifer stiffens, snatches up the talon, and examines it, narrowing his eyes. "And when were you planning to tell me about this, little angel?"

"I'm telling you now."

When Lucifer strokes his jaw again, I cross my arms, irritated. If he recognizes the talon, he doesn't let on, expression stoic until a hint of that knowing smirk returns.

"The Diviner, hmm. I will make you a deal, Astraea. Despite how you did not share this potentially significant information with me when I am the King of Hell, in the interest of punctuality, I will delay your punishment."

"In exchange for…?"

He lowers his head toward me, wings pulsing and casting shadows along my face. His eyes dilate, glimmering with rouge lust as he taps my nose to say, "For you submitting to whatever punishment I deem necessary whenever I deem necessary."

Something coils tight in my chest, warring against the flutters in my belly and the heat between my thighs—compliments of my psycho.

"More than happy to bend you over my desk now and learn if you are wearing panties underneath that taut-fitting skirt," he opts, eyes lowering to my mini skirt.

All the blood drains from my face from the implication. I have to scold the inner voice that wonders what he would do after he's satisfied his curiosity. Instead, I clear my throat, knowing I'm taking a risk because Lucifer could consider a thousand more creative punishments in the time it takes us to meet with the Diviner. But the last thing I'll do is let him get the upper hand now.

Instead, I extend mine. "You've got yourself a delayed punishment deal."

He doesn't shake my hand. My mouth drops open as he gathers my hand in his, lifts it to his lips, and rubs them across my knuckles. With his warm flames curling across the curves of my body, I almost don't care what the punishment is. Almost.

"Isn't it ironic for Hell on Earth to have a Black Market?" I wonder as Lucifer guides me down the decrepit stone staircase. On each side, enormous stone pillars stretch to the cavernous ceiling. "How can anything be worse than um…hell?"

Lucifer sniggers and lights a hand at the small of my back. "I allow for more unethical and nefarious enterprises in the interest of luring certain clientele to my domain while stimulating economic growth."

I blink, then throw him a look. Before I can ask anything more, we reach the end of the staircase that leads to a stone walkway into a tunnel. Multiple dark figures emerge from the tunnel, holding scythes. I recognize the race immediately: minotaurs. They growl low, ghostly breath puffing from their nostrils. Brands cover their naked, musclebound chests and roam along their arms.

Instinctively, I push my claws through my fingertips while shoving my angel teeth through my gums. I don't get the chance to beat my wings. Instead, Lucifer grips my left arm and turns to shake his head, brows threaded in a low warning. Once the minotaurs advance toward us, Lucifer lifts his wrist to reveal his gem-plant. They immediately part before him, bidding us entry into the tunnel.

"Surprised you had to show them anything, oh great King of Hell," I say inside the tunnel.

"You forget one of my other titles: Prince of Lies. Let's say it's not merely a figurative term."

"So, you're in disguise?"

He winks. "To all except for you, sweetheart."

"Why the charade?"

"I prefer to maintain a low profile." He folds his hands behind his back casually. "It affords me discretion so I may inspect more anonymously in case anything goes beyond nefarious or unethical."

Uncertain of what to expect, I place a thin amount of trust in Lucifer. I imagine one can't sift, or he'd have done it already. Silence fills the spaces between us, finding every nook and cranny of the tunnel. I hug my arms as we progress, my blood chilling from the shades taking various forms along the walls. Not simply shadows. Another security measure, the specters mean one thing: this tunnel and surrounding areas were once catacombs.

Feeling eyes on me, I catch Lucifer out of the corner of my eye, inspecting me far more than the tunnel. Giving into the anxiety, I start picking at my nails again but stop when warmth spreads along my wings. I swivel my head, straining my neck to where Lucifer's flames caress all my feathers. I'm about to open my mouth in protest, but once the flames latch onto the gold, I gasp. Prisms erupt within the tunnel, dancing along the walls and causing the specters to scatter from the light. I can't help myself. Heat rising to my cheeks, I do a twirl, thrilling in the sight of the spinning prisms.

My laughter echoes throughout the tunnel. "I'm a mirror ball!"

Lucifer shakes his head with a chuckle, then touches the small of my back again. "Wrecking ball would be more accurate. Oh, and Astraea, you were nearly right about the irony. No one calls it the Black Market." He winks again.

I think it may be the first genuine smile I feel for him.

The Market is nothing like a normal market. No, it's more of a hive—if a hive is enclosed within a domed cavern the size of a small mountain. It takes my breath away. All sorts of races mull about the lower levels where vendors bellow and growl for attention, selling everything: scales, talons, armor pilfered from high demons, lavaleaf grown from the pits of hell and famed for being the spiciest flavor in all Gemterra, baby dragon eggs but the dragons that wouldn't grow larger than dog-sized, maps of secret routes to the elite citizen homes in Hell on Earth, tickets for famous daemon meetings, and I eventually lose track.

We pass one of the large hive combs as I call them, where I pause. Dozens of cheers resound from a pit fight between a demon and a fae.

"Give him the horns!" My voice is swallowed by all the other cheers. Lucifer rolls his eyes and drags me away while the fae body slams the demon. I dig my heels in, leaning back to catch one more glimpse, grinning and pulse racing when the demon shoots up, horns stabbing the fae in the midsection like he's a shish kabob. Make that a pix kabob.

My skin crawls from a reaper demon advertising executions. Sweat breaks out on my hands while my wing muscles harden, but Lucifer takes my elbow, steering me away. "Lower-level reaper, Astraea. The executions never stick, and the soul always travels back to where it came from," he explains.

My mouth dries, but I nod, taking him at his word because I don't want to imagine anything else. Several vendors sell rows of exotic caged animals like chimeras, hellpups, imps, firebirds, and even mini-hydras. Remorse twinges inside me at the sight of the caged creatures. As incredible as it would be to take a hydra home as a pet, I can't help but feel for the animals. Freedom is what I crave most. I shiver at the thought of my worst fear: of bars locking me down. Wings should never be caged.

Lucifer leads me to the far end of one of the upper hive levels and to a dark, long alleyway where a row of small houses rest with large, arched gaps in the stone—windows but with no glass and doorways with no doors. Confused, I taper my brows, tensing as he urges me into the far left house and dips his head to murmur close to my ear, "I hope you enjoy the tour, Astraea."

Only once we enter do I understand what he means. Emerging into the open space, I tuck my wings closer than ever to my back, tightening my feathers. Hooked all along the walls and erected in massive glass jars like organic trophies are numerous pairs of wings. Casual as insect parts. My breath seizes in my chest, and I fall back against Lucifer, who grips my hips to steady me.

Because every set of wings is moving.

THIRTY-FIVE

THE DIVINER

—ASTRAEA—

The first thing I want to do is fly like a bat out of hell out of here.

All Lucifer does is lower his wings, relaxed, before cupping my shoulders and breathing through my curls, "Steady, sweetheart."

Fear shoots through me, turning my nerves raw. I take a few deep breaths, internally ridiculing myself when I've been in far worse situations than this. I curve my fingers to the anchor of my collar tattoo, giving Sammy a half-smile when he nudges my fingers with his soft scales. My smile grows when he slithers his tongue along my fingertips in small, encouraging kisses.

A figure emerges from the adjoining room garbed in a form-fitting gown the color of pure gold—so bright, it reminds me of winter sunlight streaming upon the Celestial Mountain pools. A contrast to her skin as dark as a mourning shroud, black and sacred as tranquil midnight. Hundreds of tiny braids spiral down her back, decorated in gold thread coiling through their expanse.

Statuesque, taller than me but not as tall as Lucifer, she moves with a supernatural grace beyond any race I've witnessed, whether fae, vampires, or witches. Not even archangels carry themselves with as much fluid serenity as she does. When she turns to the wall, back to us, I gasp from the scars. Knees weakening, adrenaline spiking, and flesh crawling, I part my lips, awed by the six scars. In the center of her back, three eternal wounds descend in a precise curve on the right and three on the left, forming a near-circle of mutilated flesh. They have one meaning.

"It's rude to stare, Astraea," the former angel, the former seraph, chastises in a dark, smoky voice without turning. Immediately, I bow my head in shame, but she taps her chin and selects a pair of wings from a wall hook. White and feathered, hundreds of black pearls adorn the edges and tips of the wings. Stunned, I drop my jaw as she binds two ribbons tight to loop around her shoulders and underarms.

The Diviner wears wings.

Once she turns, the Diviner wrinkles her nose and advances to me. "Don't give me that haughty expression, little goldy."

I balk and lower my head once more because she deserves it. Because propriety demands it even if she is wingless and no longer bears a halo. That is obvious from her skin bereft of any scintillation that would prove an inner, celestial luster. When I muster the courage to peer up again, the Diviner is staring down at me. Or at least what I believe was staring until I notice her orbs are milky and white as a spirit.

Huffing, the Diviner crosses her arms over her chest and tosses a stray braid over her shoulder. "Oh, come now, Astraea, I know I may be the first seraph you've ever seen and a wingless one. But surely, dear Abaddon shared…oh!"

Her brows lift, and I shift my weight and rub my arm, uncertain if I'm more uncomfortable by my lack of knowledge of the Diviner or how she referred to Abaddon as dear.

"Well, if that's your primary concern—" she scoffs and waves a hand. Panic bolts through me until she sniffs and gestures to the wings on the walls. "For your edification, little Miss. High and Mighty, most of these were gifts. Others were conjured, others were designed. All serve as a method of payment. After all, I didn't stab my eyes out, suffer the razing of my wings, and get cast out of heaven to do all this for free."

I open my mouth to apologize and to ask a follow-up question, but she turns on me and snarls, "Well! You are the outspoken sort, aren't you? No, I won't ask for your wings as payment. Honestly, Lucifer, didn't you tell her anything?" she snaps.

"You should know, Divyna, I always love watching you make your introduction…and your triumphant impression on first-timers." I hear the smile in his voice and turn to raise a brow at him. He winks, offering me that knowing smirk and a familiar glint in his eye, prompting me to shake my head in disbelief and heave a sigh.

"Humph," Divyna mocks him and waves a hand to the adjoining room. "That damnable charm was my first downfall all those decades ago. Rest assured, I won't make another mistake." She stops in the entryway to the next room, so abrupt, we nearly collide. "If that was a mistake, sign me up for outright sins!" she voices, the tone and pitch changed from the deep smoke to a lighter chirp.

When she spins on a heel, I drop my jaw, mouth slack from how her eyes have transformed into a fiery haze. No less blind, but the sunrise orbs confess a vast change. So do the veins glimmering to her skin's surface. Her eyes roll to the ceilings as more veins emerge, mirroring the same color as her eyes.

Cautious, I approach, tilting my head to the side, wing edges curling to mimic how I lift my fingers to her. Lucifer remains behind me. His warmth and those flames lurk nearby, but he doesn't interrupt. I get the sense I'm on the receiving end of a joke he and Divyna are playing. I turn back to her.

"Boo!"

Startled from her outburst and the sparks erupting from Divyna's chest, I leap back, colliding with Lucifer's chest. He throws his head back and laughs, deep and heated, and for once, I find myself smiling up at him. This playful side of Lucifer doesn't include sexual implications, mockery, or secret-keeping what I should damn well know. I shiver from the strange warmth pulsing through me to raise the hairs on my arms. For a half second, he meets my eyes with one brow lifted in knowing curiosity, but I spin around to face the Diviner again, preventing myself from lingering.

Her veins undulate like ribbons of liquid flame as she addresses me, "Don't you mind, Divyna, dear star. She was born with her halo shoved up her ass."

I beam at the Diviner, narrow my eyes, and wonder, "And who are you?"

She peers over my shoulder. "Didn't tell her?"

Behind me, Lucifer shrugs. "More fun this way."

"It's nice to see you smile again, old friend. A true smile I haven't seen the likes of since…" she trails off, but when she simpers, her eyes turning heavy with lust, I know exactly what she's implying.

Swinging half around with my chest tightening, I knit my brows together and huff, "Is there anyone in Hell on Earth you haven't fucked?"

He grins. "You."

I guess I deserved that. I try to hide my smirk and burning cheeks. When the Diviner loops her arm through mine, I startle from those feathered wings brushing my gold ones. "Come along, Astraea."

She leads me into the adjoining room where more wings coddle the shelves. However, this one hosts ledges with lanterns, crystals swinging from dangling ropes hooked to the ceiling, incense burning from organic holders, floor couches, and a marble altar nestled near the fireplace. The swinging crystals catch the lantern light to flicker prisms along the walls and floor. I take a deep breath, inhaling the scent of sage, finding it ironic as it's a demon repellant.

On the altar, various colored crystals form a circle with a five-pointed star in the center, alternating with dried flowers and herbs. Within the spaces of the star itself are little bones with tiny runes inked in swirling patterns. The energy, the magic of this place, prickles the hairs all over my body. Tingles tease goosebumps upon my skin as I take in the rest of the altar. A flint rests on one corner, a bowl of what appears to be salt crystals on the opposite corner, a feather upon the bottom right corner, and a stone chalice filled with wine on the final corner. Every element represented.

What the hell is she?

"To answer your question," interrupts the Diviner, patting the back of my hand while Lucifer trails us, "I am the witch demon of our dynamic duo. Divyna is the seraph—well, fallen seraph, but don't say it to her face. When we were born, our mother gave me the birthname Delia Gravemore, but our father chose Divyna. I prefer the name Del or Graves if you must. Since we share this body for survival, I put up with

Divyna's need for adornments to remind her of her feminine seraph glory while she endures my more masculine identity."

"Oh!" I smile, nodding. So, not a "she" after all. "I take it your mother is half-demon and half-witch," I hint and squeeze his hand, knowing he can hear my thoughts. Or at least predict them.

Del inclines his head to the Devil, who reclines upon a long, black floor couch, kicking his legs onto its expanse and folding his hands behind his head. "I like this one, Luci. You bring her back anytime. She's adorable." He squeezes my hand and motions to the opposite couch. At first, I dart my eyes between the couches, pausing. Del drags me back with him until I'm sidling against him. "I appreciate your respect, my dear. From birth, we'd shifted between worlds, races, languages, and histories. And when our gift came along, it became too overwhelming for one mind. So, it compensated."

I beam at Del and gesture. "With you."

He nods. "Yes. But the seraphs forced Divy to choose. Rather than lose her wings, she remained in the Celestial City. She kept me a secret for many years and protected me until she couldn't do it any longer. Or put up with those infernal, idiosyncratic seraphs using her. She gouged out her eyes—a shameful sin for any seraph who must hold to the standards beyond perfection. She did it for me. They took her wings and cast her out."

Chewing on my inner cheek, I debate before my tongue runs away with me. "Was it worth it?"

Del's features shift. The gleaming veins fade while his shoulders and limbs tense and posture. Divyna. "To sacrifice one part of my identity to preserve a greater part was the hardest sacrifice I've ever had to make. But I love Del more than I loved my wings. Yes, he is worth it. Our love is worth it every day. And I collect the wings and wear them to remind myself he is always worth it. If the day comes when you are faced with such a choice, Astraea, I know you will have the strength to choose the right one. As I did."

I purse my lips, anxiety tempting me to pick at my nails, but I restrain myself. Divyna's features shift once again while the burning veins return.

"Now, give me your hands," insists Del, waving to me. "I've waited all day for you."

I don't bother asking how he knows, how they know. Instead, I fold my palms into Del's, stilling and holding my breath as he closes his eyes, presses his full lips together, and concentrates. After a few moments, Del opens those sightless eyes and chuckles darkly. "Did you truly believe that's how this works, Astraea?"

"I—" My mouth dries, and I feel my cheeks and back of my neck grow even hotter as Lucifer joins Del, then swings his legs onto the floor to face us.

Before I may protest, Del's features change again. The smile twists to a disapproving frown followed by nostrils flaring and the original voice ridiculing, "Enough with the games, Del," Divyna scolds her other identity, though her head faces me. "You've had your fun. Get down to business already. I've also been waiting all day."

Del heaves a sigh but nods, then jerks his head to Lucifer. "Payment always comes first, sweet star."

Tapering my brows, I peer up at Lucifer, who approaches and extends his hand to mine. "What payment?"

Neither of them responds. A tight knot forms in my stomach along with a dry lump in my throat as they lead me to the altar. I lick my lips, studying Del as he takes the stone chalice with the wine and urges it to

Lucifer first. I part my lips, startled when he releases his demon teeth and uses them to slice into his hand, shedding blood droplets into the chalice to mix with the wine.

"Blood or flesh, Astraea," explains Del, collecting the remaining trickle of the Devil's blood.

Apprehensive, I hesitate before offering my blood. "What will you do with it?" When he blinks, I wince and rephrase, "I mean, will you tell me what I came here to learn or other things?" I shudder at the thought of my life spread out like a scroll. Secrets and sins I've buried more than six feet deep in the tomb of my soul. Ones I don't want Lucifer to know or to hear, not when he bears the ultimate responsibility for those sins.

"There is one way to find out," responds Del, offering me the chalice.

My hand trembles as I raise it to my mouth and use my angel teeth to slash a shallow wound. It doesn't stop as I turn it over, palm down, and spill my blood into the chalice. I nearly jump when Del seizes it from my hands, tips it back into his mouth, and swallows every last drop.

THIRTY-SIX

THE DEVIL'S DRUG

—ASTRAEA—

"Seriously, why blood? Why not a fluffy teddy bear? Or a baby dragon!" I opt with a thrill.

Divyna's typical pinched expression returns, and she glowers with blood still dripping from her lips. "It's always blood. What would I do with a teddy bear?"

Incredulous, I raise my brows, jaw dropping. Out of the corner of my eye, I catch Lucifer smirking with a breathy laugh through his nostrils. Before I may retort, Divyna shoots her head back, startling me. Without shifting her gaze back to us, she lowers her fingers to the little bones upon the altar and begins to move them, arranging them like chaotic pieces of a puzzle.

One she alone understands. Something twists in my stomach. My halo burns in my chest.

Finally, Divyna lowers her head, those hollow eyes impossibly beholding me. "Mist and starlight wield the weapons of flame and shadow. The way of the marks is veiled." Her voice dips impossibly low. Wind and darkness snuff the lanterns and candle flames within the room until my halo and Lucifer's eyes are the only light. Bone-deep chills slaughter my body. Those sightless eyes do not depart from mine, and the Diviner's dark energy ripples across my skin, breeding gooseflesh everywhere. My lungs constrict, and something strange thunders in my chest. I know it's not my halo.

"Only the monster in your heart may destroy the monster responsible for the missing ones. Your worlds are fated to collide," she expresses, turning to Lucifer. And back to me as panic courses up my spine. "But only you decide what parts of you will be burned. You were both forged in blood and darkness, and through darkness and blood, will you unite. An eye for an eye. Teeth will cut teeth."

A storm crashes into me, and my hands shake from the otherworldly power. Power that comes from the unconquerable recesses of the deep—the Unconsecrated Crater responsible for the creation of all demons. The power and magic of the gravity of the earth and its elements circulate within her blood. Her final power is the cosmic force of dark matter and clusters of galaxies that gave birth to the first seraphs. A monstrous and indomitable three-way combination.

Now, I understand why she and Del live within these under-realms of death surrounded by caverns without number. The energy of this natural realm and the sacred ground of death are the spirit forces that subdue their power. Even Lucifer lowers his head, respecting their dominion, though his ruling and power are superior.

"The betrayed will become the betrayer," Divyna announces to us both until she turns her eyes upon Lucifer. "War will come from all sides. And the Destroyer…" she pauses, tipping her head back again.

Fear paralyzes me. I feel Lucifer's eyes upon me. His hellfire surrounds my body and travels in slow, warm caresses, but it doesn't matter. All of me has turned to ice in the wake of her words, knowing she's speaking of Abaddon. The one who has shared my pain as I have shared his. An unbreakable bond from that moment he'd spared me from his sword, his duty.

"The Destroyer will meet his death."

Lucifer catches me in mid-lunge, having predicted my attack. Claws extended, I scream and thrash, snarling and snapping my teeth at the Diviner. The Devil wraps a hand around my throat while the other fists into my hair, dragging me back to his chest.

"Fuck, Astraea," he whispers harshly in my ear, jerking on my hair when I buck.

But I can't control it. My body has gone from ice to an inferno. Beyond the psycho, it's like a beast has been unleashed within me. It smolders a path through my veins, leaving nothing but ash and ruin in its wake. My body convulses. My breaths turn to frenzied gasps while blood hammers in my ears, deafening everything. What the fuck is happening to me?

Lucifer cups one side of my face, brows furrowed in concern. "Astraea, fucking breathe!"

I barely hear him. I gulp, but the convulsions return. Doubling over, stomach triple-somersaulting, I feel all the color drain my face as that ash and ruin battles to escape. He pulls my hair back, twisting as I open my mouth and retch hot black liquid that burns the very floor. His hold loosens.

Without facing them, I wipe my mouth and tear out of the house until the bitter cavern air strikes my face, freeing my breath beyond that dark matter, that seraph-demon-witch triune power threatening to unravel me.

My feathers flare, sensing a presence behind me. As soon as the familiar hand touches my back, I swing around with a desperate hiss. "Don't fucking touch me!"

Lucifer steps back, hands raised in the air, wings spreading, muscles tight in readiness. "What do you hate most, Astraea? How she called you a monster, or indicated you have a heart? How we are fated to crash and burn together? Or that your precious archangel is bound for death? Hmm…too many choices, I'll wager."

"Fuck you!" I snarl and lash at him, my claws slashing at his chest, finding their mark. Lucifer jerks back, growling as he peers down at the three angry stripes dripping blood.

"Little angel…" he stalks toward me, predatory eyes pinning mine, vowing a deadly battle.

Before he can close the distance, I flare my wings out and beat them into a rabid flight. In less than a moment, I hear the pulsing of his wings in close pursuit. His hell flames encroach, his body heat lurking closer to my wings, to my back, curling a sinister warmth up my spine until a sheen of sweat coats my whole body.

Driving myself harder, I fly past the pit fight, past the reapers, past countless market vendors, until I arrive at the cage district, where I freeze in mid-flight. An instant later, Lucifer collides with me, the inertia of his wings so great, they steal the breath from my lungs. I almost crumble to my knees, but the Devil seizes my hips, claws burrowing in as he raises me and wrenches me back. My wings crash against his chest. His feathers caress my shoulders. An attempt to soothe as if he's concerned about what I will do. He should be.

Tears threaten my vision at the cages before me. I barely feel his hands on me, his fingers shifting aside my hair so he may lust-hum in my ear, hoping to calm me. The fervent heat nourishing my body, pooling to my pussy does nothing compared to the captives. The slaves in the cages smite all my senses. It shouldn't be possible. I'm too weak from everything. Between the adrenaline rush of getting caught in Lucifer's office to these hours in the Market, everything that happened with the Diviner, and even this charged flight, I shouldn't have any strength left.

Onlookers gather to watch their King as he holds the mysterious gold-winged angel. But I don't care. A raw ache racks my chest from the woeful eyes of the daemons and the humans locked in cages—all young men or women young and fit for consumption or hard labor. I read the pain in their eyes and the defeat in their shoulders. An angry heat swells inside me from the vendors barking at them until they cower in submission or present themselves to the viewers.

I ball my hands into fists. No amount of lust-humming will overthrow me now. I feel the shrill trill inside me riding the shot of adrenaline rearing up. Out for blood, I set my jaw, lift my chin, and grit my teeth. My whole body trembles.

Before I may thrust my wings out and charge forward, Lucifer tightens his grip and sifts through time and space, carrying me with him. The Market fades into particles, replaced with the swirling environment of my room within his castle where he dumps me to the floor. Knees still shaking, I unleash that trill, louder than ever. Strong enough to shatter every mirror and window in the room. Strong enough to cause the Devil incarnate himself to double over, gripping his head from the severe pain.

My body goes haywire, limbs shuddering and bones rattling from the wrath coursing through me. Growling, Lucifer rears up and opens his mouth in a deep, vibrating, and thunderous purr to conquer my trill.

My legs go weak, and I fall at his feet as he leers over me, his dominance on irresistible display. My chest heaves in full-bodied gasps from the force of his power slaughtering me. Hellfire surrounds me, encases me like I'm no more than a bug for him to fucking burn. A moth with no choice but to pursue his flame.

It comes in waves and ripples through me until my nipples pebble beyond the black bustier. My legs part, straining against the fabric of my mini skirt that bunches up until it reveals my soaked panties.

Shadow of his mighty wings assaulting me, Lucifer towers over me, grinning down at my submissive state. I shake my head violently, rebelling against the heat spiraling through me, against my body's need from that lascivious power. Why should I be surprised? He has centuries on me. I'm a fool to believe I can conquer the Devil. This is not a battle I can win by sheer force or speed. Only cunning will overcome him. Mind fuck him until I can kill him as he's mind fucked me.

So, I don't protest when he kneels before me with a sinister smile, tosses my curls over my shoulders, and pinches my aching nipple through the bustier. Instead, I arch and thrust my chest to him, determined to reap what pleasure I can in these moments.

Strong jaw set, he gazes back at me while moving my skirt up to expose my naked thighs and my weeping pussy—transparent through the drenched panties. I spread more for him. I moan and shift my body while bringing my knees up and outward, feet flat on the floor to grant him more access.

Suspicion in his narrowed eyes, Lucifer tilts his neck to the side, studying me, studying my need right before he rips the panties from my body and thrusts two fingers deep into my core.

"Oh!" I clench greedily around those fingers, dipping my head back until my curls skirt the floor until I'm rocking against his hand. He purrs his approval.

"So fucking wet, sweetheart," he snarls low against my ear. "A couple of deep lust-hums from my demon is all it takes to tame that little beast inside you, hmm?" He lowers his mouth to my breast and bites the nipple through the fabric while injecting another finger, digging in deep.

I rock more, trembling, shift from side to side. He stays latched on, tugging the erect nipple to my motion. I moan in open mockery, "Oh, yes, Lucifer. You've tamed this she-devil of an angel. Use me, fuck me now!"

"Trust me, Astraea, there is nothing I'd rather do than push into your needy, wet cunt and force my way into that tight channel. Your angelic pussy would milk me and suck me so fucking perfect, wouldn't it? I'd love stretching you so full until you've memorized the shape of my cock and long and beg for no other, knowing no other could fill you as I do. All it would take is once, angel…" he hints, adding a fourth finger and causing me to buck and hiss. "I'd fucking wreck you as I desire. Put my Devil mark on you. You'd crave me."

When he doesn't move, I drive myself deeper, desperate for friction. "And then, I'd be the fucking fantasy. Nothing but a pleasure thrall for your demonic service. Oh, my Lord, Lucifer Morningstar. Oh, great ruler of Hell on Earth, sovereign of all races, most generous and lustful of lovers, please take me now! Chain me to your bed. And use me as you will!"

He growls from my taunt and jerks my bustier down to truss up my breasts in a monstrous attempt. I recognize the desperation in his hot mouth as he tongues my pebbled nipple and resumes closing his teeth around it. I jolt from sheer pleasure. Again, he lust-hums. Moisture pools from my center. And with a powerful motion, I thrust my whole body upward, my full breast pushing into his mouth while my cunt clenches tight around his fingers as I take my pleasure.

He snarls from the orgasm I've stolen from him. Jerks his fingers out, but it's too late. I scream. I laugh and fall to my side, shivering from the pleasure tingling all my nerves. Nothing like that night on the balcony. Nothing like the impending climax charged with pain and pleasure endorphins in the hell pits with the magma geysers shooting in the background. But it might as well be both.

As he rises, moving away from me in incensed defeat, I jerk my bustier up and my miniskirt down, cover myself with the long coat, and whisper huskily, "I fucking hate you. I hate you for everything. I hate you for the slaves in the Market. I hate you for what you did to Abaddon. I hate you for the Unconsecrated Crater and the billions of lives ruined because of you." I don't stop even when he crouches, growling and gripping my hair to force my head back, my neck exposed to his teeth. "I fucking hate you for shackling me here."

"You hate me for what I do to you." He cups my mound, the heated stare of his eyes meeting mine. His power ripples across me, triggering a fresh surge of arousal. "That an angel wants the Devil."

"And you hate that you can't use me as you've used all others. You hate that you crave me as much as I crave you. More! Because while you're the gods-damned Devil with centuries of experience—the scripter of pain and pleasure, you said?—the mother-fucking King of Hell himself, what am I? A low-ranking, rejected, fucking failure of a little angel. And that drives you wild and mad, doesn't it, demon?" Fury wreathes his eyes. His hell flames crawl up and down my body, singing the edges of my clothes. But adrenaline shoots up my spine, and I continue, unhindered.

"More than anything, you hate that all you can use is my body and nothing else. You hate that you could fuck my pretty pussy, but it would be nothing more than poison to you. You hate that you can't get past my walls to what you want most. I've imprisoned you as much as you have me. No, more. I'm a fucking addiction." I laugh maniacally. "The Devil has a drug. And it's me!" I snort laughter like a crackhead on a high.

Eyes burning against mine, Lucifer grips my hair harder, brandishes his fangs, leans down, and sinks his teeth into my throat to draw my blood.

THIRTY-SEVEN

PLOTTING REVENGE

—ASTRAEA—

I whimper, quaking, but I rise to the occasion. I spread my fucking legs and arch, so he may lap up my blood. So he may drink me. I moan unashamedly as he takes his fill of me and roams his other hand up and down my body to memorize my curves. I'm proving him wrong with every sip.

He's fucking lost this battle, and he knows it.

"Someday soon, Astraea," he whispers fire and ice in my ear in a deep and low vow, "I will fuck you so hard, and you will scream my name to your heavens and beg me for mercy. And when that day comes, I'll give you none."

With one last trill, I swipe my claws across his face and grin when he leaps back, growling at me. "Look at that! I can draw blood, too, demon."

He shoves me to the floor and storms out in a Devil-sized temper tantrum, leaving me shuddering and grinning like a wild woman.

As soon as Lucifer departs, Camio enters. And Sammy eases out from the collar. No doubt, both of them were disturbed by the noise.

I feel Sammy's rough, forked tongue on the wound, licking it, sealing it closed. Smiling fondly at the snake, I soften the tension in my body and nudge two fingers under his chin. "I hate the collar, Sammy. But I could never hate you."

He warbles in that adorable serpent way and coils gently around my neck, draping his head across my left shoulder, his favorite perch.

"You okay, doll?" Camio asks, extending a hand to me, but he's not offended when I stand on my own and straighten my skirt.

I shrug and tug my curls into a mussy bun. "As good as I can be. Damn Devil dick prick." I seethe, jerking my chin to the door. "Fucking slaves…" I trail off as Sammy flicks my earlobe with his tongue.

"Lucccifer hasss hisss reasssons."

I curl my upper lip in disgust. "Yeah. He's the Devil." Complete with horns, tail, and fucking pitchfork. He needs no other reason, no justification. Nor would I allow him any. He's fucked with me at every turn, luring me into his world, charming me with his deceit, seducing me with every lust-hum from his throat.

Now, it's my turn.

Finished with my bun, I turn to Camio and nod. "I'm going to get out of this hell, Cam. I'm not going to stop until I get my revenge. I'll throw him to the Tribunal and buy myself the biggest Get-Out-of-Jail-Free card the world has ever known. And when they put his ass on trial, the world will know that a rejected angel fucked over the Devil.

"Tomorrow, the Bride Trials will begin. I've paid my price in blood. Lucifer won't know what hit him." Proud heat radiates within my chest, and my halo glows, eager to bring the Devil to his knees.

Camio shoves his hands in his pockets and tilts his head to the side, sweet eyes warming. "What can I do?"

I grin.

——LUCIFER——

I need to hurt her.

Every word from those pretty, perfect lips was fucking true. She'd ripped me apart. She'd shoved her fucking claws right through my chest, closed them around my heart, and squeezed until she felt the blood of her hatred dripping down her arm. She'd have tasted it if she could. All a lie. A lie she tells herself to avoid the demons and sins within her scarred soul. Perhaps more scarred than mine.

She's sucked the poison of heaven for decades. A bitter taste produced from heaven's grandest deception. I've got nothing on those damned seraphs.

Deep inside me, the monster rears up, roaring and burning me from the inside. We've tested her all this time. I've pitted myself, the demon inside me, against whatever power simmers inside her. Saw a glimpse of it earlier after she'd escaped the Diviner. That hot black liquid she'd retched. She spits it out or swallows it. Represses the beast with a strength I don't possess. My Unconsecrated monster craved her monster more than ever. Forged in darkness and blood as the Diviner revealed.

An eye for an eye. Teeth will cut teeth. She may have cut me first. I'll have the last cut.

Her hatred was palpable. After everything, it was still as potent and tangled up in the ancient enmity between heaven and hell. She's on one side of the world. I'm on the other. A miles-long burning bridge between us. Once the smoke clears, she will know who's the fucking alpha King of Hell on Earth.

She'll regret every gods-damn word, every cut, every fucking challenge. She'll repent on her knees with my cock driving deep in her throat and my fist in her hair until her eyes water, and she knows she's at my utter mercy. Once she's penitent and submissive, taking all my cum, then I'll worship her pussy so many times until she begs me for mercy. Finally, I'll bend her over, spread those glorious thighs, and fuck her blessed center until her halo sings the hallelujah chorus.

Astraea Eternity wants a fucking battle. I'll give her a war.

Fisting my hands at my sides, I storm into my suite and growl at the demon sluts in my bed, so they scurry away, shaking their nude little asses behind them. I strip off my robes, chuck them aside, and go to my prepared bath, heating the water until the boiling point with my flames. Regardless of the temperature, I enter, flaring my nostrils from the sharp pain because it's better than this fucking throbbing cock and my balls ready to burst.

I fist myself, cursing that little angel, imagining her delectable ass in the air right before I grip her hips and ram her hard from behind. Her chained and suspended upon my bed, knees spread for me while I impale her on my cock, and use her wings for momentum is what finally gets me off.

In the end, she'll know exactly how much I've fucked her—when she discovers the real reason she's here and how I've used Abaddon's bargain to my advantage. He'll come for her. I've sensed his destructive presence as he's tested the shields, searching for weak spots. I'll crack them. Let him come for her.

And once he tells her the truth, I'll fuck her right in front of him, collect her broken tears, shatter her further until there's nothing left but her ragged soul weeping and pleading for me to make her whole again. She'll never leave me gasping for breath or hard again. I'll fuck this addiction right out of me.

Get my vengeance on that gods-damned archangel at the same time. Finally, I'll unleash the monster inside me. I'll let him fucking rip her apart until he grabs whatever power is hiding inside her soul. He won't stop until he devours her whole.

Then, I'll be free of Astraea fucking Eternity.

Whole body exploding with hellfire, I emerge from the bath, tip my head back, and release the roar of the demon inside me—a roar of the deepest recesses of the Unconsecrated Crater itself. Enough to shake the walls of the castle and its foundation. Enough to raise the magma moat level by an inch. Enough that it will rattle that little angel down to her bones.

Grinning from ear to ear, I snarl savagely, "Let the games begin, sweetheart."

THIRTY-EIGHT

THE INTRODUCTION OF THE TRIALS

——ASTRAEA——

My blood sizzles when I eye the inner layer of my wings. A snarl finds its way into my throat. My flesh prickles. In the center of that innermost layer is a dark patch staining the otherwise gleaming gold. This has never happened before. I conclude that it's from how long I've been in Hell on Earth and with Lucifer. There's a reason angels don't stay for extended periods here.

For me, it's been one week.

I stiffen at the knowledge. In the corner of my mind, the words of the Diviner haunt me, leading me to wonder if the monster she referred to is the reason why my wings are turning dark. Am I already so fallen, so stained, thanks to my past sins, that I'm falling faster?

Shaking off the thought, refusing to acknowledge it, I face myself in the mirror, set my hands on my hips, and tap the collar. "What do you think, Sammy?" I gesture to the outfit I've chosen for the Trial Introduction when the candidates will be introduced one by one.

Sammy slithers beyond the collar, sticks out his tongue, and proclaims, "Ethereal. Ssstunning. Marvelousss."

I grin and give him a belly rub. The swathes of deep, nightshade purple fabric sweep down in a diagonal to cover my breasts. Divided like curtains with a cut-out stomach and sternum, they exhibit my light gold skin adorned with three dark gold diamond broaches trailing down to my navel. Connected to mirrored gold epaulets at my shoulders, the royal fabric cascades in a stunning cape with a train to trail behind me. Gold constellations and star patterns accent the cape and feathered gown.

"When will we get the fireworksss?" inquires Sammy, and I rub one finger along his head and down his back, smirking at how he arches.

"Camio arranged for me to be the very last candidate. I'll wear a robe over this, and as he arrives before me, I'll light it up," I boast, referencing the enhanced features thanks to Camio.

Thankfully, there are so many candidates, Lucifer has delegated a few responsibilities to overseers, choosing to visit more elite candidates. Naturally, many candidates were disqualified following a medical check. Mine was falsified, programmed into the network. Without him, this never would have worked.

Thousands have flocked to Hell on Earth for the Bride Trials—themed after the Seven Deadly Sins. So fitting. Word has spread that Lucifer will make a special announcement for the Introduction, but there's no predicting what he will come up with.

"I want to watch the ssshow, Raea," pleads Sammy, curling his head up so he may stare at me with those lidless bejeweled eyes I love. He looks so adorable as he tilts his head and sticks out his tongue.

"It's not like you can perch on my shoulder like you normally do." I shrug and chew on my inner cheek because I can't wear a live serpent around my neck like an ornament.

Hmm...I glance at the Infinit-i closet, considering the wide variety of necklaces. I lean in, peck Sammy on the head, and smirk. Maybe I can.

"This is the most ridiculous idea you've ever had," complains Camio as the private tram escorts us to the Hell on Earth arena or its unofficial nickname: the All Hell Breaks Loose Arena. With a capacity of one million viewers, complete with prime box seats nesting in hovering skyways for the highest-paying VIPs, the cheers from the arena at peak season are rumored to be so deafening, they may be heard miles away within the Vestibule itself.

"More ridiculous than sneaking into Hell on Earth, crashing Lucifer's Eighth Circle gala, and trying to assassinate the Devil?"

Camio quirks an eyebrow at me. "You said abduct."

I shrug, prop my elbow up on the window, and snort, "I changed my mind."

Chortling under his breath, Camio says, "Trouble in paradise, Astraea? Little lovers quarrel?"

I burn my eyes against his. "Better shut up, Cam, or I'll shove pineapple so far up your ass, Aamon will never stop picking nuts out of his cock." He winces at that, and I rub my finger along the chunky gold necklace in the image of a serpent spiraling around my neck. No one will know the glittery black serpent is Sammy. He darts his tongue out as if to peck my finger, but other than that slight gesture, he remains eerily still. I suppose he's had centuries of practice. Having him around my neck is another layer of encouragement for this cockamamie plan as

Camio has named it.

"If you hate this plan so much," I flick my eyes to my friend and square my shoulders, preparing for an argument, "why did you help me?"

Camio shrugs in that adorable way of his, tilting his head to the side, so a lock of his dark brown hair casts a shadow over his cheek. He spreads his lips into a soft smile and says, "Cause you're my girl. The only one who's ever straddled the line between bitch and angel. After centuries roaming this earth and reaping all the pleasures of Hell on Earth, I've never managed to find someone who makes life more interesting than you, Astraea."

"Even Aamon?"

With a sheepish smile, Camio explains, "It's different. Aamon gives me love, quiets the demons in my wrecked soul, and gives them a place to hide. He's strong enough to bear them. But you'll always be my speed demon on wings. And since I can't die, what the hell? How can I resist raising Cain with the angel in Hell on Earth, who's got the Devil wrapped around her pretty, little finger?"

I lean back in my seat and cross my arms over my chest, huffing. "Not wrapped yet. But I'll keep pulling his strings as long as I can."

"Astraea..." Camio leans in, folding his hands in his lap, his lashes at half-mast, turning his eyes serious and dark. "Take it from one who's well acquainted with Lucifer: you've played with his hellfire. You've pierced his heart with your angel sword. You've stood on your fortress walls and taunted the gods-damned Devil incarnate. He won't stop until he's returned the favor pain in full."

I can't deny the bone-deep chill crawling over me or my instinct to draw my hood up to cover my flaming curls. In respect, I listen to Camio. For the first time in our relationship, I listen far more than speak.

"He's going to throw down, Astraea. You've poked the beast too many times. You haven't fled in terror. You haven't even taken the time to study it as one would an opponent. You've challenged the very Devil who controls the monsters of the deep. And yeah, I'm scared as fuck for what's going to happen when that war is done."

"He'll never break me, Cam," I deny, strengthening my resolve, pushing out my proud chest, and raising my regal chin.

Camio shakes his head. "You don't understand, babe. I'm terrified of what will happen after he throws you to his dragons and you come back riding them like their motherfucking queen. When all is said and done, if you go to war, if hell pits itself against heaven, when that firestorm is over, what the fuck will be left?"

Camio's words still haunt me as I take my place among the candidates, understanding my feet will be aching by the time this is over. His purposeful impunctuality is another test of a mind fuck. An unfair one, but the humans among the crowd need to know what they're getting into. I'll wager many don't expect to pass the first trial, considering they've already earned renown for this simple appearance alone. They'll go onto fifteen minutes of fame and a decent marital match or a sponsorship from a VIP citizen.

Either way, the ones most likely to compete in the trials will be demons, fallen angels, vampires, fae, elves, a handful of djinn, and one little, gold-winged angel who's broken loose and going to give the Devil some holy fucking hell.

Knots in my stomach tighten. But I harness my sporadic breath, understanding the thousands in the audience are paltry compared to the population that will flood those seats for the first official trial. A sheen of sweat breaks out in my skin as if my body is soaking up all the nervous energy. Dozens of us await Lucifer's arrival. There must be over one hundred young women here. I'm in the far back row, my face hidden behind my hood. Considering Camio informed me of how many had entered, the delegates must have been ruthless in trimming the list. Not that checking it twice would have aided them in eliminating me.

The arena plunges into darkness.

Nervous energy shudders through the assembly of young women. A shiver skitters up my spine. Every trembling pulse in the arena echoes in my ears, including mine.

I flinch. Thanks to my enhanced senses, the familiar power raises the hairs on my arms, alerting me. Like a tender current, it ripples upon the wind. If it could take shape, I imagine it would spiral like graphical kaleidoscopes in shades ranging from midnight blue to a violent dawn red. The Devil's scrollwork—his essence like a signature radiating brutal dominance and supreme authority—engulfs the arena until all hush and still in its wake.

In perfect synchronization, the spotlight beams become shooting stars trained on the flying image of Lucifer in all his grandiloquence. A commanding force of thunder and hellfire. Sweet fucking mercy. I swallow hard. From the fitted black coat open and folded back to showcase the inner crimson lining and the Circassian-style buckled waistcoat, he's excruciatingly beautiful. Parted at the back, the black cape sweeps behind him like a springing serpent but never dares to compete with the great expanse of his wings.

Nor does the ruffled white ascot—not a pleat out of place—clasped by a blood ruby broach. Or the Diablo ore epaulets spanning his broad shoulders. Curved, fragmented, and sharpened as sickles, the three-spiked epaulets accentuate his horns bound by a crown of the same ore.

My throat convulses, and I wince under my hood, inhaling the scent of Vetiver and blood roses upon his silvery hair that cascades in the air, free and unhindered.

Dragon-headed cane in hand, he is the fallen classic angel meets demon incarnate with a hint of rebel pirate. Roles he owns down to his cell matter.

Both serene and powerful, Lucifer lands upon the ground dead center of the arena. The ground shakes from the momentum, gasps flood the air, and I know the audience themselves feel the force rumbling to the skyway box seats.

The ache in my chest grows extreme. I chalk it up to this damned collar, whatever bond he's infected within me. Moments after he lands, I swear he feels it, too since he flicks his eyes, roaming them in a once-over across the crowd of women as if searching—no hunting for me. When the cinched belt at his waist shifts, I gulp, understanding he also wore a serpent today. Except, he has two. Far more controlled vs. my sentient Sammy, the scarlet serpents rear up, jaws open, and fangs on full display. Their heads strike in the air—once—before they curl back to his waist.

The symbolic message, like chilled lightning, runs wild across my skin in waves of tingles. Fight for me, and I'll take you as my battle prize. A trophy bride. More than anything else, Lucifer wants that war, craves it, fucking needs it. All to prove his control and sovereignty over whoever he chooses. Beyond the threats to his empire, there is another reason for that hellbent demand to control, the dominion he wears, and the flaming temper he restrains.

Posturing high, all his limbs stiff and muscles taut, Lucifer opens his mouth to proclaim in his deep baritone, infused with thunder and shadows, "The First Trial will commence tomorrow morning! The Trial of Gluttony. Tomorrow night, I will begin the selection of winners individually for the honor of joining my bed. You will all be tested through the Trials and beyond."

Lucifer turns away, his word final and domineering.

Fear jolts my stomach at the announcement. At the same time, my stomach twists with disturbing arousal. Not born of his lust-hum or his power. Nor can I excuse it as a primal urge or natural attraction to the demon I first met on that balcony. This is deeper: a hungering desire, so monstrous and tempting, it preys on every celestial molecule in my body.

When my arousal trickles down my thighs, Lucifer stops mid-turn, snaps his wings shut, and swings his gaze to the rows of women. He flares his nostrils. Ohshitohshitohshit, I know that deep-hooded stare of a predator when he's sniffed out his prey. Or in my case, a she-predator—one he wishes to conquer and mount into submission.

Over my dead body.

With no reserve or thought to the others, Lucifer advances through the crowd. The rows of women part before him. I suck a deep breath, touch one finger to Sammy for courage, and steel my spine. Electrical adrenaline heightens all my senses. Blood rushes to my cheeks, but I hold my ground, waiting for the right moment. It may not go down how I anticipated, but I'm all for winging it.

Ten steps. I exhale, keeping my breath slow and even. Five steps. Ball my hands into fists to quell the trembling. Three steps. He growls low, shadows breeding, flames curling toward me.

Wicked smirk growing, I defiantly sweep my cape off and throw it to the ground. Igniting the gem-tech programmed into my gown, I soar into the air. A grand dare and challenge for Lucifer to follow me. After all, he's not the only one who can make an entrance.

The gold constellations erupt like a thousand flaring sparklers. The star patterns shimmer before they begin a whirling dance. Thousands of holo-cams snap upon my figure, which was exactly my intention. Once the media feeds the story of the angel bride candidate, my and Mira's work will be done. Well, almost.

I lock my eyes onto Lucifer's as he advances. Energy thrums inside me. His shadows turn his wings darker and more monstrous than ever, but they can't hope to smother my light. Heat blossoms in my chest because I've upstaged him again. A vein throbs in his forehead, so fierce, I wonder if it will vibrate beyond his flesh. He's a pissed-off tower of a fallen angel and demon. Brutal and beautiful, Lucifer is a mercurial force when tested. Camio's words lurk in my mind more than ever. *You've poked the beast one too many times.* It's how he gazes at me as if he's about to throw down right here and now. Why do I get the nagging suspicion that whatever seven deadly trials will come, they will be infinitesimal compared to the Devil's trial?

After this, he's going to throw a monumental fit. Might as well go all out. With the stars spiraling around me, I blow the Devil a kiss and smile sweetly, preparing for him to catch me. If I'd believed he would wait until the constellation sparks had faded, I was dead wrong.

Once he gets his arms around me, despite the fireworks, he paralyzes me with his stare. For the first time, I don't deadpan. Nor do I avert my eyes. Instead, I free them to roam across the sculpted angles of his face, the shadows below his prominent cheekbones, the iron jaw, back to his sensuous and sinful lips.

After an eternity of a moment, in no more than a whispering purr of thunder, Lucifer's voice vibrates into my body, "Prepare for your punishment, Astraea."

ACKNOWLEDGMENTS

Molly Phipps of We Got You Covered: You'll always be my #1 go-to for everything covers and formatting! I love how we started with *The Lord of the Rings* and our friendship has continued. Thank you for putting up with my OCD updates and too-many gifs.

Adalynd Graves: For the first cover of *Bride of Lucifer,* which I still love.

Jamie: Thank you for being my ultimate alpha reader for this book, for picking out the tiniest errors that I missed, for brainstorming with me, and listening to me ramble on about everything from plot to world-building to sexy scenes. Thank you for falling in love with Sammy so much.

Natalie/Teagan/Katherine: You have all been such champions of this book. I loved watching your gifs light up whenever you finished a chapter! And Katherine, for telling me how Sammy reminds you of Dean Winchester and bonding with Jamie about her favorite snake. Don't worry, he will get a cute hat.

Bitchy Bookworms Super Fans: To everyone from Bitchy Bookworms who fell for *Bride of Lucifer* in its infancy, joined my Super Fan group, supported me all these months while writing this book took much longer than I anticipated. You've all been so patient and amazing. And I could not ask for a more spectacular group of readers.

Other Acknowledgments: Pam Godwin and Amelia Hutchins— whatever happens, please NEVER stop writing!

Kevin: for always supporting me through everything we've been through over the past seventeen years we've been together, including thirteen years of marriage. If we made it through 2021, we can make it through anything.

ABOUT THE AUTHOR

EMILY SHORE is a best-selling author Kindle Vella author where her books have routinely made the Top Five out of 15,000 authors as well as #1 in Fantasy Romance, Urban Fantasy, Dark Fantasy, and Enemies to Lovers categories. As of 2022, she is the only Vella author to achieve three crowns (i.e three books in the Top 250).

Her small press dystopian, *The Aviary*, is a Top 100 Kindle ebook.

Emily has worked as a teen fiction awareness speaker all over Minnesota, including the annual Minnesota Educator's Academy conference.

As a bisexual feminist and a mother of two daughters, Emily is dedicated to empowering and inspiring the next generation of girls while offering spicy fantasy romance for adults. All her 2020 and beyond work features badass, queer heroines who take on dark alpha love interests.

Identifying as queer/polyamorous, Emily bridges the gap between LGBTQIA+ and cishet audiences. She goes beyond fetishized stereotypes by showcasing positive sexuality and sex-positivity while normalizing the beauty of queer/poly relationships because #whychoose?

Please subscribe to Emily's newsletter at www.emilybethshore.com to keep up with her series projects, author promos, and contests to receive fun prizes. Join **Emily's Vella Verse** on Facebook and learn how to become a supporter and receive a free signed paperback.

Printed in Great Britain
by Amazon